ONCE UPON A WINTER

Various Authors
Foreword by H. L. Macfarlane

For those who came before us, and shall remain long
after we are gone.

Table of Contents

The wintry west extends his blast,
And hail and rain does blaw;
Or the stormy north sends driving forth
The blinding sleet and snaw:
While, tumbling brown, the burn comes down,
And roars frae bank to brae;
And bird and beast in covert rest,
And pass the heartless day.
Winter A Dirge   (Robert Burns; 1781)

FOREWORD

H. L. Macfarlane

I grew up with fairy tales. Most likely you, the reader, did too. Whether they were called fairy or folk or old wives' tales – or indeed had no name at all – families all over the world spoke them to their children before those children could utter their first word. Fairy tales are a global experience.

The experience would stop there for some children. But many kids, like me, who loved those spoken stories from our parents and grandparents, would learn to read so we could encounter new fairy tales all on our own.

Then some of us would move on to *create* those tales. Even in adulthood we wouldn't stop.

This anthology is full of such people.

I am privileged to have been given the opportunity to organise, edit and introduce Once Upon a Winter: A Folk and Fairy Tale Anthology. There are some classics in here given a twist you've never heard before, and retellings of stories only the most discerning of folk tale lovers will recognise. There are also completely original stories to add to the expansive canon of existing fairy tales, which to me is a very exciting, very wonderful thing indeed.

So why winter? In truth this is the first of four planned anthologies based around the seasons, with summer, spring and autumn to follow. There is something inherently magical about the seasons: the blossoms in spring; the scorching height of summer; the golden leaves of autumn; the darkest, deepest depths of winter.

Winter, especially, is the time for stories told beside a fireplace or hidden beneath a duvet late at night. It is a time for ceilidhs and revels, for snow fights and blizzards, for food and drink and celebrations.

Inside this anthology you will find witches fighting sorcerers. Boggarts haunting young men. Little boys falling in love with faeries – or falling prey to them. Women siding with monsters against the true terrors of humanity. All set against the backdrop of snow; of cold; of winter.

I hope you enjoy every last story this marvellous group of authors has written into existence.

THE BITING COLD

Josie Jaffrey

We think of spring as the place where everything starts: grass shoots, tree buds, flower heads, sepals and petals unfurling into life as the sap rises behind the bark. It is the beginning of the sun's return, the warming of the land and the creatures that walk on it, and the awakening of the seeds they carry within them.

But nothing comes from nothing, and some things only wake in the dark.

* * *

You have always been alone. Your mother died giving birth to you, her first child, and your father followed thirteen years later from what the vicar called pneumonia but you know was really a surfeit of gin. The parish took the house and would have taken you, too, if you'd let them, but your knees were too strong to bend. You would not spend your life atoning for your father's sins. The only thing left of your childhood is your mother's charm bracelet, a chain of wooden animals strung along a leather thong. It is too precious to wear, so you keep it in a pouch at your waist as you stalk through the forest.

This is your sixth season in the wild. You have lost your puppy fat along with your illusions about the romance of living in the trees; the tips of two toes and the littlest finger on your left hand are black with frostbite. You already know that winter is a thing with teeth.

Still you stay, not just because you have nowhere else to go, but because of this.

Look.

The forest should be three colours – the black of the bare trees, the dark hue of the evergreens, the white of the frost – but in the dusk the sky paints the snow in a rainbow from violet to red and back again. The shadows are purple and blue, like dark water pooling around the tree roots.

Step.

It crunches. The day's sunshine had melted the very top layer of the snow, but the chill of the approaching evening has since refrozen it, so it splinters beneath your boots and gives way to the soft powder beneath. It anchors your feet to the ground.

Breathe.

The air is sharp with the clean scent of ice. It burns in your lungs, in your sinuses, at the back of your throat. You smell the animal skins wrapped around your chin, too, roughly tanned and now soaked with condensed drops of your exhalation. They smell of the knife-edge freedom in which you exult: on one side, the dangers of the forest and, on the other, the constant clamour of your body's need for comfort. There's something magical about the balance – not that you believe in magic. If you were starry-eyed enough to gamble your life on a magic bean, you'd be dead by now.

You were raised on the stories, though. Between your father's bottles, when the money was too scarce even to afford the bathtub concoctions of the widow next door, he would occasionally be lucid enough to tell a tale. You know all about cannibalistic witches, faeries snatching away children, and mutilated feet shoved into glass slippers for the sake of a prince's hand, blood pooling at the toes. You understand these stories because they are true: out here on the edge of civilisation, you do what you can to survive. The forest has no morals and neither must you.

But there's a difference between truth and reality; something can be *true* without it being *real*. You know they're only stories. You've seen the faerie hills and mushroom circles, but you've never believed that fantastical creatures lurked within them. The dying light of the winter sun is magic enough for you. The dying light and the prey it awakens.

You slip into the ragged pile of branches that forms your hunting hide and let yourself fade in your stillness, waiting for movement. At first, it is nothing more than a single twig poking up through the patchy blanket of snow. It twitches and you imagine that a woodlouse is moving beneath the leaf litter, maybe a centipede, or perhaps a worm has dislodged the foliage with its burrowing. You spend your life beneath these trees and if you've learned anything about the forest it's that – even in the depths of winter – the world is alive beneath your feet. You are about to look away, but a second movement has you reaching back to your quiver instead.

Whatever is pushing its way up out of the snow, it's definitely bigger than an insect. The forest floor shifts up and down like a rug over a trap door, the snow and the leaves beneath moving in a single carpet. The something must be burrowing its way up from deep in the earth, which makes you think it must be a rabbit or, perhaps, a badger. There would be eating enough on that to last you days; weeks even. You slip an arrow free from its holder and nock it to your bow.

Breathe in.

You steady the tip and sight on your target.

Breathe out.

You wait for it to breach the surface. You might have a second, two if you're lucky, to fix your aim before the creature spots you and ducks out of sight. It'll be coming out head first, which is good news if it emerges facing away from you, but bad news otherwise. It'll be alert, looking for predators, and you are nothing if not that.

You are so focussed on the spot that you almost miss the rush of deer through the conifers. They have been hiding in the arbours created by the weight of snow on the lowest branches, bending them down into natural shelters that are so secret you have walked straight past them. The deer should be hiding there still, curling up in each others' heat to weather the night, and yet they are running past your hide in a frantic herd.

Something has spooked them, but you don't stop to question your good fortune. You turn and follow them with the point of your arrow, aim and shoot, run and chase. Your head is filled with the thought of hot meat sizzling over your fire and the knowledge that with the weather this cold, you can store as many deer as you can bring down. You run.

By the time you return to the hide with your prizes, there's a hole in the earth where you saw the twig move. You were expecting the entrance to a badger sett, but instead there's a chasm ten feet wide that spills dark soil up onto the snow like a wound. You shift the two deer carcasses on your shoulders as you turn, squinting between the trees. Discomfort tickles up your spine with an intensity you have not felt since you first ran out into the forest six seasons ago. This is your home and your sanctuary.

And yet.

You shrug the deer up higher until they rub their cooling fur against your cheeks, then retreat carefully to your hut, leaving the gash in the earth behind you.

Beneath the snow, where you can't see it, a circle of death caps rings the void.

* * *

Your fire is lively, even when it starts to snow outside. The fireplace pulls well. You turn the hunk of venison on its spit as sizzling drops of fat splash onto the coals and fill the hut with a scent that calls to your appetite. Outside in your meat larder, the balance of your hunt hangs cooling in its lean-to beside the woodpile that feeds your fire and insulates your walls. There's a water butt, too, collecting rain from your roof, though its contents are frozen now. Under the snow, your garden waits for spring. This year's crop and forage is hibernating in your root cellar or pickling there in jars.

You think of each of these things in turn, the

resources you have marshalled, and you sigh happily. You are proud, because this comfort is entirely of your own making.

It wasn't always like this.

The hut you built in your first season fell into ruin before three months had passed, leaving you shivering in wet skins and waking with digits that ached and burned, then blistered and turned cold as the snow. This year you were more careful. As soon as the ground was soft enough, you dug into a sheltered bank and sank struts to prop its roof. That's your bedroom now, lined with clay and cocooned in the warm earth. You built out from its open side with wood and dirt, lined with animal skins and topped with flattened cans to make it waterproof and sturdy. Discarded metal is easy to come by at the edges of your domain, littering rivers and ditches. There is always enough to tip your arrows, tin your food and bend for your gutters.

So that's your hut, complete with crude pipe chimney and stone fireplace. Nothing in here is pretty, nothing smells fresh, and some of it itches, but it works, and you have earned every unyielding inch of it with blood and sweat and flesh. You take your mother's charm bracelet from your pouch and stroke the smooth contours of the carvings with the tips of your unblackened fingers. You think that she would be proud too.

The venison pops on its spit and you take that as your cue to serve your dinner for one. You need not share nor concern yourself with politeness, so you bite into the meat as greedily as a dog might chew a bone. Perhaps you should yearn for more company than your mother's ghost, but in moments like this you think you might be happy alone forever.

Outside in the blizzard, a hundred yards from the door of your hut, a creature made of leaves and twigs tips back its head and swallows the snow in hungry mouthfuls.

* * *

Time moves quickly at the edge of the forest. Civilisation encroaches further and further each season, and before many years have passed there are fewer deer to be had, fewer birds, fewer rodents, fewer grubs. The jars and tins you have scavenged from the river by the village are filled with the last few mushrooms you have managed to pickle and wild berries you have boiled into something almost like jam, but they won't be enough to see you through the winter. You are taller and more muscular now so your belly demands more, but your root cellar is almost empty and the meat larder full of nothing but skins and one last, precious haunch of venison. By the time the first snow comes, early and cold and more bitter than ever, you are already hungry and lean.

You return to your old haunts. You lurk in the branch-built hide and remember that glorious winter evening when the deer pelted past like a living wave, and you wish that it might happen again. You don't pray, because if you learned anything as a child in that alcohol-fumed house it was that God doesn't listen to your prayers, but you hope and yearn and imagine that if you bring the memory to the forefront of your mind and hold it there, the forest might hear and be merciful.

But the trees sing their own mournful song as the wind cuts through their naked branches like a whip. The pines keep their own counsel; the wind is their friend. It's the hazel, rowan and crab apple trees that shriek:

11

bereft of birds and squirrels and bees, their blossom dropped to the dirt this autumn without being pollinated. They need all their mercy for themselves.

You crouch within your skins and try to be still, but weeks of poor nourishment in freezing temperatures have undone you. When finally, after hours of waiting, you spot something moving in the undergrowth, the tip of your arrow shakes with your shivering.

A rabbit. Somehow, hopping its way through three inches of snow, is the fattest, whitest rabbit you have ever seen. Whatever cache of food it has stashed away, it's clearly better than yours.

You have to take three deep, steadying breaths before you can stop your arrow from weaving. When it finally points true, you are so anxious to make the shot that you fumble your release and it goes long, but the rabbit must have heard the twang of your bowstring because in that moment it turns and jumps right into the arrow's course. The point skewers the rabbit through the neck and pins it to the ground, turning the white snow crimson.

Maybe the forest heard your prayer after all.

You say a quick thank you to the air with a voice that rasps with disuse, then turn and take your prize back home. You've been driven this far by the relentless growl of your stomach, but now you've secured another day's meal you can let yourself rest. Eat and sleep. Preserve your energy. Live to hunt again tomorrow.

After making a meal of half the rabbit – you wish you could have saved more, but you're so *hungry* – you step outside to stash the remaining half in your meat larder with the venison, but the meat has gone. The makeshift door of the larder is standing open, shattered and mangled, and the skins and haunch that you have carefully preserved and denied yourself over the past months are simply gone.

Gone.

It hasn't snowed since the last time you checked your larder, but there are no tracks here except your own. It is as though the contents simply flew out, taking some of the door with them in their flight.

Gone.

Knowing that it won't last long enough, you store the remaining rabbit in your root cellar and curl up in your bed, wondering at the possibility of a thief without feet.

* * *

You sleep long and late the next day, feeling the weight of your misery, so it's not until evening that you make your way back to the hide. Maybe the forest will be merciful again, you think. Maybe yesterday's rabbit has friends.

When you arrive, you try to pinpoint the spot where you felled yesterday's dinner. It should be easy to see – the snow was stained red – but there's nothing here now except a freshly-dug drift of soil scarring the snow. It is unpleasant in its familiarity. You try to reason away the coincidence, but your instincts know what your mind tries to deny: the gash in the earth is the same size, and in the same spot, as the one you tried to forget in the year of the deer. You'd returned to it after that night and found nothing but the flat forest floor, so you'd almost convinced yourself that it was a dream. A dream of earthbound leviathans moving beneath your feet.

Perhaps you're dreaming now. Perhaps the haunch of deer is still safe in your meat larder and the newly-tanned skins are waiting beside it to line your bed when it's too cold to leave the hut. Or maybe you've been so long in the cold that you're seeing things that aren't there.

Giving up on the rabbits, you abandon the hide and walk to the edge of the chasm, insisting to yourself that it won't seem so ominous once you know the whole of it. It's only the night, and the mystery, and the fact that the venison thief has made you worry.

You peer over the lip and have to catch your weight on your bow, digging one end into the snow. The devastation is worse than you thought.

The hole is wide only because it is deep, so the spoil has spread out around it. It funnels from a broad mouth into a deep vertical tunnel, so deep that you can't see the bottom of it; it fades into a darkness so complete that beyond twenty feet or so you can't distinguish the walls of frozen earth from the emptiness between them. Around the sloping edges, drifts of snow are spattered with blood and white fur. It looks as though whatever dug this hole has also found the rest of your rabbits.

You hear the crunching noise before you notice the shadow lumbering towards you. It's as tall as a tree, moving with the unsteady gait of a newborn fawn as it lurches into the clearing. Its bones are branches, its flesh a moving morass of dead bugs and worms, its skin the pulpy paleness of rotting petals. In the joint of an elbow, you recognise the wooden planks that are missing from the door of your meat larder and the half-tanned fox pelt you left there to dry. When it reaches the hole, it doesn't so much kneel as collapse to the ground in a pile of limbs that move independently of its control, bending into impossible shapes before reforming into something new.

14

You wondered where the creatures of the forest had gone and here is your answer: they've been disassembled and rearticulated into this. When it scrapes the snow from the ground and shovels the rotting earth beneath into its mouth, it does so with fingers made of squirrel bones and tipped with rooks' beaks for claws. Its teeth are shards of rock and flint lancing out of muddy gums, its face a patchwork of leaves, feathers and insect carapaces that glint like tar in the moonlight. There are snail shells in place of its ears and spiderwebs trail across its face like a veil. It eats the leaf litter in gulps as big as your torso, stomach never swelling, jaws never stopping, and you know that its hunger will never be sated. You don't know what it is, but you know that you have to stop it before it destroys everything that keeps you alive.

You draw an arrow and let it fly. It lands in the creature's cheek with the thunk of metal into tree bark, peeling apart the leaves that cover the wooden skeleton. You expect retaliation or at least acknowledgement, but the creature doesn't look at you. Instead, it looks at the arrow, pulling it free to examine the metal tip. Then, deliberately and slowly, it puts the arrow into its mouth point-first and chews. You let loose another arrow, and another, again and again until your quiver is empty, and each ends up crushed between its flint teeth and swallowed into its bottomless belly.

It is relentless. It is unstoppable.

It will eat the forest whole.

You run without looking back.

* * *

After that, you don't go out after dark. When you return in the daylight to the spot where you saw the creature, there is nothing but level earth and the snow that covers it. It is beyond your comprehension, so you choose to ignore it.

Until spring comes, and the forest begins to change. The plants that rise from the earth are deformed in places, plated with foil and speckled with shot that twinkles in the sunshine. Your garden spits out spinach that hardens to metal at its tips. The flesh of an errant spring lamb is threaded through with wire-like veins, making it inedible. The radishes you grow are lush and fresh at their roots, but the stalks and leaves are covered with tiny splinters of iron that drive themselves into your fingertips when you harvest them and take hours of careful work to coax from your skin. Your home is seeded with these foreign bodies, lurking unseen in places that were previously free from hazard. You can no longer trust the earth and you grow thin on its meagre fruits.

But outside the forest, life seems harder still. The roads are lined with graves, so many that most remain unmarked weeks after they have been filled. You are not the only one struggling to stay alive, nor are you the only one looking to the forest for sustenance. Trees are cut from its edges as the towns creep ever further towards its heart and your hearth. At the same time, you're finding shining sheets of wrapping material in the forest and bottles in the rivers, both made from something new, resilient and brightly-coloured, sometimes pliable, sometimes stiff. The townsfolk call it plastic. You collect the bottles and fill them with water from the clear spring by your hut, the only source from which you'll drink; the surface of the river now glints with multi-coloured oil that tastes like burned vegetables and makes you vomit.

You strip and save what plants you can over the next few seasons, thankful that at least the autumn blackberries and nuts are free from corruption, and settle in for the hardest winter you've ever known. You've dug a new, secure meat larder and you fill it with what you can, hunting only the animals that belong in the woods; the livestock you poach from the surrounding farms is so laced with metal that you abandon it for the crows. You don't think too hard about why this should be. You're busy trying to stay alive.

The first snow comes hard and fast, freezing alpine strawberries on their stalks and potatoes in the ground before you have a chance to dig them all up. You tear open the black flesh of your frostbitten finger on the flattened tins you use to excavate the crop – you can't feel the pain in the dead flesh – but it's all for nothing because the potatoes defrost into a rotten mush that fizzes with a fermented smell that reminds you of your father. It makes you so sick that, despite your hunger, you carry the remains away from your hut and scatter them in a clearing for the birds. You're angry enough and sickened enough that you pay no attention to the dusk, nor do you hear the creature approaching. When you do, you freeze as still as the icicles that drape the trees around the glade.

The creature walks past you, as though you are invisible.

It's quieter this year, smaller, barely twice as tall as you, but it still walks in the same shambling half-stumble, lurching as though it is only one gust of wind away from collapse. It drops to its almost-knees in a heap of dizzying disassembly and scoops the mess of fermented potato into its mouth along with the snow, the leaves, the twigs, and the shining wrappers that now litter the forest floor. It, too, is hungry, for even the leaf litter is thin. There has not been a mast year for as long as you have lived.

As you watch it shovelling, wondering whether you should run or stay and fight for the remains of the forest that it is devouring, your eye catches on a spray of small wooden shapes amongst the ruined potatoes. Your hand slaps against the pouch at your waist, the pouch that – now you feel the ragged edges with your fingertips – you realise has broken, spilling your mother's precious animal charms across the ground and into the fermented mess that reeks of your father's sour breath. You watch in horror as the creature scoops the delicate carvings into its metal-tipped claws and swallows them whole.

You feel a snap in your chest as something breaks loose, then you're running towards the creature without thinking, thumping at its side with balled fists, catching your knuckles on metal mesh, broken plastic and the occasional bone. When you finally collapse exhausted beside the impassive creature, it turns its glass eyes towards your bloodied hands and blinks once with eyelids made of blue eggshell. Its pinecone nose shifts up and down. Then slowly, its frame writhing with leaves and dirt and teeth and crushed cans and bottle caps as it rearranges its form, it brings its face down to your hands. You are too tired to fight it now, so tired that you almost welcome its attentions, but the bite and swallow you are expecting never comes. Instead, the creature reaches out with a tongue made of fabric and fur and licks the blood from your fingers, one by one.

This task completed, it turns away to gobble up the last of the ruined potato, then gets awkwardly to its feet and ambles away, leaving you alone in the snow.

It has left no footprints in its wake.

* * *

In the spring, the trees put forth branches ornamented with shining sweet wrappers and tiny wooden animals that nestle like flowers among the leaves, and you begin to understand that the creature is not the enemy you believed it to be. You harvest a handful of the charms and make a necklace from them, stringing deer and rabbits and hedgehogs and badgers in miniature around your throat.

* * *

It's been years since you last approached the creature. The forest is little more than a copse now and there are cities where the towns once stood. People press in from all sides, rambling along deer trails that are now empty of their original denizens, crushing strange hybrid mushrooms beneath their feet. It's been months since you last saw the slightest trace of a rabbit, and the birds have all but deserted the forest, yet the people keep on multiplying. So far you have kept them away from your little hut with judicious planting of holly and other discouraging shrubs, all of which bristle with sharp metal thorns and plastic spikes, but you know it won't be long before the interlopers chase you from your warren. Maybe you should go, you think. If there are so many of them, there must be more food out there than there is in here.

Or so you imagine, but then you see exactly what they eat and what it has done to them. A couple of them cross your path not two hundred yards from your hut. They're clad in dangerous colours – red and pink and orange – but their skin is snow white and so translucent that you can see the veins snaking across their cheeks. One has a metal plate where his eyebrow should be and the eye beneath it looks wrong. The other's hair glints with coloured lights that run along the shell of her ear like water flowing uphill. It is grotesquely beautiful, but the skin around it is rotten and waxy. Their faces gleam with oily sweat. They're loud, shouting and squinting at each other as they stomp through the undergrowth with their guns, boxier and less elegant than the one your father had before he sold it for gin. This is no way to hunt, but that hardly matters because there are no animals left here to kill. There are precious few trees to form their habitats, and every one is corrupted in bark, root and branch. In these straitened days, you must scrape morsels of plant matter from plastic and metal and glass to make your meals.

But what you watch the city people eat is worse. They unwrap it from shining leaves of plastic and bite into bricks of paste that smacks distastefully around their mouths as though it is sucking the moisture from their gums. When they leave, you take their abandoned wrappers from the ground and lick the reflective insides. They taste of nothing at all.

When the cold comes, the people leave. It's just you out here now, you and the creature that the first snow brings. You see it in the distance sometimes, moving between the trees outside your hut, but you don't leave your sputtering fire long enough to risk meeting it. There is little for either of you to eat, but you try to abstain, understanding that it is more vital that the creature eats than that you do, knowing that its hunger today means no food at all for you come the spring. You live on the mouldering remains of your root cellar and are frugal with every scrap that the forest still offers.

Your abstinence takes its toll. Without wood to burn, without leaves to fill the cracks in your walls and without the warmth of new animal hides around you, the cold is insurmountable. You lose five more fingers to frostbite, leaving you with only the thumb and index finger on one hand, index and middle finger on the other. You can still use your bow, just, but this is small consolation; there's nothing to shoot at except metal-plated trees. Your dead fingers hang from your hands like rotten carrots and burn with an ache that screams through your bones. It feels like you are dying with them.

When the frostbite blisters swell and pop, nothing soothes the pain except icing your fingers with snow. The cold numbs them, giving you some blessed relief. You have a vague memory of being told not to do this as a child, but if you were ever told the reason then you have forgotten it. You don't realise that rubbing your frostbitten digits with handfuls of ice is just killing them quicker, hurrying the cell death into your bone marrow. They look entirely black now, but they feel better, so you are surprised when you wake one morning under mouldering skins to find that they are missing. A brief search locates them in your bed. During the long, cold night, your fingers have amputated themselves at your knuckles, leaving nothing but glistening raw flesh behind.

It takes you all day to clean the stumps of your hands in the water of the forest spring – the one resource that remains clear and uncontaminated – and bind them in old rabbit skins that you have scraped clean into thin leather. It is dark by the time you go out to bury your dead fingers, and the creature is waiting for you. It is hunched and distorted, netted with mesh and packed with artificial detritus that will not bend into the shapes its contorting body requires. Its ears are glass bottle-bottoms, its fingers are plastic pipes and its shoulders are crowned with painted tin-can epaulettes, but these aren't ornaments; they're awkward pieces of a body that is no longer functional. Metal limbs spark as their parts scrape against each other in desperate attempts at rearrangement. Rubber screeches against glass, raising the last few birds from the synthetic tree tops in pathetic mimicry of their former flocks. Here and there you see a glimmer of nature in the creature: its teeth are real this year, perhaps bovine or perhaps human, and they are anchored by flesh. It has clearly found something living to eat, but not here. There is nothing on the forest floor except bundles of wire and glass encased in plastic shells. You don't know what the devices are, but you know they've been multiplying over the past few years along with the people. Now they litter the forest floor in heaps: objects of all shapes and sizes that shine and beep and flash with lights.

The creature is not deterred. Mindlessly, it picks up a handful of them in clumsy fingers and brings it to its soft lips. The metal shatters its enamel teeth, but still it crams the pieces into its mouth, smashing the devices into shards of plastic and wire that stick in its gums. It bleeds, but if it feels the pain at all then it doesn't show it.

You wait until it has swallowed its empty meal, then feed it your frostbitten fingers, one by one.

* * *

Winter ends, but it may as well not have bothered. Nothing natural grows in the forest. In truth, it is not much of a forest anymore, but a valley instead. The trees are few and stunted. Unable to sustain the weight of their metal branches on a patchwork construction of plastic and tin, they crumple at their bases and topple to the ground, smashing apart the glassy grasses at their feet. The few birds that hatch from the cellophane eggshells in their boughs grow foil feathers on flesh that is black and dead. You see no rodents or deer at all, but you find a blistered rabbit's foot that appears to have amputated itself from its owner. You do not consider this talisman to be lucky.

Over the coming years, there is almost nothing for you to eat. You have given up on growing your own fruit and vegetables – they are filled with plastic seeds and wire filaments. Instead, you survive on nuts and the apples stored in your root cellar, holding your nose as you eat them sparingly in an attempt to ignore the fermented hum of their flesh. Supplementing this with rare carrion, you waste away through what should be the fattest months of the year. By the time the first snow arrives, you are too starved to do anything but lie in bed and slurp at the last dregs of your nut porridge.

The creature comes to you like a lover on his knees, though it is no taller than you now. It crouches at the side of your bed as its artificial body barks out a series of squeaks and wails.

It is hungry, you know, because you are hungry too.

Its eyes are plaintive; they reflect your own in their metallic depths. You see your hurt there, your desperation, and know that it is nothing compared to the ravenous agony the creature feels. There is nothing of the forest left in it, just oil and shine and veneer. It may still be able to stand under its own power, but it is dying as surely as you are.

You feed it the last of your porridge, ladling the cold mixture between its blade-like teeth and then, at the end, letting it chew up the wooden spoon and bowl as well. You feed it the animal hides from your bed, which it rips into shreds then swallows in greedy, slurping strings. It eats the walls of your hut, gulping down stone and wood and fibre, then returns to your bedside. You laugh as it paws with glass fingertips at the leather that covers the stumps of your hands, then you unwrap the brittle stuff and feed it that too, and the clothes from your back, and the charms from around your neck, one by one.

When it turns towards your metal chimney, you call it back. It shouldn't eat that, so you must give it something else. You've been keeping the knife beneath your pillow for weeks, waiting for the moment when you had strength enough for this final act. It is time.

You will not see another spring. But with luck, and with one proper meal, the forest might.

* * *

In the spring, the valley is a carpet of poppies, blood red and lush in their profusion. Beneath the ground, metal acorns crack open to send up sprouts that are unmarred by human interference. They will grow tall and strong in time. Around them, burrows are filled with breeding creatures of every shape and size, each made only of flesh and blood, with one small exception: each has a small wooden simulacrum of itself that hangs from an ear, or a tail, or at its neck.

You have been prolific. When Winter comes again, there will be plenty of you to satisfy his appetite.

24

Josie Jaffrey is a fantasy and historical fiction author who writes about lost worlds, dystopian societies and paranormal monsters (vampires are her favourite). She has ten novels published so far, along with lots of short stories. Most of those are set in the Silverse, an apocalyptic world filled with vampires and zombies. She's currently working on vampire murder mysteries (the Seekers series) and a YA series about the lost civilisations of the Mediterranean (the Deluge series). Researching the latter is the first time she's used her Classics degree since university.

Josie lives in Oxford with her husband and two cats (Sparky and Gussie), who graciously permit human cohabitation in return for regular feeding and cuddles. The resulting cat fluff makes it difficult for Josie to wear black, which is largely why she gave up being a goth. Although the cats are definitely worth it, she still misses her old wardrobe.

THE MATCH GIRL

Rebecca F. Kenney

Gammer drew her final rattling breath as the sun rose on the last morning of the year. It was a hazy sun, pink and cold and frosted at the edges, so pretty that Ember wanted to stare at it, but Gammer had warned her that the brightness would scorch her eyes.

Scorched eyes seemed like a less painful fate than facing the shriveled, sunken reality of Gammer's body on the saggy old mattress. Ember gritted her teeth and tried to squeeze out a few tears – but Gammer had been ill such a long time. Weeks of changing the old woman's soiled clothes and spooning broth between her wrinkled lips had sapped every soft emotion from Ember's body. She was cold and frosted at the edges, like the sun.

There was nothing left in the house. No food, no money, no supplies. Nothing but the stock of small boxes printed with the words "Gammer Gray's Long-Lasting Sulfur Matches" in curling letters. "Extended burn, guaranteed to strike when wet."

For as long as Ember could recall, the tiny second bedroom of the house had been packed from floor to ceiling with those boxes, but she'd never seen Gammer making any matches. Every time she asked where the matches had come from, Gammer grunted and shrugged.

Over the past three years, since Ember's eighteenth birthday, the supply of matches had dwindled. The stacks of boxes grew shorter, and no new boxes appeared to replenish the ones Gammer sold when she tottered to town once a month. Gammer had begun to complain that few people in town would buy from her anymore – that she had to go over to the next town, or sell batches to traveling merchants.

Eight weeks ago, instead of going to sell matches, Gammer had collapsed back into bed, muttering and incoherent. Ember had considered making the town trip herself, especially when supplies began to run low, but she did not like to think of the old woman dying alone.

Every time Gammer had traveled to one of the towns, she'd chained Ember to the bedpost and left her there with a bedpan, a cup of water, and some bread. Ember had spent long hours wondering what would happen if some malevolent brigand crashed through the door and discovered her. Would he stab her and leave her to bleed out while he stole what little they had? Would he seize her hair in his fist, kiss her, and tell her he was there to rescue her?

Ember's thoughts had strayed to many salacious and heart-pounding places while she sat on the floor of the cottage, running her fingers along the edge of the shackle around her ankle. But in her worst moments, she feared that no one would ever come, and that she would shrink to bones and die on the threadbare rug. No one would know or care that she'd gone from the world.

The longest Ember had ever had to wait was three days. At the end of those three terrible days, Gammer had stormed into the cottage and thrust the key into the lock of the shackle, grumbling about witch hunts and how it used to be easier in the old days. "Had to travel farther this time," was the nearest she'd gotten to an apology, and she had made Ember clean up the mess from the overflowing bedpan.

But that night, Gammer had grown slow and loose-tongued on the contents of a brown bottle, and she'd talked about how she used to be powerful, beautiful, and rich. "I summoned dread things, and I drank their powers," she'd said. "Sometimes I didn't fulfill my end of the bargain. And I got away with it too." She'd choked on a chuckle and insisted that Ember help her to bed.

The very bed she died in, twelve weeks later, on the morning of the last day of Ember's twentieth year.

Ember wrapped Gammer in bedclothes and took her outside, to the eaves of the forest where there was a half-crumbled stone wall. By chopping a little way into the frozen ground, and by piling up broken stones from the wall, and by covering everything with chunks of brittle snow, Ember got the old woman buried enough. She might have to do the job better in the spring, when the ground thawed. Or maybe she would go and live in the town, and never come back to the cottage again.

Spurred by the thought of *town*, Ember layered on the few clothes she had – a thick dress, a scarf, and two heavy shawls. She packed up the rest of the matches and slung the bundle on her back. She knew how much to charge, because Gammer had always grumbled, "Bunch of miserly snipes, those townfolk. Won't part with five pennies for a pack, nor four. It's three, or they walk away. A nasty, contentious, superstitious lot. We're better off without them."

Ember pondered those words as she stuffed her feet into socks and old boots that leaked knife-sharp cold through cracks in the toes. She mulled over those words as she made hot tea, poured it into a bottle, and trudged away from the cottage, along the faint dip in the snow that marked the trail to town.

Her socks were soaked within minutes, and she chewed her lips, wondering whether she ought to stay in the cottage. But there was nothing left – she had eaten the last of the cornmeal with the last few grains of salt that very morning. There was nothing but tea, a handful of sugar, and the wind whistling sharp and wicked through gaps that she and Gammer had stuffed with straw and rags.

So Ember walked all morning, while the sun ascended, turning crisp and pale yellow in the faded blue sky. She walked under branches laden with snowy froth, and over stone bridges spanning sheets of blue ice. She walked until lines of smoke traced across the pale sky, until dark rooftops and chimneys peeked over the white hills.

Her heart thrilled with terrified excitement. She paused, set down her bundle, and wrapped her head carefully in one of the shawls to conceal the long ringlets of her red-gold hair. According to Gammer, such bright curly hair attracted wicked men.

Gammer had spoken of a street corner where she used to sell her wares – near the town square, across from a baker's shop. Ember decided to find that same corner and offer up the matches for sale at three pennies a box. Then she would have money.

Money was magic and power. Money could get her lodging, food, and books – maybe even some warmer clothes. Then she must find work. She could cook and clean, chop wood, build snares, garden, mend, and forage. Surely there was someone in need of those skills.

Her first steps onto the snow-crusted cobblestones felt like springtime. She stole glances at the passing townsfolk through the shawl's raveled edge. Her gaze darted from side to side, taking in the rows of two-story houses while she listened to the ringing stamp of horses, the clanking rattle of wheels over stone, the creak of frozen snow under leather soles. Along the street twisted the tempting fragrance of sizzling onions, hot fresh bread, and melted sugar. She could smell the sweating flanks of the horses, the acrid reek of dung in the gutter, a whiff of unwashed body from a man who swept roughly past her.

Heavy soft clouds had crawled across the sun, and from them floated large white flakes, feathery in the air and wet against her cheeks. Ember had never seen anything so beautiful as the quaint brown buildings and the black cobblestones fringed with frost. Flecks of cottony white drifted down like a New Year's Eve blessing.

No one paid her any attention, which loosened the knot of coiled tension in her stomach. She found the town square – a stretch of broad paving stones around a frozen fountain. The scent of cake and buns rolling from the baker's shop made it easy to spot. She stood on the street corner across from the bakery, a step or two into a blue-shadowed alley, and she unslung the bundle of matches and set it down on the snow.

The knot in her stomach tightened again as she realized she would have to call out to the people passing by, to catch their attention and sell her wares. She'd never spoken to anyone but Gammer, though she'd read a few books with dialogue in them.

Grimly she took a box of matches in hand and held it out. When a woman walked by, Ember tried to say, "Matches, three pennies a box," but her voice was a terrified wisp.

She tried again, and managed to croak the words loudly at a man, who glanced at her, startled, and hurried on his way. For hours she tried, arranging herself in different positions, trying different tones and words. The blue shadows in the alley behind her deepened, and the windows around the town square began to glow rich amber, spilling gold onto the cobblestones and onto the crusts of snow.

Ember was shaking with cold. Her fingers hurt, right down to the bone, and the tip of her nose had lost all feeling. At least back at the cottage there was firewood, and walls, and some semblance of warmth, though the fireplace smoked terribly. Out here, there was no protection from the savage cold that bit through her shawls and her skin, or from the hunger in her belly that gnawed her insides.

Weak and desperate, she caught the sleeve of a woman in a green coat. "Please, could you tell me where I might get warm?"

The woman jerked her arm away and walked on.

With numb hands, Ember fumbled with a box of matches, managing to slide it open enough to extract one match. She struck it sharply, heartened that she could feel the grating vibration through her fingers. They weren't entirely dead to sensation yet.

The match spurted hot and bright, and she dropped the box so she could cup her other hand around the flame. Its heat was like a love letter, singing to something deep in her bones.

True to the lettering on the box, the match burned for nearly a full minute, but eventually it burned down. When the dying flame touched her fingers, it didn't hurt, but soaked into her skin and glowed there for a few seconds. Fire had never pained Ember, though it had seemed to sting Gammer whenever she'd come in contact with it. Once Ember had asked why the two of them were different in that way, but Gammer had only grunted and shrugged. There was no drawing an answer from her unless she wanted to give it.

Ember let the blackened match fall in the snow, then bent to pick up the box she had dropped and the matches that had escaped it. As she bent, her fire-bright curls tumbled out from beneath the shawl.

"You shouldn't let matches get wet," said a voice. A male hand reached down, collecting a few of the matches.

Ember recoiled like a threatened cat. The young man straightened and smiled, holding out the matches he'd picked up.

"They're special matches," she muttered. "They strike even when wet."

"Is that so?" His eyebrows lifted. "I've never heard of such a thing."

His face creased in an appreciative smile as his gaze

traveled from her face to the curls spilling over her breast. But two other young men came up behind him and gripped his arms, pulling him away. "Are you mad?" one of them hissed. "Everyone knows you don't buy those matches!"

"Those are the witch's matches," added the third boy. "They show you foul, sinful things. I struck one for my mother's candle once, and up sprang an image of the tanner's daughter, stark naked and dancing! My mother cuffed my ears so hard I couldn't hear for a week. She thought I'd been dabbling in the dark arts, you see."

"Come away," said the second boy, eyeing me suspiciously. "Come away, and leave the witch's spawn alone."

The young man who'd helped Ember with the matches shrank from her, his eyes darkening with caution and hostility.

As the trio walked away, Ember puckered her cold lips, trying to keep tears from escaping her eyes. Her first time speaking to a man, and it had ended as bitterly as Gammer had warned her it would.

The three young men must have spread word of her presence, because no one passed near enough for her to call out or touch them again. When villagers noticed her standing there with her boxes of matches, they circled wide or crossed to the other side of the street to avoid her.

After a while no one came down the street at all. One by one each shop was shuttered and locked.

Far down the street, nearly at the end of sight, Ember could make out a small chapel with open doors, admitting dark figures for a New Year's Eve service. She thought briefly of creeping into the building with the church-goers and enjoying a bit of warmth; but the sight of the cross atop the spire sent a twist of nausea through her stomach. She felt an unaccountable revulsion at the idea of going inside that place of God.

Besides, the villagers would likely have turned her out. Witches would not be welcome in the house of the Lord.

Ember shifted further into the alley, trying to avoid the bitter sting of the wind that rushed through the town square. How she longed to pass straight through the doors or walls of a house and enjoy the blessed warmth inside! It was cruel how many buildings shed smoke into the sky and light onto the street, yet there was no room for a single slim girl.

She struck another match and held it closer to the alley wall, with some idea that it might reflect the heat back at her – and she nearly screamed when the stone began to glow and melt away in the heat of the flame. The match seared a fist-sized hole right through the stone, revealing the warm room beyond. Ember could see an iron stove much larger than the tiny one in Gammer's cottage – large enough, it seemed, to fit a whole person inside. Brass fittings gleamed on its doors. And then someone whisked past the hole the match had made – without even seeming to notice an opening *right through the wall* – and clanked a pot onto the stovetop.

The match blackened and curled, its last bit of heat fading into her fingers.

Ember stared at the blank wall, stiff with shock.

She lit another match and held it to the wall again, hoping to catch a glimpse of the same room. Once more the stone and plaster melted at the center. The closer

34

Ember leaned to the wall, the wider the hole grew. She could see the big shining stove, though part of it was blocked by a woman's back – a bustled skirt and a row of trim buttons and a neat knot of shining hair.

The match went out.

Scarcely daring to breathe, Ember crossed the alley and tried two matches against the far wall. Their twin flames sank a wider aperture into the stone, and through it she could see a big room with a broad table draped in white. In the center of the table sat a plump roast goose with crackly brown skin, tucked into a bed of translucent onions and steaming potatoes. Gingerly Ember reached past the twin flames and probed the hole in the wall.

Her finger went through it.

Impossible, of course. Unless those young men had been right, and there was something odd about Gammer's matches. Something witchy, something magical.

The matches went out, and her finger sprang out of the wall, bounced back by some opposing force. At least it hadn't gotten stuck in the stone – but it tingled unpleasantly.

Ember lit another match, intending to look into the room with the goose again – but as she moved the match toward the wall, she wished she could see a room with a Christmas tree, like the one she'd read of in a tattered book Gammer had brought her. The book had been lying in a gutter, Gammer said, and half its pages were smeared and torn, but Ember had devoured what was left of it, many times.

The wish entered her head, and the match glowed against the wall, but the room beyond the opening had changed. Instead of the roast goose and the table, there stood an enormous Christmas tree. Candles were tied to some of its branches. Ribbons, strings of berries, and popcorn chains slithered through its boughs. The tree seemed to move, approaching the hole in the wall, swelling against the aperture as if it was trying to break through and come to her.

But there wasn't enough room, and the match went out.

Ember's feet were leaden by this time – heavy blocks void of sensation. Her knees kept knocking together, and her jaw ached. Her fingers were so cold she had to put them in her mouth before lighting another match.

She was dying of cold. Dying, in a town full of people, full of houses swelling with heat and light, bursting with fragrance and food. She was dying, because they were too frightened, too comfortable, too careless and cruel to let her in.

Perhaps the magic of the matches was all in her head. Perhaps she was hallucinating as her body shut down from weariness, hunger, and cold. But if Gammer's matches held some real power, they offered one last chance for survival.

They seemed to create a path to things she wished for. If she lit enough of them, maybe she could get her whole body through one of those holes and go somewhere *else*, somewhere warm and welcoming. This pretty little town was a tomb, a maze of icy walls inhabited by soulless drones.

Ember emptied a whole box of matches, then another, and more. She piled all the matches she had left against the wall of the alley, and she formed the wish in her mind.

A wish for a place of warmth and kindness, a place of provision and generosity, of love and freedom. She wished for safety and food and *books.* For *home.*

She repeated the wish again, whispering it through trembling fingers. She held the wish in her mind while she struck one match and tossed it among the others.

They all went up in a riot of flame. The stones of the wall glowed orange, liquefying and receding as a hole opened, spreading wider – Ember could not see much of what was beyond it but she had to hurry through. This was her last chance. When the matches went out, she would die.

With a cry she threw herself at the hole, crawling on hands and knees through the flames. The fire caught on her clothes, burning them away shockingly fast, as if they were flimsy paper or crackling dead leaves – but Ember felt no pain. She wriggled through the hole, writhing out naked on the other side, her hair glowing as violently as the fire that licked her body.

She felt the tingle of the hole closing behind her, and she yanked her feet free of it as with a hiss the matches all went out at once, and the portal they'd made disappeared.

Ember lay curled on her side, facing the white stone wall through which she'd come. She could barely bring herself to get up, or look around.

"Are you going to explain yourself?" A smooth voice from somewhere behind her startled Ember, and she pushed herself half upright.

A man stood by an enormous ebony fireplace, in a room of pure white stone threaded with veins of scarlet and silver. Coiled horns sprang from his black hair, and he wore a robe of black velvet and white fur. His eyes glowed amber in his dark handsome face. Though he was frowning, his full lips pulled aside as Ember arranged her abundant hair over her chest to cover herself.

"Are you my gift from Saint Nicholas?" said the man. "But I forgot – demons like myself are never visited with gifts, unless they be lumps of coal. Ever so useful, lumps of coal. But not nearly as lovely as you."

Ember rose, trying to conceal certain parts of her body with her hands. "Demon?" she whispered. "I must have wished wrong. I wished for warmth and kindness, generosity and freedom – safety."

"Wished?" The horned man strode to a nearby sofa – more luxurious than anything Ember had ever seen. He picked up a rich red blanket from the curved arm and tossed it to Ember. Gratefully she wrapped herself in it.

"Yes, I – I used my Gammer's matches," she said. "They are long-lasting, and they strike even when wet. I thought there was nothing else special about them until I used one to warm myself, and it – made a hole in the wall."

"Diabolic sulfur," said the demon, nodding. "We use it to create passages from our world to the human one, or to go quickly from place to place inside the human realm. Did your Gammer never teach you its purpose, little demoness?"

"Demoness?" Ember recoiled against the wall. "I'm no demoness."

"But of course you are. Only a demon can wield diabolic sulfur. To a human those matches would simply be matches – though they might occasionally give the user a glimpse of their inner desires."

"That's what the boys meant," gasped Ember. "And that's why fire doesn't burn me."

The man came closer, his handsome features softening. "You really knew nothing about all this, did you?"

Ember shook her head. Words piled up in her mind, sentences and questions contorting through her brain, but she couldn't voice any of it. Not yet.

"Come." The demon laid a warm hand on her arm. "I'll take you to my sister. She'll make sure you're properly dressed, and then you can join us for dinner. I'd wager this Gammer of yours was a witch. She probably stole you years ago, perhaps as vengeance against some demon who refused to do her bidding. We may be able to read your power signature and determine to which demonic family you belong – but even if we cannot discover your origins, you are welcome to stay here as long as you like."

Ember let him guide her through the room and into the elegant mansion beyond; and as she walked with him, she smiled. Already she was warm down to her bones, and a latent energy simmered along her veins, as if something had ignited during her baptism of fire, her passage through the hole in the wall.

Perhaps she was in Hell. But to her it felt like the most beautiful kind of Heaven.

Rebecca F. Kenney writes fantasy romance about monster girls & guys and the people who kiss them – usually with aspects of Irish or French mythology woven into the mix.

Santa Claus is Coming to Town

Bharat Krishnan

Eagle's Landing is the typical American suburb: HOA-regulated lawns, backhanded compliments if a neighbor sees your car outside ("Oh, you're so resourceful. I wish I could use my garage for storage too! Ed insists on cleaning it out each week.") and – tonight – commentary on the appropriateness of using Diwali lights for Christmas.

There's a light snow, but the windows in mom's shiny red RAV4 are down because I like feeling the flakes fall on my body. The white pinpricks of frozen rain are cold and sometimes feel like slaps from heaven, but somehow they're still inviting, even irresistible. My mom pulls into the cul-de-sac where Mr. Krishnaswamy lives and I hear him arguing with the president of our Home Owner's Association, Sandy White.

"Lights are lights," he grumbles. His nostrils flare as

he climbs down a ladder, having finished streaming the lights alongside the roof. "Why would I buy two different sets of them?"

"Because you've got two holidays," Sandy responds. "Magenta and blue are so pretty for Diwali, no one's contesting that. But Christmas is red and green; everyone knows that!"

"I'm not putting up and taking down all these lights twice within a month."

"Look, don't shoot the messenger; I'm just saying there've been complaints from the neighborhood."

Balling his hands into fists at his side, he exhales and throws them above his head. "Sandy, you're the president of the HOA. You *are* the neighborhood."

"Oh, well, thanks."

Sandy's a grownup and married and maybe related to royalty for all I know, but me and the boys never call her Mrs. White. She just looks like a Sandy, or Stupid Sandy if we're complaining about some new HOA policy that prohibits frisbee golf within 0.2 miles of a house or something. Even now, with Mr. Krishnaswamy yelling at her, she's blushing just because he acknowledged the reality that she is the HOA president. Hearing our car pull into the driveway, she turns her head and smiles, one of those big fake ones that drive me nuts.

"Debra and Carter! What are you doing at Mr. Krishn...err..."

Mr. Krishnaswamy sighs behind her, sticking those hands back into his pockets. "Carter's been friends with my son for over a decade, as you know."

"How fun!" Her face lights up like the lights on Mr.

Krishnaswamy's roof.

"Is there anything else?"

"Um, yes, one last thing..." Sandy's eyes find something fascinating on the pavement as she says her final piece. "You're not allowed to write on your front door..."

"Sandy, I need you to hear me." Stepping toward her, he lifts her chin and turns it to the threshold of his home. "It's my property and I can do whatever I want to it. Now if you'll excuse me, as you've seen, we have guests."

As he waves her off, she huffs and makes such a racket that a neighbor placing salt on his driveway across the street hears her.

"It's just, no one even knows what that means: *Nale Ba*. Why do you write it on the door each night?"

"It means come tomorrow, as we've told you before. Sandy, please, you know that HOA regulations don't apply to religious practices. I'm begging you: care about something else."

Leaving her at her car parked on the cul-de-sac by his mailbox, he turns and thanks my mom for bringing me over before telling her he'll drive me back later. The last things I see before he closes the door are my mom walking away and those words in another language: Nale Ba.

* * *

"Carter's here!"

The sound of a closing door attracts my best friend, Vignesh. He's a little clumsy and geeky, and I prefer hanging out at my house because his kinda smells weird,

43

but I don't have an Xbox.

"Hi, Carter!" Vignesh runs down the stairs so fast he almost trips over himself and rams his face into a wall. He looks to his dad, palms together like he's praying.

"Can we play Overcooked?"

"Did you finish your homework?"

"Yes."

"I'll check it after dinner."

"Thanks! Come on, dude."

Taking me by the hand, Vignesh rushes us upstairs to the Xbox in his room. I hear his dad talking to his mom as we leave.

"You won't believe what Sandy has a problem with now..."

Vignesh's bed is cluttered with books from school and the library. I toss a few to the floor to make room for us to sit as he powers up the TV. A big poster of Ryan Agarwal hangs near the window, right where Vignesh's eyes would be as he wakes up each morning.

"The great big hope for Indian NBA fans," Vignesh explains, handing me a controller. "He's committed to Stanford. Me and my dad expect big things."

It's hard to fathom the 6'6" Indian from the poster when the tallest Indian I know is Mr. Krishnaswamy, who once asked my dad for help grabbing a jar from the top of his pantry.

"This is the game I was telling you about yesterday."

Vignesh smiles so wide you'd think someone told him school was cancelled. I can't bear to tell him I thought "overcooked" was code for some fighting game.

As he clicks on the menu screen, I see pictures of people making meals in a kitchen. Who actually wants to play a cooking game?

"How do you play?"

The game is actually high stakes. People put in their orders for burgers or sushi or whatever. You fill the orders within a time limit, frying meat and cutting tomatoes and boiling rice. It's like taking a school test, only fun. And we get to work together.

"You fry the beef while I cut veggies and do dishes," I tell him.

Vignesh's smile is infectious; I've caught it too after playing a couple of rounds. "What did you ask Santa to get you tomorrow?"

I can't help but laugh. "You believe in that stuff?"

"Santa? Sure. My mom mails my letter each year."

"Your mom is lying to you."

Vignesh stops playing. I see a burger burn on the fryer and wince. He's my best friend and all, but he's also a baby sometimes.

"Moms don't lie."

I remember the time my mom told me her car wouldn't start unless I put on my seatbelt. I can't tell him that, so instead I pick up a science textbook from the ground. "Think about it logically, man. How is one dude going to get to all the houses in the world in a few hours?"

You ever ruin the myth of Santa Claus for someone in real time? It's like telling a person they have cancer. I find myself actually hugging Vignesh as he heaves in air, and I have to remind myself he has asthma. He wipes a

45

booger on my shoulder. I pretend not to notice.

"Why...would...she...*lie* to me?"

"Some adults, they think it's better for you to believe in silly stories than understand the truth."

That's what Mom told me when I discovered the truth and she forbade me from telling Kara, my sister. She's turning eight next month; that's old enough to know the truth in my book.

"Hold on to your innocence a bit longer," Mom said. "Don't be in such a hurry to grow up."

That's rubbish. Growing up means cooler things, more freedom. I can't wait.

We carry on in silence for a bit longer. As the game goes on, we stop making burgers and sushi and make burritos instead. The orders get more complex. This person wants beef and cheese and tomatoes. That person wants lettuce and rice and pork. The ticking timer mocks me.

"I wonder if there's Indian food in this game, too," Vignesh says. "What if you have to, like, make bhindi masala or something?"

"Gross." I laugh. "It's a good thing you can't smell food through a TV." The words are out of my mouth before I realize they're offensive. I'm two for two. And on the night before Christmas. If Santa was real, he'd be switching me from the nice list to the naughty one. Vignesh looks like he might cry.

"Hey, man, I didn't mean anything by it. Lighten up."

He's breathing loudly, looking for his inhaler. If he has a panic attack I won't be able to play with him for the rest of break. That means no Xbox.

"Of course I like Indian food," I lie. "Mom brought me over for dinner, didn't she? Would I agree to that if I thought it stinks? I was just joshing you!"

It's enough to calm him down. Maybe not all lies are bad.

We're called down for dinner and I have to catch Vignesh as he runs down the stairs to make sure he doesn't trip over himself again. Personally, I've never run toward food. And this meal? Entering the kitchen takes me back to when Kara still needed her diaper changed. Something is bubbling on a pot at the table for four. I look inside and see green liquid that reminds me of the time Roger Hernandez puked in recess after we dared him to eat earthworms and he actually did.

Above Mr. Krishnaswamy's seat looms a portrait of a fifth resident, some Hindu god with an elephant head and four arms. The adjoining living room has a statue of another four-armed god holding a mace and sword. Those are cool. When dad takes me to church all I learn about is forgiveness. Lame. Maybe weird is better. I take another smell of the room as Mrs. Krishnaswamy scoops out some green goop and puts it on my plate. Nah.

I barely touch my food.

"It's creamed spinach and cheese," Mr. Krishnaswamy explains, seeing my plate.

Spinach? It's Christmas Eve! These people are mental.

"Ravi, I can make something else..." Mrs. Krishnaswamy is already on her feet when her husband grabs her hand.

"Shubha, Carter is fine." He faces me and adopts

47

that tone where a parent isn't mad, just disappointed. I try not to gag on his moral superiority and the smell of dinner. "It's important to try things from other cultures. Don't you think it's strange you and Vignesh have been friends for so long and this is the first time you've been over for dinner since kindergarten?"

I'd begged mom to pick me up before dinner, but she's at yoga class right now. Whatever.

I put on the same smile as when a teacher asks me if I had a good summer. What made it good was the fact that I didn't see them at all. "I'm just a light eater, Mrs. Krishnaswamy, but it's really good!" I take a bite of the green mix with some rice to make it look convincing. It doesn't totally suck.

"See?" Mr. Krishnaswamy smiles watching me take a second bite. "We have so much to teach one another. For instance, while Christmas is so celebrated in the Western world, Indians actually regard it as one of the scariest days of the year."

Vignesh fidgets in his seat. He must've heard this story a million times. One thing our dads have in common: they love repeating stuff. And they go nuts when you ask them to do it.

"Really?" My eyes widen to the size of Bambi's. "Why's that?"

"Let me tell you the story of the Nale Ba...a witch with onion-shaped earrings and pitch-black hair that falls down to her legs haunts the streets of Bangalore at night, the city where the Krishnaswamys are from. Her skin is the color of dried blood, and her eyes glow in the dark." Mr. Krishnaswamy turns off the lights for effect and steps toward me.

So far, the scariest thing about this is his breath.

"Centuries ago," he explains, "she was murdered on the eve of her wedding, on Christmas Eve, in fact."

I lean in. If I'm going to feign interest, I might as well commit. Maybe this'll help me land a part in the school play next year. "She was murdered?"

"People didn't like that she was marrying a white man."

Hmm. I've got friends who won't even let Vignesh in their house because of their parents' prejudices, but you never really think of it the other way. Interesting.

"They burned her at the stake."

"Like the Salem witch trials?" It's both weird and cool that opposite sides of the world would agree on the same form of punishment for witches.

"Yeah, like that."

"And what about the guy? Did they kill him too?"

Mrs. Krishnaswamy places a hand on her husband's shoulder, standing to speak. "Different stories say different things. In some he escaped, in others he died with her."

No happy ending? Disney couldn't make a movie of it. That's a shame. She sounded badass.

"So, what's the Nale Ba?"

Mr. Krishnaswamy chuckles as his wife continues. Vignesh is almost under the table at this point, crawling further with each minute the story goes on.

"The witch has no real name, but we call her Nale Ba. It means "come tomorrow" in Kannada. A few years after her murder, the men responsible started to disappear."

"What happened to them?"

An alarm from upstairs starts ringing before she can answer me.

"Ravi?"

"Let me check on it." He grabs a flashlight from the kitchen and heads upstairs. The noise is deafening. I take the opportunity to sift some of my food onto Vignesh's plate while everyone's distracted. It was good, but it wasn't great. Besides, I've got a reputation to maintain. Mr. Krishnaswamy emerges minutes later; the sound is gone.

"It's starting to come down a bit harder out there." As he opens some blinds, I see the snow's picked up speed. "Some snow blew into the attic. Bad weather and piping. Just as bad a duo as gas and fire."

I hope I don't have to spend the night here. Vignesh is cool and all, but it sounds like they're an hour or two away from losing power. We couldn't play Xbox in that case.

"Anyways," Mrs. Krishnaswamy said, continuing with his story, "the men kept disappearing and no one could figure out why. All that was left of them was their burnt clothes."

Vignesh is now fully under the table. Was he embarrassed or scared?

"Hang on." I remember the fight Mr. Krishnaswamy had with Stupid Sandy. "You've got Nale Ba written on your front door."

"You're a smart kid," Mrs. Krishnaswamy says.

I smile at the praise.

"Eventually, the mayor discovered writing that phrase on your house kept the witch away."

"Why?"

"It means 'come tomorrow,' right? Unlike men, she asks permission and respects your wishes." She takes my open mouth as a sign I want more food, doling out more on my plate. "The Nale Ba loves Christmas because it's the one holiday where we encourage a stranger to break into our homes."

"If the witch asks permission, why does anyone say yes?" There's a tremor in my voice I use the food to try to hide.

"That's the scariest thing about the Nale Ba. She can adopt the voice of anyone you know, the people you trust most. What would you do if she impersonated your dad and came knocking at your house?"

I think of all the times dad has made silly voices when telling me stories. I try gulping down the food and my fear. "I'd know the truth."

Mr. Krishnaswamy turns the lights back on, seizing me by the shoulders. "I hope so. For your sake."

His voice and touch shake me to my core for the briefest of moments. Vignesh's head is all that's visible above the table. I sigh in relief that my doubts will be a secret between me and his dad.

"It's just a fun story, Carter. Come, get your things and I'll drive you home."

As we leave, I notice the front door more now that I've heard the story. Nale Ba. It's written in Canadian (No, that's not right. Kannada?). Squiggly lines that look like a mix between numbers and cursive. Snow has wiped some of the lettering off. Globs of the wintry mix have piled up on the Krishnaswamy porch.

"I'll rewrite it when I return," Mr. Krishnaswamy says.

Ignoring him, I run to his Honda Accord and leap inside. Mom will be so smug when I return. She told me I'd be cold and yet I refused to wear my cap and gloves. I wait as the car heats up and Mr. Krishnaswamy brushes some snow off the top and mirrors. I text Vignesh to fill the silence: *next time, let's play Rainbow Six.*

"All set?" Mr. Krishnaswamy pulls out of the driveway. 7:40 means the sun's been down for a while. With his headlights on, I see which neighbors have free time on their hands and which have lives. The more intricate peoples' Christmas lights, the more obvious it is they have nothing else to do.

As we pass my neighbor's house, a rocking Santa hoisted on a small pole and strung up with lights calls out to me. "Do you belong on the naughty list, Carter?" Even with the windows closed, I hear the voice echo in my head.

"That's a cool trick."

"What's that?" Mr. Krishnaswamy turns his head to look at me and steer the car onto my road.

"My neighbor hooked that Santa up to his Wi-Fi or something, right? How else do you get that voice? It must be motion activated."

"You kids and your gadgets."

He pulls into the driveway, saluting my mom as she opens our screen door for me. "Thanks, Ravi!" she says. "Tell Shubha I said hi!"

Opening the door, I hear Mr. Krishnaswamy tell me

to help my dad shovel the walk tomorrow. He grunts and pulls away when I tell him Dad'll just hire someone to do it for us.

"Come in before you get sick, and wipe your feet on the mat!"

I take a moment before obeying Mom, looking at how the snow is sticking now. There's enough to make snowballs. Digging my bare hands into the layer of white, I ball some up and ignore her scolding. I throw it at the neighbor's Santa and miss.

"Do you belong on the naughty list, Carter?"

"Hey, the voice changed!" I pull Mom's yoga pants in excitement as I wipe my feet off before entering the house.

"What are you talking about?"

"The Santa next door. It sounded like Mr. Nichols in the car, but just now that was Uncle Earl. When'd he have time to hang out with Mr. Nichols?"

Mom rolls her eyes and tousles my hair.

Our Christmas tree towers over everyone, impossible to miss as soon as you open the door. Lights from some fancy boutique store are strewn across it and presents from friends and family wait patiently below to be ripped open. The smells of buttery rolls and honey ham and cinnamon frosting embrace me as I walk through the kitchen. Kara offers me a cupcake overflowing with icing as I sit next to my dad and serve myself.

"I was about to put this stuff away," Mom says. "Didn't you eat enough at dinner?"

"Indian food is gross." There's too much food in my

mouth. I sound like I'm underwater.

"Carter!" Mom tousles my hair again. "That's not a nice thing to say. You know, I didn't like yoga at first, but it's done wonders for me. And actually, it's from India!"

"Let him be," Dad says. He's reading the paper, not even looking at me. But that's the thing about Dad; I don't need to see him to know him. "It's good Carter knows his preferences so early."

I think back to Mrs. Krishnaswamy's question: *Would you know if the Nale Ba impersonated your dad?* Of course I would. And besides, what am I thinking? The Nale Ba isn't real.

"Well," Mom says, "finish quickly. It doesn't look too bad outside yet. We can still make the 8:15 service."

Kara squeals in delight. She loves going to church, especially if it means she gets to stay up past her bedtime. Weirdo.

* * *

Pastor Cal read from the Sermon on the Mount: "For where your treasure is, there will your heart be also. Is not life more than food, and the body more than clothes?"

At almost twelve years old – practically a teenager – I know he's laying it on thick.

"Let's go." Dad's just finished scraping snow off the dashboard, tapping his foot outside the church while Mom tells the pastor goodbye. Strapping myself into our RAV4, I see the same rocking Santa my neighbor has.

"Do you belong on the naughty list, Carter?"

Even with the car several meters away and the noise

of others shuffling out of the church, I hear Pastor Cal's voice come through it clear as day. There are no lights strung up around this one. I struggle to see what's supporting its weight; there doesn't seem to be a pole or anything holding it up.

"Let's go, honey. I just wanted to wish Pastor Cal a Merry Christmas."

Our car pulls away. But the voice remains in my head.

I share a bedroom with Kara. I asked for my own space last year and saw Dad frowning as I mailed a letter to the North Pole. One of several ways I knew St. Nick wasn't real.

"Goodnight, my prince and princess," Mom says.

My smile is as fake as Santa. Princes don't share. Sometimes I wish Mom and Dad only had one kid again.

"Goodnight!" Kara chirps.

Lights out.

Kara rustles around in bed, as loud as the emerging storm outside and even more annoying. "What do you think Santa's bringing? Do you think we laid out enough cookies? Do you think I was good this year? Do you think you were good this year? What do you think is his favorite movie?" Her queries come with the speed of the snowballs I launched at Freddie in the church parking lot before service began. Looking through our window, I see the Santa next door is totally covered in the storm.

"Snow's picked up."

That gets Kara out of bed. "Do you think Santa will get hurt? Should we go help him?"

"Kara, Santa isn't real!"

She starts crying. I shouldn't have yelled. Mom will be here soon if I can't make it stop.

"Hey." I get into her bed, hold her to my shoulders. "I'm sorry. I lied."

"You lied?" She looks up at me with eyes from some anime show.

"I just wanted you to stop talking."

"Why don't you like me?"

The question stops my heart. By all accounts, she's awesome. My own personal cheerleader.

"What makes you think I don't like you?"

The threat of a meltdown has dissipated, but she's still rubbing her snot on my flannel pajamas. "You never play with me anymore."

Kids. I've outgrown such things, but the truth would hurt too much right now. Maybe not all lies are bad.

"What if I stay up, huh? Make sure that Santa's okay?"

There's that smile again, as if she's a character from *Spirited Away*. She nods and lets sleep transport her to a world where fairy tales exist.

* * *

Christ.

I look at my alarm clock: 2 a.m. Despite my best efforts, sleep seized me. This won't happen again when I'm a grownup.

Looking out the window, I see the weight of the snow on trees has caused some branches to break off in the yard. I hear the wind uprooting Mom's holly bushes. What started as a few harmless white flakes has turned into a deadly blizzard within hours. Gathering my thoughts, I open the bedroom door and make my way downstairs. I can still catch Dad in the act.

"Have a holly, jolly Christmas, it's the best time of the year."

Music is playing from the basement. The door under the stairs is open. I look in and see nothing but blackness.

"Dad?" I call out, but no one answers. The tree in the living room is adorned with red and green lights crisscrossing the branches, but all the gifts are missing. Did Dad take them downstairs? I step on a squeaky stair, grabbing the bannister for support, and that's when the power goes out. I shriek, but luckily no one's there to hear me.

Luckily?

Where is Dad?

"Do you belong on the naughty list, Carter?"

Dad! He's at the front door.

I call out. "You fixing the power?"

I can see his nodding head through a side window. He's got a sack over his back. Relief flows through me like the cool breeze outside, slapping me in the face and bringing me to attention.

I go to the door. "You locked yourself out?"

"Locked out." His voice is like a warm cup of cider. I can't help but smile.

"You want me to open the door?"

"Open the door." His eyes speak to my soul.

"You have presents?"

"Presents." He shows them to me, a bag so big it masks his face.

"Will you admit you're Santa?"

"Santa." He points to a big red hat on his head. Amazingly, the blizzard hasn't knocked it off his head. In fact, there isn't one drop of snow on his entire body.

I open the door and let him in, grab the bag of gifts and rummage through it as he wipes his feet on the doormat. "Dad, you got me the neighbor's rocking Santa? How'd you do the voice?"

There's no rocking Santa, though. Actually, there's just one gift in the entire bag.

"What is this?"

And that's when I see her.

The Nale Ba, the witch. She has long black hair that goes down to her shins and onion-shaped earrings that glow red and gold in the dark. A blue sari is draped around skin the color of dried blood. She grabs my arm and her long fingernails cut into me. The cut goes deeper than mere skin, though, opening a wound within my soul that I know only she can heal. Tears stream down my face.

"Listen," she rasps. Her voice slides through bone and flesh to enter my heart and seize it, forcing me to obey.

I can't help but comply with her every desire. It takes all my strength to lift up my head, my ear cocked toward the stairs, though my eyes remain locked with hers.

"They can't hear." She whispers the words.

I scream anyway. No one comes.

Our time together will be a secret no one ever discovers.

"I've watched you all day, hoping." She sounds so sad I want to apologize. "You are not my beloved."

The white guy she married?

"I'll keep looking. There's always next year."

Does that mean she'll let me go?

"Oh, no, my dear boy." Her eyes tell me she can read my thoughts. "Though I couldn't enter your friend's house at first, I saw you from the window. And when the snow smeared the words off their front door, I snuck in and even had the palak paneer you wasted."

A lump the size of coal forms in my throat.

"Do you know what the perfect dessert is to wash down spinach and cheese?"

The back of my neck burns as my body lifts off the ground. I'm floating. The Nale Ba turns from me, placing her one gift under the tree with a note.

"The gift is for Kara, an iPhone just like she wanted, but the note is for your parents," she explains. "Want to know what it says?"

I can't answer. I can't breathe. The lump in my throat is suffocating me.

"Sometimes, it's better to believe in silly stories than try and learn the truth. Sometimes, ignorance really is bliss. Make sure to teach that to your daughter."

She opens her mouth, revealing fangs I know will tear my flesh apart, and the last thing I see is the white snow flying in the wind outside, oblivious to the harm it'll leave for others to try and fix tomorrow.

Bharat calls himself a professional storyteller and amateur cook. After 10 years of working in politics, he tried to explain how the country went from Barack Obama to Donald Trump by writing Confessions of a Campaign Manager. Then he wrote Oasis, a desert-fantasy novel that examined what makes a family and how refugees should be treated.

Bharat is always looking to make a political statement with his writing because he knows politics seeps into every aspect of society and believes we can't understand each other without a firm, constant understanding of how politics affects us in all ways.

In 2021, he released Privilege: A Trilogy, an #ownvoices thriller about an Indian-American set in modern-day NYC.

A Pea Ever After

Adie Hart

I've seen a lot of strange things in my time as a District Witch, but even I wasn't expecting a man-sized peacock to open the castle door. My fist hovered in the air mid-knock for a few seconds before I remembered my manners, brushed the snow from my hair, and smiled politely.

"Good evening," I said. "May I come in?"

The peacock looked flustered, in much the same way as a chicken looks flustered if you open the coop before dawn, except that he attempted to disguise it by straightening his rather elaborate brocade jacket. He glanced at the clipboard he held in one wing.

"We're not expecting anyone tonight," he said, but he sounded worried, not cross. Sometimes when people saw the District uniform they closed their faces and their doors abruptly, but this peacock just seemed stressed. It *was* quite late. I'd normally never think of arriving at a host's house – or castle – without sending word ahead, but the snowstorm had made rather a hash of my travel plans. Terribly impolite, but I was still leagues away from the village of Oakvale, where I'd been headed, and this was the first building I'd spotted in hours. I just wanted to dry off, warm up, and sleep. The law said any homeowner owed hospitality to a District Witch in need, but I hoped the owners of this castle wouldn't find my timing too rude.

The peacock was still running his eyes over his clipboard and muttering to himself. I had thought to do the official introductions indoors, once I had feeling in my toes, but it didn't seem as though he was going to let me in without some explanation.

"I'm Elsie," I said. "I'm here to –"

The peacock startled suddenly, tail exploding outwards for a second.

"My lady!" he cried, waving me in. "I apologise for not recognising you. Come in, come in." He bustled me through the door and before I knew it I found myself dripping my way up several flights of stairs behind a plump peahen in a mobcap and apron.

"Just a little further, dearie, that's it, and you'll soon be tucked up all cosylike in bed." That sounded delightful, but something was niggling at me. "Shouldn't I present myself to my hosts first?"

"No, no, we'll see if that's necessary in the morning," came the reply, and before I could wonder what she meant, she opened a door and my brain stopped working. Inside the luxuriously decorated bedchamber was the most enormous, most pillowy, most deliciously squishy-looking bed. There must have been six mattresses, all stacked on top of each other. I couldn't think about anything other than kicking off my boots and snuggling down under those fluffy covers. I barely noticed as the peahen helped me out of my wet clothes and into an embroidered nightgown, towelled off my hair, and guided me up the little set of wooden steps to settle in the bed.

"Now then, dearie," she said. "You be sure and call me the moment you need something, yes?"

I mumbled something affirmative as I sank into the softness. There were warm wrapped bricks at the bottom of the bed. I'd never been more comfortable.

"At any time," she said, rather forcefully. "Please, as soon as you wake even a little bit."

I would have replied, but honestly, I was already asleep.

* * *

"Wake up, wake up, wake up!" trilled a high voice in an aggressively sing-song manner. I blinked against the sudden stab of light as a silhouetted figure swept the curtains open. Clearly not content with assaulting my eyeballs, they swept the covers off the bed in one swift movement and lunged for the pillow I was curled up on.

"I'm up!" I cried, scrambling down the steps at the side of the bed. Years of District training had largely suppressed my instincts to panic when under attack, but I'd never been at my best first thing in the morning, and it had been a long night. I'd been so deeply asleep I hadn't even heard anyone come in.

Under the guise of stretching and yawning, I examined the intruder. She was a tall woman, somewhere in her middle-fifties, with silver-streaked brown hair in an immaculate knot and a figure women half her age would kill for. Oh, and a large pair of silver wings fluttering behind her.

"Good morning, madam," I said politely. If I'd known my host was a fairy, I would have been a lot more careful to set up my wards before I'd knocked. Such a beginner's error. Well, I'd just have to be on my guard now.

She waved a hand dismissively. "How did you sleep?"

"Wonderfully, thank you. Well, until you –"

"Wrong answer," she sighed, cutting me off. "I don't know what's wrong with princesses these days."

"I'm not –" I started to protest, but she barely noticed.

"Never mind, can't be helped. Get yourself dressed and come down to breakfast."

Before I could reply, she swept from the room. I got the impression she was the sort of person who swept everywhere.

* * *

I followed a peacock footman down to the breakfast room, feeling awkward in the bright green velvet gown I'd found laid out for me. Someone had cleaned and dried my coat and boots overnight, but there was no sign of my practical District uniform dress, with its ankle length wool skirt and smart collar; instead, I'd been laced into this frippery by a peahen maid. I tried not to trip over its elaborate train, hoping the rather daring neckline would be enough to keep everything where it ought to be. I'd ignored the matching silk slippers in favour of my boots, though. They'd be hidden under this ridiculous skirt, and a witch always needs to be able to run.

The footman (footbird?) handed me over to the same butler I'd met the night before, who bowed magnificently before ushering me through the door. Sat around a table heaped with food were three young women, all wearing identical dresses to mine and chatting while they ate. Beside me, the peacock rustled his feathers and coughed politely, and once he'd caught their attention, he announced:

"Presenting Princess Elsabetta of Accasia!"

Oh no. That definitely wasn't right.

"Um, I'm not –"

But he was already gone. Did no one in this castle ever let you finish a sentence?

"Welcome," said one of the young women, waving me over to the table with a smile. All three of them were stunningly beautiful, but she was the most polished somehow, exuding confidence and elegance with every movement. Even the violently green gown suited her, making her brown skin glow. As I sat, she introduced herself as Princess Intisar of Kisia; the tanned brunette with the incredibly blue eyes was Princess Harriet of Marland, and the youngest, who had hair as red as autumn leaves, was Princess Arrianora of Iveria.

"Elsabetta is a beautiful name," said Princess Arrianora. I thought she was probably around seventeen, several years younger than the rest of us. Her smile was polite, but not quite as effortless as the smile of the Kisian princess: I assumed the ease came with years of constant practice.

"It's just Elsie," I protested, accepting a large cup of

tea from a footbird.

"Oh, of course," she said, visibly relaxing. Her natural grin was a little lopsided, which made her look much more vibrant. "Everyone calls me Nora. The whole thing is a bit of a mouthful."

"And we can't be *your-highness*ing each other all the time or we'll run out of breath," added Harriet. Intisar nodded her approval.

"That's kind," I said. "But really, it's just Elsie. Elsie Cooper, District Witch. There's been a mix up – I'm not a princess."

"Thank *goodness*," breathed Intisar. "Someone's finally come." They looked at me with new interest.

"Are you in disguise?" hissed Nora delightedly.

"Wait – you'd requested a District investigation?" I'd thought this was just a house party and a case of mistaken identity, but things were getting stranger and stranger. What had I walked into?

"No, we haven't had a chance, with the snowstorms so bad. But we were hoping our parents would be getting worried. Who sent the message, in the end?"

"I'm sorry," I said. "I don't know – I don't even know if there was a message. I wasn't sent here officially, I just got caught in the storm and needed somewhere to stay."

Their faces fell in unison. Even their frowns were pretty.

"But I'll help now I'm here. Tell me what's going on."

But before any of them could reply, the door opened again and in swept my early morning visitor (I had definitely been right about the sweeping).

"Ah," said Intisar. "I'm pretty sure she'll explain it all herself."

The fairy woman was as imposing as I remembered. Even if she hadn't had those phenomenal wings stretching behind her, she still would have been one of those people who take up all the space in any room they're in. She swept her gaze over us, and smiled icily.

"Good, you're all *finally* here," she said, which was rich considering I was sure she'd waited until she could make an appropriately dramatic entrance. "Ladies, we have a new arrival, as you can see. Please make her feel at home – although don't forget, she's your competition!" My confusion must have shown on my face, as she laughed. "Ah, but I get ahead of myself. Princess Elsabetta" – she continued speaking over my squeak of protest – "let me introduce you to the reason we're all here: the divine, the delectable, the deeply *available* Prince Percival."

You'd think it would be quite hard to miss a whole six foot two of lanky, floppy-haired prince, but he must have been caught up in all the sweeping-in, because I hadn't noticed the young man standing beside her until he gave me a sheepish wave. I waved back, feeling rather silly.

"I know, you're wondering how he's still unattached. Really, we quite despair of him." She chuckled, but there was an edge to it that implied there was rather more truth in her words than humour. "I, in case you do not know, am Lady Prudence, advisor to Queen Isabelle, and since Percival's very birth I have been toiling tirelessly to assure my godson of his Happily Ever After, as I did his mother, and her mother before her, and so on. And yet! No princess has been worthy of this sweet, this noble, this wonderful boy, and so here you are, the cream of the crop."

"More like we're who's left," muttered Nora in my ear, and I stifled a snort. This wonderful boy, I noticed, was doing his level best to fade into the wallpaper. I guessed he was about my age, which seemed a little too old to still need a fairy godmother.

"Madam, there's been a mistake," I said. "I shouldn't be included in this – I'm not who you think I am."

She just laughed lightly at me. "Oh, I've heard that one before! But there's no need to be humble, dear, even if your kingdom is rather small. You're as valid as any other royal. Now, we'll hear no more about it."

"But –"

"No more." Suddenly there was steel in her voice, and I decided it would be better to stay quiet. At least I could investigate this a little further if I played along.

"Where was I? Ah yes. My dears, you are competing for the hand of Prince Percival." Lady Prudence beamed around the room like she was expecting gasps of awe and a round of applause. Receiving neither, she pursed her lips and continued. "I thought a classic test would show which of you was the most delicate and princess-like, but clearly, royal standards are not what they used to be. You all failed, even our newcomer."

"What test?" I asked. Had I made some error with the cutlery? I'd only just woken up, for goodness' sake.

"Why, the pea!" she cried. "Not one of you felt the pea underneath your mattresses. You should have been utterly unable to sleep, bruised black and blue from feeling it."

"A pea?" asked Intisar incredulously. "That bed was a mile deep."

"And a *true* princess would have felt it regardless. I was hoping dear Elsabetta would be successful, but never mind. Aren't we lucky those storms mean you're all still here?" She fixed her winning smile firmly back in place. "Let me tell you how the rest of this contest will proceed."

What I gathered from her elaborate presentation was this: she planned to hold another trial in order to decide which of us was the perfect princess, by some standard of royal behaviour known only to her. While she thought of something appropriate, we were to wait and practice our princess-y traits (which I wasn't entirely certain I possessed), and get to know Prince Percival; if he expressed a preference for one of us, that would be "taken into consideration", which sounded ominous. I didn't like to think what her plans were if the preference wasn't mutual. As she expounded on his many virtues, the eligible prince himself blushed harder and harder. Not the usual arrogant type, then. And were those ink stains on his hands?

"Ah, and I notice some of you have some magical affinity," said Prudence. "It won't count against you, but just so everything's fair, I've put a dampening spell on the castle, so don't bother trying to magic your way to the top. It won't work." I flicked a levitation spell at my teacup, but she wasn't kidding. It remained resolutely on the table. That was going to make things very difficult.

"It will be like a little holiday for you," Prudence said. "It's just that at the end one of you will be betrothed!"

"And if we don't want to participate? May we leave?" I asked, and was met with a peal of laughter from Prudence.

"Oh my dear, you're welcome to try! But somehow, I simply don't believe you'll make it through the snow." As if by command, an icy wind slammed one of the grand windows open, and a flurry of snow began to speckle the floor. By the time Nora and I had wrestled it closed again, Prudence had left.

* * *

For the next few days, we saw no more of Prudence; it seemed she was going to leave us mostly to our own devices. Intisar, Nora, and Harriet welcomed me into their group, which was a relief. People often see a District Witch or Wizard as some kind of untouchable outsider, rather than someone who's there to help, and while objectivity can be useful on an investigation, I was secretly grateful I didn't have to rattle around this draughty castle on my own.

They were good company, too, far less stuffy and proper than I'd expected from my previous experience of royalty. None of them had known each other before arriving, but they'd become close after spending the last two weeks alone here; their attendants had all fallen ill as soon as they arrived (I put another item on my mental 'suspicious' list), and were recuperating in the servants' quarters, so it was make friends or moulder here alone, I supposed.

Intisar was incredibly sharp behind her polished exterior, and was always ready to amuse with some dramatic tale, whether about her twelve brothers and sisters or some ancient hero. Nora and Harriet were alike in their wicked humour, though Nora was quite content to sit and play her mandolin or read, while Harriet felt cooped up and frustrated without her usual twice-daily horse ride and weapons practice. She seemed to have more energy than a yearling dragon; although we checked every day for a way to get her outside to train, all the exterior doors were frozen shut or blocked with snow, and every time we opened a window it iced over instantly. Harriet settled for running laps of the hallway wearing her nightgown and an old pair of the prince's boots she'd cajoled from one of the footbirds. I joined her once, thinking it would be good not to get too soft, but found myself left behind and panting after only a few minutes.

In the evenings, we commandeered a parlour to hole up in, building up the fire to keep out the chill that suffused the castle and talking well into the night. I learned that this wasn't the first time any of the princesses had been sent off for a 'visit' that was a thinly-veiled excuse to introduce them to possible spouses, but they told me that they were usually activity-packed affairs with dozens of eligible young royals of all genders, intended to create lots of mingling opportunities; it wasn't at all usual to have everything focused on marrying off the host.

And trials were unheard of.

"Maybe in my grandmother's time," said Nora. "But who's going to put up with being tested like that, in this day and age?"

"Us," said Harriet morosely. "We haven't got any choice, have we?"

It was well after dark on the third night, and we'd begged a bottle of peapod burgundy from a footbird. Now the four of us were draped across the common room in a fashion that would have horrified Prudence, if she'd seen. Intisar was stretched out on one of the sofas with her feet in Harriet's lap, while Nora sat sideways in a plush armchair and dangled her legs over its side. I was curled up in front of the fire, enjoying the warmth beating on my back; I missed my warm, practical dresses more than anything.

"I wonder what kind of trial she'll stick us with next," said Nora. "Do you think she'll tell us, or try to trick us again? Oh no, do you think she's testing us now?" She tried to sit up straighter, but just ended up spilling her wine.

"Oh, come on, let's not ruin a nice night," said Intisar. "Have I told you about the time at Prince Martin's house party when the Countess of Spondheim fell into the fountain?"

She launched into a stream of colourful, incisive gossip, and although I laughed until my sides hurt as the girls traded stories, I ended up feeling glad no one really cared about the romantic affairs of a District Witch; the scrutiny seemed exhausting. Eventually, the conversation turned from gossiping about suitors past to dreaming of suitors future.

"I'd like to rescue a beautiful princess," said Harriet dramatically. "A real classic, you know, fire-breathing dragon, impenet - imprene - a tower that's very hard to get in, the works. I can just see her there, gazing up at me adoringly."

"My heroine," sighed Intisar, feigning a swoon, which was impressive considering she was already lying down.

"Zactly," said Harriet. "An oldie but a goodie."

"So Percy's out, then?" I asked.

"Percy is *out,*" she said. "I only came 'cause I thought there were going to be princesses."

"There are princesses," I pointed out.

"Yes, but we're not supposed to be looking at each other, are we?" said Intisar. "We're supposed to be competing for Percy."

"Well, I don't want him," laughed Nora. "He's so old!"

The rest of us all squealed at this, and Harriet threw a cushion at her: Percy was twenty-six, the same age as Harriet and only a year older than Intisar and me. To a seventeen year old, though, we all must have seemed positively decrepit.

"It doesn't matter anyway, does it? Elsie's going to sort it all out and none of us will have to marry Percy," said Nora.

A cheer went up from all three of them, but I stilled, realising the weight of my responsibility. I still didn't know if another DW was coming to investigate, so it was up to me to somehow prevent a deeply unhappy marriage without offending a fairy. But Harriet interrupted my worries.

"What about you, Elsie?" she asked. "Who do you dream of?"

"I don't know," I admitted. "Someone smart, I suppose, and kind. Someone who doesn't mind me going off adventuring – or maybe someone who'll come with me."

"Pft, that's too vague," complained Intisar, and she started describing her perfect partner. While like me, she didn't seem to care about gender, , the rest of her list of desired attributes was long, extremely specific, and wildly improbable. Soon we were all laughing again, and it was a long time before we made it to bed. But two things were clear:

None of them wanted to marry Prince Percival.

And they wanted me to tell him.

* * *

I found him in the library, of course. I'd learned over the last few days that wherever there were books, there was likely to be an inkstained Percy lurking nearby, and we'd bumped into each other several times when browsing the shelves. At first we'd been awkward around each other, but once I'd revealed my true identity he'd warmed up considerably, and it turned out that he, too, was good company. He was always willing to share what he was working on (mostly translations of ancient legends, which were fascinating), as long as he could pepper me with questions about life as a District Witch: the people I'd met, the cases I'd solved, the places I'd seen. Quite often, we didn't even notice the afternoon slipping away until one of the footbirds had to fetch us both for dinner.

His desk was covered in open books and more quills than I'd ever seen. The one behind his ear was especially jaunty. I sat down across from him, and after a few minutes of helping him figure out a difficult verb, I realised I was just going to have to come out with it.

"There's no nice way to say this, Percy, but none of us particularly wants to marry you."

"Oh, charming," said Percy.

"It's not you, I swear, you're perfectly – I mean, it *is*

you a bit for Harriet, but I think you'd say the same about her – what I'm trying to say is that you're very nice but –" I could feel the blood rising to my face as every scrap of my diplomacy training fled the room.

"Do go on," he said, pressing his lips together hard.

"Look, you're a prince, which is lovely, and you're very good-looking, which is not guaranteed, I can tell you," I said.

"Mm-hm," he said, lips flattening even further. He looked about as comfortable as I felt, shifting in his chair as if he couldn't wait to get away. I'd really made a hash of this.

"It's just that none of us is really in the market for a husband, however attractive you are and...and...you're teasing me, aren't you?"

A guffaw burst out of him and he flopped forward onto the table, shoulders shaking. "Oh, curses, I wanted to see how long you could keep going!"

Prince or no prince, he deserved the swat I gave him. "You beast!"

"I'm sorry, I'm sorry!" he cried, hands flailing in defence. "But you do have a point, about the marrying. I'm not exactly thrilled with the arrangement either, but Aunty Pru is just so hard to stop once she gets started. She got this glint in her eye when Mother got sick, borrowed my favourite quill and a stack of envelopes, and three days later the first princess arrived."

"You mean you didn't sanction this entire contest-slash-hostage situation as a celebration of yourself? I'm shocked."

"She means well, Elsie, she's just... she thinks I'd be happier being the kind of prince she's used to. The kind that slays dragons and marries princesses."

"She'd love Harriet," I said dryly. "But you're not that kind of prince?"

"Put it this way: she never even asked if I liked girls before she more or less kidnapped you all for me."

"Oh. Do you mean...do you not like girls?"

"No, no, I do!" It was Percy's turn to blush furiously, which I felt was well deserved. "I just mean, none of this seems to be about me. It's like she's got a picture of her perfect godson in her head and it doesn't matter what I want. I'm not saying I don't want to get married ever, you know. But it's not as urgent as Aunty Pru's making it seem, and I'd like to meet someone who shares my interests, not just whoever she deems most princess-y. What does that even mean?"

"I'll let you know when we find out," I said. "But in the meantime I'm glad we're all on the same page." I grinned at him, and gathered my things. "Let's make a plan later. I need to go and stick my face in a snowdrift after thinking you were going to have me beheaded for insulting you."

"Hey, I'm hiring you as my new ambassador. You'll be a real hit at state dinners."

"Beast," I shot over my shoulder with a smile as I left.

"Terror," he returned. "Oh, and Elsie?" I paused at the door. "You're right. Harriet and I would be *horrible* together."

* * *

We didn't have time to make plans, however, as Lady Prudence swept into lunch a few hours later and

77

announced that the next trial was starting. Before we knew it, our plates had been whisked away and we'd been herded down to the kitchens. A very large peahen in an apron clucked and grumped from the doorway as Lady Prudence took over, extinguishing the great fire with a wave of her hand. She clicked her fingers, and six footbirds traipsed in, carrying urns nearly as big as their own bodies. Each of them dumped the contents onto the hearth, until there was a five foot pile of assorted... peas? I couldn't keep the confusion from my face.

Prudence looked triumphant. "This is a much more modern trial," she said. "A friend of mine had a princess go through this very thing just a few years ago. There are six colours of pea here: sort them all back into their separate urns before nightfall. Whoever finds the golden pea is the winner."

Before we could even respond, she was gone again. I wondered why she didn't go the whole hog and do the traditional puff-of-smoke thing. The footbirds plunked down their urns with some relief and filed out, and I sank to my knees with a groan and started sifting through the peas. If only I could use a spell!

"Elsie, wait," said Nora, and when I looked up they were all smiling.

"What are you so happy about?" I asked. "Come on, this is going to take us hours."

"No, it isn't," she said. "Watch this."

All three princesses closed their eyes. Intisar muttered to herself; Nora sang quietly; Harriet let out a piercing whistle.

"Every good princess has a bird companion for moments exactly like this," said Intisar in her most

78

proper voice, but she spoiled it with her delighted grin.

"But isn't that magic? Won't it be blocked by Prudence?"

She shook her head. "It's all training, like you can do with any animal. The only magic is in the birds, to let them hear us at any distance. Hopefully since they're outside the castle that ought to be fine."

Nora opened the nearest window, which promptly iced over. She swore in a very unprincess-y manner. "We forgot about the wards. How will the birds get in now?"

Though the ice was too thick to see any details, we watched as three small dark shapes came swooping through the storm and hovered just outside the window.

"Elsie, can you do anything?" Intisar said.

I clicked my fingers for my usual flame spell, but the dampeners were still in effect, and nothing happened. Practical it was, then. Prudence had extinguished the hearthfire, so that was no help, and though a tinderbox was standard issue for District Witches, I wasn't in the habit of carrying it around the castle, so it was sitting unhelpfully in my bag upstairs. I looked around for a heavy implement.

"Wait, tell your birds to back up. Let Gerald do his thing," said Harriet. A moment later, a small hole began to appear in the ice, the edges licked by what looked like flame, though that made no sense. When the hole was large enough, a small red head peeked through curiously. But where I was expecting feathers and a beak, I saw scales and a blunt snout. He shot through the hole, followed by two streaks of white and brown feathers, and all three companions barrelled into their respective princesses.

Nora kissed the head of a snow white dove; Intisar stroked a small, sleek hawk; but I was most interested in Harriet's companion, who was currently trying and failing to burrow down the top of her dress. He settled for draping himself around her shoulders.

"Your bird companion is...a dragon?" asked Nora with awe.

"It's a little unorthodox, I know," said Harriet, with a sideways glance at Intisar.

"I think it's brilliant," said Intisar, and Harriet beamed. "I want to hear all about how you bonded."

"Later," I said. "We need to get to work."

The companions made short work of the peas, deftly sorting them into their urns as the girls directed and praised them. Feeling slightly useless, I had Gerald light the stove and set to making us all some tea. We were sipping it and playing a lively game with some cards Nora had found in a drawer when Prudence swept in at nightfall. Seeing the spotless hearth and the urns brimming with coloured mounds, her face lit up.

"Wonderful! What was it this time, mice? Ah, birds – a classic," she said, spotting Nora's dove and Intisar's hawk perched on the backs of their chairs. "Well done, my dears. And who found the golden pea?" We all looked at each other. We'd left the companions to it, and had completely forgotten about the pea.

From Harriet's lap came a sheepish chirrup. The little dragon tapped his chest with one claw, then hung his head.

"Gerald," Harriet said in a tone that wavered between warning and laughter. "Did you eat the golden pea?"

Gerald burped happily.

"I'm sorry," Harriet said. "He hasn't really got the hang of the hoarding thing yet. He just eats shiny things – it's why I never wear any jewellery. We could wait for it to –"

"No need," said Prudence hurriedly. "I'm quite content to say that if *your* dragon found it, that makes you the w–"

"Oh no," said Harriet quickly. "I couldn't possibly claim the credit. No one can really own a dragon, can they? That just wouldn't be fair, and I can't win if I don't deserve it." She turned to the rest of us for backup, and I could see the panic on her face.

"Yes," I added. "That would be terribly unfair."

"We'd be devastated," said Intisar, fluttering her eyelashes like she was about to cry. We certainly would, I thought, though not for the reasons we were implying. If one of us was going to be forced into marrying Percy, Harriet was the last person it should be.

Prudence looked around at the four of us, all doing our best to look sad, and sighed. "Fine," she said. "We'll just have to hold another trial."

* * *

We had pea soup for dinner for the next three days.

"I suppose the kitchens had a lot to use up," Intisar said, stirring her soup slowly, "but I'm absolutely sick of peas."

"I shall never even look at a pea again once we get out of here," declared Harriet. "The woman has a pea obsession."

"Oh, I can explain that," said Percy. "Ever since I was tiny Aunty Pru's called me Pea. Said it was a special connection between us, having names beginning with P. I think she wanted Mother to name me after her, but she said no."

I laughed. "Yeah, I don't think I'd be that keen to marry Prince Prudent. It's not very dashing, is it?"

"I thought you didn't want to marry me anyway?" he asked.

"Well – no, but – oh, you beast, I'm not getting into this again." I threw my bread roll at him – and immediately regretted it. That was the only part of dinner that didn't taste of peas.

"Worth a try," he laughed, handing me his own roll without batting an eyelid. "Anyway, I think all this pea stuff is supposed to be, well, me-themed."

Now that I thought about it, there were an awful lot of pea-based items around the castle. The pea green gowns. The endless pea dishes. Sweet peas in every room. The – I whirled in my seat and pointed at the nearest footbird.

"Have you always been a peacock?"

He looked pained (or as pained as he could, around his beak). "No, my lady. Lady Prudence thought it would be entertaining to have us match the theme."

She'd transformed the servants. My blood iced over. I had already been determined to sort this castle out, but now I was furious.

* * *

The second week passed much as the first. Harriet talked Intisar into helping her haul a couple of swords off the wall of the great hall, and the two of them sparred every morning. "To keep our hands in," Harriet said, though I suspected that Intisar's interest was less in her own physique and more in Harriet's.

Meanwhile, Nora befriended every servant she could find, helping them with tasks too delicate for wings in return for them teaching her the local folk songs. And Percy and I spent most of our time tucked away in the library, researching weather spells and fairies and marriage law and anything else we could think of that might offer a spark of inspiration. Whenever we found a likely spell, I tested it, but Prudence's magic dampeners still seemed to be in effect, and I never got even a spark.

When it got too dark to read easily, we'd decamp to the parlour, where we'd play games, or talk, or Nora would play us outrageous versions of traditional ballads on her mandolin. Intisar and Harriet taught me and Percy to waltz, but once we'd more or less got the hang of it they mostly partnered each other, swirling around us twice as fast as we could manage; it seemed Percy and I had four left feet between the two of us, and we ended up knocking everyone into a laughing heap more than once.

It was lovely, in a strange way. But the next trial still loomed.

* * *

We had slightly more notice of this trial, as Prudence interrupted our morning training to herd us all out of the great hall. When she summoned us back an hour later, we found the whole space had been cleared, and a sort of maze laid out across the room with rope. Scattered across the floor were thousands of peas. Prudence and Percy stood on a raised dais at the end of the hall, which seemed much larger without all the furniture. He waved to us, and I waved back, but dropped my hand, cheeks heating, when I noticed no one else was responding.

"Interesting," said Prudence, raising an eyebrow at Percy before turning to address us. "Your highnesses, welcome to your next test. The first princess to ascend the dais and claim a kiss from Prince Percival will be the winner."

"That's it? It doesn't seem very difficult." Harriet asked. With her long legs and determined stride, she'd need to hang back to lose this one.

"Ah, but only the very daintiest steps will allow you to proceed. A true princess could walk without disturbing the air." said Prudence. She expounded for some time on the virtues of delicate deportment, but the effect was undercut somewhat by Percy, standing behind her, punctuating her speech with mimes and gestures. The princesses had the benefit of their schooled smiles, and only their eyes betrayed their amusement, but I couldn't help laughing aloud.

"You find this funny, Princess Elsabetta?"

"Oh no," I said in my best excited-princess voice. "I'm just delighted to have another chance to win such a *wonderful* prize." Behind Prudence, Percy faked a swoon.

She tsked at me disapprovingly. "A true princess does not display such vulgar feelings. Now. There's no time limit on this one; I have too much to do to stand and watch you all, but I will return when I feel a foot on the dais. Percival will remain. May the best princess win." And with that, she swept out.

"Any ideas on this one, Elsie? It looks like it's going to be hard to avoid anyone winning," said Intisar.

"And what's she on about, anyway? How hard can walking over peas be?" Nora scoffed. But when she took a step onto the polished floor, the hard peas skittered away under her feet and she landed with a bump. I leapt forward to help her up.

"Elsie," Harriet said as I guided Nora back to the clear space. "How are you doing that?"

"No offence meant, but you're not exactly more delicate than Nora," added Intisar.

I grinned. Daintiness wasn't exactly a necessary quality for a District Witch; we were more likely to be trekking through thick forest undergrowth than tripping lightly across ballrooms. I raised my hem to show everyone my feet. Even though every morning the pea green slippers were laid out with my dress, I always ignored them. With my sturdy uniform boots on, all I had to do was tread down hard and the peas stayed more or less steady.

"Ha! You don't need to be dainty at all, you just need to be prepared," Percy said. "Now that's *my* kind of princess." We all looked over at him, startled. "Er, if I wanted one," he added awkwardly.

"Show me your shoes," I said, and the princesses all stuck their feet out obligingly. Harriet, of course, was wearing the pair of Percy's old boots she'd borrowed, since we'd been interrupted in the midst of sword practice. But Nora and Intisar, far more proper than us, had stuck to the provided slippers, which were tissue thin.

"Percy," I called up to the dais. "Stop standing

around like a decorative lump and chuck us your boots." To his credit, he didn't question me, just bent down and undid his laces.

"Watch out below," he called, and threw the boots across the room; unfortunately, his aim wasn't any better than his dancing, and they landed in the middle of the room.

Harriet shook her head as she went to retrieve them. "My word, Percy, even if I liked men that would have put me off marrying you."

He stuck his tongue out at her. "I'm a thinker, not a thrower."

"You'll never make it across with those slippers," I said to Intisar and Nora. "You'll have to share, but if you wear one boot each and we tie your middle legs together, you can balance each other as you go. Harriet and I will hold on to you and help."

So it was as a strange seven-legged beast that we crossed the great hall. Some of the corners were a little finicky, but we hopped and staggered our way through the maze until we were finally standing below Percy. He reached down to help me climb up, but I batted his hand away.

"I appreciate the chivalrous instinct," I said, "but we have to do this all together, remember. Ready, everyone?"

As the four of us took simultaneous steps up onto the dais, Prudence appeared in a puff of pink smoke. I almost cheered – she *did* have an entrance that wasn't sweeping, after all! – but refrained when I saw the thunderous scowl on her face.

"What are you *doing?*" she cried.

"Will you look at that," I said. "We all won."

"This is ridiculous," said Prudence. "A draw? These tests aren't supposed to be...to be broken like this! I won't stand for it."

"Well, Aunty, I can't marry all of them," Percy chipped in. I glared at him for daring to even put the idea in her head.

"I'll simply have to set up another trial," she said, waving him off like an irritating fly.

"No!" we all shouted, and she flinched.

"What do you mean, no?"

"We mean no, Aunty." Percy said. "Please, no more trials."

Prudence looked delighted. "Oh, Pea, have you made a decision? I admit she's not the one I would have chosen for you but I'm willing to discuss it –"

"No, Aunty. This isn't fair on anyone. I won't marry someone who doesn't want me, and these four have been very clear on that subject." He held up a hand as she opened her mouth. "Yes, yes, I know, how could they not see my endless charms and so on, but the truth of the matter is that I don't want your help on this."

"Well, excuse *me* for trying to do you a favour," she said haughtily. "I never thought I'd see the day when a godchild of mine would reject their happily ever after."

"But if you'd ever asked, I would have told you." Percy sounded exasperated. "My happily ever after doesn't look like being forced into marriage with whichever random princess passes your tests – no offence, girls. That might be the traditional path, but I'd rather find my own way."

Prudence looked like she was gearing up for a tirade, and silver sparks began to flicker around her. I racked my brains for anything I'd learned in the last two weeks that might stop us all getting turned into toads.

"Excuse me, Lady Prudence," came a small voice from beside me.

"What?" Prudence snapped.

"My apologies, but if Percy doesn't want your help, I do," Nora said, shaking.

"What are you doing?" I whispered.

"Nora, no," whispered Percy.

But she continued, her voice getting stronger. "All I want is to be able to attend the university at Leifeld. I want to be a bard - I have the talent, I know I do - but my parents keep trying to force me into marriage. I'm only seventeen. I - I could really use a fairy godmother."

It was like all the anger flooded out of Prudence at once. Her eyes lit up and her whole demeanour softened. It was quite endearing, though strange.

"My dear child," she said, in a sweeter voice than I'd ever heard her use. "You're in need, and I can help. If I'm no longer needed here" - ah, there was the steel again, flashed at Percy - "then I'd be honoured to make your wish come true."

Percy smiled, putting a hand on her arm. "Thank you, Aunty Pru, for everything, but I'll be okay on my own. You're always welcome to visit, though, and I know Mother will want to see you often."

"My sweet Pea," she said, softening enough to kiss him on the cheek. "You grew up while I wasn't looking." She wiped a tear from her eye, and turned briskly to

Nora. "Come on, then, girl, let's get you your dream." She took Nora by the arm, and a cascade of glittering sparks fell around them as they began to disappear. "To Leifeld!" she commanded.

"Goodbye! I'll write!" came Nora's cheerful voice as the glitter dissipated.

* * *

We spent the rest of the day checking on the servants (now human, completely overjoyed), and the unwell attendants and queen (now healed, thoroughly confused), and removing every trace of peas from the castle before toppling into our magnificent beds, exhausted.

When I woke, I couldn't put my finger on what was different. It was only once I'd dressed (in my beloved uniform, which had finally been returned to me; I would never wear pea green again) that I realised what it was: the skies were no longer grey. I flung the window open to feel a soft breeze on my face, then waggled an arm out into the fresh air. The snowstorm had broken – or been dismissed. I clicked my fingers, and my satchel hovered in the air. Prudence really was gone.

I knocked on Harriet's door, not terribly surprised when Intisar opened it and welcomed me in. Harriet was packing, clothes and weapons scattered everywhere, Gerald the dragon draped around her shoulders. Intisar's bag sat neatly by the bed, as perfectly neat as its owner.

"You two heading home?" I said.

"Well, I am," Intisar said. "Harriet thought she might come with me for a bit."

Harriet cackled. "Harriet thought she might come

with you forever. Or did you forget I proposed to you last night?" She wrapped her arm around Intisar's waist.

"That's marvellous," I said. "But what happened to rescuing a girl from an impenetrable tower?"

"Well, turns out we were both trapped in one, and we rescued each other from boredom. Shame about the lack of dragon, though." She grinned.

"You can always let Gerald menace me a bit," Intisar said. Hearing his name, Gerald stretched up from Harriet's shoulder and nibbled happily on one of Intisar's earrings.

* * *

Percy and I waved Intisar and Harriet off from the front steps of the castle with many goodbyes and promises to stay in touch.

"I should probably be on my way," I said, hefting my satchel onto my shoulder once the carriage was out of sight. For some reason, it was hard to look Percy in the eye. I would be glad to see the back of this place, but I'd miss his company terribly. It was nice having someone else to read with, and bounce ideas off, and even to dance badly with. In fact, I was pretty sure I'd miss Percy more than that glorious bed, and that was saying something.

"I'm leaving, too," he said nonchalantly, and I noticed for the first time that he had a leather pack at his feet. "With Aunty Pru off looking after Nora, and my mother back to full strength, there's no need for me to stick around. I know you girls were stuck here for weeks, but I've been here my whole life. I want to make some of my own choices, for once. I think I'd like to see some of the places I've read about." He rubbed his chin. "But

I'm not sure where to go first Where are you off to?"

"I should probably continue on to Oakvale. Before I got stuck here, I was on my way there to investigate a goblin infestation. And once I've sorted that out, I'll be heading back to the District Office to report on all... this."

"That sounds fun," said Percy with a grin.

"Oh, no, it won't be, there's a lot of paperwork. Well, the goblin part might be fun – and it's always good to have a spare pair of hands – not that you'd want to come – but it would be nice to have someone to talk to if you did, and it would definitely be useful to have you on hand at the Office to give your side of things – not that I need you –" Oh, what good was all that negotiation training when he made my brain trip over itself like this?

"Elsie," said Percy.

"Yes?" I replied, flushing furiously.

"You can just say you'd be miserable without me."

"Oh, you beast. Is there any time you're not fishing for –"

"Because I'd be miserable without you." My world shuddered to a halt. My mouth fell open. I could only stare at him as he grabbed his pack and shouldered it.

"I don't think I've ever seen you speechless before," Percy laughed. He held his hand out to me. "Shall we go?"

I've faced a lot of difficult decisions in my time as a District Witch, but honestly, some choices are easy.

Adie Hart is a lover of stories and the words behind them. With a background in the history and literature of the Ancient World, and an abiding love of classic fairy tales, she writes everything from fun fantasy adventures to dark mythological retellings.

When she's not writing, she can usually be found reading, gardening, or trapped under her large cat!

The Snowdrop

H. L. Macfarlane

Toby was seven when he saw snow for the first time with his own two eyes. Real, tangible snow – not the kind he'd seen on TV or at the cinema with his grandparents. Cold to the touch, for you could *touch* it, and piled up higher than he could stand where it had fallen at the edge of the woods.

He didn't know what to make of the snow at first. It was February, after all; eager, early springtime flowers had already begun to emerge from the ground as it thawed. Toby's grandparents were even more surprised to see the snow than he was.

"There's been no snow here for twenty-two years," his grandmother, Nora, said.

Edward, Toby's grandfather, nodded sagely. "Twenty-two years."

It was in this way that Toby decided the appearance of snow after twenty-five entire years must signify that something important was coming. So when his grandparents trussed him up in a thick winter coat (with a sweater underneath for good measure), a pair of gloves, a woollen hat and his favourite pair of red boots and sent him outside to play, Toby did so with some trepidation.

He hadn't wanted to go outside in the snow alone, but his grandparents said they were getting too old for the cold. In truth, Toby knew they weren't. Edward was greying a little at the temples – Nora called him a 'silver fox', though Toby didn't understand why – but other than that and some lines around their eyes, Toby didn't think they looked anything like his friends' grandparents.

They didn't have bald heads or snow-white hair or stooped backs like Sarah's grandpa or Lee's grandma from school. Then there were David's parents – Toby didn't like David much – who to Toby looked barely younger than his grandparents.

But still, they told Toby they were too old to play in the snow, so Toby ventured into the back garden alone.

He was cautious and careful at first. Toby's boots crunched through the unbroken layer of white that covered the lawn, unsure at first but gradually growing bolder with every footstep. Eventually the sheer delight of the cold, glittering snow was too much for him; Toby began bounding through it in his effort to sink as far into its depths as he could, yelling and whooping and laughing all the while.

But the snow on the lawn was only a few inches thick, and too soon Toby grew bored of jumping through it. So – stumbling a little on legs unused to being half-frozen – Toby made his way to the trees that bordered the garden.

The woods.

Toby knew very well not to venture in there alone. But the forest itself was not what had caught Toby's attention; beneath the bows of the first line of dark trees was a veritable hill of snow that Toby had been eyeing from the kitchen window all morning.

Toby gazed up at the tall conifers above him just as one shook off the blanket of snow covering its needle-shaped leaves, sending the stuff tumbling to the ground. He understood, then, how the snow was piled highest beneath the trees.

Understanding how things worked was one of Toby's favourite things in the entire world. He asked his grandparents endless questions, often to their delight but sometimes to their despair, too. His curiosity was insatiable, his list of questions never-ending.

What created the sun?

Why are people warm but rocks are only sometimes warm?

How old are you when you become a grown up?

Why do you sometimes tell a lie?

But of all the questions Toby asked, there was one he never dared utter.

Where are my parents?

Toby had friends at school, after all, and he loved his grandparents dearly. He wasn't lonely, he was sure.

He didn't need parents.

After launching himself into a particularly high snowdrift, Toby snaked and wriggled his way out through the other side of the drift and landed in the entrance to the woods. He was barely out of his grandparents' garden; they wouldn't mind. With a giggle he shook snow from his shoulders in an imitation of the fir tree, then took stock of his new surroundings.

It was in this way that Toby came across a patch of late winter snowdrops. He had been watching them emerge from the undergrowth for days before the sudden snow hid them from his vantage point in the kitchen, which had annoyed him immensely. He was keen to see the flowers when they eventually bloomed.

Today, it seemed, was that day.

Each and every snowdrop appeared identical. Their delicate, drooping flower heads were tilted south, towards the sun. Toby's grandfather had told him about that – how flowers always followed the sun. Toby couldn't blame them. He loved summer and warm days, too.

The snowdrops glistened in the late afternoon sunshine; though the sun's rays were weak, they were sufficient to melt any snow that might have clung to the tiny flowers, resulting in thousands of water droplets clear as crystal resting on their petals. Toby rather thought it made the flowers look as if they themselves were made of jewels instead of plant matter.

Being careful not to squash any of the snowdrops, Toby stooped onto hands and knees to further inspect them. He couldn't pronounce most of the parts of the flower hidden inside the petals that Edward had taught him over Christmas. His grandfather was what was called a 'botanist', Toby recalled, scrunching his nose at the thought of the word.

"Bot-an-ist," he mouthed, testing the complicated word in his mouth. "Botanist," he said with more confidence. "Botanist."

Toby would be sure to demonstrate to Edward just how well he could pronounce the man's profession when he got back. He would be pleased.

Toby reached out to touch the largest, most beautiful of the snowdrops, intending to at least try and vocalise exactly what all the parts of the flower were called, but his gloved hand was clumsy against the petals. His bullish touch caused the snowdrop to shiver and squeak.

Squeak?

For a long moment Toby did nothing but stare at the wet grass directly beneath the snowdrop. After a few seconds, a movement between the blades caught Toby's eye, but though he peered and peered to try and get a better look, he could see nothing from where he crouched. So Toby took off his glove and slowly, carefully, sifted his tiny fingers through the grass, searching for whichever bug must have fallen from inside the flower that was capable of making such a squeak.

But there were no bugs to be found. When Toby's fingers finally swept across an object that did not feel like grass or frozen mud or flowers, something told him not to squeeze his hand around it: some instinct he could not understand at the tender age of seven. Instead, Toby gently encased the object in his hand and turned his hand palm up, towards the sun. He did not know why – only that it was the right thing to do.

Against a heart that was beating furiously and excitedly, Toby unfurled his fingers to bear witness to whatever it was he had found.

It was a girl.

A tiny, tiny girl, dressed in pure white like the

snowdrop she had emerged from, with dark brown hair curling down her back all the way to her feet. She could not have been more than one inch tall.

It was only Toby's age that prevented him from believing he must be hallucinating. He trusted that the minuscule girl currently clinging to his thumb in her unsteady attempt to stand up was real. For why wouldn't she be real? Toby could see her, and he had heard her, and now he could feel her almost weightless presence scurrying across the palm of his hand.

She was tiny, but she was real. That was the end of that.

"Hello," Toby said quietly. He wanted to lift the girl up to his eyes in order to see her better, but he absolutely didn't want to scare her. This feeling came from personal experience: two months ago, Toby had insisted he was big enough to go on the fairground rides constructed in the village square every Christmas. He had been a mere spectator to the rides before then, eyes gone wide with wonder at the flashing lights enticing him to sit inside a spinning cup or atop a lavishly decorated horse.

His grandmother had taken him on a rollercoaster shaped like a caterpillar, but when it had reached the top of the track Toby had screamed and clung to her in terror. Nora had warned him not to look down.

Toby had looked down.

Down, down, down, where the people below him had looked almost as small as the girl currently standing on his palm. Toby had not stopped crying until his feet touched the ground once more.

And so it was that Toby did not lift the tiny girl

dressed in white more than three inches from the spot where he had found her.

She looked up at him. Or, at least, Toby assumed she was looking at him – her facial features were too small to see. She held her hands up to her mouth.

"Hello!" the girl shouted, though it was barely a whisper in the wind. "Can you lift me up?"

Only now that he had permission did Toby eagerly comply, fighting his jittery excitement to raise his hand to his face as slowly and carefully as he could manage.

Up close, the tiny girl looked to be about the same age as Toby. Her dress wasn't just the same colour as a snowdrop – the folds of the fabric matched the shape of one, too. Around her neck Toby could just make out a shiny green pendant. She wore no shoes.

"Why are you so small?" Toby asked her, though it was the kind of question his grandmother would have told him was rude.

The girl put her hands on her hips and seemed to huff. "Why are you so big?" she squeaked.

"I'm...well, *I'm* small, too," Toby admitted. "But I'm only seven right now. I'll get bigger."

"I'm seven, too!" the girl exclaimed in delight. "And I will also get bigger. Much, much bigger."

"You will?"

She nodded matter-of-factly. "I can't be big and live in a snowdrop, though, can I? Sometimes being small is useful."

"You live in the snowdrop? Don't you get cold?"

"The petals close around me like this," she said, wrapping her arms around herself to demonstrate her point. "Then I'm as warm as can be!"

Toby thought that sounded quite nice, but he still preferred the idea of sitting by the fire in the living room. "I'm Toby," he said, remembering his manners. "What's your name?"

The girl seemed to literally sparkle at the mention of his name. She twirled the skirt of her snowdrop dress. "I'm Galana. You can call me Lana!"

"Ga-la-na." Toby tested the name on his tongue just as he had with the word *botanist*. "Lana. It's nice to meet you."

"And you, Toby."

A shiver wracked Toby's frame, then, and he glanced back towards his grandparents' house hidden by the snow drift.

"Are you cold?" Lana asked.

Toby nodded.

"Then we should go inside!"

"*We*?" Toby cocked his head, confused. "You want to come with me?"

"How can we play if I don't come with you?" Lana said, as if it were obvious. "But you will have to be careful carrying me back with you. You almost squashed me when you knocked my snowdrop!"

"I'm sorry," Toby said, very seriously. With his free hand, he searched through the contents of his jacket pocket until he came across a small glass jar complete with a lid that came off with a satisfying *pop*. It used to have a candle in it; Toby's grandfather had given it to him when the candle melted away. So Toby could look at beetles properly, Edward had said. So Toby could study living things just like him.

Toby had never used it before; he wasn't too interested in beetles. But Lana was not a beetle, and Toby didn't want to squash her.

"How about this?" he asked Lana, proffering the glass jar for her to climb into. She smiled a tiny smile for him.

"That will be perfect...for now."

"For now?"

Another smile. The pendant around her neck twinkled. "You'll see."

* * *

When Toby rushed back indoors it was all he could do to remember to remove his red boots, jacket, hat and gloves. His little candle jar was hidden underneath his jumper; something told Toby he had to keep Lana a secret.

"Toby!" Nora cried when she caught him skittering from the kitchen and up the stairs to his attic bedroom. "Where do you think you're going? It's dinner time. I was just about to call you back inside to –"

Toby didn't hang around to hear the rest of his grandmother's complaint. The moment he reached his bedroom, Toby closed the door and breathlessly placed the candle jar below his bed.

He opened the lid, then gently tilted the jar so Lana could climb out. "I won't be long," Toby promised. "I will eat my dinner *so* fast."

"Can you bring me some?" Lana piped up. "I'm starving!"

Toby eagerly agreed.

Dinner was sausages, chips and beans – Toby's favourite. He'd eat it every day if he had his way. Edward prided himself on the fact the sausages came from the local butcher shop ("Only the best will do!") and the chips were handmade by his wife from Maris Piper potatoes ("Accept no substitutions!"). But Toby didn't care about any of that; he was only seven. Sausages, chips and beans were all sausages, chips and beans to him no matter where they came from.

"Can you cut these for me?" Toby asked his grandmother after trying and failing to chop up his sausages. He was much better at it than he used to be but, even so, the knife felt clumsy in his hands. Perhaps it was because he was too excited.

Nora frowned. "Whatever happened to biting them off the fork?"

Toby usually ate his sausages that way, but how was he supposed to sneak some up for Lana if they weren't cut up?

"I want to be a grown-up," Toby said, pointing at his grandfather's plate: the man had cut his sausages into perfect slices of equal size.

Edward laughed at this, then ruffled Toby's hair. "Most grown-ups don't go to this much effort. I just prefer them this way."

"Then so do I."

"Since when?" Nora asked, shaking her head in amused disbelief. "Honestly, Toby, whatever is going on with you today?"

"I'm different than I was before," Toby said, shrugging, because he was. His grandparents didn't need to know why.

Though it was clear his answer left both Edward and Nora more confused than anything else, Toby's grandmother complied with his request and cut up his sausages. He'd brought down the candle jar and hidden it in his trouser pocket; when his grandparents weren't looking Toby popped a slice of sausage into it, then two, then three. He stuffed in a chip for good measure, but ignored the beans.

After wolfing down his food – Toby had promised he'd be fast – he leapt from his chair and ran upstairs.

"Toby –" his grandmother began.

"Thanks for dinner!" he shouted, cutting her off. "I'm going to bed!"

"But it's barely five!"

The closing of his bedroom door was all the response Toby gave. After struggling to pull a chair in front of the door to prevent his grandparents from barging in unannounced, Toby bent low beside his bed, then pulled out the jar full of food.

"Lana?" he called out, searching for her beneath the bed. For one horrible moment he couldn't find the tiny girl, and his heart broke, but then she emerged from behind an old box of Pokémon cards that belonged to Toby's uncle.

"You took your time!" Lana scolded as Toby beamed at her. She plonked herself down on the floor in front of the open jar, then sniffed appreciatively at its contents. "Although you brought me some good food, so I'll forgive you."

One slice of sausage was almost the same height as Lana; she precariously balanced it on its edge, then bit into it eagerly. Before Toby's very eyes she made quick work of the morsel, then moved onto the next one.

"You eat a lot," he observed. "Maybe even more than me."

"I have to so I can get bigger," Lana got out around a mouthful of food.

"That's why Grandma and Grandpa tell me to eat a lot, too."

"Grandma? Grandpa? Not your mum or dad?"

"I don't have a mum. Or a dad."

Lana scoffed. "Everyone has a mum and a dad."

"Where are yours, then?"

With a tiny hand, Lana pointed to the window. "In the woods, of course!"

"Will they be scared that you're not in the snowdrop?"

"Oh, no." Lana polished off the third slice of sausage, then moved onto the chip. Toby had no idea where she was putting it all. "They always know where I am. Everything in the woods is connected, so I'm safe."

Toby liked the sound of that a lot. "I don't know where mum and dad are," he admitted. "I don't remember them."

Lana considered this as she polished off the chip. "Then it's good you have Grandma and Grandpa. You have to thank them for the food; it was delicious!"

"I thanked them for dinner already."

"Then that's good. It's important to have good manners."

"Did your tiny parents in the woods say that?

Grandma says that *all* the time."

At this Lana laughed, then ran over to Toby's sleeve and tugged it until he lifted her up to his face. She stretched her arms up high. "My parents aren't small," she said. "They are as big as your human grown-ups!"

With a scrunched-up nose, Toby digested what Lana had just said. "Your mum and dad aren't...human?"

"Nope."

"So you aren't, either?"

"Nope."

"So what are you?"

Lana twirled on his hand. "Something else!"

That was enough for Toby. "Can we play now?" he asked.

"Yes," Lana said, so they did.

Even when Toby's light-up clock told him it was seven then eight then nine o'clock, he and Lana didn't stop playing. Their evening largely consisted of Toby making a town for Lana out of his building blocks and Lego according to her detailed instructions, and then Toby was tasked with finding her. It was something he was adept at – it was as if he simply *knew* where Lana was, and that was that.

But once ten o'clock struck, she let out a yawn. "I'm tired," she said. "Can we go to bed?"

So Toby washed out the little candle jar and covered the bottom of it with cotton wool from the bathroom cabinet and placed it on top of his bedside table near his pillow. Lana settled into the jar, her dress rendering her almost invisible against the fluffy fibres.

But Toby knew she was there, which was good enough for him.

"Good night, Toby," Lana called out.

"Good night, Lana," he replied. Sleep took Toby as soon as he closed his eyes.

* * *

"Get up, Toby!"

Toby rubbed at his eyes, confused by the unfamiliar voice. Then he felt something jump up and down on his stomach, and he remembered all that had occurred the day before.

"Lana?" Toby called out. He cast his gaze down his bed and realised what was jumping on him.

Lana. Only she was no longer a mere inch tall.

She had grown over five times that.

"I told you I'd get bigger!" She grinned at the shocked expression on Toby's still-sleepy face.

Now Toby could see the small-but-no-longer-tiny girl more clearly, he realised Lana had long-lashed brown eyes to match her dark, wavy hair. There were a handful of pretty freckles sprayed across her face, and when she smiled at Toby her cheeks dimpled. The pendant around her neck shone a little brighter than it had the day before.

In his entire life Toby had never loved anyone other than his grandparents but, in that moment, he knew he loved Lana, too.

"The jar is too small now," Toby said rather uselessly, waving at where it lay abandoned on his bedside table.

106

Lana giggled. "I'll need a new bedroom, then, it seems!"

Toby could hardly believe what he was hearing. "You're going to stay one more night?"

"Until the snow melts," Lana said, clambering over Toby's stomach, chest and shoulder in order to jump onto the windowsill. He knelt up to look through the glass, too, wiping away the frost that had built up during the night in order to see properly.

Outside in the garden, Toby's footsteps were imprinted in the snow, leading to the woods. A surge of disappointment filled his heart at the fact no new snow had fallen.

"Until the snow melts?" Toby parroted back to Lana.

She nodded. "So shall we play?"

And so, once more, they played.

It was surprisingly easy for Toby to conceal the little forest girl from his grandparents. It was Monday, which meant Edward was working at the university in the city and Nora was baking cakes to bring to their local bakery the following morning. Normally Toby would be at school, but it had been cancelled due to the snow.

More and more he was growing to love the stuff.

Toby and Lana played outside until lunchtime, making little-and-large snow angels and playing hide and seek at the edge of the woods. Then Toby burrowed through the snowdrift to make a network of tunnels for Lana to crawl through, and they pretended a dragon was after her. Only Toby, the mortal giant, could save her, by crashing into the snow to steal her from the dragon's lair.

In the afternoon, Toby hid Lana in his blanket and read his favourite books to her: Toby was very good at reading. Even his grandfather said so, and he read the most complicated books Toby had ever seen. Between all his reading and learning how to talk from his grandparents, Toby knew he spoke differently from his school friends. 'Formally' was how his teacher put it. But Lana spoke the same way, so Toby was happy not to feel like the odd one out when he was with her.

"Who are you reading to, Toby?" Edward asked when he returned from work and discovered his grandson lying by the fireplace, wrapped in his favourite wool blanket and reciting the words to The Magician's Nephew.

Toby barely glanced at him. "Just nobody."

"Just nobody?" Edward laughed. "How about you read to me after dinner?"

"I can't," Toby fired back. "I'm busy."

"He's been like this all day," Nora murmured to her husband, kissing him on the cheek as she did so. "Barely saw or heard him since breakfast!"

Toby ignored his grandparents talking about him, and remained silent during dinner in favour of eating as quickly as possible in order to return to his bedroom. Lana was now much too big for Toby to steal scraps of dinner with which to feed her, so Toby had taken it upon himself to steal half a loaf of bread and a jar of jam from the pantry ahead of his own dinner for her to eat, instead.

When Toby returned to his bedroom, she'd eaten every last crumb of bread and speck of jam.

"That was lovely," Lana said, smiling at Toby as he

quickly opened and shut his bedroom door and replaced the chair in front of it. "I do love strawberries, and I haven't had any since summer."

"You can just buy some from the shops," Toby said, hoping his knowledge of how to procure food would impress Lana. "When I go with Grandma tomorrow I can buy you some fresh ones."

Lana's eyes lit up, and she clapped her little hands together. "That would be delightful!"

That night, Toby found an old fish tank in the attic store cupboard and stole a cushion from the living room sofa to put inside it to make a comfortable bed. Lana curled up inside the tank at ten o'clock on the dot.

"Good night, Toby," she said, yawning.

"Good night, Lana," Toby said. Unlike the night before, Toby forced himself to stay awake simply to watch her fall asleep. Her pendant softly pulsed green, green, green, until it was all Toby could see. But eventually his eyes grew heavy, and before the clock reached eleven, Toby was fast asleep, too.

* * *

Toby was amazed and elated to find Lana sitting by his pillow the next morning, no longer five inches tall but instead the height of a human baby, like Paul-from-school's new little sister.

Lana patted Toby's hand. "What will we do today?"

"We can –"

"Is that you up, Toby?" Nora called through the door. "We should get to the shops now that the snow's melted a bit!"

Toby stared at Lana in horror, then turned to look

out of the window. Sure enough, the snow was beginning to thaw; he could see patches of grass on the lawn, stark and green against the melting white.

"Strawberries," Lana whispered to Toby. "You promised me strawberries."

Toby felt like crying. "But the snow –"

"Why waste the time we have worrying over tomorrow, or the next day, or the next?"

It sounded like something a grown-up would say. But Toby knew it was good advice, even if what he really wanted to do was throw a tantrum. So Toby got dressed and promised Lana he would be back very soon, and glumly followed his grandmother to the car.

"Whatever is wrong with you this morning, grumpy guts?" she teased.

"Nothing," Toby grumbled.

"Aw, Toby, you're too young to be grumpy! What can I do to make you feel better?"

At this Toby perked up. "Can I have a big picnic in the garden? With strawberries?"

At this Nora burst out laughing. "I don't see why not! Though it's a bit cold for us to sit outside. How about –"

"No, I don't want you to be there."

"You don't...seriously, Toby, what's going through your head lately?"

Toby didn't reply. Though it was clear Nora wanted to know what was going on after a long moment of scrutinised staring she nonetheless indulged her grandson's request.

Lana and Toby dined that afternoon on peanut butter sandwiches (he giggled profusely at Lana's attempt to chew through the stuff), apple slices, deliciously salted crisps, fresh orange juice and chocolate-covered biscuits.

And, of course, strawberries.

"Did your grandma ask why you wanted all this food?" Lana asked, leaning against the snow drift with a satisfied sigh. They were using the snow to hide from the prying eyes of his grandmother, but it was rapidly melting; Toby knew that, tomorrow, it would not make for a very good shelter.

Toby shoved the thought of melting snow to the side. "I never ask for anything normally, so she just bought it for me."

"Toby!" The forest girl tutted loudly. "You can't treat your grandma like that. *Or* your grandpa. Or anyone you love, for that matter."

"But I can't tell her about you!"

"And why on earth not?" Lana crossed her arms over her chest. Though she wore nothing but her snowdrop dress and her glowing green pendant – which had both gotten bigger alongside her – Lana did not seem to be affected by the cold at all. Toby had asked her why and she'd simply smiled at him.

She wasn't smiling now.

Toby looked at his gloved hands. "I don't know."

"Yes, you do."

"Well..." He thought about his words very carefully. "What if I tell Grandma and she doesn't believe me? What if –"

"Are you scared I'll disappear if you tell anyone?"

"Yes."

It was something Toby hadn't understood before now. Lana was real, after all. She was right there in front of him. But she was strange, with her rapidly growing body and origin in the woods, and Toby had a book all about a little fairy girl found inside a flower.

Was that what Lana was? A fairy? Toby wanted to ask her but was afraid to do so.

With a rustle, Lana got to her feet and stood in front of him. Even with him sitting and her standing she was still shorter than Toby, though it made him wonder, excitedly, if Lana would finally be the same size as him the following morning.

She looked up at him with her lovely brown eyes full of secrets. "You can tell her if you want to," Lana said. "I don't have to be something you keep to yourself. I won't disappear before the snow melts."

A lump filled Toby's throat and he struggled not to cry. "Do you *have* to go then? Can't you stay?"

Lana said nothing.

That night, Toby made a bed for her in the bottom of a large box which had originally housed books; he tossed them unceremoniously across the floor of his bedroom.

"Good night, Toby," Lana said when the clock struck ten o'clock.

"Good night, Lana," Toby said, though he didn't want to utter the words. For if the day never ended, then Lana would never have to disappear from his life, and Toby could be happy with her forever.

* * *

When Toby woke up the next morning, he almost didn't want to open his eyes. But a reassuring weight on the edge of his bed made his decision for him.

Lana sat there, swinging her legs and grinning at him. She was exactly the same size as Toby.

"Let's play," she said, taking his hands in hers and squeezing them excitedly.

"I don't know how to sneak outside without Grandma seeing you," Toby admitted. Perhaps, if he'd shown Nora his unnatural friend when Lana was still impossibly small, his grandmother would believe that the girl wasn't human. Now that Lana looked like an ordinary, human seven-year-old, Toby felt certain anybody looking at her would think she had simply run away from home.

But Lana seemed unperturbed by Toby's problem. "Get dressed and fetch us breakfast," she said, "then meet me outside. Now I am bigger I can use my magic."

Toby's eyes grew wide as saucers. "Magic?"

"Yes, magic! Like this." Lana's hand against Toby's faded until he could see straight through it.

He yelped in fright mixed equally with wonder. "Your hand went away!"

"Not away," Lana giggled. "Just invisible. See? You can still touch it, can't you?"

Toby realised that he could. "So you'll sneak out? Can you be very quiet?"

She nodded. "Yes, so be sure to get me more strawberries from the kitchen to feed my magic!"

At breakfast, Nora did not question why her grandson was already dressed up to go outside. But she *did* take his hat and gloves off.

"It's too warm for those," she insisted, pointing outside. "All the snow has gone. The wind's coming from the south now; it really feels like spring! How exciting, Toby. I know you hate the cold."

Nothing could be further from the truth now that Toby understood what the cold and the snow brought with them. Glumly he shovelled cereal into his mouth, while his grandmother watched him, at a loss for what to do.

With a gentle hand, she reached out to stroke Toby's cheek. "What's been going on with you, Toby?"

"I can't tell you yet," he said, because that's what he'd decided.

"*Yet?*"

He nodded. Toby didn't want to think about tomorrow or the next day or even that evening, just like Lana had told him. If today would be their final day together, then he had no time to talk to his grandmother.

With a resigned sigh, Nora allowed Toby to raid the pantry for all the food he could carry, before letting him out into the garden. Toby felt bad that he was keeping his grandmother in the dark, but he wasn't ready to tell her about Lana. One day he would.

Just not yet.

Toby didn't bother searching for Lana; he ran straight for the patch of snowdrops in the entrance to the woods. The snowdrift was barely a puddle left upon the earth.

He bit back a sob.

"I brought strawberries," Toby called out. "And chocolate!"

Lana appeared from behind a tree to sit surrounded by the snowdrops. The green pendant around her neck shone from within as if it held a light all its own, brighter than it had been the day before, or the day before, or the day before.

"Let's eat and play one last time," Lana said, so they did.

As they ran through the trees chasing each other, Toby learned that the woods were only dangerous if one went into them with bad intentions; so long as he was good they were safe to him. The creatures of the forest would make sure of it.

But Toby didn't want any other creatures protecting him. He only wanted Lana.

As the sun dipped lower in the sky, Lana's pendant grew brighter.

"Why is it glowing?" Toby asked, suppressing a shiver which told him the sun was about to set. He desperately didn't want it to set.

Lana played with the pendant in her hand, a sad expression painted across her lovely face. "It's telling me my time is up."

"But – but it isn't ten o'clock yet!"

A giggle. "That is my bedtime, not when I have to go. My family want me back now."

"Can't I come with you? Can't I? Please?"

Tears welled in Toby's eyes; he didn't know what to do or what to say to change her mind. Lana couldn't go. She *couldn't*.

Lana took a step towards Toby, then another and another. Before he knew it she'd wrapped her arms around his middle and patiently waited for Toby to return the hug. He gripped onto her with shaking arms that never wanted to let go.

"I can't stay," Lana whispered. "And you can't go. Your family is here, Toby."

"But I'll never see you again!"

At this Lana gently pulled away from Toby's grip to smile at him. The glow from her pendant lit up her eyes, turning them molten and magical. "Who said anything about never seeing each other again?"

Toby was flummoxed. When *had* Lana said this would be the end? "Then...when can I see you again?"

"When we are both bigger." Lana brought her hands to the back of her neck and unclasped her pendant. Slowly she placed it on Toby's palm and closed his fingers over the shining jewel. It was reassuringly warm to the touch.

"When we are both bigger?" Toby echoed back, transfixed by Lana's eyes and the heat in his hand and the beating of his heart.

"When we are both bigger," Lana said. She kissed Toby on the cheek and then, when Toby made the mistake of blinking, she was gone.

Leaving Toby alone in the woods, the warmth in his hands and far more searing heat spreading across his cheeks the only proof Lana had ever existed.

That night Toby cried and cried and cried. His grandparents asked him what was wrong but he couldn't tell them.

Not yet.

Not yet.

Not yet.

* * *

Toby was almost thirty when it snowed again at his grandparents' house.

No; *his* house.

Edward and Nora had moved closer to the city to be near Toby's uncle, Fred, along with his wife and twins. Fred had been studying at university when Toby was small before moving abroad to work for many years, so he wasn't that close with the man. It didn't help that, whenever he had a drink or two in him, Fred made a point to complain about his no-good sister and her equally no-good boyfriend running off to god-knows-where and leaving their parents to look after Toby.

He meant it as a form of support for his nephew: *you* don't need them; *we* don't need them; everyone the family loves and needs is right here. Toby knew Fred's intentions were good, but still it hurt his heart to hear such a thing. It only served to feed the creeping sadness that had bloomed in Toby ever since he was a child.

For not everyone Toby loved and needed was currently in his life. The green pendant tied around his wrist was the only proof he had that the person he most wanted to see in the world ever existed in the first place.

Though he wasn't close with Fred, he was still happy his uncle would have Edward and Nora nearby to help him with the twins. They had done an excellent job raising Toby, after all.

And it meant he got the house by the woods.

Toby's grandparents had initially planned to sell the house. The surrounding area had become something of a tourist trap, with very few permanent residents living there. It was therefore to their complete surprise when Toby asked if he could live there, instead. His job was remote; all he needed was a good Wi-Fi connection and he was good to go.

And besides, Toby and the woods had some unfinished business.

It was still snowing when he arrived at the house – a late February snow that covered the garden in several inches of white. It hadn't snowed for twenty-two years.

Just like when he was seven, Toby took this as a sign that something significant was meant to happen.

Toby barely wasted any time dropping off his bags inside the house. He knew exactly where he needed to be, and didn't want to waste more time than he had to before he got there.

A month ago, the green pendant around his wrist began faintly glowing. Toby had known, then, that his wait was almost up. He was bigger. A full grown-up, in fact. With every day that the pendant grew brighter, he felt his heart and spirits lift.

Now the jewel was as bright as it had been the day the little forest girl said good-bye.

Behind a snowdrift – it looked so small to his adult eyes, though Toby knew his seven-year-old self would have deemed it a mountain – and between two towering conifers was where Toby found the snowdrops he knew would be there. Crouching low, he rubbed the velvet petals of the largest, most beautiful of the flowers between his thumb and forefinger, his touch delicate in a way a young Toby could never have managed. He touched the snowdrop and he thought of her.

Toby thought of her and then she was there.

"Galana," he said, testing the word in his mouth just as he'd done all those years ago. "Lana."

A bell-like laugh. "You certainly grew bigger, Toby."

Toby closed his eyes for a second, inhaled, then stood up to greet her.

Galana was fully grown, just like Toby, tall and lithe and dressed all in white. For a moment she looked like a stranger in all her ethereal beauty. But the dark hair tumbling down Lana's back in flowing waves, and her lovely brown eyes, and the freckles on her face, and the way her cheeks dimpled when she smiled, were identical to the way Toby remembered them.

It was her. It was really her.

A long moment of silence stretched between them as they looked at one another. Then Toby stepped forward just as Galana did, too, and he wrapped his arms around her as soon as he reached her.

"I waited, like you said," Toby murmured into Lana's hair, squeezing her as close to his chest as he dared. "I waited and now you're here."

"And I waited, and now *you're* here," Lana replied, tilting her face up to smile at Toby. His heart swelled with so much heat and happiness he rather thought it would burst.

When Galana's lips brushed his, Toby was sure he must be dreaming.

"Come and meet my parents," she whispered. "They are eager to meet you."

"Will you meet my grandparents, too?" Toby asked, when Lana pulled out of his arms – too soon, much too soon – to take his hand and lead him into the woods. "I am afraid I have *yet* to tell them about you."

She laughed. "Of course! I wouldn't make a very good wife if I didn't meet your family, Toby."

"My – my –"

"Unless you don't want to get married?" Lana cut in, a tragic, stricken expression painting her face. "If you don't want to –"

Toby almost tripped over his words in his urgency to correct Lana. "I want to! It's all I could ever hope for. I've loved you from the moment I met you."

When Galana laughed again it reminded Toby, somehow, of the snow. "I love you, too. I've loved you for so long. So let's not waste any more time; I rather think we've both waited long enough to be together, don't you?"

Toby had never agreed with anything more in his life.

As they walked hand-in-hand through the woods, a trail of snowdrops grew behind them. Connecting Toby's world to Galana, and Galana's world to Toby.

Hayley Louise Macfarlane hails from the very tiny hamlet of Balmaha on the shores of Loch Lomond in Scotland. After graduating with a PhD in molecular genetics she did a complete 180 and moved into writing fiction. Though she loves writing multiple genres (fantasy, romance, sci-fi, psychological fiction and horror so far!) she is most widely known for her Gothic, Scottish fairy tale, Prince of Foxes – book one of the Bright Spear trilogy.

Silverfoot's Edge

Ella Holmes

My mother once said to me *love is an edge you will fall over*, and she was right.

I think about it often as I walk the woods. She is dead and shrouded in the earth, and I feel her with every bare-footed step through the dirt. Winter frosts the soil, makes it cold to the touch. I welcome the bite. Mother is not the only one I have lost this season, though she, at least, we found dead by the hearth with her needle in hand, poised forever at the point of threading. Matthias is simply gone.

As the daughter of a Lord I am not allowed out of the keep without an escort, but there is little my guards can do when I slip out like a bird taking flight, silent and swift. *I will find him,* I tell myself. A silent mantra, over and over, so many times my bones hum with it. People go missing in the Silverfoot forest as easily as fish in water, and some come back the same, but Matthias has been gone for weeks. I cannot wait. I will find him, like a hook.

My mother was not an easy woman to please, and as I walk through the Silverfoot forest, I remember how easily she took to Matthias when she saw how we shared meals, rode our horses, and danced together at supper. It must stand for something, that a woman as hard-won as my mother would give her blessing to us when there were more beneficial matches to be made.

The words I tell myself – *I will find him, I will find him, I will find him* – do nothing to soften the bite of shock that tears a cry from my chest. A frozen pool lies before me, black in its depths except for the man sleeping in the ice, still and sallow as cold wax. Matthias. My Matthias, with his scarred eyebrow and unruly autumn hair, his face as calm as if he floats in nothing more than a gentle dream. The chill gnaws my skin red, but I beat at the ice with my fists, over and over. Solid as stone, it does not crack.

I beg for Matthias to wake, my chest tight and heaving. Heat steams from me but it is not enough to melt the ice. With my next breath I notice the stillness of the woods – not even an insect chirrups.

"He wandered into my woods, bearing no gift," a singsong voice says. Bone-white head tilted like a bird listening for worms in the soil beneath her feet, a slight woman stands at the edge of the pool. She is one of the good-folk, almost cutting in beauty, with skin as lustred as the silver of my father's sword. "You have disturbed little Sorrel's home. She would have your teeth for it."

Though surprise hollows my stomach, I do not allow my voice to fall through it. "I am sorry," I say. I have heard the stories. Everyone knows the three rules when it comes to the good-folk: do not disturb, do not displease, do not dispel. The crust of bread and hard wedge of cheese I carry in my pocket is for just this purpose, and I lay them on the ice with shaky hands. "Please, accept this offering."

A small bark-skinned creature darts from beneath the woman's ivory skirts and steals my offering in a single swipe. Their limbs click like the snapping of little branches, running a shiver down my spine.

The little-folk, with clothes of moth wings and beetle shells, tilt their heads as though I am a book to be read sideways, silent in their watching and all of them shorter than my knee. The barken creature nods to her kin.

"Sorrel says it is gift enough," the good-woman says. The air is colder for her presence, snowflakes falling light and large as fluffy dandelions. "You may keep your teeth, and have three answers of your choosing."

Oh, I was not expecting this. There are stories of good-folk playing for bargains and tricks, but I did not think...my fingers wring the soft thick wool of my dress for the right questions to ask. "How can I free Matthias from this ice?"

The woman smiles, a harsh purple curve against the pale of her skin. "All things for a price," she says. "I seek a snowflake of the smallest measure, whose shape shall unlock a greater treasure. Ask another."

"How shall I know which snowflake to bring?" Morning snow already falls, and the edges of each flake twinkle like stars before they melt around us, yet somehow Matthias's pool is frozen solid.

"My folk shall follow you, and weigh them." This amuses her, casting her answer like bone runes and watching my reaction.

Desperation lilts my voice, shaky as a lilybird's call. "How shall I find it before I die of old age?" There is no answer offered to this question, just as there is really no choice to make. Still, I ask another, painting the air with it. "What are your rules, and may I have your word that Matthias will wake, in full health, the moment he is freed?"

"I knew you were clever." The good-woman's head once again cocks, as though her smile weighs it down to one side. Perhaps she hears my heartbeat through the ice as much as I feel it throb in my feet. "I swear it," she declares. "Just as I swear that if you do not find the snowflake, and you do not find it alone, he will remain in the ice forevermore."

As her promise settles over me, raising each hair on my body with its magical prickling, resolution swells in my chest like a bulb ready to burst through the soil and brave any season. Did I not love him with heart enough to risk myself in these woods to begin with? I could not imagine a world without his silly stories, or sharing each sunset while he says, *another day spent with you, Maeve, is another day I am happy.*

He was always finding flowers to give me, and as I look down at his frozen body in the dark ice, my eyes catch on the purple petals of a bluebell bunch in his colourless hands. I had not seen them through my desperation to free him, but now they are all I can see; those delicate petals he picked for me despite the danger. I fell over love's edge long ago.

"I will do it," I say. How could I not?

There is no great flash of power, only a sound like creaking wood, then she is gone. I feel the eyes of the little-folk settle on me like the first drops of rain.

There is nothing to do but begin.

Our old healer Hollythorn's cottage is now empty and lies close to Matthias's icy bed. It is well hidden, but the little-folk tell me they will spell the path so only we can find it. Before I go there, I run back home, sneaking through the stone halls and into my chambers. It is still too early in the day for the household to wake, so I prepare a pack of clothes, oats, and other supplies without trouble. I must do this task alone, and if I tell father what has happened, he will never let me out again.

I keep my letter brief. I am going north, to the people in the mountains. Perhaps I will learn from them how to weave a better cloth so we might decorate the dining hall with finer images, I say, by which time my heart may be healed, and I shall return home.

I leave the letter on my bed atop the scarlet quilt my father made for me when I felled my first bird. He is as good with a needle as mother was, as he is with a sword and bow. I have him to thank now, for while I live in the woods I will have the means to fend for myself using the skills he taught me. As I leave the castle I take a fur-lined cloak, a dagger, and a light sword. The good-folk are not the only things to be feared in the woods, and I had best be prepared.

Hollythorn's house is cosy enough, the walls whole and whitewashed, the thatching thick, the central hearth full of ash but surrounded by heavy stones. I drop my bedroll, pack, and sword onto the wooden pallet by the door before turning to face the snow. Where does one look for a special snowflake in a land covered with them? There is no direction better than any other, so I simply catch the snow as it falls, or find flakes on leaves and bushels and present them to the little-folk that follow me.

One, with a head of orange grass, perches on the edge of a rock as I pluck snowflakes from the weeds along a bubbling stream. Voice soft as a whistling wind, he tells me his name is Foxen, that he was named for the creature whose sense of smell can find food even when it is buried deep in the soil. He turns his twitching brown nose to the snowflakes I find, then huffs them away.

Sorrel, whose home I disturbed when I found Matthias, weighs the snowflakes in her hand and throws them to the air with a displeased sigh. Poppy-cap holds them up to his starless night-sky eyes, then drops them on his head, wearing them in his red-petalled hair like a crown. Again and again I find the prettiest, smallest, shiniest flakes.

Again and again, they tell me I must find another.

"What task is this?" I ask, stooping to collect firewood for the night. The sun has already begun burrowing into the horizon. "That someone should find the one snowflake in all the world...what could such a delicate thing ever be worth?"

Sorrel clicks her tongue and stirs the soil at her feet with a twiggy finger. "It is worth your man, is it not?"

I cannot argue with that. I would search the world for a single breath of air if it meant Matthias might breathe again.

"So small a thing, yes," Poppy-cap says slowly, "but so big a thing to Brinae."

"Hush!" Sorrel hisses.

Foxen steps behind a fallen tree, blending in with the grass around him. "You should not speak of this," he says to me. "Find the flake, then go home."

"Brinae?" I ask, shifting the heavy wood in my arms. "Is that the good-woman's name?"

The yellow grass on Foxen's head bobs in confirmation. "Old. Very old."

"And powerful," says Poppy-cap.

Sorrel's *shhh* cuts like a blade swung through the air, and we do not speak again until we are inside the healer's house, sitting around the central hearth. There are pots in the back room which I use to cook oats from my provisions, the little-folk fashioning spoons and bowls from the air when I say it is time to eat.

Sorrel sits beside me. "If you are as clever as Brinae believes you to be, you will either find the flake she seeks and return home with your love, or you will stop your search and go home anyway. She is bound by her word, but if she hears us speak of her, she will not be kind."

Poppy-cap hides his eyes behind his hands. "Years and years, this goes on and on –'

Sorrel's hiss halts his words, and we sit in silence once more. Questions come to me like storm rain; they are cold and persistent, a flood of confusion. Walking in the woods seems a gentle task, but I am bone-weary, so I clean my bowl and settle for sleep.

"I will find the flake," I say, laying on one half of the bedroll, covering myself with the other. "I will."

The good-folk's mutterings follow me into sleep, but it is Foxen's that chases me into a nightmare.

"I am afraid of that."

* * *

The days pass as quickly as flat stones tossed across water, each one the same. One month passes, then two, then three, so fast I begin to dread the oncoming spring. Each day I search. I check my traps. I build my fire and thaw my hands before it, cold from presenting snowflakes to my companions – it is easier to work without gloves.

Soon, they help me in other ways. Sorrel refills the bucket of water each morning; Foxen sniffs out the best place to lay my snares; Poppy-cap sings songs in a language I don't understand but feel in the marrow of my bones. One such tune draws tears to my eyes, and having woken that day with a sadness even Foxen's warm honey brew could not wash away, I collapse back on a damp log and let myself cry.

The sun is bright and blurs through my tears, reflected a hundred times over in the puddles of thawed snow. Winter is leaving for spring, and the hope I held so fast to my heart is leaving with it, while the part of me that misses my father grows heavy with guilt. I cannot go back until my task is complete, for Father has always sought to protect me, sometimes stiflingly so. More than that: I am finding I am more a woman of the woods than the daughter of a Lord.

Poppy-cap and I walk to the lake where Matthias still lies frozen even though the forest's soil already thaws, and I talk to him with the hopes that he can hear me. I tell him how much I miss his skill on the harp, and his story-telling too. It would give me strength to hear him sing but once while I wait for the snow to return.

"But for now," I say, "you will have to hear my tales of the woods, though they may worry you." Sitting on a stone with Poppy-cap at my side, I tell Matthias of the fat worm I stepped on yesterday, how it squished so wet and thick between my bare toes that my stomach curdled. "He would laugh at that if he could," I tell Poppy-cap, and Foxen who joins us. "Then he would fetch me a cloth and warm water for my feet, all while telling me some made-up story of a trodden worm being a sign of good luck, just to make me feel better."

Foxen sniffs. "He is too good a lad to be stuck here."

"Like us," Poppy-cap whispers.

It is just as well Sorrel is not here to stop our talking. I hold Poppy-cap's little hand in mine as I think through all that has been said. "Brinae has trapped you somehow?'

"Trapped, snapped, wrapped in her magic." His poppy flower hair wilts as he talks. "But she too is caught in a snare"

"A snare she wants to break," says Foxen.

I think back to my meeting with Brinae, to the words she said to me. *I seek a snowflake of the smallest measure, whose shape shall unlock a greater treasure.* Oh, but of course. "The greater treasure she seeks is an end to her entrapment?" It is half-question, half-thought. "What will she do with the snowflake when I find it?"

"When?" Foxen repeats with a sad smile. "You have not given up?"

"No," I say. "Will you tell me –"

"Questions lead to answers lead to consequences," Sorrel's voice sounds from behind us. Her barken skin is as dark as her tone. "There are hours left in the day and few flakes left on the branches. Come."

And thus I search until winter abandons us, and

spring invades.

* * *

The woodland flowers turn their faces to the sun each day, and I try to do the same, even though I miss my father. With no snow to search, I sneak into the castle's staff quarters and slip letters for my father into the messenger's pouches. He will be pleased to hear from me. Rumours swarm the household; I have run away to marry another man and scorned Matthias, and my father is heartsick for it. According to Janis in the kitchens, I have always been curious and strong-willed, so it is no shock that I would travel far away for a time.

I only wish I could tell Father how long a time it will be.

Spring carries on with a soft hum; the length and persistence of it grows irritating. I long for the muffling of snowfall. Though the little-folk need not stay with me during these months of colour and warmth, they do. We fall into a routine of waking, gardening, walking, and cooking. They bring me provisions of fresh bread, assuring me it is not spelled to transform me into a bird or make me dance until my feet are ground to the bone, and I split it between us with each meal, now out of kindness as much as caution. Into summer, Matthias grows paler in the ice.

Sorrel, though she is kind, still does not let us talk of Brinae. Her manner is as rough as her barken skin, and we all try not to brush up against it, as the trees gild themselves in autumn's orange and gold, lest we end up splintered.

In the thick of the Silverfoot forest I venture out to the traps I set the day before. My companions have gone for the day, as they sometimes do, for reasons I am not

131

privy to. As I track my path, I leave small offerings of dried fruit for the others who do not show themselves but who I know to be lurking. Befriending the little-folk has not made me forget the rules we humans so strictly live by.

I do not disrupt the mushroom rings and hollylark wreaths half-buried in the soil, do not displease the creatures that make themselves known as I pass by, do not dispel the ones who choose to follow me for a time.

Between two oak trees is my trap, a weak hare squirming with its foot caught. With my dagger I grant it a quick and clean death, keeping as much blood from the fur as I can – it will make a nice new shirt for Foxen, should he wish it.

A twig snaps, betraying someone's presence. But there is nobody here, from what I can see. Even the little-folk are gone. I take the hare and reset the trap for tomorrow, but the hairs on my neck stand up, prickling all the way to the tips of my ears. A sharp cry rings through the air – Sorrel's voice. I dart through the trees, light on my feet until I see a black form that stops me in my tracks.

Sorrel, one foot at an odd angle, holding a large branch between her and a great black wolf.

Its amber eyes break away from Sorrel to look at me, slathering yellow teeth bared. My father told me what to do should I ever encounter a wolf, and as I raise my arms and spread my cloak, I can hear him telling me how to make myself bigger in the face of such hackled danger.

"Stay still," I whisper to Sorrel. I should back away, but I cannot leave her.

The wolf raises its tail, so I raise my cloak even further from my body, not once looking away from its eyes. My heart pounds to the same unsteady rhythm as the wolf's growls as the three of us remain still. The wolf's lips pull back further, and I remember the dead hare in my left hand.

"Please, do not harm my friend. Take this instead," I say softly, and toss the carcass with a flick of my wrist, careful not to move too much. It lands but seven paces away. "I caught it this morning."

The black wolf sniffs the air while I lift my cloak higher still. Sorrel's injured leg twitches at her side, sap leaking between the splinters of her wound. I am not sure she would make a tasty meal. The wolf agrees; he dips his head and takes the limp hare in his mouth and disappears behind a shadowy copse of hazels.

Sorrel turns and looks wide-eyed at me, almost like a babe whose bottom lip can't decide between curving up or down. "You helped me."

"How could I not?" I reply.

And with that, she is gone.

She returns at supper time and helps me cook a broth of wild garlic and mushrooms where she would normally sit in front of the fire, staring as though seeing something other than flames. While Poppy-cap and Foxen bicker, we portion supper into bowls and tear the bread loaves for sharing. It is so different from home, where I am a lady and not so free to serve myself food, or roam about our land without an escort. I am thinking of how I could live out here with Matthias once I free him when Sorrel speaks.

"The old-folk," she whispers, "other good-folk, that

is, do not like Brinae."

I do not want to put her to flight, so I remain silent.

Sorrel stirs the pot, even though we have ladled everything out. "She is tricky. She wants control. She thinks the old-folk – her folk – should do what they will with everyone else, just like before." A pause. "But there must be balance, so the old-folk banded together and locked away most of her power, cursed her with the task she has now given you."

Poppy-cap takes his bowl of broth and bread, his flower hair drooping low and springing high as though not sure what to do. "Thought it was secret. Thought we couldn't say."

"Hush," Sorrel mumbles. It is hard to tell by the bark of her skin, but her cheeks seem to pinken. "Brinae has seen how you solve your father's riddles when you ride your horses, how you have made contraptions from the most unlikely materials to help those who need it, without hesitation. You fixed a farmer's wagon with nothing but branches and dry grass, broke up an argument with measured tact and kindness. Can't you see, Maeve? It is your compassion and your cleverness Brinae sought."

"And Matthias?" I dare to ask.

Foxen nudges my dangling hand with his wet nose. "She made the bluebells sprout, knowing he would pick them for you." He stands behind me, as though still afraid Sorrel will reproach him for speaking.

She does not. She hands him his bowl of broth and we move to the fire, where the light is brighter and the air warmer. It will soon be winter again, and I remind myself of this when the night grows cold. Matthias is waiting for me. We eat, and my friends paint a picture.

"If she gets the flake, she will have her powers again. All of them," says Foxen.

Poppy-cap shakes his head. "Has control of most us folk anyway. Little choice, little will. We dance to her tune."

"Do you not have powers as she does?" I ask. "Could you not lock her in ice as she did Matthias?"

Foxen glances at the door. "Having power is one thing; succeeding is another."

I open my mouth to ask another question, but Sorrel cuts me off with a hand on my knee. "Talk, and we will know. Do you understand, Maeve? We will all *know*." She looks at me, waiting for my understanding.

So I cannot ask my friends for help even if I want to. I nod. But that will not stop me. If Brinae wants me for my cleverness, I will be clever. Somehow I will, though the thought of leaving the woods and going back home after so much freedom sets a new chill in my bones.

* * *

Since dawn I have been here, desperately scraping the ice with my sword, and it has left no more mark than a whisper would to a cliff-face. I overheard talk in the stables when I stole some of the rider's oat and sweetmeat provisions. Father has taken ill, and I could not risk seeing him, so I came to Matthias instead, needing to see his face, missing the feel of his arms around me. I tell him everything, about even the part of me that wishes we could live out here amongst the trees and wildflowers. His face is patterned with frost. What will he look like next year?

I scrape the ice again and again to no avail. The air

snaps with a sudden chill. For a few heartbeats, I simply stare at my autumn-haired love, feeling for all the world like there is no choice here, and there never was.

"You have not yet found the snowflake," Brinae says without kindness.

I face her. "I will not give up."

"I would think," she muses slowly, "that if this man meant anything to you, you would have found it by now." Her words hit me like the first swipe of a cat's claws – a provoking scratch I wince at.

My cheeks burn hot and angry, but I keep my voice calm. "I love him and I will not give up. I will search forever if I must."

"I pity him."

"You put him here," I say without thinking.

Brinae raises her chin. "But whose fault is it that he remains?"

Tears claw my eyes. I know she is only trying to anger me, but I can't help feeling as though I have indeed failed him. I turn away from the good-woman and kneel over Matthias, whose sleeping face would beam at me if he were awake, whose dimples would show if he could grin, whose forehead would dip with three little lines if he could see the tears in my eyes. I lay my hand on the ice above his face, where his cheek is freckled with twinkling frost.

An idea strikes me, sharp and frightening as the silver gleam of my sword.

"I see it," I say, still looking away from Brinae. "The flake – it is here, buried with Matthias. I am sure of it."

"You think me a fool?"

"Apologies, good-woman, I meant no insult." I stand and face her, that she might better believe me. "But does it not make sense? That the thing you search for should be hidden under your nose, frozen with the very thing you spelled yourself?" The fear and desperation that shakes my voice is my only weapon, and I use it like a bard wrings a pleasing tune from his harp. "You called me clever, and this is what I would have done. I would have twisted the terms of your deal, made you the one to keep your own punishment."

Brinae's eyes narrow, her silence choking the forest to stillness. "Someone has told you."

I realise my mistake too late, but I can fix this. "Someone did, yes, but it changes nothing. I wish to save Matthias by finding the snowflake for you. What you do with it is not my business and I would never presume to ask about it."

"Do you know what it is like," she says quietly, "to live with half of yourself missing? Taken away to ease the fears of others?'

Yes, I want to say. Matthias is my other half, and she has taken him away. But there is a gentleness to her voice, like a fledgling bird's first hesitant chirp, so I do not. "I am sorry you have suffered this way."

"No matter," she says. "Once I have the flake, once I have all of my power again, there will be peace."

"Peace?'

"Yes, girl." Her pointy chin juts the air. "With me in control, there will only be peace and order. Everyone and everything has its place, and I will put them there."

My throat tightens. This is not what I want at all – but how am I to choose? Save Matthias, or save the little-folk, my new family?

Brinae clicks her fingers and several little-folk appear, chief among them being Foxen, Poppy-cap, and Sorrel. They look at their feet, then at her, both brave and deferential to the good-woman.

"Tell me if she is lying," Brinae orders, standing uncannily still.

Foxen says, "She does not lie."

Poppy-cap nods.

Brinae focuses on Sorrel, and it is then that I remember. Brinae controls the little-folk. She can make them dance to any tune she wishes. "Tell me the truth of it, Sorrel. If this is a trick, snap the twig of your littlest finger."

Sorrel looks at her hands, sending my heart into a panicked flight. She has no choice. It is all over. But then she straightens, like a sapling earning its bark overnight. "Maeve has not uttered a word against you, and only wishes to find the flake and free her love."

It is the truth; I let out a breath. The other little-folk chitter amongst themselves, saying *it must be true, the flake must be in the ice! It is just the sort of trick the other old-folk would play.*

"I do not have the power to unfreeze the pool, but I will succeed." I say this to Brinae, but I hope my friends understand. "All I need is a chance."

The good-woman lays a bone-white palm to the dark ice at the edge of the pool, and Matthias sinks. Before I can voice my fear, the ice beneath her hand shifts into a staircase. She extends a hand, not in offer, but in order. Of course she wouldn't trust me not to go down first, armed with my sword. I unsheathe the blade, and she demands Poppy-cap carry it away before I take a deep breath and descend.

Matthias lies on a platform of ice, his body frozen in sleep, hands clasping the bluebells over his chest. But which flake should I choose? The one on his shaven chin, or on the blue skirts of the bluebell sprig?

"There," I say, pulling the flowers from Matthias's hands. They slip free easily; they were always mine to begin with. I point to the single white frost flake on the topmost flower. "This is the one, I am sure of it."

Brinae stands at the top of the stairs. "Bring it," she orders, and a clacking of barken feet upon the icy stairs follows.

Sorrel comes to my side, but I am not so foolish. "Please, good-woman, come down and wake Matthias so we might leave this place in peace. I swear I shall hand over the snowflake when he is awake, and we have reached the top of the stairs."

A heavy moment passes. Brinae walks soundlessly down the dark-ice steps, and I stand at Matthias's side as she blows a chest full of air over him. In an instant, the frost on his skin fades, and his hair lolls on either side of his face, finally free to fall. I grip his hands as they warm, and when his fingers tighten around mine it is all I can do not to sob. His eyes – oh, they have never been so brilliantly green until this moment, when they finally land on my face.

"Maeve," he says, light with breath. "You got my flowers."

Oh, how can I do this to the little-folk? "I did," I say, brushing the tear-blurred copper curls from his ear. "All is well, my heart. Can you stand?" With an arm under his shoulder, he sits up on the icy platform. He moves with the sluggishness that comes from waking, and my heart roars with relief that he seems otherwise unscathed. "Come, to the top of the stairs. That's it." Walking step by step beside him, the bluebells remain fisted in my free hand.

The forest is bright with sun, as though it has come to light the way home. Brinae follows us up the staircase, her steps light and unfaltering despite the long gown that pools at her feet in swathes of shining, ivory fabric. Sorrel clasps her barken hands in front of her, meeting my eye as I bring Matthias to the surface of the pool. Foxen's nose twitches, and his head jerks as if catching something in the air. Poppy-cap's petals stand at attention, his little hands gripping the too-big hilt of my sword in his hands.

"The snowflake," Brinae says. "You are at the top of the stairs, now give it to me."

I swallow, not moving from the topmost stair so she cannot yet exit the cavern. "Should I not give it to Sorrel, for weighing?"

"It matters not who weighs it, girl."

"Then I shall give it to Foxen, whose sense of smell is far greater than mine." Anyone but her. My heart shoots through with fear; what will Brinae do if she gets the flake? Foxen nudges my leg and I fist the bluebells. There is only one way we will succeed, and it is by surprise, by being the opposite of what she thinks me: clever.

I gently push Matthias towards the edge of the pool, and hold out the sprig of healthy bluebells to Foxen. Before he can sniff the snowflake, I turn and kick Brinae in the belly. Her breath shoots out of her mouth as she falls, tumbling back down into the dark cavern of ice. The stairs begin to melt, water rushing. Foxen steps forward to help me but slips – down the first few stairs.

"Foxen!" I grab his hand and haul him up, while the other little-folk approach the pool. They place their hands atop the melting pool, and I slip and slide us over to the safety of the soil, to the comfort of Matthias's arms.

"Quickly!" Sorrel shouts. Fingers of ice reach out from their hands, refreezing the pool. Brinae clambers up the stairs, trying to speak but swallowing mouthfuls of gushing water instead. If the little-folk are not fast enough she will make them do her bidding again. She will control us all.

"I lied," I quickly say to Foxen. "I do not know where the flake is."

His yellow-grass head shakes. "It matters not. Brinae will..." He sniffs, once at the air and once at the stem of the bluebells. "Maeve – oh, Maeve! You *have* found it!'

He sniffs it again, as though he cannot believe it. Nor can I. Foxen takes the flake to the water's edge, and one by one the little-folk hold hands; the darkwater creaks like old wood as it begins to freeze again – but of course! The flake contains Brinae's power. The little-folk raise their arms to the sky, and a chill breeze wails through the trees, growing so strong that it snatches the flake from Foxen's delicate fur hands.

"Catch it!" Foxen yells. "Catch it and destroy it!'

Matthias and I chase the flake around the freezing pool, his height allowing him to reach – and miss the flake as it blows by. I jump into the air. Brinae's shrieking is muffled beneath the ice as it hardens around her. The flake blows away, around my head and up high into the sky before floating down like a feather. How are we to destroy it?

"Maeve!" Matthias shouts, and throws me my sword.

I catch it by the cold steel hilt and arc it through the air, slicing the flake in two with a bright burst of light.

For a handful of breaths the forest lies still and silent, watching as Brinae's pale form stills in the ice, trapped forever. The little-folk watch on until they are sure she cannot move, smiling with all of their bright teeth and dimpled cheeks. "Thank you," they all say in a chorus of gratitude and gasped surprise.

"But how did it work?" I ask, looking to Matthias beside me, and Sorrel in front. "Could the old-folk not have destroyed the flake themselves?"

Poppy-cap laughs, high as a tiny tinkling bell as he puts Matthias's hand in mine. "Strange is love. Powerful and strong."

Sorrel squeezes my free hand, eyes wide and watering. I bend down and hug her to me, fighting back my own tears of joy and sadness. "Thank you, my friend," she says into my ear.

One after another, the little-folk tug at my winter pants, my cloak, my littlest finger, before disappearing back to their own world.

Foxen pushes his wet nose into my palm, and offers a smile worthy of his name when he looks between Matthias and me. "We will see each other again, Maeve," he says.

"I hope so." I smile, a curve weighed down by sadness. My mother said love is an edge, but she did not tell me just how sharp that edge could be.

Poppy-cap, with his starless night-sky eyes and flowery hair, is the last to say goodbye. Like a babe longingly eyeing a sweetcake, he stands between two trees, and hesitates. "No goodbyes. No farewells," he says.

Matthias gazes down at me and squeezes my hand. "I think, if Maeve agrees, we shall not stray too far from the woods – if you should ever wish to share a warm meal again. I owe you much, for everything you have done for us both."

I mimic Poppy-cap's nodding head, overcome by the knowledge Matthais heard every word I spoke over him. "I would like that," I say. Then to Poppy-cap, "You will always have a place at our hearth."

The red flowers on his head spring high and bright, and Matthias and I can't help but smile as he dances away.

Afterwards Matthias holds me – presses me into him with a gentle insistence that I cannot refuse, repeated thrice over with each shaking breath that he exhales into the silence of the Silverfoot forest. He kisses the top of my head. "I shall never be parted from you again, Maeve. Where shall we go that is not too far from here?"

I look up at him through the tears in my eyes. "I know a little healer's house that would be perfect."

Ella T. Holmes is a fiction and fantasy writer from Australia. Her passion for storytelling began at an early age and is greatly influenced by her lifelong interest in history, folklore, and an appreciation for typefaces of the serif variety.

When she's not writing, she's thinking about it! Either that or she's as lost as Alice down a rabbit hole of research pertaining to a new and suddenly acquired interest. She writes for the Y/A and adult market, and her works include themes of love, family, trauma, and healing.

Several short stories by Ella can be found online in literary journals across the web.

THE STORM HAGS

Caroline Logan

Catriona Grant flicked the ash from her face and tried for the thousandth time not to think of the lips that had kissed her there, almost a year ago. She tried not to remember the laughter that had filled the walls of her croft house or the hands that would have warmed her on a cold winter's night like this. Instead, she stoked the fire, then tucked herself back into her wool blankets and stared numbly into the flames.

Life had become an endless rotation since the almost-end. She'd wake up with the dawn and do her best to scrape together some food, then her evenings would be for the ghosts. They lurked in the shadows, silent witnesses to everything she'd done. But those spirits she could deal with. It was the one who *didn't* visit that haunted her.

She'd saved the world, once. They'd told her she was The Chosen One, that she was their only hope. So she followed the prophecy – had sacrificed everything she had – and the apocalypse was averted.

And where did that get me?

There had been celebrations at first. She'd been called before the king and he'd toasted her. Children had thrown flowers at her feet. They'd given her jewels and beautiful dresses. Now they sat languishing in a trunk. She'd tried to trade them when she'd returned to her village, but it had been no use. Starving people have no need for trinkets.

So off she went, right back to the life she'd had before. Except now there was no laughter, no teasing smiles. Just a sad girl and her lonely house. It became clear very quickly that everyone else just wanted to move on and forget. And that meant forgetting The Chosen One, too.

Catriona swiped at her cheeks, thinking again of the last good day. The day before her world had turned upside down.

She'd woken safe, nestled in strong arms. She didn't remember what she'd said – only that she'd rushed out to watch the snow fall like ivory feathers, imagining a flock of birds overhead. The forest had been peaceful. She'd returned to a pot of tea whistling on the fire and a crooked smile that made her warmer than the flames.

How had it all gone so wrong? They'd heard whisperings in the village of a curse, one that could destroy the whole kingdom. Never did they think it could relate to them.

> Son o' seven 'n' seventh son,
>
> Born under th' fresh moon,
>
> Though unaware 'n' innocent,
>
> Will surely spell yer doom.

They'd joked about the rhyme, when they'd first heard it. There must be thousands of seventh sons, of seventh sons, born under a new moon. But then they'd heard the second half of the prophecy and their fate had locked into place.

But the maid wi' locks white like ice,

Can save th' kingdom's heart,

Slice through th' cursed's chest, avert

Th' end before th' start.

Catriona pulled on her ivory hair and let out a whimper. Her mother always said her daughter had been gods-blessed and many others had told Catriona the same since. But from the moment she'd learned her destiny, she'd known the gods had forsaken her.

In the days before the world almost ended, the ground had cracked. It was the fissures that led the holy men and women to Catriona's door. The midday sky had turned black as night and, in front of her whole village, she'd been made to do the unthinkable.

I can't, she'd told him.

You have to. You have to save them all.

But just before she'd plunged that dagger into his chest, he'd made her promise. Promise to keep going. Promise to live in the new world without him.

Catriona's eyes slid to the window. Outside, snowflakes were barely drifting through the dead trees. *Keep going.* Now was as good a time as any.

She stood, letting the blankets drop from her shoulders and immediately felt the chill. *Set the traps, collect the snow and then you can come back inside.* These were the tasks which would keep her fed and watered. The bare minimum. Then she could go right back to the ghosts.

Not bothering to change, she wrapped her thick coat over her nightgown and slipped her feet into boots that were slightly too big. Her gloves went on next. One finger was missing, but they were better than nothing. Finally, she raised the hood over her white hair and grabbed the pail. Then, taking a deep breath as if she was about to plunge into water, she opened the heavy door.

Immediately, the snow and wind whirled around her and she threw herself into the night to keep the heat in the house. Catriona slammed the door behind her but didn't bother locking it. There was no one else out at this time of night. And if someone really wanted to get in, she doubted the bolt would keep them out anyway.

Her feet crunching against the snow was the only sound as she stomped into the woods. She set the bucket down near the treeline, ready for when she came back and ducked under the scratching branches. Then she pulled out her knife.

In the summer she could have fished in the streams nearby, but the ice cover was thick at this time of year. Now she had to rely on catching the few animals that weren't hibernating; rabbits, pheasants, and squirrels were up for grabs, if you knew where to look.

She waded through the heather and into the heart of the forest where the trees were evergreen – a reminder that there was life in this snowy landscape. Doing her best to keep her hands steady, she stripped some branches from a large fir and set to work. It was only when she'd finally got the springy wood into a loop that she heard a noise in the distance.

Catriona held still, straining her ears for the sound. At first, she thought the haunting melody was a bird but soon it was clear that the song was far too human.

She straightened slowly from her crouch, her heartbeat almost too loud to hear the voice. Catriona scanned the dark woodland, searching for the singer.

And then, over her left shoulder she saw movement, just as more voices joined the first.

A group of women were darting between the trees. As Catriona's eyes focussed on them, she realised they were dancing, laughing as they spun each other.

Run home, a little voice told her. But it was as if a stranger piloted her body. She found her feet moving forward, towards the dancers. They had chosen a clearing, allowing the full moon to cast its glow on them as they pranced over the snow. The women were young and dressed in long, flowing gowns of lace so fine it looked like spider webs. Each wore antlers atop their brows but they didn't seem to feel the weight as they swung each other around in a jig. As soon as Catriona cleared the treeline, they smiled at her, but didn't stop their dancing.

What are they doing? Catriona wondered, enraptured by the movement. And then, as one, they flung their arms out.

As if they'd thrown them, icicles appeared on the closest branches, dripping down the boughs like gems. Then the women lifted their skirts, revealing bare feet which they stamped down upon the ground. From these points frost spread over the forest floor, encasing the fallen pine needles in white.

Storm Hags, Catriona's numb mind supplied. She'd

been told as a child of these fae. They brought winter to the world each night and left their work for the humans to discover in the morning.

The women slowed their movements, coming together to hold hands in a line. The closest of them turned to Catriona and held out her palm.

"You should come with us," she said, in a voice as soft as the wind.

"Why?" Catriona asked, clutching her coat tighter to her chest.

The Storm Hag's eyes twinkled. "Your heart is frozen like ours. You can help."

Catriona recoiled. She'd helped the world enough, hadn't she?

But the Hag seemed to understand. "We can show you the truth of it."

The truth about why I saved them? Hadn't she been wondering that very thing for a year now?

Catriona stepped into the clearing and, before she thought better of it, slipped her hand into the Storm Hag's. The woman's touch was ice, sticking Catriona's gloves to her skin. Panic rose from the tips of her toes and up her body like a wave. What was she doing? She should leave. But the more she tried to pull her hand away, the tighter the Hag's grip became.

Stop, Catriona wanted to scream, but before she could open her mouth the women moved, all of them breaking into a run. Her arm was almost pulled out of its socket as she was hauled along with them, her feet slipping over the frozen ground. The Storm Hags sprinted through the woods, darting between the trees gracefully. And everywhere they raced was covered in a layer of thick frost.

Catriona's breath huffed out in gasps as her eyes darted from her surroundings to the woman who still held her hand.

As if sensing her gaze, the Hag looked over her shoulder and grinned. "Are you not enjoying our run?"

"I'm frightened," Catriona choked out.

"You should be," called the woman. "But there can be pleasure in that. Look down."

Catriona's eyes fell to her feet, which she'd ignored in the snatched conversation. Now a new terror clutched at her chest. Her boots were no longer touching the ground. Her legs were still moving as if she was running, but they merely worked uselessly in the air as she continued to be pulled along.

"We're flying," she gasped, not quite believing it still.

The Hag nodded. "Now up we go."

The leader of the group jumped and then she was sailing into the air, pulling her companions up, up, up with her. Then it was Catriona's turn as the Hag holding her hand raced into the sky. Catriona could do little as she was dragged from the forest floor and into the black abyss above.

I'm going to die. I will fall or freeze or choke. But as she flew, she took stock of her body. The Hag's grip was secure. She was warm inside her coat, warmer than she'd been on the ground. And her lungs were filled with sweet, cool air. As soon as she realised this, her movements slowed. Now, instead of dashing desperately, she allowed the Storm Hags to pull her along. Now she was swimming through a night-dark loch and all around her were stars, lighting their way forward.

On and on the Storm Hags ran, until something tall and white loomed up ahead. The leader changed the angle of her body and the group began to descend, their feet brushing the tops of the trees as they found their way to the ground. Catriona braced for the impact of the hard soil but they landed gently.

The Storm Hag holding her let go of her hand and Catriona snatched it to her chest, half expecting it to be frozen solid. But whatever spell the Hags cast was still working; she was as warm as she'd been in the air.

"Where are we?" she asked, gaze darting around the dark forest.

The Hag nearest her only pointed up and Catriona's eyes followed her finger over the trees. Towering into the blackened sky was a building made of pale stone. It appeared whole, with turrets and parapets, and flags bearing a crest she did not recognise. But then she blinked and the walls were crumbling, the banners torn and shredded.

"What magic is this?" Catriona breathed. One moment the castle was a fairytale, the next it was a wreck. And despite the flickering image, there was something else that had Catriona's hair standing on end. The forest was deadly silent.

"What you see are the remains of a great kingdom which came before yours," the lead Hag said.

"But how is that possible?" asked Catriona. "Our kingdom has been here since the start of time."

The Hag shook her head. "Before you there were others and before them were more still. Kingdoms rise and fall as often as the sun."

Catriona's mouth opened and closed in shock for a moment before she was able to rasp out, "What happened to them? How did their kingdom fall?"

"The world ended."

"But we're still here."

The Hag nodded and then held out her hand to her sisters. Catriona stood by numbly as the Storm Hags began their dance anew, her gaze flickering between them and the ruined castle. How many people had died when this other kingdom had ended? Why didn't she know about them? She thought of the people in her village, in the capital. Things were hard for them, but they were so full of life compared to this place. It was a stark reminder of what could have been if she hadn't fulfilled the prophecy. Except... if all kingdoms fell like the Hag said, did that mean their own doom was inevitable? Had her sacrifice really saved them? Or had she only bought them a few more years?

The Storm Hag's dancing slowed and Catriona realised these woods were now covered in a thick layer of frost, like those beside her house. She pulled her coat tighter. Her body still felt warm on the outside, but there was a chill creeping deep into her bones.

"Let's go," said the Hag nearest, holding out her hand once again. Catriona blinked down at it before slipping her palm into the other woman's once again. This time, when the Storm Hags began to run, she did not fight it. As they lifted into the air once more Catriona looked over her shoulder to where the castle was. She kept her eyes on it until they'd climbed over a mountain and the building was no longer visible.

On and on they flew, over forests that had already seen the Storm Hag's frost. After what seemed like hours the lead Hag angled herself, turning their formation towards a glow on the horizon.

Is that the sunrise? Catriona wondered.

But then she recognised things on the ground below. A snaking river. Three hillocks in a row. A road leading from the forest and into a town. And then she understood. The glow was from the capital, from the torches they used to light their streets.

The trees dwindled and then they were flying over farmland. From this height the fields looked stitched together like a patchwork blanket of golds and greens.

The lead Hag dipped and then they were floating down once more, landing in the middle of a sea of grass. Catriona's feet brushed the blades before she, too, touched down gently amongst them. She shook out her limbs, feeling heavier than she had before they'd taken off. Her back was aching and her vision did not seem as clear. *You're just tired,* she told herself, before turning to watch the Storm Hags.

As before, the women spread out into a circle and began their dance. Catriona watched them mesmerised at first, but then it dawned on her where they were standing. This was someone's farm. They were standing amongst their crops, their livelihood. And then the Storm Hags threw out their hands, casting their ice all around them.

"Stop!" Catriona shouted before she could think. "You're killing everything." Indeed, the plants all around them curled inwards under the frost. She didn't know much about farming; had they already harvested their food? Or was she watching their one hope of survival die?

The lead Hag paused in her dance. "And in the spring, there will be new life. Sometimes things need to end so others can begin."

And so they began again, dipping and turning and spreading winter where they went. But as they ran and danced, Catriona watched with alarm as the Hags changed. Their skin wrinkled and became papery, their hair became as white as Catriona's. When the woman held out her hand to Catriona once more, it was frail and creased. And, when Catriona went to take it, she realised in horror that her own matched. She too had aged.

Her voice came out in a croak as she said, "You told me you could show me the truth. What is it?"

"We can show you, but you must realise it," said the Hag. "You're at the end of your life. What was important?"

But before Catriona could answer she was being pulled into the sky once more. Over the fields they flew, straight to the jagged crests of mountains to the north. And to the east, the first rays of sunlight peeked over the horizon.

This will be my last day alive, she realised with a bone-deep certainty. She was too old now. So she drank it in; the land she had saved once upon a time. Tears raced down her cheeks as she flew. What *had* been important? She knew in her heart the answer.

When they finally landed upon the mountainside, Catriona was bent and weak. She let go of the Hag's hand and stared around with failing eyes. They were amongst trees again, but in the centre of the clearing sat something made of stone. She drew closer and realised it was a fountain. In the centre, water bubbled out of a hole, trickling down into a pool large enough to bathe in. And to her surprise, the Hags began doing just that. One by one they approached the fountain and splashed the water upon themselves. And, in the morning light, Catriona saw them change once again. Their skin smoothed, their hair darkened. Each Hag emerged from the pool looking as young as she'd first seen them.

Then the Hag who'd been holding her hand asked her question again. "What was important?"

"Love," said Catriona. "But that was taken from me."

The Hag smiled. "Take it back."

Catriona's gaze snapped back to the fountain, and she knew what she had to do. Lifting the skirts of her nightgown she hobbled over the frozen ground and headed straight for the bubbling water. With a cry she launched herself into the hole, diving into the well.

The water that engulfed her was as warm as a bath, but she didn't allow herself to enjoy the heat as she kicked her way down into the dark. Her lungs screamed for air and the pressure popped in her ears, yet she didn't stop. Down, down, down, until she had no idea which way was up anymore. Then, finally, when she thought she'd be lost in the blackness forever, she glimpsed a light up ahead.

Catriona broke the water with a gasp, throwing her arms out to grab the lip of the pool. Her pale hair clung to her face, and she scrabbled to clear it from her eyes so she could see where she was.

It was another forest, but this one felt familiar. Deep cracks gouged the ground, radiating out from a single point. A crowd stood amongst the trees, hushed as they stared at a figure kneeling in the dirt. And all around them, the snow fell like ivory feathers.

Catriona pulled herself out of the water, her clothes plastered to her body as she found her footing. She drifted forward, as if in a dream, not feeling the cold. Now she was closer, she could tell the figure was a man. And then she was running. He turned his dark head and she choked out a sob. No one in the mob spoke as she approached him, not until she was right where she'd been almost a year ago.

Then, a holy man held out a knife to her and the midday sky turned black as night. Around them, she was distantly aware of torches being lit as she took the dagger from his hands.

"Fulfill the prophecy, maiden, and save us all," said the holy man.

Her hands shook as he stared down at the knife. And then she raised her eyes to the man kneeling in front of her.

His face was as familiar to her as her own. Catriona had thought she'd never see it again.

"Slice through the cursed's chest," said the holy man beside her.

Tears slid down her cheeks again. "I can't," she said. But she wasn't talking to the holy man.

"You have to," said her love, on his knees as if he was begging. This whole year she'd avoided his name, trying to cast it from her mind. Finally, she allowed herself to think it.

"You have to save them all," said Reid, and her heart broke again for him. Here he was, ready to sacrifice himself, for people he'd never met.

But Catriona shook her head. "I tried that once and it didn't work. Now I want to try something else."

Reid stared up at her, confusion plain on his face, but before he could ask her what she meant Catriona turned and plunged the dagger, not into his chest, but into the heart of the holy man.

Catriona felt the fabric and flesh give way under her blade, bringing back memories of when she'd done this once before. It had been Reid's chest then, his eyes she'd watched drain of life. Now she looked into those of the holy man as he blinked in shock. She dropped her hand from the dagger's handle, leaving it embedded there.

Seeing what she had done the crowd began to scream, but Catriona paid them no mind as she grabbed Reid's hand, forcing him to stand and run with her, away from the clearing and the riotous mob.

"What did you do?" he huffed out as they raced over the churned soil.

"I made a different choice," she said, leading him back to the fountain. "Trust me." Then she once again launched herself at the water, pulling him in with her.

* * *

Catriona watched the smoke through the window, the only evidence of a kingdom ending so very far away. There would be another, she knew now. And just because the kingdom was doomed didn't mean all of the people were. They'd survive, adapt, build anew. It had happened over and over again. *Kingdoms rise and fall as often as the sun,* the Hag had said.

She felt a warm hand on her shoulder and leaned into it. A roughened thumb scraped against her cheek. It

158

had been a year since they'd fled, finding themselves in the abandoned castle she'd visited with the Storm Hags. They'd both earned their calluses repairing the building, making it liveable. But it had been their smiles, their laughter, their love that had turned it into a home. A place to wait out the end of the world.

"I have to leave tonight," said Catriona. "It's the first day of winter."

"But you'll come back?" asked Reid.

"Once we've done our job."

That night Catriona left to dance with her sisters, covering the world in frost. And when the sun rose the next day she slipped into the fountain, finding her way back to her love and their new beginning.

Caroline Logan is a writer of Young Adult Fantasy. She is currently working on her Scottish fantasy series: The Four Treasures. The Stone of Destiny, The Cauldron of Life and The Sword of Light are out now, with the final book – The Spear of Life – scheduled for release in October 2022.

Caroline is a high school biology teacher who lives in the Cairngorms National Park in Scotland, with her husband and dogs, Ranger and Scout. Before moving there, she lived and worked in Spain, Tenerife, Sri Lanka and other places in Scotland.

She graduated from The University of Glasgow with a bachelor's degree in Marine and Freshwater Biology. In her spare time she tries to swim, ski and paddleboard, though she is happiest with a good book and a cup of tea.

The Boggart of
Boggart Hole Clough

Jake Curran-Pipe

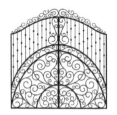

The mind and the forest are almost indistinguishable. For centuries mankind has sewn its complete unknowing of itself and the world into these ancient trees. To them the forest means life, fertility, the divine feminine energy of creation and love. But it is also the home of fear, of sadness, of decay. Where one life rots amongst the lichened logs another is blooming with delicate petals in the sunshine.

The mist-wreathed clearings lie as still as the mind, in a perpetual state of lingering, waiting for something to disturb it. If you are lost in the forest you wait for the light to guide you; it's no coincidence that happiness and knowledge are symbolised by light. The warmth from the sun offers safety – the promise of leaving behind the unknown.

Jordan wished for the sun.

His ears rang like a distant house alarm, causing the muscles in his back to tighten with anxiety. In all his tumultuous life he had never heard true silence; his childhood home welcomed the nightly purr of an approaching bus to comfort him as he drifted off to sleep, as if it were a snoozing cat on his chest. Distant yells, bangs, snippets of techno from a passing car, all perfect in their decibel and rhythm, all soothing. But now it was him, and just him, amongst the barren trees and frost-capped mushrooms. Not even the rustle of a wintry wind to keep him company.

He wished an owl would hoot.

In the silence, Jordan was very aware of his body: the drum of his heart, the ringing in his ears, the twinge in his thigh, the streams of alcohol coursing through his veins. Another empty bottle clenched so tightly in his hand he was sure it would soon break. He closed his eyes and exhaled a billowing draconic mist into the bitter night air.

"Where's the fucking gate?" he muttered through chattering teeth.

He threw the glass bottle to the ground where it landed with an unsatisfying thud in some frostbitten mulch. Through the thick darkness and his spiralling eyes he could just make out the path that would eventually lead to the park's gate. A stiffening finger rummaged in his pocket for the gate-keys. The icy metal bit his numbing thumb. He groaned and began to make his way to the path.

The ringing in his ears grew louder; the silence tried to drag him further into the dark. But he wouldn't let it.

The crunch of his shoes against frosty leaves.

The pathetic half-whimper of his shortening breaths.

The jingle of the keys in his pocket.

He fought off the freezing silence with all his might. Icy spectres loomed between trees, waiting for him to succumb to the stillness. If there was noise, there was safety.

"There we go," he mumbled.

The path straightened out toward the towering wrought iron fence that was nestled between glistening brick walls adorned with frost. In gold lettering, it said:

BOGGART HOLE CLOUGH

Well, Jordan could only read it backwards.

He pushed himself into the gate, stumbling on his feet as the sturdy barrier rattled. He fumbled with the key in his pocket and, after several attempts, was able to pry open the lock of this ancient barrier. The threshold between the forest and the real world. A car zoomed past with a sharp burst of rap music. He smiled to himself; he was at the entrance closest to his mum's flat.

With the hardening soil Jordan was only able to open the gate a fraction. He slinked through it, careful not to rip his parka.

"Shit!" He nicked his hand on a spike.

The up-hill walk was a struggle as Jordan tried to keep on a straight line and avoid falling into the sporadic traffic. He had no idea what the time was but it felt like that dark corner between midnight and dawn.

He arrived at the block of flats. Luckily the main entrance was operated by an electronic fob; no need for an embarrassing escapade of trying to fight a tiny key into a tiny lock. He stumbled into his childhood bedroom, still laden with posters of dinosaurs, the solar system and Billie Piper.

Despite being close to freezing only twenty minutes ago, Jordan flung off all his clothes and threw himself on to the bed. The gentle heat of the radiator next to his bed slowly warmed him up like a pig on a spit roast. Within an instant he was asleep.

* * *

In his dream, he was back in the forest. An owl was hooting. He kept seeing a small, spindly creature moving swiftly between the branches above like a monkey made of ribbon. It was whispering something he couldn't quite hear.

* * *

In the early morning glow Jordan's eyes began to flutter with the rays of sun that filtered through his curtains. In that limbo between slumber and consciousness, Jordan kept his eyes scrunched up tight and tried getting back into his dream forest. *What was that creature?*

Jordan felt something cold and clammy against his cheek.

He groaned and tried turning away but the clamminess stayed.

As Jordan's consciousness crept out from his mind he could feel long grooves laying on his cheek. The shortest, stubbiest one gave a slight nudge. The cold, clammy flesh rubbed against Jordan's warm, dry skin.

His heart leapt when he realised a hand was cupping his face.

He jolted awake, his left foot hitting the bleed valve of the radiator.

"Fuck!"

The clamminess was gone.

Whatever was there, he didn't want to see it. He buried himself under the duvet like a cowardly ostrich.

He kept his eyes closed and waited for the sun's light to brighten. Waited until he was far away from twilight and safe in the morning shine. He knew the sensation must have been imaginary but he'd rather stay ignorant. Maybe it was his mum?

A few hours later Jordan woke up once more. Head tight, hangover throbbing.

In the haze of his eyes and the glare of his phone, he could make out a text from his mum, who worked in the café of Boggart Hole Clough: *YOU LEFT THE BLOODY GATE OPEN!*

Back to sleep.

Deal with that later.

* * *

Knock-knock

Knock-knock

Jordan rubbed his eyes with the heel of his palms; he felt like absolute shit.

"Hello?" his voice cracked, throat lined with phlegm.

Silence responded.

Though Jordan decided to actually get out of bed this time he already knew today would be a write-off. The churning nausea in his stomach and the throngs of pain that crowded in every corner of his head let him know that today was a duvet day. Jordan thanked God that he didn't have work until tomorrow and could avoid his mum until she got back from her second job around midnight.

The thought of the park made him jolt for his phone to see if the text his mum had sent was real. He had a knack for reading text messages in the early morning that sleep would eradicate from his short-term memory. He always, half-jokingly, told his friends that contacting him between the hours of 6am and 10am would be a fool's errand.

He caught a glimpse of his hands. Scarlet red with blood stains so dry that they had cracked where the channels on his palms were. He looked like a grotesque palmistry ornament. He ran to the bathroom to scrub them clean, cursing the spikes on the gate. With no sign of infection he stumbled back to his bedroom.

His heart sank as he read his mum's early morning text. He glanced at the current time – 10.30am. She would have been working for hours already. The damage had been done. He thought that he better go down and apologise to her...

But first, a brew.

Jordan groaned a histrionic bellow as he clambered off the checkered duvet. For a moment he was back in his Deansgate flat with Ciaran, ducking from a pillow that his boyfriend would launch across the airy bedroom. *You're such a drama queen! No, I'm not, I'm genuinely in pain!* The encroaching walls of his childhood home in the red-bricked suburbs felt sepulchral in comparison to Ciaran's glass-walled apartment that would allow Jordan to see out to Greater Manchester, Cheshire, Lancashire *and* West Yorkshire. Every corner of the pristine palace let light dance upon each shiny surface; the only shiny thing his mum owned was a second-hand kettle.

How much can change in just a week.

The hot water rolled to a boil as he leant on the kitchen counter.

His eyes wandered to the small window that offered a view of the block's garden. Since moving back in a week ago Jordan came to realise that this was more a fly tipping hotspot than somewhere you'd nurture a row of sunflowers. A pink tricycle caught his eye, and he smiled, thinking of all the kids' toys that his mum used to nick from other people's gardens. She would always spray paint her loot a bright pink; a way of disguising the stolen goods.

As the kettle rattled and hissed towards its boiling climax, Jordan bent over to the fridge.

"Eugh," he moaned, his stomach curdling at the unwanted buckling.

He pulled out a half-pint of green milk - the only thing on the shelf along with a cheese-string and some broccoli.

"Definitely a takeaway day," he mumbled.

Jordan put a splash of cold water into the hot tea and then poured the milk as he glanced once more at the garden's pink tricycle. Raising the mug to his lips, he smirked at what he thought was an impressive life-hack: adding cold water to a tea or coffee makes it instantaneously drinkable.

As Jordan took a mouthful of the drink, he felt a bitter sharpness stab at the walls of his mouth. Chunks of curds squelched in his teeth; his tongue revulsed at the acrid burn of rotten milk. Before Jordan could properly compute what had happened, his stomach was already making decisions for him. One retch later and he was face down in the sink, puking up a vile cocktail of rotten milk, last night's vodka and the golden nuggets of sweetcorn from yesterday's lunchtime jacket. Tears pricked at his eyes.

I only bought that yesterday!

Once he'd emptied his guts, he looked at the half-empty bottle of milk. The use-by date was five days from now.

"What the –"

He kicked open the bin and threw the milk carton amongst empty Pot Noodles. Devastated, he made himself a glass of water and sat on the battered leather couch he spent his childhood picking at. He pulled out his phone and saw that, along with his mum's text, he had missed five missed calls from Ciaran. All from last night.

"Fuck off," he muttered.

He opened the text thread between himself and his mum and started drafting an apologetic response. After minutes of typing and deleting, typing and deleting, he decided he would try and speak to her in real life.

He glugged another glass of water, scoffed a crisp sandwich, and grabbed his parka. The road to Boggart Hole Clough felt a lot quicker than last night's pilgrimage. Downhill and sober, Jordan's journey took a matter of minutes.

* * *

He entered the Clough - a Northern English word for ravine that he once had to explain to Ciaran - and made his way to the Lakeside Café where his mum, Debbie, busied herself in a workshed-office-thing that stood proudly with the "Do Not Feed the Wildfowl" and "Lives Not Knives" signs. He knocked on the door; the wooden rap reminded him of the knock on his door this morning...

"Come in, cock," said a nasally voice from within.

This was another word Jordan once had to explain to Ciaran. A term of endearment up North that Essex posh boy Ciaran couldn't quite get his head around.

Jordan opened up the door to find Debbie, a woman in her mid-sixties, sorting out a pile of ropes used for summer sports days. Jordan cleared his throat.

"Oh, it's you..."

"Hiya. I'm so sorry for not locking up last night."

She sighed.

"I told you the first day that you must *always* lock the gate. You're lucky I even trusted you with the keys, Jordan. It's bad enough what happens when the gates *are* open; you can't be letting things in willy-nilly. Or out for that matter. How long were it even open for?"

"I - I think I got home around two."

"Right, well, I got there around eight, so that's a good few hours," she sighed, a worried brow framed her eyes.

"I -"

"What on Earth were you doing in here?" Her face

169

had the usual look of loving disappointment. "Do I even wanna know? I hope it wasn't what you lot like to get up to!"

"What do you mean, us lot?"

"You know," she whispered. "*Mandy*! Your generation can't seem to get enough..." She smiled, impressed she knew the lingo.

Jordan scoffed. He couldn't believe what just came out of her mouth.

"Now, I mean no offence by that my love," his mum continued, "you know I was on as much acid as the next person at Thunderdome back in the day. I just don't want you high at my – *our* – place of work..."

"It wasn't drugs," he half-lied, "I wasn't...doing that."

"Well, the park shuts at dusk. That were about 4pm yesterday. That's nearly twelve hours you were in the Clough last night..." Her brows furrowed in either confusion or concern.

Jordan tried to piece back together his night. He was definitely in town somewhere. And around midnight he remembered being on a bus...

"Look, Jordan, I don't mind what you do in your spare time, you're an adult now. Just don't be swanning about the Clough after hours."

Jordan nodded and apologised.

"And if you *ever* decide to come here again at night you *must* make sure the gate is locked. I'm being serious." Her perennial smile was nowhere to be found.

His mum looked down at the latte on her desk. She sniffed it and nodded her head in satisfaction before taking a sip. "Seems like we're alright. Now get lost and

I'll see you tomorrow, love. Enjoy the rest of your day off. Our Maxine said she's gonna pop in tomorrow."

Jordan's mum's cousin. A woman who spent the 80s and 90s falling out of clubs in an attempt to be the Madchester version of Patsy Kensit, then spent the 21st century squandering her wages at the Belle Vue greyhounds. The kind of person who's a great laugh but you'd never believe a word they said.

On his way back to the Clough's exit, Jordan watched a kaleidoscope of puffer-coated children throwing pebbles onto the thick shelf of ice that had covered the Boating Lake. The shrill giggles caught at his temples, the latent hangover beginning to throb in the nothingness between brain and skull. A small dog was yapping at nothing nearby.

He went home via the corner shop for another pint of milk. He shook it around in front of the bemused shopkeeper, inspecting it for any signs of souring. As he reached the steps before the block of flats, a red-headed woman in a ponytail and green parka stood facing the door.

"Bethan?" said Jordan. His heart panged.

She turned around and smiled. "Pardon?"

"S-sorry, I thought you were someone I knew..."

Bethan was Ciaran's sister. Her bright red hair was always in a swishy pony.

He remembered last night's missed calls. He remembered Ciaran shouting at him.

"Bethan's a nice name. Better than my one," she laughed. "Do you live here?"

"Yeah, just recently..."

"Aw, lovely!" She smiled. "I have to run but maybe I'll see you around?"

Jordan's brain fog couldn't properly compute the situation. Before he could even get a good look at her face she had already rushed past him. He spent the rest of the day curled up on the sofa watching television. Programmes about home improvement, buying a villa in Spain, re-doing the garden; the kind of thing that's only found after the fifth page of the TV guide. He liked the perky drone of the presenters, allowing him to move focus from the bubbling cauldron in his stomach.

It was approaching five o'clock in the afternoon, and Jordan's eyes were beginning to haze. He turned the volume down slightly, not fully committing to switching the telly off, and gently dozed.

* * *

He was in Boggart Hole Clough. Only this time, Ciaran was with him. He stood by the Boating Lake shouting but Jordan couldn't hear what he was saying. It was like a mute scream one omits in a nightmare. Ciaran's eyes bulged with horror as long, black strands of spectral ribbon slinked between his legs, around his torso and twisted around his neck. Jordan was frozen; his arms and legs heavy under an invisible weight. He tried to call out to him but he suffered the same voiceless scream.

Black curls engulfed Ciaran's face as they lurched him to the ground. Jordan could feel tears pricking at his eyes as the slithy, serpentine creatures dragged Ciaran to the depths of the icy lake. Jordan's eyes were petrified and hazy, staring out to the lake where the gentle bubbles of Ciaran's last breath danced on the glassy surface.

As the black entities slithered their way towards him Jordan felt what could be described as cold hands rubbing themselves up and down his legs, his torso, his neck, his ears. They were grabbing and pulling, grabbing and pulling, as Jordan struggled to move against them. A freezing finger and thumb grabbed his earlobe and yanked; he finally screamed.

Jordan realised he was no longer dreaming.

He shot upright, knocking a glass of water off the table. The room was pitch-black except for the static flickering from the television that coated the walls with frenetic cobwebs. His eyes stung like he'd spent the evening crying; his heart raced as he remembered the cold finger and thumb that had pulled on his ear lobe. He put the big light on, flooding the room with a yellow glow.

Not a single shadow.

He wanted to speak out, but didn't want to make his presence known.

So Jordan shut the curtains, not even looking at the window in case he saw something he didn't want to. The bulbous-eyed creature that Ciaran had become clawed at his mind, desperate to be released and be present in the living room. The crack in the living room door bled the hall's darkness; Jordan didn't want to step foot in there. He shut the door properly and sat back down on the sofa.

A cup of tea, he thought. And teleshopping. That would calm him until his mum came back from her shift at Yates.

As he opened the fridge, the curds of rotting milk looked back at him.

Knock knock

The faint tapping woke Jordan from his sleep. The teleshopping channel was flogging tote bags with matching scented candles. It sounded like glass, the tapping noise, and at first he glanced at the window. Daylight was struggling to emerge from the chintz curtains.

"Who the hell..." he muttered, clambering up from his den.

Remembering the spectre in the woods from his dreams, he was hesitant to open up the curtains. But the glimpse of the pink tricycle drew him out of his phantasmagorical state.

Jordan checked the oven's clock and saw he had half an hour to get down to the Clough to start his shift in the café. Why didn't his mum wake him? He washed his face and doused his body in cheap deodorant before legging it down to Lakeside Café.

* * *

Whilst chopping mushrooms with a leopard-print knife, he still couldn't get his mind off this morning's dream. Jordan *never* remembered his dreams but this one felt different. He shuddered at the visceral physicality – the clammy hand on his face, the tugging on his earlobes. It reminded him of those poltergeist films. He hadn't told his mum about the rotten milk. She would turn it into a way of blaming him.

"Mum..." he said, his throat dry and desperate for water.

"Yes, Sleeping Beauty?" she replied, juggling three

fry-ups at once.

"Is this place haunted?" he said, immediately laughing at the notion.

"Of course, love, why else do you think it's called Boggart Hole Clough?" she laughed, plating up the bacon.

"Pardon?"

"I mean, the clue's in the name, isn't it? You know...boggart!"

"What's that?"

"Don't be silly, Jordan –"

"Mum, I swear down what the fuck is a boggart?"

His mum scoffed in return and plated the rest of the fry-ups. She took them out front as Jordan continued chopping mushrooms.

"Maxine, our Jordan's just asked if the Clough is haunted," he heard Debbie laugh.

Jordan smirked at his own idiocy. Ghosts didn't exist, what a stupid question.

"Our Maxine wants to see you," said Debbie in a sing-song voice, poking her head into the kitchen.

Jordan wiped his hands on his apron before draping it over a chair. He came into the café to find Maxine sat filling her face with a breakfast muffin.

"Hiya, Jordan, love. Your mam said you fell asleep on the couch last night."

"Yeah..."

"Big night or just a lazy git?"

"I –"

Jordan's ears flushed with heated rage at being called lazy. Several café patrons laughed at Maxine's comment.

"Anyway, what do you mean you've not heard of the boggart? Did you not educate the boy, Debbie?"

"Our Maxine loves the supernatural. I never got involved in all that shite," smiled Debbie.

"Have you seriously never heard of boggarts?" said Maxine. "Well...people think there's just one that lives here. But I'm certain there's loads. I had this friend at school – remember Karen Busby, Debbie?"

"Her with the teeth?"

"No, that's Karen Braithwaite. Karen Busby was the one who did the whip-round for Boov 'All 'Ospical but five months later she had a new conservatory. Anyway, me and Karen Busby was playing here one day back in the 70s. Out of *nowhere* was this vile shriek. At first I thought it were a woman, and then a fox. But it screamed again and again and again. We thought, 'what the blinking hell is doing that'. It was only the afternoon so we weren't scared or owt. Anyway, Karen goes, 'ey, look where we are' and I goes, 'what?' and she goes 'right by the brook.' Well, I fucking shit meself, Jordan. That's where the boggart lives. Well, one of them anyway. So we legged it. Never been over there since."

She nodded her head in the direction of the brook and did a faux–shiver.

Jordan looked on, his mouth slightly agape. There must be some sort of generational gap with the fear of this apparent boggart.

"You saw the...boggart?"

"No but we heard it flippin' screaming!"

"But what *is* a boggart?"

"A spirit. They love to torment. They linger in hollows, under bridges, in the sharp bends of a country lane. They're all over Lancashire. Waiting for a vulnerable person to latch on to. People follow the sounds of a boggart and never come back out of the woods. Dogs can sniff 'em out, though. So if you have a dog you're alright..."

"What do they look like?"

"Depends...some people say a child, a monkey, a goblin...the thing is, if you see it, you're not long left for this world. Especially if you give it a name."

"A name?"

"Aye, if you name it, that's it attached to you for life. You'll never escape it."

Jordan looked around the café to see the other patrons nodding in agreement.

"There was one in Moston that had a name," said Debbie over the counter. "Nut-Nan. Apparently it drove a family insane and they moved away. Poor things were dairy farmers too..."

"Why's that relevant?" said Jordan.

"When a boggart latches onto you," said Maxine, "their presence is so foul that milk rots."

* * *

The rest of the day, Jordan kept quiet in the kitchen. He chopped away at the vegetables, channelling his anger at Maxine calling him lazy. His mum tried making small-talk with him but he couldn't remove himself from the frozen forest in his mind. Could he have disturbed something in the woods by leaving the gate open? From fairytales he knew that iron was supposed to repel creatures like fae folk and witches; did it also keep boggarts from escaping into civilisation? Was the boggart with him in the house? He couldn't believe he was even considering this as a logical notion. He felt like the stock non-believer in a horror film; the skeptic that always gets killed by the monster.

* * *

It was the first time in a while that Jordan and Debbie had been home at the same time. They got a chippy and watched a cheesy 80s thriller together. Jordan kept noticing tiny patches of blood on his hands he hadn't been able to scrub off yet. He followed the scarlet stains around his palm, looking for the scab of the small wound that caused it.

There was nothing.

* * *

He was back in Boggart Hole Clough. No Ciaran this time. No hooting owl. No slender primate slinking between the branches. No curling black ribbons of preternatural composition. Just him and the trickling rhythm of a brook nearby.

"*Jordan,*" said a whisper from the trees.

He froze, in fraternity with the leaves of a holly-bush. The red jewels glistened with powdered frost that caught the soft moonglow. His body felt a calmness that can only be inspired by nature.

"*Jordan,*" it whispered again. But it did not frighten him.

It sounded feminine. Raspy. It had the same texture as the bitter wind that rustled evergreen leaves. The

Clough was still and silent in the numbing winter; a stark, bright beauty swathed in silver. He never considered its elegance before now.

His eyes were drawn to the gentle brook that passed through the Clough. The gibbous moon reflected in distorted ripples. Jordan felt safe. He pictured an ethereal goddess made of moonlight watching over him and the Clough. There was no boggart here. How could a place of such serenity be haunted by a devilish spirit?

The brook turned red.

Scarlet ribbons flowed amongst the grey rivulets of icy water. Deeper and darker the brook became until its whole body was consumed by a brownish-red hue. The sharp tang of metal.

Maxine's pallid face floated past him. Her eyes wide and bloodshot with terror, lips blue. A fleshy, black stump where her neck would be.

* * *

The screams lurched Jordan from his sleep. His mum stormed into the bedroom.

"Jordan -"

He sat up on his elbow.

"Why didn't you tell me?" she said, her eyes wide like Maxine's in his dream.

"What?"

"You stupid boy!"

" *What?* "

"The bloody milk that's what -"

"What are you on about?"

"It's rotten! I could have put that in my brew!"

"It wasn't rotten when I –" he stopped.

Debbie looked at the contorted look on his face. He looked down and saw the glisten of fresh blood upon his palms.

"What..." she muttered, stepping back.

Jordan's heart began to beat at a rapid pace. His throat tightened and the burning sensation of vomit bubbled like a cauldron in his chest. He burst past his confused mum, grabbed his shoes and rushed out of the flat. It must have been around four in the morning. Debbie would have just come back from her shift at a club in town.

The echoes of his trainers bounced against the magnolia walls of the stairwell.

"Jordan!"

He ran out into the night, his flimsy pyjamas doing nothing to protect him from the drizzle and winter wind. Running down toward the Clough, he leapt over the wall and stumbled into the mud, his knees catching the fall.

Jordan ran and ran.

He wanted to call Ciaran.

If he stopped running he would be sick.

But he had to make sure.

Jordan ran past the Boating Lake, past the Lakeside Café and towards the brook that Maxine said she and Karen Busby never dared return to. The brook that appeared to him whilst he slept. The brook where Maxine's face had emerged from the icy ripples. He ran down the path, the light drizzle melting away the twilight frost so he didn't need to worry about slipping.

In the moonlight he saw a woman standing by the brook. Ginger hair tied back in a ponytail.

"You!" he called out.

The woman turned around. Her smile was wide but her furrowed brow gave her a look of menace.

"What was it you called me?" she asked in a raspy hush, "Bethan...such a nice name."

Don't give it a name, echoed Maxine in Jordan's head.

"Are you...I thought...?" he couldn't believe the thoughts racing through his mind.

"Thought I'd look different? I can do. I can look like anything," she said with an air of calmness and severity.

"Why me?"

She laughed. She stepped forward.

Jordan stumbled back and patted his pockets, looking for a phone that wasn't there.

"You want to ring him, don't you? Did you think he could help you?" she giggled.

How did she know?

She raised her arms to shoulder height, outstretched as if pretending to reach for him. Jordan felt stiff and frozen in the small of his back; he tried to move his legs but they were as stubborn as fallen logs. She spread her hands wide, ivory fingers darkened as they grew longer and longer until they were pitch black twirls that slithered through the air like haunted snakes. Her blue eyes bulged, turned yellow; her skin sprouted sprigs of onyx until her whole body was consumed by a wiry black fur. Her body levitated off the ground as she floated toward Jordan, her arms and legs moving in a slow, thrashing rhythm. Her grin vicious and sharp, as wide as a lion's.

"You...you killed Maxine. I saw you in my dream," muttered Jordan, fog emerging from his chattering mouth.

"My dear, I didn't kill anyone." Her voice was deeper now. She slithered around his neck and between his legs. Around his body, inspecting every inch of his being. "*You* did."

Jordan's fists clenched.

"You see, when you left the gate open, I was able to leave. I followed you. You smelt like death. Death and destruction. It made me curious. It made me angry that something so foul would be let inside the Clough. *My* clough. I could smell your rotting stench of death and followed it all the way into the city. That's where I found this..."

In the cloudlike ribbons of black emerged a grey severed head.

Ciaran.

Jordan's breath caught in his throat. The boggart laughed a throaty laugh.

"Tsk, tsk. Don't you remember? Don't you remember slicing through this poor man's neck? That's why you left, isn't it? That's why you ran away...that's why you ended up here that night. His blood on your hands."

"Stop! Stop it!" He tried to break free from the boggart's supernatural grip. He hadn't even realised her prehensile limbs were wrapped around his legs.

Ciaran's head disappeared back into the aether.

"And the poor woman last night. What could she have done to *you*?"

He saw Maxine's head floating in the brook. Whether it actually *was* there, he didn't know anymore.

"Don't you see, Jordan? I can't have you here... you're a scourge on this land. You're a vessel of anger and violence. And now I have to get rid of you –'

"You tricked me," Jordan mumbled as the boggart's limbs wrapped around his neck. "You made me name you!"

"Oh, how easy that was. I copied the visage of a girl in a photograph I found by that poor man you killed."

Flashes of attacking Ciaran in his flat struck Jordan's mind's eye. The burning rage from the argument that signified the end of their relationship. *I couldn't have...I wouldn't have...*

"I didn't! I didn't!"

"Shh...you'll wake the birds," said the boggart as the formless entity wrapped itself around Jordan's mouth and dragged him into the Boating Lake.

* * *

Debbie switched on the morning news and shattered her favourite mug as she collapsed to the floor.

Her son. Her only child.

Wanted for the murder.

His fingerprints, which were already on file from a troubled youth, had been found on the decapitated body of Ciaran Dorritt in his Deansgate flat. And also on Maxine Fairclough, whose headless body was found strung up on the Boggart Hole Clough gate early this morning.

Debbie's face was ashen; gaunt. She tried to compose herself but the tears kept flowing as Jordan's phone kept going straight to voicemail.

But don't worry, Jordan.

I'll look after her.

Jake Curran-Pipe was born in the Canary Islands and raised in Manchester, UK. He currently lives in London and is a theatre producer focusing on developing new writing.

Ever since he was a child, he has written stories as a hobby but only recently realised that he had the skills to turn it into a career. He loves writing in the realms of fantasy and horror but will occasionally dabble with mystery, bildungsroman and romance. He likes to use a Northern voice in his work as well as incorporate elements of his Scottish heritage. The characters he creates always belong to communities rarely represented in mainstream speculative fiction as he wants to see more positive diversity in fantasy and horror.

Around the Hawthorne Tree

Jenna Smithwick

Every year the village mimicked the earth, turning in on itself in a quiet slumber as the first winds of Winter blew in from the sea. People shuttered their windows and piled under blankets to wait out the worst of it, and when the ground warmed again in the Spring the whole place seemed alive with the bustling of market days and hours spent in the meadows. Our village was the envy of the neighboring lands; even when Cailleach blew her harsh breath across the coast no one was ever truly afraid.

Not when we had our Solstice Queen.

The Solstice Queen planned the food for the festivals, divvied out jobs to our neighbors, and spun tales about faery-trees and creatures that hid in a copse beyond the stone gate. The adults listened to her with the same rapt attention of the children at her feet.

"It's from the berries I plucked from the Faery tree,"

she told them. "The fruit is blessed with magic that will keep us well through the Winter."

I rolled my eyes every time she said it when they placed the crown upon her head and called her their Queen. For they were superstitious folks, and I had trouble believing in things I could not see.

And yet I watched her, and I listened, for she had a way of telling tales that made time stop. She was so full of life, her hands moving with her words, invincible. Our Solstice Queen. That's why I could not believe it when she took ill.

It came on softly at first. Her hands slipped on the mortar she held, spilling mashed bits to the floor. Then she started limping as she made her rounds to the homes of nursing mothers. Within months she was bound to her bed, and we had no choice but to accept that it would not be long before we'd feel the absence of her tales, the magic she brought to life.

The first Winter she stayed in bed was the worst I could remember. There was no festival without the Queen. Snow fell in sheets across the land, covering the thatched roofs, permeating the walls and leaving everyone chilled as they rose in the morning. Winter crops succumbed to rot; root vegetables withered beneath the Earth. Mothers cried and clutched wailing babes to their breasts. They were hungry – so hungry – and the darkness seemed to stretch out forever. It went on like this until the villagers unfurled from their homes when Spring arrived, worn and weak from the brutal months.

They mourned the imminent loss of the Solstice Queen, their wise healer.

I mourned the fact that I would soon have to live in

a world without my mother.

But time stopped for no one, and the wheel of the year turned again, leaving us to hold our breath at the highest point of Autumn before the world tipped to Winter once more. We heard whispering threats in the winds that blew through crisp leaves; this year would be harder than the last.

It was market day, two days before the next festival, and I turned my face away when the other villagers looked at me, their smiles never quite reaching their eyes.

"Sinead," they'd prompt me, "is your mother any better? Was she able to get the berries?"

I had to wave them away, for my mother had not left her bed, and she never would again. Still, they vexed me with their begging, desperate for the berries. I wished to laugh in their faces – to tell them that the stories were just stories, that they would be better off focusing their efforts on keeping their food stores full and sealing any cracks in their home to keep warm.

"I saw Finian's mother at the market today. She patted down my hips and told me they would make for an easy birth," I told my father as I unwrapped my shawl and dropped my basket near the hearth. If he wished for me to marry now that I was of age, he never pressed the issue. He stayed by the fire, puffing his pipe, a lost look on his face.

"Perhaps you should give Fin a chance," my brother laughed behind me. "He may be your best hope at finding a husband who allows you to wander through the gardens all day."

"Shouldn't   you   be   worried   about   making

188

arrangements for your own bride?" I retorted, and his face grew red around the mustache he was trying to grow. It wasn't fair, and I knew it. For though he wished to take a wife it was not possible while he still lacked the means to support a family.

"I'm sorry, Aiden," I murmured, pushing past him, wishing to escape the conversation. I had seen how the girls from my childhood withered in their marriages, how their wrists grew thin as they served everybody but themselves. I did not wish to eat last at every meal, I did not wish to be pushed toward something that made my stomach flip over just to think of it.

My mother's room was still a comfort to me, even as a sick room. I closed the door behind me and stood at the window. A wren perched on the sill, but it flew off with a great gust of wind and a robin settled in its place.

The small bird looked at me, its chest puffing, and I nearly remarked to my mother how it was like one of the stories she told when I was young, where a robin became the Oak King and chased Summer away. I held my tongue though; I did not want to get her started on stories. Instead, I fastened the shutters against the cold and walked to her bedside where she slept.

"I have blessed thistle and fenugreek to help Niamh make more milk," I said aloud, dipping my fingers in my leather pouch to pinch the herbs. "But what she really needs is food...she can't feed the babe when she's starving herself." I sighed and sat next to my mother's frail body, her collarbones peeking out above the collar of her nightgown. It was strange to see her hands so clean when they had always been stained with herbs and dirt.

"H-ha –" she wheezed, her jaw working to make words.

"Shh, mama, it's alright. You should rest," I whispered, ignoring the sting of tears behind my eyes. I smoothed her hair back from her face.

"Hawthorne berries, I need you to remember," she choked out. My heart pounded against my ribs at how weak the words sounded. "*They* need you to remember."

I stilled my hand on her forehead. "Shh, it was just a story, mama." She was a fine healer, a wise woman, and I knew she could not believe her own stories. It was the illness. I kissed the top of her hair; she smelled sickly sweet, like the women who died in their birthing beds. "I'll recite your stories when I return home," I promised, before making my way to Niamh's house.

No one came to the door. I stood there for several moments, my ears not picking up any of the baby's wailing cries. He was a fussy thing, and who could blame him? He was not getting enough milk to fill his belly. I knocked twice more and pushed the door open. I'd known Niamh since we were babes ourselves; she wouldn't mind.

The house was quiet – too quiet – as I stepped past the ash-covered hearth. Her husband was likely out collecting wood. A strange clacking sounded from the small room past the hearth. I peeled back the curtain and saw Niamh in her bed, the baby at her breast. My stomach dropped at the sight, the sheen of Niamh's face, her gown soaked with sweat.

I reached my fingers toward the babe, afraid of what I would find, but his chest rattled beneath my fingers. He was breathing, but pale and listless.

"Niamh," I whispered.

She smacked her lips, delirious with fever. They would both die. The herbs I carried and the tinctures I'd made were useless. Niamh gripped my wrist with a sudden burst of energy.

"Take up her mantel, Sinead," she panted. "We cannot make it through Winter without our blessings from the Solstice Queen."

I wanted to say something, anything to soothe her, but I could not. Her eyes snapped open, too big and too blue for her gaunt face.

"Your mother must have told you how to get there. How to trick the fairies so you could collect from the sacred tree."

"She did not," I managed. "They were only tales, Niamh. I heard the same stories that you did."

She loosened her grip and fell back against her pillow.

"Oh. I'm sorry." She turned her head to the side, tears spilling down her cheeks as she closed her eyes once more. "I only hoped there was another way."

I stoked a small fire in her hearth and stormed out of the house. I pressed my hands to my stomach, a wave of nausea washing over me. I wanted to run as far and fast as my legs could carry me. I wanted to leave this village and this feeling that they all expected something impossible from me.

The sun was sinking in the sky; in two nights it would hover and hold its breath before plunging us into the dark of Winter. It would be a season without hope, even if my village had tried its best to seek protection, throwing branches of rowan and oak in offering to bonfires and singing into the night.

But what if I could give them more? What if I could bring them the berries and at least they'd have their hope to get them through? I did not believe in magic, but I believed that people tried harder when they had something to hold on to. It was why so many people were currently losing their grasp.

A fine plan if only I knew where the faery tree grew. I pressed my hands to my eyes at the thought. It was impossible. I hadn't lied to Niamh – my mother passed no secrets down to me.

I was not meant to be a Solstice Queen.

A familiar chirping caught my attention as a robin flitted by. It stopped on a nearby branch and seemed to look at me before flying off toward the woods. My mother would have remarked on how many robins we'd seen today, a sure sign that Winter would be moving in fast.

I sniffed at the thought. She could weave a tale around any casual observance, leaving little gems of stories wherever she went.

When the wren is chased away by the Winter king, where the robin flies you can find the Faery ring...

The line from one of her stories rang through my head and I stood outside of Niamh's house stock-still. *It would be silly to follow a little bird because of a bit of lore,* I thought, and turned away.

A shriek pierced the quiet air. The hair prickled along my arms and up the back of my neck. *Niamh's babe,* I thought, but then my mouth went dry. I had heard her baby's hungry cries, and this was something else, a screaming lament that death was near.

Banshee. The word bounced around for a moment

in my memory and I tore off to the woods where the robin had flown, moving as fast as my legs could carry me along the cobblestones. I had to get away from that sound. Cold air stung the bellows of my lungs as I passed the homes of our village, snuggled close together. I made it all the way to the stone border of our lands where they backed up to the forest and I slipped through the space between the rocks.

I had been here with Niamh before, when we were just girls daring each other to look for faeries behind stumps, or treasure hidden beneath tree roots. We never ventured far though; the children of the village knew to stay on the cleared path. Otherwise we could be taken deep into the woods and never seen again.

I didn't believe the tales of faeries switching out children or taking young women as their brides. I knew the adults were only trying to frighten us into obedience.

So why are you so afraid? a small voice whispered. *Perhaps, deep down, you hope the stories are true.*

I was afraid because there was real danger in the woods, from thorns that could catch on clothes and cause wounds that festered or the chance that you might lose your way once you got deep within. But I was Sensible Sinead, and I would not be afraid of things told to children in their nurseries. I took one last look at the sun dipping toward the horizon and made my way inside.

* * *

I pulled my cloak tight around my shoulders, willing my feet to keep moving even though the forest grew thick around me, and vines and underbrush forced me to step gingerly as I moved deeper.

I turned back to check my path; I had travelled so far that I could no longer see the entrance. I would need to make it back before nightfall, but I refused to turn back. Not when time was running out.

Something cold dropped on my head and slid down to my ear. Small white dots fell from between the tree cover overhead and landed on my hair. "Snow," I whispered to the trees, as if they could hear me. *But how?* It was unusual this early in the year, and I was too deep in the forest. I held up my palm and caught the flakes in my hand.

A hollow tapping came from one of the branches and I squinted to see better. The robin was nearby. "Oh, it's you," I said, with the strange sense that the creature was listening. "Are you going to help me find the tree? The one with the small red berries upon its pale branches?"

The bird let out a small sound as it flew away, and I picked up my skirts to follow. "Wait," I called after it, lonely and tired as I attempted to keep up the pace. My foot caught on a root protruding from the forest floor, and I staggered past branches that scraped at my sides until I fell forward to my hands and knees.

A sob bubbled in my throat. I didn't believe in any of this yet here I was, a fool chasing a bird through a forest on the brink of one of the longest nights of the year. My breath puffed out in a visible cloud, hot air against the chill of the day that was slipping into twilight. Footsteps sounded from behind me, and I made a futile effort to stand, my dress catching on bare branches.

"Sinead, is that you?" a familiar voice called out to me, and a moment of sheer terror melted to relief as my brother appeared beside me.

194

"What are you doing here, Aiden?" I asked as he pulled me to my feet.

"I could ask you the same, but I think I know the answer." He glanced about the path then checked my hands for any cuts. "Mother was worried when you did not return from Niamh's house, so I went to find you. When I saw how poorly she was, I thought you might come here."

"But how..."

"She is my mother too, Sinead. She sang me to sleep with her stories just as she did for you." He closed his hands tight over mine. "I'm sorry I teased you about Finian."

"And I'm sorry I poked at you for not being wed yet. You'll make a fine husband someday."

"You must know, you don't need to marry him, or anybody else. When mother and father..." He pressed his mouth into a flat line and sucked a breath in through his nose. "I want you to know you will always have a home with me when they are gone."

The woods seem to stand still around us, the snow falling softly on his shoulders. I dipped my chin and wrestled my hands free from his grip to wrap my arms around him like I used to do when we were young. We stepped apart and looked around us, the last threads of daylight unraveling.

A small breeze floated past my ear, lifting wisps of hair as a small brown and red blur flew past. I followed where the bird landed upon an archway comprised of two tree limbs that stretched out until they touched and wound their way around each other. I moved forward, holding my hand out before me to touch the knotted wood structure.

"I think this is it."

My brother's throat bobbed as he swallowed, and he did not ask me how I knew. The robin flew beneath the arch of branches, and I crouched down to look at the passage they created. A bitter wind licked across my cheeks and hands, forcing cold air up my nose. I shivered at the breath of Winter that lay ahead.

"I think you are right," my brother said, his teeth chattering. "I think we might find it here."

We ducked and stepped through, the world growing colder the moment our toes crossed the threshold. The woods were silent here. No singing in the trees – not even the song of my friendly robin could be heard. There was nothing save our breaths coming in sharp gasps, clouding the air with white mist.

"Sinead," Aiden warned, holding a hand to my shoulder to steady me as my shoe slipped against something slick. "Watch your step."

I looked down and felt my eyes go round as a web of ice shot several paces across the earth as I stepped forward. With every step the lace pattern of ice wove together until it formed a sheet that crushed the ferns and dying greens beneath its cold glass floor. I would not look at my brother; I did not want to see his face. If there was magic in this place it would remain unreal so long as I did not acknowledge it.

We walked like this for quite some time, our arms locked together and neither of us daring to speak. We walked despite the cold that nipped through our shoes and the unnatural snow that wet our clothes. We walked until the timber around us parsed down and bare branches left gaps through which we could see a clearing further ahead. The blank canvas of snow between the scraggly limbs took up more of the scenery until the woods opened into a glade where everything was blindingly white and bright as mid-day.

I could no longer tell the time; I wondered how long we had walked. The expanse was clear save for the tree in the center of it all. Its vibrant berries stood in stark contrast to the neutral world of white and grey around us.

"I thought it would be a great beast of a tree," Aiden murmured. I did not reply, but I agreed. The pale, slim trunk that rose from the earth was not what I'd imagined: with its sickly branches reaching out and holding so many berries it was a wonder they did not all drop to the ground. Perhaps the way it stood defiant and fruitful against the rest of the dying woods was why people thought it was full of magic.

"Let's split up," I said, ready to head back home and eat a bowl of stew. I did not want to be in this uncanny forest any longer. "Fill up your pockets – I did not bring a basket." I shot him a warning look so that he would not challenge me as I unwrapped my cloak to fill with the bounty.

I fell into a rhythm, standing on tiptoe and plucking the berries to toss them into my cloak.

"There are so many," I called out to my brother. There was no answer. The quiet of the glade held no response. I listened closely; I had not noticed how the sound of his breath and the crunch of his boots against the snow had died away.

I circled the tree, searching across the entire space, and found nothing. I went around again and again until I was dizzy, and nausea threated to overwhelm me. I searched the line of trees that surrounded the place. Like my brother, the path back to home was nowhere to be found. I steadied myself against the ash-colored trunk of the Faery tree and closed my eyes shut.

I did not want to let myself believe that details of my mother's tales were true, but if they were then we had surely committed a crime against the Faeries by stealing from their sacred tree. A line from a story blazed across my memory.

The faeries were so busy dancing under the moonlight that they never took notice of the girl picking the berries from their sacred tree, and so she was able to bring back baskets and baskets with the magic to keep the village safe through the winter.

I slumped down in the snow. My sensibilities had told me that I needed to get home before dark, but my mistake lay in arriving too early. We were trapped here because I was so unlike my mother. I had never bothered to take her words – her stories – to heart.

I would never wear her crown and be the Solstice Queen.

"I didn't know it was all true," I cried to the wind. "Mama, why did you not tell me they were real?"

A small hum of noise echoed across the empty space and I sat up, wiping my nose on my sleeve. The robin rested in the branches above me, its beady eyes following my movements as I dug my cold-numbed fingers into the snow to unearth a rock. I brushed it off and chucked it toward its tiny figure.

"You silly little bird!" I shouted. The robin flapped its wings in response. "Did you lead me here to take my

198

brother? Why not take me, instead? I do not care. I cannot go home without him. That would be worse than showing up empty-handed before my people!"

Hot tears were dripping down my cheeks but I blinked them away, the world blurring until I realized that I was no longer alone. People – no, they were too beautiful to be people – *faeries* floated by; their gowns of gossamer and petals swished on the air as they waltzed by in a circle. The moonlight shone overhead, its light sparkling on the snow. Their dance had begun. I got up and no one seemed to notice me in my plain attire, my loose dress and too-tight shoes, but I felt as out of place as the Hawthorne tree looked in its glade.

The air smelled sweet, like the violets Mama sprinkled on sweet breads, and I noticed that the cold air felt nice against my skin. A human face stood out amongst the rest. *Aiden,* I thought, but I stopped myself before I shouted it.

Never give a faery your name. My mother's advice was clear in my head, so instead I stepped closer to the circle of faeries as they made their way around, hoping to grab his attention. It would be a difficult task, judging from how he gripped his partner's waist, how his eyes were glued to the faerie's flawless face.

A hand clapped my shoulder and warmth buzzed through me.

"The Solstice Queen," the man – *faery* – announced. He was tall, with pointed ears that peeked from beneath brown hair. His skin was fair; he glowed beneath the moon.

I shook my head. "I am not her."

"But you will be," he said, a half-smile forming on

his lips. "Come. Dance with me." He held out his hand and I studied his fine attire – the brown tunic and trousers, the red vest tied with gold string – before I glanced down at my own. "Do not worry about that."

He waved his hand before me and my plain beige dress transformed before my eyes, into a gown of silken ivory petals. I touched my hair and a petal fell away. My feet were bare now, but the cold no longer bothered them. He extended his arm out once more and this time I took it. I could not insult him, and I needed to get close to my brother.

The faery spun me out into the circle, our steps seeming to bounce and float from the earth in time to a song I had never heard before. His eyes – warm gold ringed with green – stayed on my face until I rested my forehead against his chest. He was so beautiful that it was hard to look at him for long.

"After hundreds of years it was not until this moment I realized how lonely I have been," he said. "I have watched you for some time: the steadfast daughter of the last Solstice Queen." His smile was sharp enough to cut the night.

"If you knew her, why did you not take her away like you have with me and my brother?"

"Because she was a cunning woman and honored our ways. Besides...she was in love with a plain human man, and I do not like to interfere. She would not have been happy here."

"How honorable," I huffed, and allowed him to turn me through another round. It was warm in the circle, pressed close to him, and I liked how his voice sounded like the wind through a willow to my ears. "Can you save her?" I asked, thinking of my mother's light. The way she beamed as she handed a new mother her fresh babe.

The way she lit up my whole world from the moment I was born.

"I cannot." He sounded genuinely sad. "She will die this year, and you will be the new queen."

"I do not wish to be the Solstice Queen," I said against his chest. "Couldn't the Hawthorne berries save her?"

"No. It is her time. But here you would never have to think of it again. You could stay and be my Queen instead."

I looked up at him and knew, without a doubt, that I was staring at the Faery King. The memories of my mother's light sputtered in my mind, leaving me only with visions of her sick room: spittle on her chin pink with blood; the scent of her sweat; the overwhelming dread of what was to come. I was content to stay here. Happy to dance and drink wine and feast on berries and never, ever have to remember the winter death that blew in from the sea or my mother frail in her bed.

I stopped my questioning and let the music take over my thoughts, no longer remembering how we had started dancing in the first place.

A sharp cry cracked through the enchantment of the dance. I froze in the Faery King's arms. I had heard that cry before.

The Faery King slid his hand beneath my chin to lift it. "Look at me," he coaxed. "Pay no mind to that."

The waltz picked up again and I could not remember why I felt such dread. I searched frantically around me, not quite knowing what I was looking for until my eyes landed on my brother.

The cry started again, a high-pitched wail that brought my mind to sick babies and mothers dying in their birthing beds.

"I think I must go," I said, and pushed away from the Faery King's embrace. If *he* was real then so was the banshee's lament.

"You wish to leave? I do not see how it is fair for you to steal from my sacred tree, then insult me further by refusing my hand." The Faery King peered down through his lashes. "Besides, you will not be happy there."

"It doesn't matter," I said, for it did not.

The music stopped. The ethereal beings did too, and they all turned to face the King, to study the human who had breeched their territory. My brother was among them, the spell broken for him as well.

"Sin-" he stopped himself, his face twisting around my name as he remembered my mother's wisdom. I turned back to the King.

"I will come back," I swore, "but my people need me. If you have watched me then you know I am true to my word. Please. I must keep my word in this matter, too, or else no one will honor your name at the Solstice feast. Let us go."

He lifted his chin at the last part of my statement and sighed deeply, frost coating the sleeves of my gown. "We have a deal." With a flick of his hand the world turned black around me, the moon swallowed by the night.

Cold stabbed at my lips and palms as I pressed myself away from the ground, spitting out a mouthful of snow. My shoulders shook as the frigid air hit my skin. I felt too weak to stand so I crawled, shaking, until I found my brother. He groaned as I rolled him onto his back.

"I must have hit my head." He rubbed his neck. "How long have I been out?"

"I cannot be sure." All I could think of was the Faery King, our dance, and how the world had seemed to drop away. The sky was stained an inky blue now. "I think it's close to dawn."

"Where did that come from?"

I looked to where he pointed; a basket woven from willow catkins sat beneath the tree, filled to the brim with red berries.

"I found it nearby," I said, which wasn't a lie. "I will bring it back someday."

* * *

We made it home after sunrise, our mother sitting up in her bed, worry in her eyes. Her expression softened to something like pride when she saw the basket that we carried between us.

"There is no time for the wine," she said, smiling weakly before falling back against her pillows. "Boil some water and make some jam, then spread it on thick slices of bread for the festival."

I busied myself and recited her stories as I did so, the old ones that were now layered with something new. Something that was hers and mine, too. Eventually I heard her fall back into a peaceful sleep.

When the jam was ready we had plenty to share at the festival. I fed Niamh and the babe with a spoon until their cheeks grew full and rosy again. That year my neighbors danced around the bonfires and placed my mother's crown upon my head as they made me their new Solstice Queen.

It was an easier Winter than the year before; people dug up root vegetables the rot had spared, and found hidden stores of food they thought they'd lost, and Niamh's babe grew plump with milk.

Hardly anyone took ill that Winter, and most people made it out alive. The only person I mourned that year was my mother. The loss of her cast a shadow over everything for some time. An undercurrent of sadness appeared at unexpected, random moments; at my brother's wedding or the time I tasted a perfect loaf of bread, warm from the oven.

The wheel of the year never stopped though, and I kept myself busy. I visited nursing mothers and brought them tinctures. I delivered my nieces and nephews and helped to feed and bathe them and sing them to sleep with my mother's stories.

Some days I wished to ask my brother if he ever remembered our time in the Faery circle, but the words always froze on my tongue with some strange magic. It was lonely to keep the secrets of the forest, and yet there was a thrill in telling the tales of the Fae, in hoping the children would grow up and remember them.

The knowledge would keep them safe when they took up my mantel, if only they pieced it together the way I had. I was always more careful after that first year slipping into the woods after the moon rose, when the Faery King would be engaged in a dance.

Sometimes I looked out my window and caught sight of a robin on my sill. It always called me back to the time when I was asked to be the Faery Queen, and a feeling of longing welled up in my throat. It was something I could never explain.

A faery cannot lie, my mother's words whispered to me, but a part of me still denied that bit of information. *He didn't mean it, it was just a trick to trap you there,* I reminded myself year after year until I grew very old, and my nieces and nephews had children of their own.

One day as I prepared for the festival coming in three days' time, a jug slipped from my knotted hands and shattered on the floor. A robin chirped at my windowsill, and I wiped my palms against my skirts before I followed its call. I sighed to my winged friend, my eyes watering with the memories I'd held on to for so long.

"It is nice to think you might remember," I said. "I think it is time to return something." I made my way to the cupboard where I pulled out a basket, unworn and shiny despite its age. I carried it from my house, and no one noticed me, or my bare feet on the cold ground. It had been years since I had begun to be forgotten, save for at the night of the festival where I still reigned Queen. But I was a Queen who had grown tired of her crown. I walked all the way to the forest, alone as I had been on every trip except for that first Winter. By the time I made it to the Hawthorne tree I felt the weight of every year, every memory.

I set the basket down and collapsed in the snow, closing my eyes against the cold until a warm hand pulled me to my feet. My skin was smooth and unblemished where it twined up with the set of long, slim fingers interlaced with my own. My body was young again, everything as it was during that first visit except for the hair that strayed from its plait and fell around my face.

"You have returned, my silver Queen," the Faery King laughed, and pulled me to him. My footsteps felt light, the weight of what I carried falling from my shoulders as he wove his fingers through my silver hair. "I've loved watching you earn this," he whispered, stroking the long braid that still held the wisdom of years gone by.

"I told you I would," I said simply, and waltzed around the Hawthorne tree where I found the quiet peace of forgotten memories. The tales the village would tell on the coldest nights were all I left behind.

Jenna Smithwick is a writer living in Virginia Beach with her husband, two sons, two wild cats, and one sweet pup.

She has an M.A. in International Studies, but she's more interested in the stories that tie communities together than foreign policy these days. Jenna writes Gothic romance and horror for adults and is always interested in new spins on old tales.

When she's not writing you can find her teaching yoga or reading a romance novel on the beach.

The Best Girl This Side Of Winter

Laila Amado

On the morning of the last day of classes, Weda didn't know yet that her winter holidays were irreversibly ruined. The girls of Oakleaf Academy filed into the school auditorium in neat, impeccably dressed pairs, a feat only achievable under the relentless supervision of teachers. Waiting to take her place in the assigned row, Weda squirmed – the stiff, checkered dress she wore was the latest fad at the school, but the prickly woolen fabric itched against her skin. She wished there was a way to scratch the spot right between her shoulder blades without drawing attention. It proved impossible, but admiring looks directed at the dress somewhat alleviated her suffering.

At last, the teacher holding the placard with the name of Weda's class motioned them towards their row. A line of plush-backed chairs curved gently above the stage and Weda followed the girl in front of her to the designated seat. She sat down, taking care to smooth the folds of her dress, and looked at the so-far empty stage. The lights were low, waiting for the ceremony to begin, but behind the lectern where the Headmistress was going to deliver her speech the end-of-year projects that had made it to the final round – clockwork robots, miniature zeppelin mobiles, flower arrangements, and glass sculptures – sat in a neat row.

Oakleaf Academy held this competition each year and the girl whose project won the most voices received the coveted title of "The Best Girl". Just thinking about it made Weda's heart beat faster. Everybody wanted to be friends with the Best Girl. She got invited to the coolest parties, had her photo published in the Daily Gazette, and represented the school at the Mayor's summer ball. She was important.

In the dimmed lights, Weda could see her own project sitting alongside the others. She had spent hours laboring over its construction and she was sure it was a winner.

The lights on the stage went on, and the Headmistress, dressed in a red flowing gown, came up to the lectern. The pompom of her beret glittered gold. She pushed up her spectacles and launched into the traditional end-of-year speech – top grades achieved, competitions won. Weda barely listened, her attention focused on that most important part of the ceremony where the name of the Best Girl was to be announced.

A spotlight focused on the leftmost project, a replica of the school's tower clock. It was neatly executed, but the voting score announced by the Director was unimpressive. The light moved on.

It hovered from one project to another; the closer it moved to Weda's project the harder it became to breathe. Her stiff dress felt positively suffocating. But when the Headmistress ripped open the envelope with the votes and announced the score, Weda felt her heart swell with pride. A girl in the next seat, whose name she didn't remember, congratulated her in a loud whisper.

Weda was almost up from her chair, eager to claim her prize, when she noticed an unopened envelope in the hands of the Headmistress. Another project. Positioned at the end of the stage, right behind the lectern, it was hidden from view and Weda had not seen it.

The envelope ripped open. Weda couldn't believe her ears – the voting score for this unnoticed project far exceeded her own. Face red she slumped in her chair, trying to pretend that she hadn't been going anywhere in the first place. Up on stage the winning girl claimed the prize and the whole auditorium erupted in applause. Making her best effort not to cry, Weda couldn't wait for the ceremony to be over.

***

At last, the Headmistress dismissed the assembly and the girls rushed towards the exit, all semblance of order forgotten. A whirlwind of girls – dresses, hats, and cute little handbags – flooded the school lobby. The prize-winning girl sailed from the auditorium surrounded by a crowd of admirers. Weda pouted.

"Hey, Weda, nice dress," came a voice from behind her. She turned around to see Amalia, the undisputed queen of their class. Weda was surprised the girl even knew her name.

Amalia stood surrounded by her ever-present

entourage, hair arranged in a shiny crown on top of her head. She held out a hand with a pink envelope pinched between thumb and forefinger. "Here," she said. "I'm holding a midwinter party at the Royal Cup Teashop. You're invited." Weda yipped, snatching the glossy envelope. Being invited to one of Amalia's parties was the dream come true of every girl at the school. She opened her mouth to thank Amalia, but she was already gone, lost in the crowd. Envelope in hand, Weda made her way towards the exit from the crowded lobby. Perhaps the day wasn't going to be so terrible, she thought.

She was wrong.

***

Weda slumped on her bed, cream colored frills trampled by the heel of her shoe. "But why," she wailed, looking up at her mother, "why do I have to spend the holidays with Grandma?"

"Because she has injured her leg and needs someone to help out."

"Why can't you go?" Weda spat the words out.

Weda's mother sighed and pointed at her own rounded belly. "Because the baby is going to be here soon. Weda, you know that perfectly well."

"I don't have a winter coat."

"I'll buy you one."

"But I don't even remember Grandma. She only came here once, when I was little."

"All the more reason to catch up," Weda's mother said and turned to leave the room.

Weda rolled her eyes and fell backwards onto the

211

bed, sprawling like a beached starfish. Outside, the spires and towers of Acamont City – pink, cream, and lilac – blushed in the light of the setting sun. She was going to miss everything: the shops in their holiday decorations; special deals at the dress factory; hot cocoa in little cups on the promenade and, most importantly, Amalia's party. She'd probably never be invited again. Her life from now on was utterly pointless. Weda sobbed and rolled over, pulling the duvet over her head.

***

The little plane rattled and creaked making its labored ascent over the Kolmarg mountains. Strapped into her seat Weda peered out of the window and past the rotating blades of a propeller. The fields and rivers of the flatlands surrounding Acamont stayed far behind and, beneath the plane's battered wing, there was nothing but the ridges and valleys of the mountains painted in graphite black with pale veins of snow snaking down from the caps. Lulled by this wearying pattern, by the constant buzz of the engines, the overheated air of the cabin, and the chickens clucking in the crates in the back of the plane, Weda fell into a heavy sleep.

When she opened her eyes again an endless white flatland stretched down below. The aircraft climbed further and further north, and the whiteness stretched uninterrupted. Weda had never imagined there being so much empty space in all the world. In Acamont it snowed for, at best, a week out of the entire year; the streets became slippery with sleet but never turned white.

But here winter reigned supreme. Weda couldn't help feeling dwarfed by its overwhelming presence.

The plane leaned on the right wing, taking a wide

212

turn, and began its descent. Far below a village – surrounded on all sides by a snowed-over forest – was a small dark speck against the vast, unblemished whiteness.

Another turn, the aircraft descending in a downward spiral, and Weda made out the tall walls surrounding the village, built from massive logs so dark they looked almost black. Four towers rose above the wall. Weda imagined Grandma's village to be like the candy towns displayed during holidays in the window of her favorite confectioner's shop or like the illustrations in the books she read when she was little, not like a gloomy castle with forbidding towers and a locked gate. No wonder mother never brought her here. Weda's mood sank along with the plane's altitude.

The airship slid lower and now Weda could see a small group of people standing in the wide clearing between the forest and the village wall. She wondered which one of them was her grandmother.

"Welcome to Wintervale," said the pilot from the cockpit. The plane lunged downward, causing Weda's breath to catch, and rolled to a stop in the middle of the snowy field.

So that was it. Weda unclasped the buckle of the belt holding her in the chair. Legs stiff from the long journey, she made her way past the barrels and the chicken crates. The door in the back of the plane was open and the pilot had already unloaded her suitcase along with a bunch of lumpy bags and bundles. Weda climbed down the short metal ladder and came face-to-face with her Grandma.

The old lady sat in a most peculiar transport – a high-backed chair positioned on top of a pair of long skis. Grandma's left leg, covered in stiff plaster, rested in a contraption of leather belts. Her white hair was rolled up in a bun, and a shawl wrapped around her shoulders like a soft cocoon. She smiled, and a network of fine wrinkles ran from the corners of her eyes like sun rays.

Next to her stood a young boy about Weda's age, with a freckled face and disheveled hair the color of copper coins. He grinned and waved so enthusiastically that Weda felt compelled to wave back.

The third person on the field was a massive, bear-like man in a sheepskin coat. He picked up the bundles the plane delivered with no visible effort and, before Weda could object, snatched up her suitcase and stuffed it under one of his massive arms.

Weda attempted a polite curtsy to greet her grandmother, just like mother had taught her, and almost tumbled over into the snow.

"Hello, Weda," said Grandma, brushing away a small tear from the corner of her eye. "I'm so glad to have you here. Let's not stand in the cold. Come on, Odric, give me a push." The redheaded boy grinned even broader. Weda hadn't thought it was possible. Grabbing the handles arching from the back of Grandma's chair, the boy turned her around to face the village.

"Odric here has been a great help," said Grandma.

"It's not a problem. Not at all," said the boy, pushing the sled down the hard-packed snowy path. On both sides of the narrow walkway a blanket of snow lay undisturbed and fluffy like candy floss.

"Stay on the path, Weda," warned Grandma over her shoulder.

Their small procession moved towards the dark walls

of Wintervale. Up ahead Odric pushed Grandma's chair; it moved forward with monotone squeaking. Weda trudged along and, somewhere behind, the bear-like man carried the bundles and her suitcase. They moved at a brisk pace yet the village remained resolutely far away – in the uninterrupted whiteness of the snow, the distances were difficult to judge.

Without the suitcase to occupy her hands and no one to talk to Weda soon became bored. She dragged her feet after the sled, hands stuffed deep into the pockets of her new coat. Cold air bit at her cheeks and nose. She tried hopping along like they did back home in a game of hopscotch, but it wasn't much fun on her own. Her attention drifted to the banks of snow on both sides of the path, deep and soft like a featherbed. Thinking that it might be fun to fall into all that softness, Weda turned and made a giant leap.

She flew through the air, freezing air burning in her nose, and landed knee-deep in the snow. It glittered all around her with a myriad pin-size diamonds. All of a sudden the far-off forest no longer seemed so distant. It leaned towards Weda, long and naked branches extending like black, crooked fingers.

Stunned, Weda sat in the snow and stared at the beckoning woods.

Then, quite unexpectedly, she was airborne.

Weda has completely forgotten about the bear-like man walking behind her. Now he lifted her from the snowbank and set her back on the path. "Stay away from the snow," he grumbled. Weda thought his voice sounded very much like that of a bear, too.

Puzzled and a bit ashamed, Weda hurried up to catch up with Odric. Grandma didn't seem to notice anything amiss and the rest of the journey to the village passed without any further adventures, welcome or otherwise.

***

The walls of Wintervale towered high, built of humongous logs darkened by severe weather and time. Here and there metal braces holding the structure together glimmered silver through the cover of snow. A smaller, hidden door opened in the tall gate for their small party and they walked through.

Within the enclosure the village of Wintervale was a labyrinth of winding streets. Narrow houses with pointed roofs huddled together under the pale, overcast skies. Weda's gaze trailed over the bright murals painted on their facades: red sun rising over the snowy treetops; arctic foxes with sweeping, fluffy tails; birds of wind and fire, and the dancing figures caught up in the colorful carousel of aurora lights. Fascinated, she stared up at the paintings until she walked straight into Odric, who had come to a stop in front of Grandma's house.

The house stood wedged between a bakery and the residence of a seamstress, indicated by a row of dancing scissors painted on the facade. In comparison to the other brightly painted buildings, the mural on Grandma's house looked modest and almost subdued. The narrow exterior, a deep indigo blue, held no other pattern but the scattering of bright yellow dots imitating stars in the shape of a constellation Weda didn't recognize. She thought it looked like a tall woman holding a sword.

Odric ducked inside the dark doorway and re-emerged carrying a pair of crutches. Grandma rose out of her sled chair and, together, Odric and Weda helped

216

her up the steps. The bear-like man deposited Weda's suitcase in the hallway and bowed out.

The house was surprisingly warm, and smelled of vanilla and cinnamon buns from the bakery next door plus something darker. Something *woodier.*

Books.

They lined the shelves that rose up from the floor and disappeared into the darkness above. Weda craned her neck to see but couldn't make out where the shelves ended.

Odric rose on tiptoes and whispered something in Grandma's ear. She laughed. "Well, why don't you tell her yourself? I'm sure she wouldn't mind."

The boy turned to Weda. Twisting a pair of thick woolen gloves in his hands, he blurted out in rapid fire, "Would you like to go to the ice rink tonight? There's going to be dancing and skating and stuff. It's going to be fun. Promise."

Weda doubted she would enjoy it. Then she looked around, taking in the gloomy foyer and the steep, boxed stairs leading upstairs – a miserable comparison to the zephyr pink skyline of Acamont in her bedroom window at home. The thought made her want to cry. "Sure, why not," she ended up saying.

Odric grinned again, even wider than before. "Great!" he said, tumbling out of the door. "I'll pick you up at nine."

Leaning on the crutches, Grandma took off her coat and shawl. "How about you go get settled in your room, Weda? I can't make it upstairs, but I asked Odric to leave the door open. You should have no trouble finding it."

Weda nodded. Grabbing the suitcase by the handle, she dragged it up the dark wooden stairs. Old, polished steps creaked under her feet. She found her room on the top floor of the house. It was a small, cozy bedroom dominated entirely by a giant bed with a patchwork duvet. Two over-sized pillows towered by its headrest like a mountain ridge.

Weda sat on the floor, in the middle of a patterned rug, and pulled the suitcase towards her. She unclasped the latches and the lid fell back, revealing the tightly rolled-up sweaters and thick socks packed by her mother. Weda dragged out a prickly woolen sweater and a pair of flannel pants. She was supposed to sort through the items and place them neatly in the chest of drawers by the bed, but the very thought of it made her sick. She tossed the sweater and the pants aside and climbed onto the bed feeling, more than anything, sorry for herself. The spiderweb of fine cracks ran between the dark brown ceiling beams. Weda's gaze traced the patterns formed by their lines: hulking bears and racing reindeer, barren trees and skiing hunters, and above all of them, a rainfall of stars.

Eventually she must have slipped into a dream, for the stars above her were no longer paint and plaster but precious, shining gems.

***

She woke up feeling hungry. Outside the sky had turned a deep, dusky blue. Weda sat up on the bed and listened but the house was just as quiet as before, save for the gusts of snow battering the panes of a small window across the room. She slid from the bed and made her way downstairs. In the kitchen a pot-bellied saucepan puffed on the stove but, other than that, the room was empty. Weda called after Grandma but there was no response. Perhaps she decided to take a nap, Weda thought.

She ventured down the dark corridor, going deeper into the house. At the end of the hallway stood a single door. Quietly – so she wouldn't disturb Grandma if she was indeed sleeping – Weda turned the handle and slipped inside. The bedroom was as empty as the kitchen.

Weda looked around, taking in a bed under the dark blue canopy, a painting of a snow owl above the fireplace, and a vanity dresser with an oval mirror. On the wall opposite the bed a sword in a leather scabbard hung supported on two metal hooks.

Weda approached to take a closer look. The scabbard looked old. An ornamental floral pattern with inlays of blue and white gemstones ran up its length and continued on the sword's handle. Weda had never been interested in sword and daggers and weapons of any kind, but here, in this darkened bedroom, she felt an odd fascination with the sword and reached out to touch it.

"It belonged to your ancestor, you know. The fabled Guardian of Winter. A great-great -grandmother of mine, if I'm not mistaken," said the voice behind her. Weda jumped. Grandma stood in the doorway. "Legend has it, her sword kept the darkness away from these lands." Grandma sighed and added. "Perhaps there's some truth in it."

"This pattern," Weda said. "It's so pretty. Does it run along the blade as well?"

Grandma shrugged. "I wouldn't know. No one could pull this sword free from the scabbard except for the Guardian and none in the family have inherited the gift.

Sometimes I think that's why the winters are becoming darker and longer with every year." Grandma's voice turned softer, pensive. She spoke about Wintervale and the forests around it, how they'd changed without the Guardian's protection, growing wilder and stranger, but Weda had already lost interest. She trailed after Grandma into the kitchen, helped her set the table, ate the stew and apple pie, but all she could think of was which of her sweaters she should wear to the ice rink later that night to be on top of local fashions, and whether or not there was going to be candy floss.

**

Weda was helping Grandma with the dishes when there came a knock on the door and, minutes later, Odric flew into the kitchen, a flurry of snowflakes dancing in his wake. Cheeks shining red, he puffed as if he had run a mile. Grandma laughed. "Leave the dishes," she said, ushering Weda out of the kitchen. "Go, have fun."

At night, glowing gas lanterns illuminated the narrow streets of Wintervale. Weda was surprised to see so many people outside. Alone and in groups, laughing and singing, they followed the same route she and Odric did.

"Is it always so busy here at night?" she asked.

Odric shook his head. "No, not really. But it's the Night of Stars, the festival of midwinter." A bunch of older girls wrapped in bright woolen shawls shoved past them and Odric shot them a dirty look. "Let's speed up," he said. "Or all the good places will be taken."

They ran. Weaving through the crowd, Weda and Odric dodged collisions and laughed, slipping on the icy patches, until finally they erupted into a small square. The spire of Wintervale's city hall wasn't anywhere as grand as the spires of Acamont, but it shone with strings of lights and a whole canopy of lanterns spread outward from it in a dazzling, luminous web. Beneath, an ice rink glimmered, clear as a mirror. Around it a makeshift scaffolding of wooden benches bustled with a gathering crowd. Up ahead, someone yelled Odric's name.

A minute and they were enveloped by a group of kids. Weda could make out flushed faces, frosted glasses, soggy mittens, an assortment of woolen scarves and bobble hats. The group carried Weda along. All together they slumped on the benches at the far side of the rink. Below them, half a dozen couples whirled in a complicated dance, the sharp blades of their skates cutting trails into polished ice.

"They're competing for the mayor's prize," Odric shouted in her ear. "Once they're done anyone can go down and skate." Somebody pushed a small package into Weda's hands. "Oh, these are good," said Odric, stuffing his fingers into the paper bag.

Weda peeked inside the bag. Big round berries, yellow with one ruddy pink side and covered with sugar, sat in the paper nest. Gingerly she tried one. The flavor exploded in her mouth, sweet and sour against her tongue. "What are those?" she gasped.

"Snowberries," said a girl in a red hat on her right. Jia. Her name was Jia, Weda remembered. "They grow in the forest and are only good to pick in winter. If you taste them in the summer, they're just bitter and hard. So we let them sit on the bushes until it's cold. Maybe you can come out with us to pick them some day."

Odric choked on a berry and shook his head.

"What?" Jia rolled her eyes. "It's not that dangerous."

Weda was curious what was so dangerous about gathering berries, but at that moment the dancing stopped and the mayor – a plump little woman – trotted up on stage. "Shh," Odric hissed. "She's going to announce the winner."

A hush descended over the ice rink crowd. The mayor launched into her speech, but Weda did not hear a single word. She was captivated by the strangest object in the woman's hands. A sharp-petaled flower? A star? Translucent, it glowed bright as sunlight.

"What is that?" Weda whispered, leaning into Odric.

"It's a falling star," he whispered back. "Sometimes, at night, you see one coming down from the sky like an orb of fire. They're rare though, not easy to find once they land in the forest."

Weda stared. If she could bring home something like that, she would undoubtedly become the most popular girl at school – lost Best Girl prize and a missed party notwithstanding.

"Hey, want to skate?" Odric's question yanked Weda out of the daydream. At first she balked. Having tried skating only once before, she worried that she would look stupid in front of everyone, but Odric's enthusiasm was catching and Jia, the girl in the red hat, brought her a pair of spare skates that fit quite nicely.

Then the other kids – Roy, Hetta, and Mien – took turns helping her skate, and Weda discovered that she wasn't bad at this whole skating thing. She actually enjoyed it.

By the time Odric delivered her to Grandma's house the night was a black velveteen curtain punctuated by the silver pinheads of stars. Grandma was asleep in her bedroom, soft snores drifting down the hall. Weda made her way upstairs and dove under the patchwork duvet. Drifting off to sleep, she thought of falling stars racing down towards the roofs of Wintervale in all their shining glory.

***

The days stretched from there, full of snow and sunlight. Weda helped Grandma around the house, although it didn't seem like the old lady needed a lot of help. In fact she was surprisingly efficient for someone with a broken leg and, for the most part, seemed to want Weda out of her way. More often than not she would send her out to have fun with Odric and his band of friends. They skated on the rink, drank hot cider in a little pastry shop off the main square, and played board games in the attic of Jia's house.

They even went skiing once or twice. A trail was treaded around the outer walls of Wintervale, demarcated by blue and red flags, and they raced along its length, going in laps. Weda wondered why no one ever skied towards the forest but didn't find a good time to ask. She was under the general impression that the residents of Wintervale did not like the forest much.

The mystery of this animosity notwithstanding, Weda was surprised how much she was enjoying herself and her unusual winter holidays. She never had so many friends – even if they didn't care at all what she wore or how many prizes she'd won.

One day, when Odric was dropping her off at Grandma's house, he said, "Say, would you like to go on a night watch with me?"

"What's a night watch?" Weda asked, perplexed.

Odric pointed at the top of the village wall, just visible beyond the roofs of the houses. "Up there," he said. "There's a walkway. All the adults of the village take turns holding the night watch. Having a look out."

"Look out for what?"

Odric shrugged. "Anything no good from the forest. My dad is making the rounds tonight. He promised to take us."

Weda was still puzzled. "Are we going to walk around the wall all night then?" It didn't sound like a lot of fun.

"No, of course not." Odric's face flushed red again. "They won't let us. It's not really a real watch for us kids. But we can sit in the tower and play board games and have hot cider and snacks."

Weda supposed this sounded considerably better. She hadn't had the chance to go up the wall yet, either – hadn't even known there was a walkway – so she nodded in agreement.

***

Odric picked her up at the agreed time. They hurried down the now deserted streets towards the village wall, squinting against the oncoming snow. The last houses dropped behind, and the wall loomed over them, black outline against the indigo blue sky. Odric rapped on the panel of a metal-studded door Weda had never noticed before. It swung inward and a tall figure in a leather overcoat ushered them inside. Odric's father. They hurried after him, going up the winding stairs of the tower. The steps seemed to go on forever, up and up and up. This was the tallest staircase in Wintervale; panting and winded, Weda was sure of it.

At long last they reached the top. Odric's dad pushed open a low door and a blast of cold air hit Weda in the face. She gasped. They were standing on top of the wall. On her right the chimneys on the slated roofs of Wintervale puffed smoke up into the night. On her left lay darkness. She could barely make out the outline of the forest, a darker patch of black against black.

"Tell you what, kids," said Odric's dad, pulling a woolen hat deep over his ears. "We're going to walk one strip of the wall, right up to that tower over there." He pointed to a boxy silhouette in the distance. "You can camp there and I'll go on with the watch duty. All right?"

They nodded and trailed after his receding figure. The stars over their heads hung low, fat and bright. Weda had never seen them that way before, yet her gaze kept drifting to the forest beyond the wall. With every step, it seemed to be getting closer.

They walked and walked and the deepening frost bit at the tip of Weda's nose and her cheeks. There was nothing to see on the wall but darkness and the stars and, if she were entirely honest, Weda couldn't understand what it was that the adults of Wintervale came up here to look out for.

She was relieved when they finally reached the tower. From the outside it didn't look like much, but inside the fire roared in the fireplace and a barrel of hot cider sat on the table, filling the small room with the warm scent of apples. Jia and two younger boys Weda had never met before sat around the table. A stack of board games towered in the middle.

***

It was a fun night. They played checkers, jackstraw, and two rounds of merchant's luck. In the middle of the third round Weda lost her bets and had to drop out of the game. Bored, she drifted over to the couch by the tower's only window and sat looking at the night sky.

A small bright dot appeared in the darkness over the forest. It bloomed into an iridescent orange light as it fell down, for a brief second illuminating the jagged outline of the treetops. Weda leaned forward, nose pressed against the cold glass of the window, just as another star tumbled from the sky. They came down like a fiery rainfall, one after another, painting the night in fantastic colors.

Plastered to the window, Weda couldn't take her eyes off the fascinating sight until a strange feeling of unease forced her to look down. At the foot of the tower stood a strange man. He was dressed like a denizen of Wintervale out for an evening walk, in a thick jacket and bulky pants. It was strange to see him standing outside the village walls all alone but, other than that, he looked normal enough.

Until, in the light of a falling star, Weda saw his face.

A layer of hoarfrost covered his features like crust and his beard hung with icicles. But worst of all were the eyes. Inky black – no whites – they stared right up at Weda. She couldn't look away until a shutter came crushing down in front of her face, obscuring the view. Odric stood next to her, his face grim.

"What was that?" Weda gasped.

"One of 'em. Dead hunters. I'll go find Dad."

Weda caught him by the sleeve. "What do you mean 'dead hunters'? How are they dead?"

Odric sighed and Weda thought that he looked very sad. At first it seemed he wasn't going to tell her anything, but then he spoke. "There's a tradition among Wintervale hunters. They don't like no funerals, don't like having to expire in a sick bed. So, when a hunter feels that death is close, through illness or old age, he or she picks up and goes away into the forest for their last hunt. They never come back, letting the forest take care of their last minutes and of their bodies. Only, you see, lately...they have been coming back. Like this." He gestured towards the closed window, pulled on his hat and tumbled out into the night of the walkway.

In the distance a horn wailed. One, then another.

Weda went back to the table and Jia poured her a cup of hot cider. They settled in front of the fireplace on a pile of blankets, watching the flames dance. "They think there's a darkness in the forest, deep inside. Something evil that corrupts the forest and everything inside it," Jia whispered. Weda didn't respond. She kept thinking of the empty eyes staring up at her, the memory sending cold shivers down her spine.

Eventually, the heat from the fireplace and the warmth of the cider settled her nerves and lulled her to sleep. As if from a distance, she heard Odric come back and climb into the pile of blankets on the other side of the hearth, and then she heard nothing more until the bright sunlight of the morning woke her up.

They were rolling up the blankets when Odric's dad came in from the watch. In the light of day, with the same freckles and ruddy red hair as his son, he looked much less severe than the night before. "Hey kids, I heard you had a bit of a scare last night," he said and smiled. They all puffed their cheeks and shook their heads, trying hard to show how unaffected they were by the dead hunter's appearance. Odric's father smirked. "I know you're all brave, but I still feel a bit responsible.

Let me make it up to you. How would you like to go snowberry picking tomorrow? That'll be much better than sitting in the dreary tower all night."

"Dad, are you sure about this?" said Odric, looking very serious.

"Don't worry, son. Your friends will be perfectly safe," said his dad.

"It *is* perfectly safe," said Jia in response to Weda's unsaid question. "We always follow the trail and the adults are there to look over us. Besides, the hunters never show in the day time. It's going to be fun."

Outside, the forest glittered white and silver, not a trace of darkness left from the night before. Weda found that she was in agreement with Jia and Odric's dad. It was going to be fun.

***

All day Weda could think of nothing but tomorrow's adventure and even went to bed early to shorten the wait, but all through the night she kept waking up, turning and tossing in her bed. In her dreams she saw snowberries, round sides gleaming with starlight, and the orange arrows of falling stars racing towards the roofs of Wintervale. She saw herself on the stage of the school's auditorium, the blooming flower of sky fire in her hands, and the adoration on the faces of the other girls and the teachers alike. Wouldn't it be incredible if she found a falling star on their forest walk today? She imagined Odric would be very proud. His red hair and freckled face figured in her dreams as well.

All through breakfast she was uncharacteristically distracted, spilling and dropping things at random. "Weda, you're walking in your sleep. Are you sure you should be going to the forest?" asked Grandma.

Weda shook herself. "No, no, Grandma, I'm not sleeping. I just can't stop thinking about it. The forest. I've never been there before."

Grandma pinned Weda with her gaze. "It's not good to stumble around that forest all dreamy. Remember to stay on the path." Weda promised that she would be careful but, now and again, she caught Grandma looking at her, eyes pensive.

Weda finished breakfast and ran to the village gate where a small group of kids assembled before departing on a berry-gathering trip. Four adults dressed in heavy overcoats flanked them on all sides. Weda joined the group, squeezing in between Odric and Jia.

One of the older women watching over the group handed out snow shoes: large, oval contraptions Weda found rather funny. Most of all they resembled rackets used in a popular ball game in Acamont. She struggled putting them on, but eventually managed with the help of Odric.

They marched across the snowy field in the direction of the forest. About halfway across Weda realized that she hadn't ventured so far from the village walls since the day she came here. Her stomach made a little excited somersault at the thought.

The little party plowed its path through the snow, finally reaching the border of the forest. A breath of colder air brushed Weda's face as if the temperature under the canopy of ice-white branches had dropped a few degrees.

Weda looked around in awe. She had never been in a winter forest before and now she felt as if she'd walked straight into a fairytale. The forest around her was so pretty; she struggled to understand why Odric and the other denizens of Wintervale seemed wary of it.

They followed the adults up ahead until they reached a small clearing where a scatter of low-set bushes sprawled, spreading into the trees. Tiny silver leaves covered the branches of the craggy bushes and, amid the leaves, plump yellow globes of snowberries shone in the sunlight. Woven baskets in hand, the kids ran towards the bushes.

Weda found a patch to herself in the far corner of the clearing and began picking berries. She picked and she plucked and every third berry never made it into the basket but went straight into Weda's mouth. She could swear nothing had ever tasted that good. She kept moving along the length of the bush, picking more and more berries, and before she realized it ended up at the very border of the clearing.

She looked around to check where the other kids were – none were close by – and that was when she saw it. A bright speck of light just a short distance away, between the trees on her right. She squinted, not sure that she wasn't imagining things, but the light was still there, winking and glimmering.

A falling star! Weda couldn't believe her luck. Of course, she remembered Grandma's warnings and Odric's furrowed brows when he talked about the forest, but the woodland around her seemed magical, not dangerous, all pristine white and glimmering silver. And the star was almost within her grasp. Surely she wasn't going to get in trouble if she went to fetch it. If she was back really quick.

Weda cast another look around. Jia was talking to a

couple of adults. Odric was stuck elbows-deep in a particularly large snowberry bush. No one was looking in her direction. She took a small step away from the clearing. Nothing happened. The sky didn't come down on her head. In fact, stepping off the path turned out to be very anticlimactic.

Quietly, she moved in the direction where she'd first seen the star. The closer she came the brighter it burned. From the shortened distance Weda could make out its brilliant, crystalline facets. It looked a little like honeycomb. A very beautiful, perfectly proportioned honeycomb.

Weda knelt in the snow. She took off her glove and reached out for the star. This was a dream come true; her eyes watered with excited tears. But just as her fingers locked around the glowing crystal – expecting scalding heat and finding none – she heard a low, menacing growl.

Weda looked up. A hunching figure stood between the trees. Face and clothes covered with a thick crust of ice and brown blood, its mouth gaped open in a snarl, teeth too big and sharp for a human. But worst of all were the eyes, the whiteless black spilling from the sockets in a spiderweb of pulsing, inflamed veins.

The dead hunter uttered another growl and lunged forward. Frozen to the spot, Weda stared at the monster's expanding mouth with elongating canines. She squeezed her eyes shut, waiting for unavoidable pain. It did not come. There was the sound of snow crunching under running feet and a loud thud.

Weda opened her eyes and saw Odric, hair flaming red, hitting the dead hunter with a large stick. The creature hissed and fell back, then lunged again, swinging its hand with enormous, crooked claws. In the distance she heard the shouts of adults running towards them. In slow motion Weda watched Odric wield his stick again and then the claws of the monster caught him in the side, tossing him away like a ragdoll.

A second later the adults were upon the monster. Weda saw burning gas torches in their hands spitting blue fire. In a blur, she saw axes coming down on the creature's disfigured head; she heard the hiss of fire taking hold, the remains of the abomination burning like a bonfire with an acrid smell that made Weda gag. She registered one of the women scooping her up from the snow bank and Jia crying.

Stunned, she watched a man in a brown deerskin coat lift Odric's limp body off the snow, his head hanging lifeless from the man's arms.

***

They brought Odric to his parents' house. By the time the stunned and shaken procession reached the door of a two-story building painted with the bright red tails of fire-birds, the whole village knew what had happened. A somber, murmuring crowd filled every nook and cranny of the house.

From behind the elbows and shoulders of adults in the congested bedroom doorway, Weda could barely make out Odric's red hair on the pillows and the dazed expressions on his parents' pale faces. Her own grandmother was in the bedroom, too. Propped in a chair by the side of the bed, she was busy bashing up some herbs in the pestle. The mortar ground against the pestle's stone bowl and the bitter, pungent scent seeped into the hallway.

Weda did not know how long she stood in the

doorway. Adults kept coming and going. The mayor's assistant with a box of sweet pies. A doctor with a fat, leather case. Two hunters with rifles and a box of protection charms. If it wasn't for her stupid wish to get hold of the falling star none of this would have happened. Her legs felt like lead, but she couldn't leave. Shame and guilt burned in her cheeks, covering them with red blotches.

Somewhere in the house a clock rang nine and Weda saw Grandma make her way through the still-crowded doorway. People parted to let her pass. Leaning heavily on one of her crutches Grandma slid her arm around Weda, turning her towards the exit. They made their way downstairs in silence. Weda pushed the chair the way Odric did and, just like him, rushed to open the door and then help Grandma up the steps.

In the kitchen Grandma sat down heavily in the chair by the table. She looked tired and old, defeated – the first time Weda had seen her that way. "Is he going to be all right, Grandma?" Weda asked, her voice barely more than a whisper.

Grandma was silent for a long while. Then she shook her head and a small silver tear slid down her cheek. "No," she said. "No, I don't think so. The dead one got him with his claws and its poison is spreading through his body. There is no cure for that, I'm afraid."

"No cure at all?" Tears welled up in Weda's eyes.

"Not in the village," said Grandma, the sadness in her voice palpable.

Hope stirred in Weda. "In Acamont? On the coast? Can we send the plane to bring it here?"

Grandma shook her head again. "No medicine of the living can help with this wound, as it comes from the world of the dead. Only one thing, one single thing, could save our Odric." Grandma's voice trailed off.

"What is it?" Weda asked.

"There is a tree." Grandma paused. "It grows in the heart of the forest, on an island in the middle of the lake. An apple from that tree is the only thing that can cure this wound."

Weda's eyes lit up. "But that's good, Grandma, isn't it? The hunters can go and get it and Odric will be all right."

"No, child," Grandma said. "No one has ever reached that lake but the Guardian of Wintervale, and Wintervale has been without the Guardian for a long, long time."

"But we can't just sit here and do nothing!" Weda exclaimed.

A moment of silence passed between them. Two. Three.

Then Grandma sat up straight. "You're right, Weda," she said. "I can't leave the boy to his death. After all, I'm the descendant of the Guardian. Fetch me my coat and shawl, I'll be going to the tree."

She started to get up but stumbled and leaned heavily on the table. Weda gasped. "Grandma, you can't go. You're too tired!"

Grandma sagged on the spot, all her previous fight immediately lost. "You're right, child. I'll rest a bit and go." Weda helped Grandma up and led her to the bedroom. "Just a little nap," the older woman said, lying down on the bed. She fell asleep as soon as her head hit the pillow.

Weda unrolled the duvet to cover Grandma's feet and sat on the edge of the bed. In the gloom of the bedroom she felt small and hopeless. She thought of Odric and the poison wrecking its way through his body. She wondered if he was in pain. Suddenly cold, Weda stuffed her hands in the pockets of her jacket and her fingers found something. She pulled it out. The falling star.

She must have stuffed it in her pocket when the dead hunter attacked and forgotten all about it. The star shone bright, iridescent colors playing on its facets, but Weda found that she no longer cared about it. It was just a pretty lump of crystal, nothing more. She let it fall on the carpet. It rolled away, and its shimmering light illuminated the sword hanging on the bedroom's wall. The fabled weapon of her ancestor, the Guardian of Wintervale.

She picked herself up off the bed and approached the wall. Where was the Guardian when they needed her? Wiping her nose on the sleeve of her jacket she reached for the sword, taking it off the wall. It was surprisingly light. Perhaps it was nothing but an illusion but, for a brief second, Weda thought she saw a thin strip of light between the hilt and the scabbard. Curious, she pulled at the hilt and, to her astonishment, it yielded, coming out of the scabbard shining bright as sunlight. Weda stared at the glowing blade. She had never seen anything that beautiful in her life, she was sure of it.

Disturbed by the light, Grandma stirred in her sleep. Anxious not to wake her up, Weda plunged the sword back into the scabbard. She now knew what to do.

In the dark hallway Weda pulled on a hat and scarf, then stuffed her mittens into her pockets. The strap of the scabbard fit her perfectly and the sword sat on her back, hilt showing over her right shoulder.

She had almost reached the gate when she realized she wouldn't make it far into the forest in her boots. Luckily she remembered where they stored the skis. It wasn't difficult to get into the shed – no one in Wintervale seemed to bother with locks – and grab a pair of them.

Skis in hand and sword over her shoulder, Weda tiptoed towards the gate. Luck was on her side. The guard on duty had left the little door leading outside unattended. Quiet as a mouse, she undid the latch and slipped out into the night beyond the walls of Wintervale.

Weda sped towards the line of trees, hoping that none of the adults patrolling the wall would notice her small figure. Distraught as they were, they didn't, and she entered the forest unencumbered.

White and silver during the day, it was now a domain of deep blue shadows. Weda wasn't sure where exactly the heart of the forest lay, but she figured if she went deep enough into the trees she'd find it.

She glided forward, the long strokes of her skis carrying her weight without sound. The forest was alive with the flapping wings of invisible owls, the soft whoosh of snow caps tumbling from the branches, the faraway moans of a forlorn moose. Weda kept pushing forward, working her way up the slopes and sliding down into the hollows. She was so caught up in the patterns of lifts and falls, she almost didn't notice it.

The forest going strangely quiet.

Something wasn't right. Weda sidestepped from her trail and crouched under the low hanging branches of a fir tree. For a few minutes nothing happened, and she was about to crawl out from her hiding place when she saw it. No, heard it first. The labored, wheezing sound. Breaths escaping a large body. A body that shouldn't be breathing at all.

Backlit by the moonlight a figure appeared, moving forward with a heavy, lumbering gait. Blood-crusted white fur on its snout hung in slimy tendrils under the deep, black hollows of its eyes. The bear moved past Weda's hiding place with the jerky tread of a bizarre marionette and, rooted to the spot, she watched the massive beast's labored advance. Through the gashes in its once-white fur peeked the yellow arches of its ribs. Maggots, gooey like clumps of curdled black ink, swarmed in the cavity. Weda gagged.

The bear passed by the tree and moved on but for a long while Weda heard its wheezing, rattling breaths fading in the distance. Utterly numb, she remained still in the snow heap under the fir tree. The situation was, impossibly so, worse than she imagined. The nameless evil that took root in the forest did not only rip the dead hunters of Wintervale from their secret graves; the other creatures hidden beneath the trees were not spared the same terrible fate.

Whatever power was at play here, it had no right to violate and pervert these lives and deaths. Angry tears swelled in Weda's eyes. What she saw in the forest was so very wrong. She had to make it right.

With the dead bear gone, the forest was once again alive with sounds. Weda wiped the tears off her face with the back of her mittened hand, crawled out of her hiding place, and resumed her trek into the depths of the forest.

***

She didn't know how many hours had passed since she'd set out on her journey. There was no noise but the whoosh and swish of her skis, the crackling of the snow, and the pale moonlight. The forest went on forever until the trees fell back and a lake of liquid silver spread out in front of her. Glittering and glowing in the light of the moon, it lapped gently against the shore. A bridge of three filigree arches spanned over the water, reaching up to a tiny island in the middle of the lake.

And there it was: the apple tree. Weda could see its outline, white branches reaching for the sky.

She undid the bindings of her skis and raced down the slope, towards the lake. She almost made it to the bridge when a dark shape blocked her way. Weda stopped short. It was as if the night itself and every deep shadow of the forest coalesced at the bridge entrance, tendrils of blackness weaving themselves into a tall figure. It towered over Weda and a pair of eyes – bloodshot quicksilver – peered down at her. A mouth opened in the darkness, full of needle-sharp, wicked teeth, and a voice, raspy and cold, slithered into Weda's ears.

"Ah, so we meet again," said the voice. Its breath, imbued with the sweet, pungent smell of decay, swept over Weda's face.

She fought not to recoil. "We have never met," she said.

"The Guardian. I've met her before," mewed the darkness.

"But I'm not her."

"Are you certain about that?"

The only thing Weda was certain about was that she needed to get the apple, bring it back to Odric and make him well again. "I need to get to the bridge," she said.

"You'd have to fight me for it," the darkness said.

"But I've never fought before."

"That is certainly your problem, not mine."

"But what if I lose?"

"Then you will die." The darkness exhaled more pungent rot and smirked.

It was that smirk that sealed Weda's fate. A wave of anger rose in her chest, washing away the fear and doubt. As if in a daze she reached behind her shoulder and, with a smooth movement begetting a skill Weda didn't know she possessed, drew the sword. In the heart of the forest its blade burned brighter than moonlight.

The darkness hissed and recoiled.

Weda swung, bringing the blade down. Darkness shifted, moving sideways, and the shining blade in Weda's hands cut through the emptiness. She stepped forward and caught her balance just in time to see two dark tentacles lunge, aiming for her throat. She rotated, bringing the sword down in a glowing arc; severed tendrils fell on the snow in heaps of dirty ash. Sprouting sharp spears from its own flesh the darkness screamed and charged again.

Weda parried, and so they danced.

The sword felt heavy in Weda's hands and grew heavier with every move. Eventually she faltered and the darkness laughed, a gurgling sound coming from somewhere deep in its inhuman throat. "Don't you see?" it bellowed. "You cannot win."

It stretched outwards, as if in triumph, black tendrils reaching for the forest and the sky and the moon, and that's when Weda saw it: a bulge, like a knot, at the center of the creature's monstrous body, holding the whole thing together. She gathered her remaining strength and lurched forwards, plunging the shining blade of her sword deep inside that knot.

The darkness screamed. It thrashed and jerked and writhed, but Weda held on fast, pushing the sword forward until, with the last convulsion, the darkness fell apart, raining to the ground in specks of greasy, oily ash. Weda leaned on the sword to catch her breath. The way to the bridge was now open. She returned the sword to the scabbard and ran towards the white silhouette of the apple tree.

***

She ran across the bridge and its filigree arches sang under her feet. She felt elated – the darkness in the forest was no more and the magic apples were only a short distance away. Everything was going to be all right; she was sure of it.

Weda cleared the bridge and came to a halt in front of the apple tree. She stared at it wide-eyed, disbelief mixing with horror.

The tree was dead.

Lifeless, barren branches stretched towards the moon. There were no apples. Not a single one. It took but a single moment for all hope and happiness to drain out of Weda's heart. *The tree was dead.* She wasn't going to get the apple, and Odric would die, and her battle with the darkness and her victory – those were worthless.

She stooped, hanging her head down. But a flicker in the silver waters of the lake caught Weda's attention, and she peered at the reflection of the apple tree. Upside down, in the underwater kingdom, the tree was in full bloom. Its branches were heavy with apples.

She knelt at the edge of the island and plunged her hand down into the water, trying to reach that other tree. The cold bit through her mitten and thick coat sleeve and her hand came back empty. Soaking wet and cold, but empty. The apples were out of reach and there was no way to get hold of them from the shore.

She stood up. The water of the lake at her feet undulated, serene and deadly cold. Weda thought of her Grandma and her mother and the baby brother soon to be born in Acamont. She thought of Odric and the way his bright red hair always seemed to spike upwards, as if reaching for the sun. She thought of the village of Wintervale, standing alone against the darkness. She took a step forward.

In a rush, the freezing water closed over her head. Heavy clothes dragged her down into the lightless abyss. Air left her lungs, rising to the surfaces in hollow bubbles. The cold tore through her muscles and sinews and her body came apart, breaking like a shattered ice sculpture. Dark water swallowed her, and Weda was no more.

* * *

A pale light appeared in the inky black depths of the lake. Weak and trembling at first, it grew stronger by the minute. Silver shadows rose from the lightless dark – all scaly sides and pointed fins, and the round, lunar eyes of giant fish. One came up first, then another joined her, and another until a whole shoal of carp swirled around Weda's broken form. They danced in the water around her and by the command of their fins and under the soft caresses of their mouths, her body came back together, broken shards fitting back into place, old and new at the same time.

Weda gasped and opened her eyes. She was standing on a strange, moonlit shore and the apple tree was right in front of her, branches adorned with silver leaves and blooming with a myriad of white flowers. And, amid the flowers, one ruby-red apple swayed close enough to reach. Weda stretched out her hand and the apple fell into her palm, round and perfect.

One blink later and she stood in front of a very different tree – white, barren branches shining in the moonlit winter night. She looked down. Reflected in the water, the apple tree bloomed and, around it, the shoal of silver carp swirled, glowing with a quiet light.

"Thank you," Weda whispered.

She ran back across the bridge. The skis were where she had left them what seemed like a lifetime ago. She sped back to the village, following the trail of her own tracks clearly visible in the rising sun. She broke out from under the cover of trees and raced towards the gates of Wintervale. Shouts and gasps erupted from atop the village wall but Weda paid them no heed. Abandoning the skis she ran through the now open gate, the guard following her passage with an open mouth, and raced up the street towards Odric's house.

By the time she reached the familiar door a small crowd had formed around Weda. Even more people waited by the house. She ran inside, face flushed, the shining red apple clutched in shaking, frostbitten fingers.

She pushed it into the hands of Odric's mother and the pale woman, face dawning with new hope, rushed to her son's bedside.

Weda didn't see him take a bite, but she heard his sharp intake of breath and the relieved cry of his mother before the assembled crowd swept her up and carried her downstairs and out into the street flooded with people. There was music, and balloons of all colors rising up into the air, and a cup of hot cider pushed into her hands.

Then she was sitting on the steps of her own house and her grandmother was hugging her tight.

"You know," said the old woman with a smile, releasing her from the hug. "A letter from your mother arrived this morning. The plane is coming soon to take you back to Acamont."

"Don't worry, Grandma," said Weda. "I'll be coming back next winter." She saw her place clearly now. Understood what was *important*. Not shooting stars or awards or fancy dresses or parties with the popular girls. "Wintervale is safe with me."

Laila Amado is a writer of fantasy and science fiction. She spends her days teaching, writing, helping her teenage kid navigate both senior school and a global pandemic, and, somehow, she never quite manages to catch up on her own research agenda. In her free time, she can be found staring at the Mediterranean Sea. Occasionally, the sea stares back.

Check out her website www.amadolaila.com for links to her published stories.

The Snow Trolls

S. Markem

In the faerie kingdom of Trippety Lee it was *always* springtime and it was *always* daytime (somewhere around three in the afternoon).

Time did not pass for faerie folk as it did for mortals, so everything was always green, sunny and pleasant – with just enough breeze to get your washing dry.

Nothing ever changed. Nothing of note ever happened. In fact, one might say that life was pretty dull for the average faerie.

Until, one day, the king of Trippety Lee called all the other faerie folk together for a *very* important announcement.

* * *

His Royal Highness, King Ooflaff I, had been king for as long as anyone could remember, which in practical terms meant forever.

He was a big fat faerie, almost as wide as he was tall. He had droopy eyes, flabby cheeks and sported a moustache so long it nearly reached his knees. Quite ridiculous by most standards, especially when you consider that faerie kings can choose their appearance. But faerie folk value novelty above everything else. It relieves the boredom.

On this very, very important day, the king wore bright blue britches and a glorious red jacket. He also decided to wear his crown – this was most unusual.

It was going to be an important announcement, and he wanted everyone to know it.

He sat on his throne and waited as his subjects gathered in the town square before him: centaurs, leprechauns, hobgoblins, will-o-wisps, faerie princesses. And, of course, trolls.

When he was sure everyone was in attendance, and when he sensed the crowd starting to get bored and fidgety (faerie folk have short attention spans), he cleared his throat and rose to his feet.

The heralds (cherubs) announced his intention to speak with several toots on their trumpets. It was a toneless sort of noise that irritated the ears – faerie-folk have no gift for music – but it did the job. It got everyone's attention.

"Dearest citizens," he began, "I have a very important and exciting announcement to make."

He paused for dramatic effect.

"I should like to declare that, after considerable effort on my part – and quite a bit of expense, I might add – I have, at last, invented: winter."

There was a murmur that rippled through the crowd – and then silence.

Pleased he had their attention, and reasonably sure they had no idea what he was talking about, he waved his hand. Behind him a magical gateway opened.

A magic portal was a fairly mundane occurrence in the faerie kingdom, but this one was distinctly different.

"Ooos" and "Ahhhhs" began to drift up from the crowd.

The king, always fond of a bit of drama, smiled to himself and patted his big belly.

The portal, the height of several centaurs and as wide as a dozen oliphants, was a glowing picture frame. It bordered the most magnificent wintery scene.

Picture postcard stuff: reindeer, pine trees, white foxes, icicles and, of course, snow. Tons and tons and tons of the stuff, covering everything in six inches of pure white powder.

"Dear citizens, I have created this wonderland for you! Isn't it simply marvellous? I like the foxes especially."

Silence.

Eventually a confused looking centaur raised his hand timidly.

"Yes, you there," said the king, somewhat perturbed by the lack of applause.

"If it pleases Your Majesty, may I ask, what is the white stuff that covers everything?"

The king shook his head in disbelief. Whilst he knew his subjects were not the most gifted thinkers it never ceased to amaze him how poorly travelled they were. "Why, that is snow, my dear fellow."

The centaur considered the answer for a few moments and then said. "But – what does it do?"

Many heads in the crowd nodded in acknowledgement. The concept of snow was new to everyone.

"Do?" exclaimed the king. "*Do?* It falls from the sky, of course."

"But...why?"

"Well – er – well – well – because falling upwards would be perfectly ridiculous, that is why."

The crowd gave a gentle "ahhh" as if the entire matter was now clear to them.

"Anyway," continued the king, "I have created this for you, for all of you – it's taken me bloody ages – and so you had better enjoy it!"

And with that he disappeared in a puff of smoke (a sign he was in a bad mood).

Many in the crowd turned to each other with puzzled looks. Eventually a few of the braver folk tip-toed up to the portal and peered in. But, somewhat underwhelmed and not sure what to do with themselves, eventually they all drifted away, shrugging their shoulders and shaking their heads.

Everybody – except two faerie trolls.

As with all trolls these fellows were about a foot high and naked as the day they were born, with stubby noses stuck in the middle of pug-ugly faces. They were virtually identical. In fact, all faerie trolls looked the same. It was this lack of diversity that kept them firmly on the bottom rung of faerie society.

Fortunately for us, one wore blue boots and the other yellow, which will make the whole story far easier to tell.

They could barely contain their excitement,# and so, when they felt sure everyone down to the last rabbit had left, they ran hand-in-hand through the portal.

Once through the magical gateway they moved more cautiously, chuckling to themselves at the crunching sound of the snow under their feet and occasionally turning to admire their footprints.

They squealed with delight as a squirrel clambered up a nearby tree and jumped up and down repeatedly, thus dislodging snow from a branch – it landed not six inches from where the trolls stood.

"How sweet," said Yellow Boots. "What an animated little fellow. Clearly he enjoys this winter malarkey."

* * *

After a short time they came across a sign. It was a big wooden board; painted on the board was a proclamation. The squirrel, who had decided to follow them, ran rings around the base of the sign. Yellow Boots cleared her throat and then read aloud:

Notice To All Trolls
(That Means You!)

When visiting this Winter world,
A few things you should know.
Please wear warm clothing at all times,

249

And don't eat yellow snow.

All faerie folk are welcome here,
You are free to come and go.
But once again I warn thee:
Don't eat the yellow snow.

And if you do not heed me,
Do not think that I won't know.
Cos strange things start to happen
When trolls eat yellow snow.

Appreciation of this facility is mandatory!
Visitors to this site do so at their own risk.

(All standard Terms and Conditions apply)

By order of
His Majesty, Ooflaff I (The King)

Blue Boots scratched his nose (trolls do that when required to think). "Well, this is mighty peculiar and now for some reason all I can think about is yellow snow. What on earth can it mean? He's laying it on a bit thick, don't you think?"

"The meaning is obvious, dearest. The yellow snow is more valuable and, therefore, much more delicious. And we trolls are not permitted to eat it, for it belongs to the king."

"I didn't even know one was *supposed* to eat snow."

"Of course," Yellow Boots said, full of false confidence. "Of course you do. Why – what on earth would be the point of it otherwise?"

And so Blue Boots and Yellow Boots began munching on snow. Great big handfuls of the stuff.

I could point out that trolls are non-too-bright, but I suspect you've figured that out for yourself.

After a time, Blue Boots said, "My head hurts. I have a pain in my brain. 'Tis freezing."

"Me too," said Yellow Boots, "and I have to say I do not see the appeal at all. All I can taste is water, grass and – something else that I'd rather not dwell on."

"It's given me a tummy ache."

Blue Boots sat on the ground and held his stomach. Then he remembered just how cold snow was and so decided he would stand up again. "I am beginning to think this snow stuff is overrated," he said.

"Perhaps we have it wrong, dearest," said Yellow Boots. 'Perhaps it is only the yellow snow that is worth eating. And most probably, it is magical snow. Yellow is, after all, the colour of magic."

"Why of course! I think you are right, my love. As usual, your logic is impeccable. We must explore and find some of this yellow wonder."

And so the two trolls began their exploration.

And they explored.

And explored.

And then they had a rest for a bit.

And then explored some more.

* * *

They were beginning to get bored of exploring, having spent a least half an hour doing so, when suddenly, Blue Boots exclaimed, "There, there...I see some. Quickly, dearest, follow me."

Wild with excitement and skipping through the snow, they arrived at the base of a tree where, sure enough, there was a big patch of yellow snow.

Yellow Boots knelt down to take a closer look.

"It is as I suspected," she said, with no shortage of confidence. "'Tis magical – that is most certain.'

"Why do you think so, my love?"

"Why, look, see how a faint mist rises from it. That is the surest sign of magic I can think of. And look, our little squirrel friend has followed us and is beside himself with glee. See how he jumps and hops. This is a magical spot, or I'm not a troll."

"What should we do, my love?"

Yellow Boots looked around just to make sure they were alone. "I think we should eat some," she said. "It is the most logical thing to do."

"But what about the king's proclamation? We might get into trouble."

"Nonsense, dearest. He just wants to keep it all for himself. He won't miss a little bit."

It took them at least four seconds of consideration before they began to wolf down handfuls of yellow snow.

* * *

When they had eaten their fill, and when once again they both had the most terrible headaches, Blue Boots said, "What do you think?"

252

"I don't think it tastes very nice at all. In fact, I would go so far as to say it tastes worse than normal snow."

"I am inclined to agree. The taste is not entirely unfamiliar, either, although I cannot place it."

"Perhaps the magic will be worth it. Do you feel any different?" asked Yellow Boots.

"Can't say that I do, dearest. Do you?"

"Alas, no. Perhaps we need to wait?"

"For how long?"

"The required amount of time, naturally."

"Ah yes, of course."

And so they waited.

And they waited a bit longer.

And a bit longer.

And then, after five minutes, their limited patience gave out.

"Nothing is happening," said Yellow Boots sullenly.

"I agree," said Blue Boots, clearly disappointed. "I suggest we return home. All this snow is starting to make me shiver."

Downhearted and despondent, the two little trolls trudged their way back through the snow, following their footsteps.

* * *

About halfway back Blue Boots stopped. "You know dearest, all this snow, and the cold air and whatnot...I think I need to go to the toilet."

"Use that tree over there then", said Yellow Boots.

"I won't look."

She waited patiently for Blue Boots to relieve himself.

"Oh hey, I say – dearest," Blue Boots called out.

"What is it, my love?"

"I think you should come and see this."

"See what?"

"I really think you should come and take a look. I don't think you're going to like it."

The two trolls stared at the patch of yellow snow beside Blue Boots' feet.

"Oh dear," said Yellow Boots.

"Oh dear, indeed."

S. Markem is an accidental writer of fiction. You cannot find him anywhere.

LORD OF THE FOREST

Katherine Shaw

Thunderous footsteps shook the ground. Hunting horns blared. Whoops and shouts rang out. Shotguns fired. It was pandemonium.

Anca hated all of it.

Every year they insisted on this nonsensical hunt, and every year it escalated, in both scale and thirst for blood. It made Anca sick to her stomach.

Of course, they wouldn't find the Leshii, they never did, and that would only fuel their anger more. Each time it evaded them a new crime was added to the list: spoiling the crops, stealing the livestock, spreading disease, even bringing the heavy blanket of gloom which threatened to suffocate their little rural village. Ridiculous.

"Anca? Anca!"

Oh, shit.

She prepared herself to make a dash into the

shadows between houses, but it was too late. He'd spotted her.

"What are you waiting for, girl? Get out there!"

Anca resisted the urge to roll her eyes. She might be willing to talk back to her father within the confines of their house, but he had a formidable reputation in this village, and she had quickly learned not to show him up in public.

"Must I, Father?" she pleaded, voice raised over the crowd of jeering villagers filing out towards the forest. "I don't want to be a part of the hunt, of any of this."

Her father frowned, making no effort to hide the disappointment in his eyes. Standing over six and a half feet tall, sporting a thick, dark beard many men could only dream of and wearing a large, fur-lined coat further contributing to his bulk, Casimir Skala was an imposing man, and Anca shrank under his glare.

"Daughter, do not embarrass me like this. Every man and woman without child joins the hunt, no exceptions. You know that. Now that you're sixteen that includes you.'

"But, Father, I don't-"

Casimir leaned in close, eyes blazing, his voice a low growl. "That includes *you*."

He thrust a lit torch towards Anca, the flickering flame glittering off the snow beneath their boots. "Take this. You do not need to carry a weapon this time, if you would prefer." A ghost of a smile passed over his lips at Anca's small nod. She tentatively closed her fingers around the wood, appreciating the heat as it was handed over to her. "But you must come with us, and if we happen across the monster – gods willing – you must help flush him towards those of us who are armed. Now come."

Giving Anca no further opportunity to protest, he pressed a firm hand into her upper back and urged her forwards. Her feet struggled to keep up with her father's pace as they joined the throng of villagers marching their way into the forest.

Anca pulled her fur-lined hood tight around her ears as they reached the tree line, trying and failing to block out the deafening shouts of her neighbours. It was a cacophony of misplaced anger and futility.

The swarm of bodies plunged deeper into the forest. The towering clusters of birch, oak and pine grew denser, pressing into Anca from all sides, forcing her closer to those around her with their flushed, twisted faces just inches from her own. Her heart pounded in her chest; her breath struggled to find her lungs. She tried to stop, to step back from the crowd, but there were bodies on all sides, forcing her onward.

Their jeers and threats roared in her ears until Anca felt like her head was about to explode.

She quickly lost sight of her father; the head of the hunt needed to be seen to be leading the charge. The faces around her blurred together until she was lost in a homogeneous mass of furious eyes and gnashing teeth. Finally, a narrow trail snaking off between two tall silver birch trees appeared to Anca's left, and she squirmed out of the writhing mass and sprinted into its sanctuary.

Free of the crowd she leaned against a tree, closed her eyes and took a series of long, deep breaths. Finally, the cries and shouts faded and her heartbeat settled. She could open her eyes again.

It was dark. And cold.

Anca stood frozen, bathed in the weak firelight of her single torch. She was in a clearing, surrounded by dark, looming branches which blocked out all but a sliver of moonlight.

She could go home. She'd been seen to join the hunt, and her escape from the crowd had probably gone unnoticed. She could hide in one of the neighbours' gardens and join the disappointed villagers as they made their less-than-triumphant return.

Anca cast her eyes over the ring of trunks encircling her, searching for the trail that would take her home. But the trees all looked the same, and the trail was hidden in the shadows gathered around their feet. Without the sounds of the crowd as a guide Anca lost all sense of direction. Home could be through any of these trees.

I've waited too long.

A brisk gust of wind rustled through the branches, showering her in a flurry of ice-cold snow. She couldn't stay here, shivering in the cold. Alone. In the forest. At night. She had to move.

Here goes nothing.

Anca pulled her hood tighter over her head and strode into the trees, willing herself to recognise something that would guide her home.

* * *

Grasping branches tugged on Anca's cloak and thorns ripped at her legs as she pushed her way through the undergrowth. No matter which way she turned the forest seemed to grow denser with no end in sight. She picked up her pace, fear bubbling up inside her until

259

she could feel acid rising up the back of her throat.

Anca paused to take a breath, her heart hammering against her ribs. She just needed to calm down, clear her head. As her heart rate finally settled, she became aware of a new sound cutting through the crisp night air.

Growling.

She spun around, scanning the undergrowth for the source of the noise. That's when she saw them. The eyes.

Anca couldn't move. She couldn't breathe. There was no mistaking that vicious yellow gaze; it had haunted her dreams for almost a decade, ever since the night she lost her mother. And where one was, others had to be nearby.

Wolves.

There was no time to think. Anca's heart stopped as a mass of teeth, fur and claws lunged from the bushes, powerful jaws open and savage eyes on her throat. And then...it stopped. Anca's eyes bulged as the beast shrank – no, *cowered* – back, ears flat to its head in submission. It was impossible; the wolf was afraid.

"W-what–"

A low rumble emanated from behind Anca, sending a chill down her spine. She stood, frozen, fear paralysing her lungs so she couldn't even scream.

It couldn't be.

Anca's people had hunted the Leshii for years and never seen more than a glimpse of the creature. And yet there wasn't a doubt in her mind that what stepped between her and the wolf was him.

The Lord of the Forest.

Anca's stomach knotted as she took him in. Towering over her at what must be eight or nine feet tall, he swayed towards the wolf with an unexpected grace, his large feet making virtually no sound on the soft snow. The beast let out a low whine and retreated further, lowering its body to the ground as the Leshii reached out an arm covered in thick, white hair. Anca swallowed, her throat dry. Her legs were trembling so much she thought they might give out from under her.

With the wolf subdued and slinking into the dark undergrowth, the Leshii turned its focus onto Anca. Its startling red eyes seemed to bore into her very soul, chilling her to the bone. She wanted to speak, to let it know she wasn't like the others, she didn't *want* to hunt it, but the words wouldn't come. The Leshii took a step towards her, the moonlight casting a shadow over Anca so cold it sent her teeth chattering. It leaned over, its fiery gaze holding Anca in place. She couldn't look away, no matter how hard she tried.

She blinked, and a strangled scream caught in her throat as she opened her eyes. The eyes were close now, too close. Mere inches away from her own. Two endless crimson pools drawing her in, forbidding her escape. The world seemed to lurch from below Anca's feet as her head swam, and dark shadows danced in the corner of her vision. There was no forest, no Leshii, just those eyes in the darkness. Her eyelids drooped and she strained to keep them open.

Why...why am I so...so tired?

Her thoughts faded to nothingness as an overwhelming exhaustion swept over her muscles, her legs giving out as the collapsed into the snow, the darkness finally taking her.

Somewhere, in the abyss, a gunshot rang out.

* * *

Anca stirred as the scent of springtime flooded her nostrils. She wrinkled her nose and rubbed her heavy eyes. As they fluttered open, her jaw dropped.

She was lying in a clearing in what looked to be the same forest, but where there should have been bare branches there was a canopy of lush, green leaves, and in place of thorny shrubbery there were pockets of bluebells, crocus and iris, all in full bloom. Anca pushed herself up onto her knees, feeling soft ferns and grasses between her fingers where she expected snow. The soft amber light of daybreak cast dappled shadows across the forest floor. It was morning. Anca frowned; it had been late evening when she had met the Leshii...

The Leshii.

Anca's eyes darted about the clearing until she finally saw it, kneeling at the opposite edge, its head bowed. It had its hand on something: a dark, unmoving mound. Anca crawled a little closer, as quietly as she could manage, and spotted a pair of antlers.

The gunshot.

Tears pricked the back of her eyes. Deer were trapped and slaughtered for meat, that was true, but Anca had always hated the unnecessary additional deaths that arose due to the trigger-happy Leshii-hunters every year. They didn't even use the carcasses. They just moved on, hungry for the Leshii's blood.

But what is the Leshii doing with the deer?

A shiver of disgust ran through Anca as she considered that it might be eating it, right there in front of her. But, no, it wasn't that. It was...crying. Its shoulders shuddered with soft sobs, its large, clawed hand tenderly stroking the deer's fur.

She watched, enraptured, as the Leshii laid a wreath of woven branches and wildflowers against the fallen creature's body. It was beautiful – far more intricate than anything Anca had seen in the village. She crept closer to get a better view, cringing as a loose twig snapped beneath her palm, the sound piercing the tranquil air around her. She froze, heart pounding, praying the Leshii hadn't heard.

For a moment nothing happened, and Anca allowed herself to hope. Her stomach dropped as it raised its head and her blood turned to ice as it turned its fearsome gaze upon her.

Except...it wasn't fearsome. Not anymore.

Where once there was a crimson rage, there was now a shimmer of gold. Anca was no longer paralysed in fear as this mysterious creature considered her, its expression oddly comforting.

Although he spoke no words, Anca knew he was beckoning her to him.

* * *

The days Anca spent with the Leshii bordered on bliss.

Wherever he trod, the forest sang. Anca watched in awe as animals flocked to him: deer seeking his blessed touch, wolves revering him as their alpha, even a family of bears welcoming him as if one of their own. The Leshii wasn't a monster; he was the embodiment of nature, a single thread holding the entire forest together.

Although he never spoke a word to Anca she felt like she could understand him. He welcomed her into his grove, an oasis of life amidst the frigidity of the winter forest, silently teaching her some of his skills. The Leshii was patient as he tenderly showed Anca how to craft a simple wreath from hollyhock and silver birch, a world away from what he laid on the body of the deer, but still far superior to anything she had ever made before.

On the fifth day, the Leshii took Anca beyond the grove, back into the snowy outside world. The dense canopy above blocked almost all the warmth of the winter sun, leaving the air bitterly cold. Anca pulled her hood up, following the Leshii as he weaved in and out of the trees, pointing out herbs and plants they could use to make medicines. She collected samples of each, carefully tying them up in bunches and placing them in a basket the Leshii had beautifully woven for her.

I can't believe I found him. I'm so lucky.

The Leshii strode ahead into the trees to examine a patch of fungi, leaving Anca to finish collecting rose hips in a small clearing. She took her time, crouching by the plant and selecting only the very best fruit which wouldn't harm the plant, as the Leshii had shown her.

"Anca?"

She froze, recognising the voice instantly. Her heart pounded against her ribs and she considered running, bolting into the trees and never looking back. She closed her eyes and took a deep breath, the cold air burning her lungs. Her stomach clenched as she turned, taking in the bewildered face of Casimir Skala. Her father.

"Sweet Daughter, where have you been? We have been searching for you!" Before Anca could respond Casimir bellowed over his shoulder into the trees, "Andrik! Burian! Come quickly, she is here!"

Anca's heart dropped.

It looks like my adventure is over.

It wasn't fair. Living alongside the Leshii had been a dream, an escape from the bitter drudgery of the village, where hate and misery ruled supreme. And now it was over; cut short before she had the chance to learn even a fraction of what the Leshii could teach her.

"Well, what are you waiting for, girl?" her father asked as his two surly companions emerged from the forest behind him, arms crossed. "Come, back to the village."

He took a step forwards, arm outstretched to take Anca by the arm and lead her home – whether she wanted to go with him or not. She took a hesitant step towards him and stopped. True, she hadn't had a long life, but these past few days with the Leshii had been the happiest time Anca had ever known. Peace like she had experienced in the grove was unheard of in a village wracked with toxicity. Distrust and spite poisoned even the most optimistic of people until they were consumed, left hollow shadows of what they once were. She didn't want that.

Not when she had seen what life in the forest could be like.

"No."

Casimir stopped walking, his face unreadable. Anca's chest tightened and she braced herself; this wasn't a man who was familiar with refusal. For an excruciating moment he did nothing, staring at his daughter with a face of stone. Then his features darkened as his eyebrows knitted together, his mouth twisting.

"What did you say?"

"I said," Anca began, her mouth dry under his penetrating stare. "I don't want to come back to the village. I'm sorry, Father, but I want to stay in the forest. I like it here."

Casimir shook his head and lurched forward, grasping Anca tightly by the arm. She grimaced, his iron grip squeezing almost to the point of pain.

"A handful of days in this gods-forsaken maze of trees and you have already taken leave of your senses." He moved to pull her forwards but Anca resisted, digging her heels into the snow. "Anca, stop this! You are coming home. *Now.*"

"No!" She wrapped her free arm around the nearest tree branch and held on tight. A twinge of pain struck her shoulder as her father tugged, attempting to wrench her free.

"This is insanity! Andrik, Burian, get over here and get this fool girl off this tree so we can go home."

The men advanced and Anca thrashed against the tree, desperate to shake her father off and escape her would-be captors. "Leave me be!" she screamed, kicking out to keep them at bay.

Burian moved to the right of Casimir, attempting to flank Anca and grab her while she was fending off her father, but he stopped short. Anca glanced at him, his face suddenly ashen and his eyes bulging with horror.

"Don't just stand there!" Casimir shouted at his frozen companion. "Help me with-"

A thunderous roar shook the forest as the Leshii burst from the trees behind Anca, fiery eyes blazing. He was here to protect her, she felt it. The pressure of her father's grasp fell away as she was swept off her feet, enveloped in the Leshii's arms. He clutched her close against his chest, holding her off the ground and away from these dangerous men.

Casimir's face flushed red as he beheld the Leshii. "The monster!" he bellowed, shining eyes no longer on his daughter but focussed entirely on the beast holding her in its arms. "Finally, the village is saved! Andrik, the crossbow! Burian, take a hold of yourself and move!"

This war cry shocked Burian out of his stupor. He shook his head and took a step back from the Leshii, unsheathing a heavy shortsword from the leather scabbard around his waist. A strangled cry caught in Anca's throat as the three men spread out into a semi-circle, each with a weapon pointed at the Leshii: Burian with his shortsword, Andrik with a light wooden crossbow and her father with the heavy battle axe he carried on his back. Anca had witnessed him swinging that axe down on his hunting quarry many times, and knew it could deliver a swift and sudden death.

"Stop!" she screamed, gesturing wildly from within the Leshii's gentle grasp. "I'll come, I'll come, just don't hurt him!"

"It is too late, child," her father growled, inching closer to the Leshii, the three men pressing him towards the thick trunk of an ancient pine tree. "This is greater than you or me. This is what we have been working towards for all these years. Today, I take down the beast, and free our village from its vile curse."

"Don't you understand, Father? There is no curse! You all make a scapegoat of the Leshii as an excuse for your own twisted natures. He is gentle and good!"

Casimir barked a cruel laugh. "I see he has you under his strongest spell. Fear not, Daughter! I will wrest you from his evil clutches myself."

A panic swept over Anca's body, almost paralysing her, but she was surprised to realise it wasn't hers. It was the Leshii; he was afraid. Not for himself, but for *her.* Tears pricked the back of her eyes as she felt concern for her safety swelling within him. *No,* she thought, hoping he understood. *Leave me and save yourself. Please!*

Strong arms embraced her tightly, pulling her into the Leshii's warm chest, before placing her gently on the snow behind him. He wanted her to run.

No! Leave me, save yourself!

It was no use. The Leshii stood his ground, positioning his body to shield Anca from her father.

"Ready yourselves!" Casimir's cry was low but hard; he didn't intend to end this standoff without bloodshed.

"No!" Anca cried, her voice strained and desperate. "Don't–"

Too late.

As the Leshii stepped forwards, ready to protect she who had become a part of his world, Andrik let a crossbow bolt fly. Anca's legs buckled from under her as it found its mark, plunging deep into the Leshii's chest. Into his heart.

He fell to his knees, eyes bulging as he stared forward at Andrik. The man's face paled at what he had done but Casimir was unperturbed. He let out a riotous whoop as the Leshii collapsed on his side, readying himself to make the final blow.

"*No!*"

Anca threw herself forward, over the Leshii's body. Her fingers touched the Leshii's skin where the crossbow bolt penetrated it, coming away red.

"I don't know what to do," she spluttered, stroking the soft, white hair of the Leshii's face as his eyes turned to meet hers. "Tell me what to do to save you!"

It is too late.

"No!" she cried, burying her face into his chest, her body shaking all over. "You can't die, not here, not now."

Through her shuddering sobs Anca was vaguely aware of her father's harsh shouts piercing the frigid air around her.

"Daughter, step away from the beast! Now!"

The snow crunched as the surrounding men closed in around her, but she ignored them, clenching her eyes shut and wrapping her trembling fingers around clumps of the Leshii's thick hair, her constricted chest heaving as she struggled to take a breath. She had done this. She had put this magnificent creature in danger, just to satisfy her own thirst for a better life in the forest. It was all her fault.

"Anca..."

This voice was new, and yet familiar. It was deep and rich and laced with the ancient wisdom of the forest itself.

The Leshii.

She raised her head and peered into his eyes, their usual radiance already dimming. He lifted an unsteady hand to her face and brought it closer to his, dipping her head forward so he could place his lips on her brow. At his touch, a surge of energy rushed into Anca, taking her breath away. She clenched her eyes shut, overwhelmed by the force passing through her. It was as if she could...*feel* them. The trees, the animals, down to each falling leaf and climbing ant. It was intense, and wonderful.

When Anca opened her eyes, the Leshii was gone.

She pressed her fingertips into the cold snow beneath her, eyes scanning for any sign of her fallen companion. There was only one – a fallen crossbow bolt, still slick with a blood so red it seemed to glow amidst the stark white of the forest floor. Anca traced trembling fingers along its shaft, her grief transforming into a rage the likes of which she had never experienced before.

This was his forest. *Her* forest. They shouldn't be here.

The slender bolt crumbled as she clenched her hand into a fist, the wood easily buckling in her strong fingers. She turned to face the men, eyes blazing with a burning fury. As she took in their faces, each a picture of horrified surprise, a deep rumble stirred in her chest and erupted from her throat in an earth-shattering roar.

"*Get out!*"

A smile slowly spread across Anca's face as she watched the three men turn and run, back to their village with their tails between their legs. She closed her eyes and took a deep breath, welcoming the magic of the forest into her body. This was her home. She would protect it, and they would be at peace.

Forever.

Katherine Shaw is a multi-genre writer and self-confessed nerd from Yorkshire in the United Kingdom, spending most of her time dreaming up new characters or playing D&D. She has a passion for telling the stories of underdogs who must rise up to defeat the hardships they have been dealt in life, often with a focus on female protagonists. She recently released her debut novel Gloria, a contemporary domestic thriller, and has already begun writing her next one.

You can find out more at her website www.katherineshawwrites.com

QUEEN OF THE SNOWS

Joyce Reynolds-Ward

Blink in. Awareness jolts into place about halfway down the steep slope, wind whipping icy wet snow pellets against her unprotected cheeks. No time to wonder who she is, or how she got here. She'll fall hard if she gets distracted.

Ice scrapes against her uphill ski as it grabs the hard-packed snow and brings her around. She snaps into the next turn, pushing her turns. Ignoring the ice pelting her face. Ignoring the teeth of the wind. Then an echoing, faint screech catches her ear and freezes her insides.

A *familiar* screech, one she should know well.

She digs into the ice to stop. Looks around. Wavy white snow clouds blow by in shades of white and gray.

The screech rings across the slope again. A faint,

distant line of four figures on snowboards rides the edge of the wind. The keening cry rings one last time, a call picked up from rider to rider. Longing burns deep within her – *mine, they are mine* – and she pushes off to try to catch them.

Another wave of snow blocks her vision. When it blows through, she's alone again, sliding to a puzzled stop.

Blink out.

* * *

"Saasaren."

She moans and turns in her bed, trying to worm her head deeper into the pillow.

"Saasaren."

The name, whispered in that commanding voice. *Her* name, though she hasn't known it until now.

A cold metal point presses into her arm.

"Saasaren. Queen of the Snows. I have need of you."

And with that simple phrase, memory floods back. Saasaren opens her eyes in the darkness. The cloaked woman calling her sits on the edge of the bed, her image wavering, and Saasaren knows it as a sending, not an actual presence.

A poniard hangs in the air between them. Saasaren reaches for it. The poniard ducks away. She snaps her fingers impatiently. Now she remembers how temperamental it is. She is grateful to Callan for bringing it to her. Isn't she?

"Come to me," she growls at it.

The poniard slides into her palm, and she closes her fingers around the hilt. Icestar, sigil of her power. She raises the tip of the blade to her lips, gently kisses it. *Welcome back, old friend.*

She chooses not to think about why she sent Icestar away.

"My lady Callan," she says to the sending. "What do you wish of me?"

"Jamarkte has been captured."

Saasaren frowns. "I'm confused. Doesn't your marriage make him off-limits to your Rust forces? Or have things changed while I've been cloaked?"

Callan shakes her head. "Those who capture him are not of Rust and Flame."

"The Old Ones?" Fear tingles through Saasaren. While the powers of Rust and Flame are eldritch to the humans they herd, the Old Ones herd Rust and Flame. If the Old Ones were angry, that would be most desperate need on Callan's part.

"These are not the Old Ones," Callan says reluctantly. "They attack the Old Ones as well. The Old Ones are calling upon us for help, and I – well –" She parts her cloak and pulls her garments tight to show the slight bulge in her abdomen. "The Old Ones think this child may be what these new intruders seek."

Callan's powers are great, but none who bear power can use much of it while pregnant, for fear of harming the unborn. Especially if the child is a suspected sorcerer. A sorcerer *in utero* could lash out dangerously against its parent if frightened or provoked.

"I see," Saasaren says. She traces a pattern on Icestar's hilt as silence falls between her and Callan. The poniard throbs under her soft touch, yearning for blood. *There will be blood soon enough, dearest,* she thinks to Icestar.

"Will you help me, my lady of the Snows?" Callan finally asks, breaking the silence.

"I hear and obey, my lady of Rust," Saasaren says.

Callan spreads her hands wide. "I do not want blind obedience. I have no power to compel."

"We of the Snows are our own."

"As is the Forest. Tilent has agreed to join forces."

"Then we of the Snows can do no less than the Forest. I will assemble my Court and be with you within a day."

"It may be more of a challenge than you think to tame them again," Callan warns. "The world has turned."

"My Court and I will be with you within a day," Saasaren repeats.

"My thanks to you, Queen of the Snows. Take care. Those that should walk easily with you may not do so." She bows before fading away.

Saasaren lies in bed, Icestar across her chest, assembling what she needs to know from the mana of the world about her. She discards Callan's last warning. The Queen of Rust has always been cautious. Caution brought Callan to leadership. Caution brought Callan to the unexpected union with Jamarkte and Flame. What could Callan know about the Four? Rust and Flame never have known the challenges of leading the Snows. She's confident that not only can she win back her Court – she can *rule* them.

Didn't you think that before? the mocking voice of

doubt echoes deep inside Saasaren, evoking unpleasant memories.

The world changes, Saasaren tells herself.

She hopes she's right about that. Her last ride with the Four was not pleasant. They are an unruly lot, and they hunger for power independently of her.

Fourth time's the charm, she whispers to herself. *Four for the Four.*

* * *

It's late morning by the time she drives to the ski area. Wind whips waves of snow across the parking lot as she parks. Saasaren bares her teeth to the wind as she climbs out of the car. It recognizes and bows to her, capering in respectful snowy swirls before whispering away. Saasaren pulls on her ski boots, unbags her skis, fits the helmet to her head.

The wind breathes encouragement into her ear as she strides to the edge of the first run and steps into her bindings. As her second foot clips in a low chord sounds. Power tingles up through her knees, her hips, through her shoulders to the tips of her fingers and the strands of her hair. Saasaren raises her arms high and wide, letting the jubilant cry break free from her chest, announcing her return.

An exuberant snowboarder echoes her whoop. Saasaren ignores him, extending her awareness farther.

No response.

Yet.

This is the sort of day her Court loves for riding the wind and snow. She'll have to chase them down.

She pushes off, the thrill of the chase beginning to

pulse through her veins.

Find them for me, she whispers to the wind.

A swirl of dry, powdery snow caresses her exposed cheek.

* * *

By her third run, Saasaren's worked over to the west edge of the ski area. She has heard the Court but not yet seen them.

To be expected. Once won, they're loyal. But to prove herself, she'll have to outski them. Saasaren is on high alert as she rides the second highest lift on the mountain, eyes scanning the trees. As the chair approaches the end of the lift she hears the faint cry again, far off to the side of the run beyond the ski area boundaries.

She glides away from the other skiers and riders. Pauses on boundary's edge, listening, looking. Sees the gray shadows on the slope above her.

Go, she whispers to herself and to her skis. *The race begins.*

She ducks under the boundary rope and plunges into deep, unpacked snow, riding the fall line. Her Court drops in ahead of her, angling down the steep canyon that parallels the ski area. Saasaren follows, crouching low and hard with each kneeling turn, barely turning as she builds up speed.

She finds a short cut and beats her Court down the slope, shooting out of the trees and into their midst.

"Come to me!" she screams at them. "I am Saasaren!"

They flinch away. But one rider catches an edge and

face plants into a snowbank. *Kientjen*. Good fortune to her. Kientjen's the head of the Court but loyal to her. He'll come to heel easily.

Still, he growls in defiance at her. Saasaren snaps out of her skis and unsheathes Icestar as he struggles to his feet, his gnarled and twisted face evoking the juniper that calls his spirit. She raises Icestar high.

"Kientjen!" she calls. "Submit!"

"Would have been best that you'd remained asleep, Saasaren." Kientjen growls at her, staggering sideways.

She kicks him back to his knees in deeper snow. "Swear your vow."

Kientjen bares his teeth and hisses at her. A brief doubt surges through Saasaren as she remembers Callan's warning.

No. He is mine. She rests Icestar's point on his throat.

"Swear your vow," she repeats.

"You should have remained asleep."

She presses the point harder against his pale skin. "Do I need to take your blood?"

Kientjen swallows hard. "No." He drops his head for a moment and looks back up. "I swear my loyalty to Saasaren, Queen of the Snows. I am yours to command, my lady."

One down. She steps back into her skis. This time the chord doesn't sound. She chooses not to think of it as an omen.

* * *

They ski back to the lifts. Saasaren and Kientjen

catch the lowest lift back up to the top, riding in a stiff silence until they dismount. Saasaren waits for Kientjen to reattach his free foot to the snowboard.

"Where are they running?" she asks.

"We waste breath. Follow me."

"Do not lead me wrong," she warns him, putting one hand on her waist where Icestar hangs in hidden shadow. Doubt flares. What if Callan were right about the Four's loyalties?

Kientjen snarls wordlessly and kicks off. Saasaren shrugs off her worry and follows.

This time they ride the edge of the run, not ducking away from the ski area boundaries until they're in the trees. Kientjen dives into the thickest glade, twisting through the deep powder, heading straight down into the canyon.

Before they break out of the trees, he stops. Throws his head back and shrieks.

An answer echoes back.

Kientjen points downslope. "There. Fast, to tree's edge. You'll face them there." He points at a higher angle. "I'll circle around above."

Saasaren eyes him cautiously, tapping Icestar's hilt. Doubt wakens again.

"Go! Before it's too late!"

He speaks as he always would. But she doesn't find that reassuring. Something in his eyes doesn't seem right, and yet – she has no more time to worry. Saasaren pushes off, gliding to a small snow-choked meadow at the edge of the trees. She doesn't see the rest of her Court yet, but she can hear the sobbing cry of a human.

Feeding? She wonders if she should intervene. Once fed, the Court will be harder to capture. She climbs toward the sobs, working along the edge of the trees until she finds them in a small meadow.

At this point they're playing with their food. The victim, a young, scruffy male, thrashes through the snow. His snowboard lies in pieces at the edge of the tree line, and the remaining three of her Court are herding him, only beginning to feed on his terror.

The fear draws Saasaren as much as it does her Court. The victim struggles through the snow toward her. Saasaren lets him hope until he reaches her.

Then she draws Icestar and grins at him.

His bleat changes to fear. She looks deep into his thoughts, identifies him as a ski area predator, a thief and bully. Hardly an innocent; certainly someone worth her Court's attention.

The other three members of her Court cluster nearby. She holds Icestar high. The victim cowers at her feet. She eyes her Court. Ranimak makes a grab toward the victim, and Saasaren points Icestar at him.

"Mine," she says.

"*Ours*," Dondije snarls in return.

"*Mine*," she repeats. "I thank you for your gift."

"It is no gift!" Dondije presses forward. She slashes Dondije's throat. As he falls, Ranimak leaps for Dondije's torso while Wewivek gnaws on his leg.

Saasaren lets them feed. Feeding on each other won't give them the strength of feeding on this victim.

The victim gibbers behind her. Saasaren turns and smiles down at him. Lowers Icestar's point. She ignores the pleading words, hunger rising deep from within her. This hunger is for more than blood and flesh, more than sating her stomach. She's ready to drink this one's soul.

But first, the preparation. She pulls off one white glove and yanks off the victim's tasseled cap, tossing it away. Lovingly caresses his cheek, capturing one single tear on the tip of her index finger. Brings the finger to her mouth to taste.

Experiences flood through her. Catching a ride from that middle-aged teacher, he and his pal forcing her off on a side road where they beat her up before stealing her stuff. Making off with a snowboard while a kid yells after them. Other things, dark and shadowy. Cause for dread about his ultimate fate.

No, this one's no angel. And he's a perfect treat for her return as Queen. Saasaren reaches down again. Runs her fingers through his lovely, lovely curls. Eyes his strong young body. For the moment she's tempted to take his body. But no. Such would give him power.

Instead, he'll be just what she needs to bind the rest of her Court. She holds tight onto the victim's curls as she turns her head to check on Dondije's progress. He growls and snarls as he comes back to life, biting and tearing at Ranimak and Wewivek to recover pieces of himself. She has time to feed. The three of them have accounts to settle.

She contemplates whether she should give the victim the kiss of peace before she feeds. Considers his soul, and decides against polluting herself with it. She lays Icestar against his throat, then bends and kisses those sweet, sweet curls. Icestar strains in her hand. She lets it follow its desire, sliding into her victim's heart.

The victim thrashes on Icestar's tip, screaming in

agony. At last he stills, his eyes still wide with terror as Icestar drinks his blood, still aware, still *knowing*.

She lets her lips slide down his forehead, pressing deep over each eye, before she finally sips his soul from those firm, luscious lips.

It's a mean little soul, for all that. But it gives her power. She straightens. Holds Icestar high, dripping with the victim's blood.

"This one is yours, if you renew your vows," she says to her Court.

Dondije yowls, skin drawn tight over his renewed body. He lunges toward her and stops short of Icestar's point, just enough caution remaining.

"Vows before feeding."

He quivers. She wonders if she'll have to kill him again. Wewivek and Ranimak wait. Kientjen sneers. She hadn't noticed until now that he had joined the others.

The balance of power wavers. Dondije tilts his head and works his jaws. He reaches out one hand, not toward the victim but toward her.

"*Want,*" he whispers. "*You.*"

"No."

"Not food. *You.*" He leers at her.

Kientjen laughs a short sharp bark. "The world has changed since you last woke, Saasaren."

"Worlds do not change that much, Kientjen!"

"Oh, this world has changed, Saasaren." Kientjen steps forward. "You cannot just snap your fingers and bind us back to you, even with a sacrifice. You must give of yourself."

"And who says this?" Anger pulses through her. "I am the Queen of the Snows!"

"It is a new era."

Kientjen should not be challenging her like this. Saasaren presses Icestar against his chest. The poniard remains quiet in her hand as it touches Kientjen, though it should be straining to take him. She pulls Icestar away and it glows. Touches Kientjen and the glow fades.

"What have you done?" Saasaren whispers.

Kientjen laughs again. Unstraps an ice axe from his belt and holds it high. The glow gives it away as he straightens taller than he's ever stood before. Iceshatter. Icestar's sometime matchmate, sometime nemesis.

"*Where did you find that?*" she whispers. Eons ago she'd broken Iceshatter's shaft and thrown its head into a glacier, after he who had wielded it had betrayed her one final time.

"I sought long for this," Kientjen says. "I knew a time would come when you would call us back. I wanted to be ready."

"What do you want?" Dread washes through Saasaren's veins, chilled even to her lips despite the power of the sacrifice burning bright inside of her. Iceshatter has power over her. He whose name she no longer remembers made it so.

Saasaren raises her chin high. She will not let Kientjen and the others see her fear. Icestar vanquished Iceshatter once before. One way or another, she will find a way for it to happen again.

To her relief, Kientjen hesitates. The others press close but he waves them back. "My choice!"

Dondije presses even closer. Kientjen shoves him back. Dondije leaps for Kientjen. Kientjen catches Dondije in the chest with the tip of Iceshatter's sharp pick. Ranimak and Wewivek move warily closer, lying in wait.

"Yield!" Kientjen roars at Dondije.

Dondije howls defiance.

"Yield!" Kientjen roars again.

Dondije tries to rise. Kientjen raises Iceshatter high. Red lights play up and down the ice axe's head and shaft as he brings it down hard on Dondije's head, howling curses.

Saasaren shivers as Iceshatter glows bright red. The red glow washes over Kientjen as Dondije crumples and fades.

It's the true death this time for Dondije. More than Icestar, Iceshatter seeks souls and power. She can control what Icestar does. None of Iceshatter's wielders have been able to control it.

Bleakly, Saasaren considers her prospects. Disarming Iceshatter had taken all of her power before. She's not certain she has the strength to break it again. Still, Kientjen is newly come to power. She might possibly prevail.

But it would cost time, and weaken her for what Callan needs. There must be a better way.

The glow slowly fades. Kientjen straightens up, his twisted body straightening. When Ranimak and Wewivek press close, he raises Iceshatter to stop them.

"Swear," he rumbles in a voice deeper than she's ever heard Kientjen use. "Swear to me as your King of the Snows."

They hesitate. She sees her chance and steps forward, but Kientjen is quicker.

"Do not interfere!" he snarls at her. "I'll deal with you next!" He kicks Ranimak away from Dondije's crumpled body. "Swear, damn you! Swear, or you'll suffer his fate!"

Ranimak and Wewivek drop to their knees. Saasaren hears their voices but not the words. All is lost. They're not *her* Court any more, but Kientjen's. She's wakened to a new servitude. She drops her head, staring at Icestar. Wonders what it would feel like to give herself to Icestar again. She did it before this last sleep, when she had shattered her world so thoroughly that there was no other choice. *I cannot choose that. It weakens not just the Snows but the powers of Rust and Flame.*

"Not yet," Kientjen tells them, before they fall upon Dondije's carcass. "Swear to *her.* Just like you swore to me."

When they hesitate, he shakes Iceshatter at them.

"*Swear!* On your knees to your Queen, damn it! Swear your puny lives to her!"

Saasaren jerks her head up. Iceshatter's wielder has never acknowledged her as Queen before.

"*Swear,*" Kientjen commands again, voice trembling slightly. "Crawl on your knees to her and *swear,* damn it!"

Not believing what she hears, she extends Icestar as Ranimak and Wewivek crawl through the bloodied snow to her. They swear to serve her, then kiss Icestar's blade.

I should have made Kientjen kiss the blade, she

thinks. *A stronger binding.* She'd been foolish and far too trusting. She should have listened to Callan's warning.

"He is yours," Kientjen says to Ranimak and Wewivek. "Leave no trace. Of him or of the other."

The two cautiously back away from Kientjen and Saasaren before falling first upon Dondije. Once they've settled on squabbling over Dondije's carcass, Kientjen turns to Saasaren.

"What do you want from me?" she asks.

"To walk by your side as your King of the Snows."

She can't find words to answer. The wind twirls idly, wrapping them in a snow-laden embrace.

Kientjen caresses her cheek. "I want to walk by your side," he repeats. "I want to be your King of the Snows."

"I," Her throat tightens and she can't say any more.

Why is Kientjen different from Iceshatter's other wielders?

"*Saasaren,*" he breathes. "Share with me." He pulls off his glove and strokes her cheek with bare fingers. His fingertips tremble on her lips. His eyes plead for a response. Deep inside of her, emotion stirs, something akin to what she felt for someone long forgotten in her eras of sleeping and waking.

"Saasaren. Please. This new world requires both of us to face what Callan needs." His new face is the dark gray of juniper bark. His green-gray eyes reveal a deeper knowledge than the old Kientjen. Somehow he has become even more himself, darker and more skilled than the Kientjen she has known. *Iceshatter or something else?*

Saasaren looks at Iceshatter. It will betray both of them, not just her. Without Iceshatter's presence, she would have made Kientjen kiss the blade on his vowing.

"How do I know you can control it? Iceshatter is deceitful and destructive."

Kientjen swears softly. Sheathes Iceshatter. Steps close to her. Ignores Icestar in her hand. Puts both hands on her shoulders.

"I've put it away, Saasaren. I am its master."

"For now," she whispers.

"*I need your help,* Saasaren. I can control it for now. But I can't do it alone. Share with me."

"Why should I trust you?"

His hands cup her cheeks.

"Because I have loved you from my first awareness," he says. "I have loved you since Icestar's tip called me forth. I have watched as Iceshatter's wielders tried to destroy you as it devoured them. I knew it would be different if I were the one carrying it. And when Iceshatter came to me," he shivers, "I knew this was my moment. But oh, Saasaren, I can't do as they did."

"In time you will."

"*I will not.*" He picks up her hand holding Icestar and raises it between them. "I will not follow the path of Iceshatter's predecessors. I will be its master. I will not betray you."

"So you say now."

He kneels. "Of my own free will," he whispers. "*Of my own free will.* Iceshatter acknowledges Icestar." He touches his lips to Icestar's blade. Icestar quivers but does not seek his heart. Power goes forth from her, sealing him. He releases her hand, quivering.

She trembles with him. Carefully, without looking, Saasaren sheaths Icestar. Kientjen is the first master of Iceshatter to say he loved her. The first to offer himself to Icestar.

I will have to yield to Iceshatter. She in turn will have to kneel to Kientjen, to have Icestar acknowledge Iceshatter.

Kientjen watches her, gray-green eyes steady. She looks into his depths and sees only love and a determination to win her. No previous wielder of Iceshatter has asked for this union. None have asked for her aid in mastering it.

Saasaren bows, then kneels. "Bring forth Iceshatter," she says through the dread choking her throat.

Iceshatter strains briefly toward her as Kientjen unstraps it. He growls and it quivers, then yields.

"*Of my own free will,*" she whispers, and kisses the axe. It twitches but does not seek to devour.

Kientjen sheathes Iceshatter and drops to his knees. He wraps his arms around Saasaren. She yields to his kisses. They are in their own world of ice and snow as she fiercely takes possession of his lips.

It has been a long time since Saasaren has drunk so deeply of another's heart, and never before has she let another drink of hers.

* * *

Saasaren comes back to herself in Kientjen's arms. Ranimak and Wewivek stand guard over them, Ranimak at their head, Wewivek at their feet.

Callan, she remembers, with a start. *I promised*

Callan.

"We must go," Saasaren tells Kientjen. "Callan called me from my sleep. There is need."

"I know," Kientjen says. "Icestar spoke to me. The foundations of Rust and Flame tremble, and if they fall, we fall, too. We must go. Together."

She summons up a snow-laden wind and pulls on her skis. Kientjen and the others strap back into their snowboards. With a cry, she pushes off, Kientjen at her side, the others behind them. They scream with the wind as they twist through the canyons. As they ride the storm, a fierce joy fills Saasaren.

Whatever happens, this time she will not be facing her fate alone.

She hopes it will remain that way.

Joyce Reynolds-Ward has been called "the best writer I've never heard of" by one reviewer. Her work includes themes of high-stakes family and political conflict, physical and digital cloning, personal agency and control, realistic strong women, and (whenever possible) horses.

She is the author of The Netwalk Sequence series, the Goddess's Honor series, and the recently released The Martiniere Legacy series as well as standalones Klone's Stronghold and Alien Savvy. Her most recent work, Justine Fixes Everything: Reflections on Mortality comes out on October 15, 2021.

Joyce is a Self-Published Fantasy Blog Off Semifinalist, a Writers of the Future Semi-finalist, and an Anthology Builder Finalist. She is the Secretary of the Northwest Independent Writers Association and a member of Soroptimists International.

LONG MEG AND THE
SORCERER'S STONES

M. J. Weatherall

How pleasant it is to feel the gentle pattering of cool rain, feel its power as it trickles lazily through every crevice, washing away the grime and cleansing your soul. I always appreciate it when it comes. Today is no different; I drink it in urgently.

The wind whips and howls around the moorland hill I stand upon, its primal force battering my rough exterior to no avail. The warm layer of moss and lichen creeps further across my surface, built up thicker and thicker with each passing year of inactivity and stillness. The perfect winter coat.

I watch the world go by, seasons slipping into each other with ease. Here I am unencumbered by time or responsibility – mere social constructs designed to give the illusion of worth. I could complain of loneliness but

I am constantly surrounded by my sisters and our joint consciousness.

It is winter now and the precipitation turns from rain to sleet interchangeably as the temperature drops and the heavens open above us. There is something magical about the way the snowflakes dance towards the ground, each one unique, each one only existing briefly before changing again - either melting or fusing with others to create something bigger and more intricate than themselves. I have had a lot of time to observe and marvel at nature's wonders but snowflakes are one thing that I have always admired, their time fleeting but perpetually beautiful.

It can be widely agreed that rocks don't talk. Some may scream and reek of history but that's just cosmetic. You have no idea what it feels like to be trapped, voiceless, frozen in time, forever living but never really living.

Or maybe you do. I don't know you.

The first few hundred years were relaxing, there with my sisters just chatting and coming up with new games or stories. *I spy* was banned after a while. I had time to come up with a detailed account of what happened that night and the events that set it all in motion.

As our life forces were strung together we no longer had secrets and I could piece together the whole story. While Meg was the most powerful amongst us in the thirteenth century her power was severely depleted in her last-ditch attempt to save the coven from the villainous sorcerer responsible for our eternal imprisonment. Her sacrifice bound us to the stones once our earthly bodies were vaporised.

It is often said that *hell knows no fury like a woman*

292

scorned but I don't agree. When a man doesn't get what he wants he, historically, would rather destroy it.

For this to make sense I'll recount what happened. Maybe *you* can see what our coven failed to foresee.

It was the day of the winter solstice and our coven was out in full force on the moors, at the sacred site where we complete our rituals. Our coven leader – or mother as some referred to her – was Long Meg. A fiery ginger beauty, tall and elegant. She was barely my senior and by no means the oldest woman in the coven but she was the most powerful by a considerable stretch.

It was because of Meg's beauty and power that the sorcerer was drawn to us; he desired her. Who didn't? She was, of course, intrigued by the attention of the accomplished sorcerer, and for a while allowed him to pursue entanglements with her.

Until he wanted more.

He wanted to take her as his wife. To most thirteenth century women this would have been an honour and a privilege. But Meg wouldn't enter into such a contract – being his subordinate, his personal property until the day she died. He saw this as a flirtatious challenge at first and tried to win her over, for she was the strongest and most beautiful woman for miles around.

Not only was his proposal laughed at by the coven, it was fundamentally against our code. We chose to take only lovers without being involved in continuing our line. You may think this a great feat - taking lovers and not producing any children – but I can tell you now that not all lovers are men and not all women are fertile. Magic comes at a cost after all.

It was bitterly cold on the day he came, even for the north of England: the kind of dry coldness that keeps the snow on the ground for weeks after it falls. Our ritual depicts that we are unclothed to feel the full power of the moon's rays, so we began shedding our garments like we shed the responsibility of upholding social normalcy by joining the coven, letting them drop onto the dry, crispy snow with a raspy thud. The slight breeze ruffled the golden hairs that lay in vast swathes upon my skin. I shivered instinctively, partly from the change in the air temperature around my skin but also partly from excitement.

It was the day we renewed our powers and felt the surge granted to us from the dark mother Hecate. The winter solstice provides the longest window of moonlight in the year, which is why it was perfect for charging our powers.

It was the time we were the most vulnerable and consequently the most wary.

There were scores of witches, all with nearly empty tanks of magic, gathered on the hill that evening waiting for the sun to set so that our ritual could begin.

It was part of the tradition to have a majestic bonfire, hot enough to warm our naked bodies while they lie unmoving through the night. Even though it was still early the fire had begun to burn, melting the surrounding snow and causing it to run freely down the hillside, witches gathered near to stare into the welcoming flames. It had been a cold winter so far and we had all seen the signs - it was due to get much worse. The sky had been clear and cloudless for weeks and the berries on the trees were abundant, Mother Nature's way of sparing some of her children from the starvation of a harsh and desolate winter, no doubt.

Meg sat alone, red hair tumbled like a cloak around her shoulders, staring across the fields and hills wistfully, somewhat removed from the group. I crossed to her silently.

"What troubles you?" I inquired, laying a comforting hand on her head, stroking the strands of fire from her face. Meg looked up in surprise and the breath caught in her throat. She'd been whispering an incantation. But why? She saw the revelation dawn on my face and dragged me down beside her roughly.

She began to speak but she stopped and dropped her gaze to the crisp, dying grass poking out of the snow around the rock she perched upon, deep in thought. I'd never seen her so defeated before, so I took her slender chin in my hand and lifted her gaze gently to mine.

"Meg, what is it?" I asked again, with a slight force to my tone this time. My urgency roused her.

"I am with child." She said it in barely a whisper, as if speaking the words would condemn her. I looked from her pondweed green eyes to her stomach. It was then that I noticed the witch hadn't stripped off her clothes with the rest of us and was still wearing a baggy dress of midnight black. I was alarmed that I hadn't noticed it before, blaming the cascade of red hair engulfing her shoulders.

I rested my hand on her knee supportively and thought about my next words carefully.

"The others will notice." It sounded more like a question than I intended. Meg nodded glumly. I traced a path up from her knee to her thigh delicately then laid my hand gently on her stomach, feeling the swell beneath my fingertips.

I sighed sadly. There were only two ways this could have gone. Meg would no longer be our leader if this got out, and there was no way she could pass by the night in the present company without being found out and ultimately banished.

"You wish to keep it?"

"I know not what I wish for," she replied scornfully. My fingers twitched away at the harshness of her tone. She immediately softened and took my hand in hers, stroking gentle circles on my palm by way of an apology.

"We can go away," I suggested. "Start a new coven, with new rules." Giddiness rose in her expression, and that spark of defiance that usually glinted in her green eyes returned to push her flash of sadness back into the depths, if only for a moment.

She leaned her head towards mine, slowly at first, looking from my eyes to my mouth hungrily. So close I could count every eyelash, but I didn't waste the time.

I closed the gap, my mouth landing on hers with a firm, desperate pressure. She tasted like apples, fresh and sweet. Her soft hands sent a shiver up my spine as her fingertips lightly brushed across my bare skin with no hint of apprehension. We breathed each other in through panted breaths, entwined our tongues, pressed our bodies close, gripped any flesh we could reach.

She pushed me over onto my back. The snow felt rough and abrasively cold against my naked body. She pinned me with her weight in one fluid movement, her mouth only leaving mine to emit a throaty laugh at my breathless moan, muffled by her mouth.

She had me right where she wanted me. She was the coven leader; who was I to deny her such pleasures? Her body pressed mine, unresistingly, further indenting the patch of snow, slipping her legs between mine so we became a knot of limbs.

She gathered my hands and pinned them behind my head with the weight of one of her strong arms, leaning over me, her hair a thick curtain blocking out the rest of the world.

I was completely at her behest. I didn't think much of it in the heat of the moment, my brain so rushed with other thoughts that I had no room for suspicion.

Meg's other hand teased its way around my midriff, toying with me. Her mouth left mine and worked its way along my jaw and down my throat, kissing and nipping playfully. I couldn't help but think of the life growing inside her; the swollen lump was more noticeable now her body pressed onto mine. I couldn't help but think about how it was the result of her entanglement with another.

"Hey," Meg broke my thoughts with her raspy voice and fixed, glowing stare, "Not going shy on me now, are you?"

"No, of course not." I grinned, tipping my head back to line my face up with hers, laying a fleeting peck on her full lips.

Now I was the one teasing, leaving longer between the kisses, building the tension until it was unbearable, not being able to wait any longer before her mouth came down clumsily on mine, teeth clattering and tongues intertwining gracelessly.

The taste of copper filled my mouth, contrasting in an ugly way with the fresh coldness of Meg's lips. Like a refreshing spring now tainted with the product of my split lip.

I winced at the sudden pain and drew back.

Meg took a sharp intake of breath, deeply, filling her lungs. She raised her thumb to wipe the liquid from my lips. I watched her move painstakingly slow with a strange, almost mesmerised expression on her angelic features. The pad of her thumb tickled my lip with the lightest of touches, relieving me of the offending liquid.

"I'm sorry," she breathed.

"It's nothing." I replied, not knowing that it was just the pretence of her apology. She covered my eyes with her free hand and began chanting an incantation, low and guttural, into my ear. Her warm breath was the last thing I remembered, for I was unconscious in seconds.

A blood-fuelled spell, spilt by a lover on the evening of a lunar event. Powerful magic.

* * *

I awoke sometime later.

Meg had disappeared but not before she threw a cloak over my exposed flesh. *It's too late to save me the embarrassment,* I thought. I couldn't fathom what had happened but my heart ached with betrayal nonetheless.

When I looked around the moor it was dusk. The wavering light caused my eyes to focus and unfocus constantly. Witches were milling around comfortably, catching up, swapping recipes and incantations freely. None of them had noticed that their fearless leader had abandoned them.

I stood up shakily, still feeling the magic slowing my brain and dulling my senses, before wrapping myself up tightly in the cloak and wandering into the thick of the discussions. The intense cold had time to seep into my bones in the time I'd been removed from the thick of the group and the raging bonfire we built to keep us warm.

No sign of Meg's bright red hair. I pushed on through, no doubt looking like a drunk with my glassy expression and clumsy movements, but I didn't care about that – there would be time to explain my countenance later, once Meg was found.

From what I've managed to glean from the memories of others whilst being stuck in our perpetual slumber party, what happened next was both diabolically anticlimactic but also impeccably well timed and – I cringe at the word normally but for this it is fitting – lucky.

The lunar gathering at winter solstice usually involved bathing in the moon's rays whilst chanting naked, laying on the ground with palms facing the sky. A sight to behold: scores of witches of all different shapes, sizes and colours, confident and proud.

The atmosphere was electric despite the lack of magic in each individual witch. It tingled excitedly on my skin.

I'd circled the whole of the group twice and could see no sign of Meg anywhere. Panic rose in my throat. The coven leader was missing during one of the most important events of the coven's calendar.

That was when I heard raised voices over the brow of the hill. I pulled the thick cloak even closer around me and strained my ears, not wanting to get any closer in case I betrayed my position.

"What have you done?"

"The right thing."

"You had no right! How dare you not consult me..."

"Consult you?" Meg's voice was shrill and thick with emotion, "It's my body! My life!"

"You have no idea what you have cost me." A male voice carried on the wind.

"Leave now and I will have no reason to call my sisters."

"I have more power in my pinky than the dregs of your coven combined," he scoffed.

I edged closer, sensing the shouting part was over.

"Leave," Meg said again with more force. I could feel the tensions rise, the magic in the atmosphere charged with negative energy.

"Fine. But I'll be back once I've thought of a suitable punishment."

That was the last I heard of the sorcerer's conversation. I waited a while longer until I could no longer hear the man's footsteps rustling on the crunchy white powder.

Meg let out a muffled sob. I was still angry at her for sedating me and using my blood for her dark magic but hearing her heartbroken sobs changed my feelings somewhat.

"Meg," I called gently into the darkness, stepping carefully down the decline with small, sure steps, careful not to slip on the icy hillside. The sobbing ceased almost immediately. I followed the sound of the unsuccessfully muffled sniffles until I reached her. She smiled at me sadly, once my vision adjusted to the darkness away from the fire, and I saw her green eyes swim with emotion and reflect the dancing light from the fire.

"Hey," she said apologetically, her voice soft and steady now.

I reached my hand out to touch her stomach, the feeling of new life no longer radiated from the swell. I knew that she'd needed my blood for some dark magic. I hoped it was to curse the sorcerer, but it made more sense to purge the baby since it would take less magic to do so.

I just stood there with my hand on her stomach not saying anything for what felt like an eternity, mourning the life that would have been.

"Say something, please," she begged.

"Why?"

"I couldn't bear to leave the coven. I hadn't even thought of it until you bled. It was an impulsive decision."

"You used me to murder your unborn child."

"It was a kindness! The child wouldn't have had a good life. The child of two powerful sorcerers wouldn't be healthy – the potential for evil would be too great. How could I knowingly bring that into the world?"

"What if... what if... what if..." I whispered, angry once again.

"I know you don't approve but what was I supposed to do? It's the coven's rules, not mine!"

"It shouldn't have gotten that far! Others take measures to prevent it."

"Sometimes it's not that simple."

"I know. I'm just angry you sedated me, didn't confide in me, *used* me. I would have willingly helped you if you'd asked. You know that?"

"I know you would have but...I needed to do this on my own." She lifted her hand up to stroke my cheek. I couldn't resist; I leaned into it sheepishly. She pulled me into an embrace, wrapping her long, strong arms around me protectively. I was thankful for the heat she emitted, so I collapsed into her completely. The top of my head barely grazed her nose, the perfect level for her to plant a lingering kiss on my forehead.

"We have a ritual to complete," she said after a peaceful moment, the argument well and truly out of our systems.

"I cannot wait for my magic to be restored."

"Not long now."

Hand-in-hand we walked to the fireside, the rest of the coven eagerly awaiting the return of their leader. None of them suspected the sorcerer's involvement – from the approving looks they gave me upon our return they assumed the nature of our relationship. I blushed and joined the circle around the roaring fire.

"Sisters!" Meg bellowed. "Tonight is the night we have been dreaming of for weeks, the night that we feel the magic rushing through our veins. A night of rebirth, relief and rejoicing!"

Calls of agreement went out amongst the gathered women.

"The dark mother smiles on us tonight, my sisters. Bask in her light and join me in worship."

"The dark mother smiles on *you*," the witches chanted back in unison.

The witches joined hands and began chanting the well-known restoration incantation, eyes closed, faces turned up to the moon which was now full and beaming.

Darkness had fallen quickly on the moor and nothing could be seen outside the circle of witches; the night was too close, darkness couldn't penetrate it. Moonlight and firelight bounced off the pale winter skin of the gathered women.

I chanted alongside the others, soaking in the powerful rays, letting it seep through the thin layers of my skin and energise me, saturating my cells. In those few moments our lives were merged we had the opportunity to see into each other's souls, feeling their deepest fears, most painful regrets and heart-wrenching guilt.

I probed along the line, searching for Meg's lifeforce. She must have had enough magic left to shield the recent painful event from her immediate impression. I tried to do the same but, unlike Meg, my emotions ruled me and were constantly bubbling at the surface.

The next stage of the ritual involved everyone laying down with their palms facing the sky. The fire had dried and warmed the ground beneath us pleasantly, no longer wrapped in the snow's icy embrace. The coven leader would send us into a coma-like state, an out-of-body experience like no other, where we are reminded of our earthly vessels and their role in our day-to-day lives.

Meg had made her way around slowly. I opened my eyes to meet hers before she did me, my heart quickening at her approach – still reeling from being sedated against my will to have my blood stolen for her dark spell.

Showing un-leader-like favouritism, she stooped

down over me and brushed her lips against mine briefly. A sign of apology? Love? All I know is that she was asking me to trust her. I closed my eyes and forced my breathing to slow, knowing the experience wouldn't be pleasant if I wasn't comfortable.

With a light touch on the forehead my soul was free of my body.

Floating above our pale, naked hosts we soared contentedly, the aura of our collective consciousness pale green and quiet.

Once Meg joined us in the spectral realm we began the next stage. Almost immediately after she vacated her body we felt a strong presence disturb our circle on the ground, breaking the protective enchantments surrounding our empty bodies like a straw padlock.

Intruder, one of us called. We all looked down, searching for the intruder in the midst of our lifeless bodies. It was the sorcerer, his dark robes a beacon of terror against the pure whiteness of the snow-covered landscape. Meg's presence prickled angrily.

Let me deal with this, she announced authoritatively.

Before anyone could protest we saw her body rise like a reanimated corpse on the ground beneath us. She spoke calmly to the sorcerer, who apparently wasn't in the mood for chatting. He closed his eyes, extended his fingers outwards with his palms facing down, spitting his incantation at Meg.

Time stopped.

Literally froze around us. At first we didn't see how this would affect us, being outside of our bodies at the moment of the time stoppage.

In unison we attempted to follow Meg, to reclaim

our bodies and protect our coven.

But we couldn't return. It was as if we had been locked out, unable to pass through the barrier in time. Confusion and panic spread throughout the ranks of disembodied witches.

What's happening?

Why can't we get back?

Who is the sorcerer?

Meg!

I analysed the situation, quickly realising that there was nothing we could do. It was all down to Meg - limited in power - up against a sorcerer that sliced through our protective spells like they were butter.

We watched intently as Meg fought the time spell around her, refusing to let her body succumb to the stiffness creeping up her limbs.

"Let them go!" Meg cried. "They aren't a part of this."

"You chose them over me," the sorcerer spat. "Over my baby, over *us!* This is your punishment, Meg. I'm going to wipe them off the face of the earth - obliterate their bodies so that there is nothing left to remember them by."

"You bastard." Tears were streaming down Meg's freckled face as she fought her way to him.

"You brought this on yourself. There's nothing you can say or do to change my mind."

A storm was brewing. Electricity sparked in the air around us, dark clouds seeming to appear from nowhere to block out the light from the moon and cutting off the source of our power indefinitely.

Panic flashed over Meg's face for a split second. Her fingers twitched almost unnoticeably in the dark. Her vivid eyes flashed.

Casting spells without saying the incantation out loud was something only a handful of sorcerers over the course of history had ever managed. I wasn't sure Meg could do it 'til that moment.

Thunder cracked overhead and the dark clouds threatened to burst, circling malevolently with the sorcerer in its eye.

The sorcerer made the mistake of underestimating Meg again. He wanted to goad her one more time; to gloat before he destroyed the people she cared for.

I watched with my heart in my mouth as the earth beneath the sorcerer opened up and swallowed him whole. But not before he cast his final spell.

From where we were it looked like a scorchingly dry fire pumped out of the hole and spread mercilessly across the ground, filling the area where time had stopped like a liquid. It was as if a transparent dome had been dropped over the coven's gathering.

We watched as our bodies were eviscerated, leaving distinguishably thicker black scorch marks on the ground atop the burning blades of grass, sizzling and evaporating the layers of snow all around.

A strangled cry escaped me.

Meg battled against the flames. We all prayed that she had some idea up her sleeve to save us.

Sisters, lend your strength to Meg. She needs it if she has any chance to save us! I called into the air, vibrating through each soul, rippling the message through our ranks.

We rushed down to our leader and surrounded her mortal form with our spectral ones as if that would be enough to keep the flames at bay. Bolstered by our support, Meg fought harder, feeding off what little magic we had left.

* * *

Without being tied to the stones our souls would have roamed the earth until we no longer remembered who we were, just empty, floating, ghostly husks - devoid of purpose.

Meg called the stones up from the ground, and we watched them erupt out of the earth's surface and rush up to encase us, holding us tight forever more, replacing our fleshy bodies.

The stones stand to this day, frozen in the protective circle we made around our coven leader, a constant reminder of a battle lost. Of the greed of men. Of our sisterly bond.

What happened may not seem ideal but compared to the alternative it is a thousand times better.

The thought of forgetting myself was a fear I'd had throughout my life - seeing the elderly of the village forget the faces of their lovers and children; their memories, opinions, purpose and principles gone.

Meg used the last of her power to bind our souls to the stones. Barely having enough magic to join us, she's lain dormant since the event.

Naturally our story became a local legend. In the first few years some of our fellow witches from foreign covens came and tried to break the spell on the stones but without willing hosts for us to pilot, it was useless.

People have forgotten our existence yet we live on.

<u>M. J. Weatherall</u> is one of those people who loves writing but always struggles to write about herself. She always feel like she's bragging (which in and of itself sounds like a brag according to her).

She is a young author from Sheffield who moved to the Lake District to get her BSc (Hons) degree in Outdoor Adventure and Environment. More recently she has qualified as a primary school teacher and is now fulfilling her calling as an educator.

M. J. loves climbing, kayaking and spending all her spare time in nature. A lifelong bookworm, she takes pride in growing her book knowledge (an asset to any pub quiz team to be sure!). She likes to think that she's a fun person to be around...at the very least, her cat seems to think so.

The Frost of Mercy

A. J. Van Belle

At the base of my oak, on a bed of decomposing leaves, Forsythia and I rest. My head is pillowed on her shoulder, hers against the bulge of a root. This is where I am home. In her arms I am warm in winter, where her care wraps around me and I am as snug as the seed-meat inside an acorn shell. My arm twines over her and we're two branches grown in tandem.

The day is brown and misty. The sweet scent of vegetation returning to earth mingles with the petroleum stench that wafts from the factories. I send my senses deep into our embrace, letting love and life force soak through my sister's body. I want to weep at the frailty I sense in her. Forsythia is only a few decades older than I am, and I thought we had plenty of time left together. But lately I've felt her slowing. Stagnation plagues her veins just as it does the trees.

She strokes my hair as she has not done since

Mother Cedar withered. "Entropy claims all forms in time."

I stiffen. "Don't say that."

"You've seen my elm. Half the branches didn't grow new leaves this summer." She croons the words, as if to a sapling afraid in the night. Of course I saw her elm. We said nothing of it aloud...until now.

Our small wood is hazy amber at dawn and smoke-marred bloody sky through bare branches at dusk. It is Spanish moss in thick hanks, so much so that you walk through curtains of it moving from one tree to the next. It is soil dry from drought one season; ankle-deep mud from torrential rains the next.

It is lonely. It is almost empty. Only we two remain.

We had other sisters. The last, Sylvia, left us not long ago. She went to the human world on a quest of revenge, and I no longer feel her on the air. But that is a story I don't wish to dwell on. Losses that have already happened are weak compared to the threat of losing another loved one.

"Azure," Forsythia says. When spoken in her voice my name is a drop of sweet sap. "It will be easier if you prepare yourself to let go."

Azure: a name plucked from the deep heartwood of Indo-European language roots. *Deeper than ocean is the sky.* I keep the web of time and water flowing through the xylem in my grove. The veins of all the nearby trees feel brittle to my mind's touch. The lace of clouds, tainted by smog, offers no solace.

It's winter in this curve of land along hot waters. Factories sprawl over the shores. Forsythia has been here ages and says it was not always thus. I have dim memories of brighter blue over branches but, as long as I have been alive and extending the feelers of my mind, reaching my thoughts past our grove leads me to concrete and the screaming corpses of ancient trees reduced to smoke. Their spirits never rest but become hungry ghosts, thin, spread out like fog, wondering what they forgot to remember.

When our trees grow old and die, we die with them. But Forsythia is not old. Her tree is not old. It wanes because our soils are depleted of nutrients, because our air is thick with poison from the factory smokestacks along the Gulf Coast. The festering waste of humans' pillage of the Earth is killing Forsythia's tree, and with it my only remaining sister.

But. *But.* There may be a way a dryad can live on after her tree dies.

From our shared dream-legends, from the twilight dream state we dryads access when merged with our trees and when linked to each other by zephyrs of thought, I know of a being older than the soil beneath my feet. This being is something like a dryad, perhaps. But not the same. Linked not to one tree but to the primeval essence of Forest that joins us all in the aether. In dream state, in visions of the distant past, I've seen her long fingers untwine the limbs of shadowy dryad spirits from the trees that birthed them. When those trees reached the end of their natural lifespans, those delicate deft fingers retied the dryads' spirits to new trees, young wood healthy enough to sustain them.

If common dryads such as Forsythia and me are each the spirit that animates one tree, Tilia is a living embodiment of the quantum stuff that underlies woods everywhere. She is not tied to one place, nor even one continent. She belongs to all the world.

But if my visions are real then she is one being with one body, and she can only be in one place at a time. If I can find that place, I can speak to her.

I close my eyes again, inhaling the heady damp-leaf scent of Forsythia's lovely hair. Everything goes golden behind my eyelids, and I drift into the aether on winter stillness inside my mind.

Cold replaces the musty alternating chill and dank warmth that is all the winter I've ever known. Tilia is somewhere Winter is a beast with crystal teeth and a freezing grip – one that lives where all remains white many months of the year.

I grip Forsythia's too-thin hand. The touch gives me strength, and I feel lines of energy running through the loam deep beneath my feet, a branch-pattern of invisible forethought and might-have-beens and could-bes that tell me where and how my path might cross with that of the ancient being, Tilia.

I feel the branching web travel through land only, not through an ocean. She's on my continent right now.

Forsythia presses her cheek to the top of my head, breaking my reverie. "Where have you gone, little sister?"

I open my eyes. The light is fading. In the twilight, early stars burn cold between clumps of Spanish moss overhead. I decide to tell her the truth, even though a sick twist in my gut tells me she won't approve. "Toward someone who might be able to help us." I choose to say *us*, not *you*, on a hunch she will be more likely to agree to let me go if she thinks of this as something *I* need. She won't let me take a leap of faith only on her behalf, I'm sure of that.

She stiffens, and her worry streams through me like light among tree trunks. "Show me," she whispers and presses her head against mine, reaching out with psychic tendrils in an invitation to share my thoughts and feelings and images with her. I let down my guard and allow her to see.

"Tilia," she breathes. "Maybe she's real. Maybe she's just something we all dreamed together." She sucks in a hard breath after saying "all," because we're not an "all," not anymore. We're a mere duo, and one of us is fading fast. "Either way, we let the others go when their times came. As it should be. I'm not different. Not special."

I squeeze her hand. "Of course you are. And you're all I have."

"No. You'll have to let me go when the time comes." She disentangles her fingers from mine. Disentangles the tendrils of her mind from mine, too. "Tell me the truth. If I say no, will you go anyway?"

I think a long moment. She can't stop me by force, but she has a strong will and may be able to convince me not to go if she puts her mind to it. Nevertheless, in the end, I decide once again that I won't lie to her. "Yes."

She climbs to her feet, more slowly than I would like, and paces away from me. The leaves don't rustle under the bark-like soles of her feet. She speaks with her back still toward me. "Then go if you must. Remember, though: these quests never end well in the legends." *Or in our experience.* She doesn't need to add that. Sylvia's departure and failure to return is an open wound for both of us.

"Legends aren't reality," I reply, nonsensically perhaps, given I'm about to travel an untold distance to chase a legend-in-the-flesh.

In two blinks Forsythia is back by my side, cuddling against me as if we're two little squirrelets huddling in a nest for warmth. The trees around us spread thought-forms over us like a blanket, and as pale violet darkness fades to deep indigo, we sleep.

In the yellow-gray morning I wake alone, though I still sense my sister nearby. And I know in my bones I won't take her advice to let her slip into death quietly. I wander through our grove until I find her. She sits on a rock at the edge of the stream, long brown legs hanging over the ragged edge of stone, curled brown toes dangling into the water. Her hair, the rich crimson of Spanish red oak leaves, flows over her shoulders like rivulets of blood. "Go if you're going," she says without looking at me. "The longer you delay, the less chance I'll make it until you get back."

I force my fingers into the deep grooves in the bark of the pine next to me, needing the pain to make me focus. "Don't say that."

She still doesn't look at me. "If I die before you return, you'll feel it. And you'll have to come back and manage by yourself."

"You won't," I say.

She bows her head and won't look at me. I retrace my steps to the young oak tree to which I am bound.

I press close to my oak and whisper the wordless desire to be one with it. Without movement and without a sound, it seems to sigh, and it lets me in. My body merges with my oak. Limbs become wood, beating heart becomes heartwood. Hair becomes filaments that conduct rainwater along the channels from root to twig.

For a moment, I enjoy. I become the pulse of the

oak, a rhythm slower than my heartbeat or breathing. Slower than my whole lifespan, the forest beats with a different kind of breath. This is pleasure and peace at once, surrendering individual body and spirit to oneness with the woods: a collective living being.

But a harsh rasp mars the breath of the woods. Not only Forsythia and her tree are ailing. The whole grove is weaker this year than last. We are all one.

And we are, slowly, dying. Not now. Not this season, or the next. Our decline is slow. Over the course of decades we will fade.

I can't stay. I share the thought with my oak, and I feel it sigh again. This time, the sigh is its way of letting me go. I send my awareness deep into our roots, down into the warm soil. There, tiny filaments, like threads of light, bind us to the physical world, giving us nutrients in exchange for the sugar we make. The mycelium in symbiotic partnership with us is bound to mycelium all over the continent. No one knows whether our partners could be considered one or many. They live outside the rules of individual versus group. Their consciousness blooms in an alternate dimension, even as their cells churn out the nitrogen and phosphorus we need to survive in this one.

With a focused stream of thought I tell them what I want from them. They answer by letting me pour my ethereal being into their vast network of hairlike cells. My physical body remains merged with the tree, but my awareness travels on the filaments of light. Through the warm earth, through our forest. Connected to human lawns and plantations. Going north. The soil grows chilly. The mycelium thins then grows thicker again as I travel ever northward, into colder lands less thick with humans. Into heavy northern woods. Then further north, and further, until the filaments are spiderwebs of ice in frozen soil.

She's so far away.

The mycelium does not answer in clear thoughts the way a tree might. But it answers in an echo of an echo of a feeling. One that holds something of bemusement. Something of superiority. Something I interpret, rightly or wrongly, as, *What do you expect, little dryad? That the world revolves around your neglected corner of the land?*

I find myself sprawled on a bed of snow. Even in wraith form I can feel the cold. I don't shiver – my body is far away and safe. But I feel numb and slow, taking in my surroundings one sense at a time. After feeling comes sight. I am in a thick wood, every tree bare and every twig coated in a thick layer of ice. This could be another world: a winter planet. But it is only the north of my own continent. I should feel at home.

I do not.

Next comes sound. My spirit-ears wake to this ice world at a crack that vibrates through me. Wood splinters and shards of ice rain down on me. Some bounce off my almost-there self, and some fall through me, and I tremble as bits of some strange tree travel through my spirit-heart and land in the snow, where I make no imprint on the whiteness. A few bits of ice stick in my almost-there hair, and I brush them out in an automatic gesture left over from being accustomed to having a body.

Soft footsteps crunch the snow somewhere behind me. "That should do it." The cheerful voice fills the cold air.

As my wraith-self, I sit up, a task that should be easy without a body but instead seems more difficult than usual. I turn, and the creature who treads lightly on the snow is so beautiful my almost-fingers and almost-toes tingle with fearful delight.

She is like a dryad in form and in the way she moves. But her skin is such a smooth beige she could be human, instead of a creature of rough bark. Her hair is a thick collection of ringlets and spirals of a deep, rich brown. Her eyes are a shade I've never seen – a blue that belongs to neither dryad nor human. And not to any animal of the wood. That shade of blue should belong only to the sky.

She meets my gaze and smiles, shining like the sun on snow, gorgeous and frightening in its cold. I sense in her the strength of an underground stream and the power of an entire forest of trees. She holds up a finger before me. "One moment." The words are a shock of cold politeness, out of place in these wild woods. She dashes past me, and her huntress' path leads my gaze to a felled tree.

The tree is a young oak, one that would have had another two centuries to live. Pain at the senseless loss shoots through my chest. Tilia – it *is* Tilia, I know by feel, by long dream familiarity – kneels next to the thick trunk and pulls a long, pointed stick from the heartwood. She stands and turns to face me again, running her hands over the polished wooden spear with a satisfied look on her face.

"Did *you* do that?" I suppose it's a silly question. Her expression tells me the answer. But how could a wooden spear fell an oak? And *why?*

Tilia casts the spear aside and comes toward me. "A

strong intention goes a long way when it comes to splitting wood with wood. This tree is an offering. The humans nearby don't know it, but I have a pact with them that winds into their subconscious: as long as I supply them with prime lumber once in a while they won't clearcut my section of the forest. I travel the world, making this silent deal. A bargain made is a bargain kept, when I'm the bargain maker." She snorts. "What have *you* done to protect *your* wood lately, little sapling?"

I choke down my horror and disgust. "That's why I'm here. My friend – my sister. Her tree is dying."

Tilia places herself behind a network of branches and peeks at me between their ice-coated twig-web. "Well, isn't that her choice?"

"No!" It comes out more forcefully than I intend. I should cultivate kindness with this being, no matter what I think of her deals with the destroyers of the natural world.

"We choose our trees." Tilia strokes the ice-covered twigs that frame her face. "And they choose us. We choose, and we move on to two-legged freedom when we've drunk deeply enough of the sap." She kisses the ice, a sweet closed-lip peck, and I imagine the ice tasting sugary, like the frozen heart blood of a live oak, or the juices of crushed moss. But it is only frigid water, colorless, without nourishment to offer. "Then we let our bodies go when our tree's time is done. You think you're on a quest to save what you know. But we never freeze the past in place. You've sent your roots deep enough to know that truth, sapling. You're on a quest to find the thing you thought you couldn't know."

"You're not making sense," I mutter.

She goes on as if she hasn't heard me. "You've

come from such a murky, hot place. You're alone down there, now. The places of smog and muck are a lost cause." She smiles, lips perfect and pink, face as smooth as a child's. "You already know that."

This creature knows where I came from, everything about me. I feel smaller as if, impossibly, my wraith-skin fits too tightly for my sore spirit. "I'm not asking anyone to save the whole region. I'm only asking one thing. You know how to do it, to unbind a dryad from a dying tree and bind her to a healthy one. The legends say –"

"Legends say many things, my inaptly named green-brown Azure." I jump, and the corner of her mouth quirks with amusement. Of course she knows my name. Her long fingers trace crevices in the ice that covers the bark. The gesture seems too intimate for one to do with any tree but one's own – but then Tilia belongs to all trees, doesn't she, all and none and nothing between. "Legends say I'm ten feet tall. That I've been alive since before the dawn of tree-time, since the days when plants had no vascular systems." Her eyes narrow, merry and sinister at the same time. "But there is no such thing as a time before. Not for us."

"You're not like me," I say, throat tight, my almost-trachea freezing. "You're not a dryad. Are you?"

She tilts her head back and looks up at the sapphire sky beyond the lace-trimmed branches. "Where is the boundary between dryad and not-dryad? Have all your studies in the aether taught you that, little one?"

I blink, and her gaze is fixed on mine again, though I didn't see her move. She stands closer, too, seeming weightless. I wonder if her feet ever leave prints on the earth. The big blue eyes are the same color as the sky, and I feel I'm looking right through a mind as open and wide as the stratosphere, with thoughts not bound to earthly reality.

She takes my chin in her hand, and her touch feels broad, vague, her fingers of ice light on my numb skin. "Boundaries," she says. "They are soft. Permeable. Maybe they're not there at all, at least not where we think we see them."

"I don't understand." I don't shrink from her touch, but neither do I lean into it.

"What is *you*?" Her eyes dance with cold mirth. "And what is your tree? Where do you end and I begin? Where does the mycelium that nourishes your tree end and the one in symbiosis with another tree begin? These questions have no answers. We're clouds that float and change. Your sister will not pass away, child. Her life force may change its form, but energy cannot be destroyed."

My eyes ache as if crystal snowflake webs replace my wraith-corneas. "I want my sister. I don't want to lose her."

"You never will. She'll be mist in the air, a pulse in the heart of a cedar. And an elm. And an oak. All at once. Godhead. That is her destiny: to be one with the All. That is the aim for all of us in time." She chortles and shows a dimple. "Even for me. I wonder when."

"Can you," I ask, through teeth like shards of ice, "or can you not re-bond Forsythia to a new tree?"

Tilia wanders a few steps away from me. Did she not hear?

As I open my mouth to say some other awkward, pushing thing, she spins to face me, frost-lace curls flying about her face. "That depends on you." Her words sparkle like the sunlight on snow, and a chill goes all the way to my core. "It's not a power I have. But you do."

It's a flash of lightning in my mind, something more than a vision: a jolt of electricity through every part of me. Tilia dances back, sparks of knowledge in her eyes like midday sunlight glinting off a field of snow. "Haha," she says. "Now you see."

I don't. Not yet. The flash is still too strong, blinding me. But as I blink and let the brightness fade, I see the vague outlines of what she's shown me.

She does not untie souls from one tree and bind them to another. Not so easily as in my dream-vision. No, it takes tremendous energy to unbind a dryad from her tree. As much force as...as...

"Yes," Tilia croons lovingly, sensing me seeing the shape of it. "The force behind a whole life. Your entire being is enough to catalyze the transition. No less." She grins.

I can't feel anything. "I would have to give my life?"

She strokes the ice that coats a branch. Rivulets of water stream down the branch in the wake of her fingertips. "No! You have to transform your life. At the moment you're a dryad with pretty brown skin and autumn-gold hair. How lovely...and how common. Wouldn't you like to try a different form of existence? Be the fluff that carries a dandelion seed? Or the air current that lifts it?"

I still can't feel, but my voice comes out choked. "You're awfully casual about death."

She licks her lips with a cherry-red tongue. "Death is awfully casual about its business, my seedling. Why shouldn't I treat Death the same way it treats all life?"

I look down at the lines in my wraith-palms, echoes of the lines I know so well from my physical form. Where do these lines lead? I could give Forsythia what she wants by letting her go. She wants me to go on as the last spirit sustaining our woods.

Then the day will come when I am no more, when I am part of everything, and all that was green and growing has given way to stink and ruin. That is not the life I choose: standing alone to watch my world decline.

But if I give myself away to save Forsythia's life, I condemn *her* to that existence.

Tilia shrugs one perfect, smooth shoulder. "It's your choice. I have no hand in it. I'm only the bearer of good tidings, leafling."

"I thought you were – I thought you could –"

Her dangerous grin surfaces again. "Don't believe everything you see in your mind's eye. It *can* be done. Your vision told you that much. But I'm no goddess. I'm like you."

"Except...except that you're not bound to any one tree. I'm not wrong about that."

"I was," she croons. "I'm not anymore. How did I become unbound? I see the question in your leaf-green eyes, little one. But I won't answer. That's for you to find out for yourself."

Frustration bubbles in my wraith-chest, hot and sick, like the polluted Gulf waters off the coast of Texas. "I thought you would help me." The words come out clipped and bitter, and I squeeze my eyes shut. "But I guess I was wrong." I open my eyes again. She's gazing at me, serene, unconcerned. "Can't you tell me how?"

The mycelium seems to vibrate under my wraith-feet, a low hum that speaks to me in not-words. *Come home,* it seems to say. *You're needed.* I concentrate and listen. The hum grows stronger, warming my wraith-feet until they leave the faintest prints in the snow where I stand.

Tilia keeps her gaze fixed on my face and tilts her head to one side like an eager, listening dog.

Something more comes through the network in the soil that links me to my homeland, a message of pain and fear, small first and then growing, like a fiddlehead unfurling.

I wouldn't speak again to Tilia, this maddening, teasing witch of the woods. Except that she's staring at me, a knowing look on her face. Almost amused.

"I have to go," I mutter.

"Of course you do," she replies, her words fading as I send my selfhood back through the mycelium, back to the land of my birth.

In seconds I'm home with my oak, aware of my body joined with wood and my blood running one with the sap. A heavy layer of yellow-gray clouds shrouds the land. I separate from the tree trunk and pad across the bed of leaves on feet that now carry weight and make a rustling sound.

Forsythia lies on the forest floor, curled at the base of her elm, shivering, even though here in our home grove all is brown and warm. I wouldn't recognize her if it weren't for the fact that we're the only two dryads for miles and miles. She's thinner, her hair faded to a faint auburn. I kneel and slide one arm under the crook of her knees and the other under her shoulders. Without thinking I stand and cradle her to my chest. We were of a size, but she's dwindled in the short time I was gone, and she weighs little more than a dry branch.

"You're here." Her voice is twigs grating against each other in the wind. She presses her face against my shoulder. "I was afraid I wouldn't get to say goodbye."

I rest my cheek against the top of her head. Her hair is rough. "Of course I'm here." I'm younger, but I feel motherly. Protective. "Tilia told me nothing I didn't already know." That's not true, not exactly. But Forsythia doesn't have to know the awful choice Tilia gave me, nor that the ancient proto-dryad didn't tell me how to accomplish it anyway.

"I saw," Forsythia whispers as I hug her closer. "I saw through the aether. I merged with my tree to see more clearly."

So that's why she's faded so quickly. Becoming one with her dying tree drained the last dregs of life from her. I suck in a breath so it won't become a sob.

"Open to me," she whispers. "Let me show you what I saw." Her twig-like fingers grasp the sides of my face, and she touches her forehead to mine. I let her thoughts join with mine.

And see myself as from a distance, standing upon pristine snow, in conversation with Tilia. The sky sparkles a perfect blue overhead, just as it did when I was living this scene. But there's something I didn't see: behind me, among trees grown thick and twisted together, shadows writhe, merging and coming apart, licking toward me like flames and then retreating.

"What is that?" I ask, chest hollow.

"I don't know. But it's here, too. Or something like it. Don't look for it; *feel*."

I close my eyes and try to feel, but the weight of grief presses down on my chest. Forsythia goes limp in my arms. I hug her close and kiss her forehead, but she doesn't stir. I can't feel her ribs expand with her breath.

No.

I wait a long moment, and she breathes again. And again. Then another long moment before the next breath.

This is how it is at the end. Irregular. Life sputtering out.

The few brown leaves that cling to her elm tremble in an ominous breeze.

Please. I'll give anything. I'll give up the lives of every tree in our grove if it saves hers.

There's no time left for me to do what Tilia advised. She was right, I feel it now: I know how to do it. I only have to let myself go on the wind the way I let myself go when I traveled through the earth on the filaments of mycelium. Let the wind carry me to Forsythia, and let my love carry her spirit to bond with a new tree. But she's barely breathing now, and the pulse jumps in her throat only once every several seconds. She's almost gone. Wisps of her spirit rise from her body like steam, swirling away on the wind. They disperse. It's too late for me to catch them.

Thunder rolls. It's the wrong season for thunderstorms. Winter rains here are gentle, steady. Not electric. But the season of calm is not enough to stop the sky from cracking open with my anguish.

Another roll of thunder follows the first, traveling across the gray heavens from east to west. Shadows rise from the damp earth. They're hotter than the heavy Gulf

Coast air in summer, hotter even than the factory furnaces that belch smoke into the air along the shoreline. They lick my arms, leaving burn marks. Smoke rises from the soles of my feet.

Forsythia stirs in my arms at the rage of sky-sound. Her eyelids flutter. I hug her closer. Let the sky and the shadows destroy us both now, in her last moments. Let the angry world take me, too. I'm ready.

Lightning turns the clouds into a purple dome, together with a clap of thunder that makes my ears ring. The broad spark of electricity meets the elm and a column of white light connects the tree to the sky.

The wood splinters with a crack that rivals the thunder in its strength. The hot shadows rise up taller than I, as tall as a tree, and dance in faceless glee.

With a hiss and a crackle, Forsythia's elm goes up in flame.

I back up a step, still holding her to my chest. Her eyes flutter open, green irises reflecting the sudden orange blaze. Fire races along a dry branch and lights a neighboring tree on fire. And then another.

In seconds I stand in the center of a circle of flame. The mycelium under my feet gives off a hum that I feel through my soles, and cool mud submerges my feet. The trees I've known all my life burn as brightly as the sun.

Forsythia grows warmer and feels heavier in my arms. Her breathing becomes regular. She angles her legs toward the soil and I let her go so she drops lightly to her feet and stands at my side, one arm around my shoulders.

As the fire consumes the woods I recall my hasty

thought. *I'll give up the lives of every tree in our grove if it saves hers.* We watch until the flames die when there's nothing left to burn. By now the sky is a deep purple-black, starless and silent.

"Look." Forsythia tugs at me, and we turn together. Toward my oak. The one tree still alive, set apart from the blackened, smoking stumps. It stands tall, its limbs still vibrant. My tree is the only one left, incredibly, untouched by the blaze.

Together we walk slowly to the oak. We each place a palm on the bark and feel the energy flooding the trunk. The tree is bound with my life force and, now, Forsythia's as well. The two run together like eddies in a stream, crossing over, intertwining, dancing separate dances as inseparable parts of the same whole.

"Did *you* do this?" Forsythia asks me, eyes as green and vast as our charred stubble of a wood once was. She speaks in a wondering tone that tells me she expects no response.

I saved her. But at such cost. My reason for existing was to protect the trees that have become smoking ruins around me. Now, I have my sister for as long as my young oak lives. But our shared future lies ahead as a barren wasteland, with nothing here left to protect.

A bargain made is a bargain kept. The words echo in my mind. They feel like Tilia, with frost in her voice, laughing at me from all those miles away.

A. J. Van Belle is an author living in Massachusetts with their husband, teenage daughter, and two very personable dogs.

They write for teens and adults in multiple genres, including sci-fi, fantasy, horror, and contemporary lit fic. Across all genres, their work incorporates themes of trauma, healing, and a hint at something beyond the senses.

When not writing, A. J. works as a professor and researcher in biology. They often bring their scientific expertise to their fiction and have a blast using real knowledge of fungal ecology and evolutionary history to help build speculative worlds.

Check out their work at www.ajvanbelle.com.

WINTERCAST

R. A. Gerritse

Outcast

Looking back at the moment everything changed I mostly remember the silence of the place as the artist sat behind the piano. I'll never forget that fateful moment for Mr. Belton – poor, young, disillusioned, talentless Toby. Oh, how I felt I'd ruined his life that cold winter's day.

Since then I've learned that change, like all magic, requires perfect contrast in both moment and circumstance; like finding the light we so desperately seek in our darkest of seasons. Salvation in Winter's heart? I may not have recognized it at the time, but I've become a believer.

I can still picture Tobias and how he sat staring at the blank sheets meant for notes and lyrics in front of him for over an hour. Despite the venue's poor heating, apparent from his clockwork clouds of breath, he never even shivered.

Unsurprisingly, Tobias was oblivious to the half-dozen white-clad Sparks that drifted around him like snowflakes in a storm, surrounding him with an unseen flurry of activity. Some humans have always been able to see us – if only in a passing glance – but only those with genuine talent, in whom the dream lives strongest.

I marveled at the futility of my kin scurrying below. Even in the muted light coming through the snow-covered windows I could tell by poor Toby's soulless stare that his thoughts were probably as empty as his papers. However, unlike my brothers and sisters who gave Toby's inspiration their all, I knew and accepted that his candle held no flame and never would.

Not with a thousand Sparks. He would never brighten our world, nor even this auditorium.

As far as I could discern from the available clues in the dilapidated venue there wasn't anything unique or extraordinary about this particular musician. There was nothing noteworthy about the quality of his music nor the social significance of his works; at least, nothing entitling the young man to the significant amount of effort the Sparks were spending for his benefit. Then again, significance was not a particular prerequisite for the absurd scene before me. No, this futile waste of effort was the typical nonsense that I, a Spark myself, had to deal with every day of my existence.

You see, you can usually find us Sparks wherever tortured human artists seem in need of our self-appointed calling – to provide much-needed and visibly absent inspiration. This is a tradition as old as time itself, our elders say. Without us there would be no art, they say. No creation. We, so they claim, are the muses of destiny; the heralds of creativity; the voice of divine artistry.

Still, they can never explain why our efforts never seem to be appreciated, recognized, or even, well, noticed. I'd say that would make it quite unlikely we are the sparks of human inspiration, pun intended. What a farce.

It's been a long, long time since I called bullshit on the whole ritualized tradition and stepped aside to become the voice of skepticism at the sidelines on another, quite similar Winter night.

My kin, fond of their mass delusions, never forgave me, and I have been an outcast ever since. Still, as an outsider looking in, I have never had a single regret – not with all the free entertainment I've gotten in return. Some days it's hard to imagine that the surreal madness that formed the everyday existence of an average Spark used to be my birthright.

This particular fateful afternoon in the dim New York auditorium, my brethren - as usual, obsessively focused on their task - seemed clueless about my presence as I watched them from my hiding place on the balcony. With a grin from ear to ear, resting in the luxury of a left-behind bucket of popcorn, I enjoyed both the sweet scent of my sticky sofa and the show.

Two of the Sparks below, small as our kind is compared to the average human, had climbed on Tobias' right shoulder and stood softly humming an out-of-tune melody into his ear, their slender glowing forms perched like tiny guardian angels. They seemed unbothered by the knowledge that Toby would never be able to hear them – which, given their lack of musical prowess, in all fairness, was probably for the better.

Two different Sparks stood on Tobias' other shoulder, whispering what seemed to be random nonsensical rhyme words. The last two sat hunched over the virgin pieces of paper scattered across the top of the piano. One yelled instructions to his 'colleagues' on the shoulders, the other drew invisible letters on the blank paper with his finger, as if teaching the tortured artist how to write. The mere futility was highly amusing to watch.

I wished Sparks could eat so that I could have some of the popcorn in which I sat to complete the experience.

Look closely, Harold, I thought. *If this is our so-called 'glorious purpose,' be glad that you abandoned it.* Even though I never felt regret for turning my back on my kind's calling, deep down, the uselessness of it all still pained me. *Is this truly all there is to our existence? I refuse to accept that.*

It angered me to no extent that I seemed to be one of the few who could see the futility of it all and that I was the only one of the enlightened who actually stuck around. There had been others before me who had seen the truth but they never stayed. Maybe they felt it too painful watching our kin waste their existence. Maybe they left to chase some higher purpose I had yet to grasp. Maybe they lacked that little scrap of attachment to their heritage that I still seemed to have for reasons that even baffled me. Whatever their motivations to leave and never look back, it left me desolate and lonely.

Below, the two Sparks on top of the piano started pointing at random piano keys. "Idiots," I muttered. I must have spoken a little too loudly for, all of a sudden, I felt all eyes in the room except Tobias' bovine saucers turn my way, immersing me in a cold front of disapproval. *The show's over, I guess; it was fun while it lasted,* I snickered to myself. It was time to play my society-given role – the asshole. I rose from my bucket and swung my feet over the balcony railing, perching myself on the edge where all could see me, and gave my estranged kin a nice long slow round of applause.

"Great work, guys. Seriously. You are such shining examples of Sparkdom, such radiant muses. I bow to your gifts of inspiration. Just look at how much you've already accomplished here with young Tobias Belton. Good show."

If looks could kill – or Sparks could do harm, for that matter – I'd probably have toppled from the balcony right then and there and been maimed in, oh, probably six different horrifying ways. But it only egged me on. I know, I know. I've never been a particular saint, and my decades of solitude did not much help my bitterness. I did mention I became a bit of an asshole, right?

"The true artistry here is how you manage to magnify Toby's lack of talent," I said, laughing. "I mean, c'mon, look at the guy. He'll never amount to anything and you're just rubbing it in! Do you actually believe that your unfelt and unseen, incompetent meddling could ever make a difference? No matter how many off-key notes you whisper to him or how many piano keys you point at, you cannot Spark what is not here. You can dress him up in Christmas lights, and still he'll never shine. So why bother?"

As usual, as I'd seen a thousand times before that moment, my kin responded in their infuriatingly spineless, passive-aggressive way, which is how our kind have always handled outcasts like me. They turned away and ignored me, unaware of the irony of how much their action resembled how their chosen subject did not see *them*.

I grunted. I know. 'No regrets.' That's what I told you, and for the most part, it is true, but to be ghosted by your kin wherever you go still stings. Never enough to self-doubt, but more than plenty to despise, well, everything – yourself included.

It was a silent, slowly simmering resentment that had grown into a dark passenger over the decades of my banishment. For no apparent reason, this deep and bitter sense of discontentment chose this otherwise unremarkable moment in my existence to boil over. It released something so disturbing, so dark and ugly that it shaded the very room as it slipped from my lips and took an ominous, monstrous shape.

"He will never be anything more than a talentless loser."

A chill ran through me as the last word left my mouth, its echo cascading from the cracked plaster walls of the venue, set against a chorus of shocked gasps from the stage. I felt – actually *felt* – the moment that my words, like hungry predators racing towards their prey, reached Tobias and connected.

To my astonishment and utter horror – and to an even greater extent to the astonishment and horror of my kin – I'd been heard. By a human. Not with the prophesized words of inspiration our kind are supposed to deliver, but with the harsh and ugly detonation of a nuclear, unwelcome truth.

Two Sparks fainted, and all of them turned white as sheets. None, myself included, dared to breathe as we watched Tobias swallow hard, shiver, and hang his head. A single tear ran down his cheeks as he stood from the piano and, with defeated posture and step, exited stage right, without ever looking back.

"What did you do, Harold?" someone whispered behind me. Still in shock, I turned to find the Cardinal, the first of my people, staring at me with a grim look of disbelief and fear. "How could it be you, Harold? And, Allspark help us, how could it be so...dark?"

Then, something cold struck the back of my head and, with the sensation of a thousand lightning rods drowning out my consciousness, my world turned white as the snowy streets outside.

Catalyst

When I came to I found myself in the central square of our capital, bound to the frost-covered Tree of Life, stuck neck-deep in the only earthly material that can hold a Spark – resin. Night had fallen, and I sat alone in the heart of Sparkdom, without so much as a guard. Not that there was any need for one; I couldn't have escaped my transparent prison had I wished to waste the effort.

The thousand light decorations for Mid-Winterfest sparkled through my tear-filled lenses. From the base of the tree empty, snow-covered streets stretched and curved between the countless shuttered dwellings – like inverted silhouettes mirroring its darkened branches, reaching the furthest corners of the village.

In utter silence, the very night seemed to hold its breath.

What did I do? I marveled. *And how?* With complete disgust, I recalled the soul-chilling feeling that had come over me the moment I damned young Tobias with my unguided spite, derailing the mortal's destiny. *That was not supposed to happen. We're not supposed to actually have influence, are we?*

The consequences of my unintended gruesome act hit me like a freight train. For most of my existence, I'd rebelled against the very idea that we Sparks were even able to communicate with the human world. Not only had I been proven wrong, I felt like I might have doomed us all. Had I perverted the Spark gift with my selfish defiance, unknowingly releasing a new evil into the world?

"Faceless keeper of all Sparks, guide me through this heart of Winter. Tend to me so I may tend the light to earn my place in your night sky," I whispered, at the time unaware of the strangeness of these words or their origin, this apparent prayer – words no Spark had spoken before.

Ignorant of prophecy, I wallowed in the agony of my juvenile behavior and its dark repercussions until, at dawn's first light, the whole Council of nine elders finally came for me. Watching their white-robed forms and their procession of followers approach across the virgin snow on the town square, I felt empty, defeated, and damned. I'd gone over every bleak consequence of my apparent ability and was fully aware of the monster it made me. I was ready to accept any punishment. Never could I have foreseen what came next.

"The Council has discussed yesterday's revelations under the light of the Gods," the Cardinal spoke. "For several centuries Sparkdom knew of your coming, Catalyst. We knew that someday one would arise, a Wintercast, who could change the threads in the great weave of existence and bring balance. One who could recognize and redirect mortal purpose. We just never assumed..." The Cardinal swallowed and wiped his dry but reddened eyes. "Pardon our ignorance, Catalyst. Forgive us. Please forgive us!"

With a bowed head, the Cardinal sank to a knee in the snow. As the rest of the Council of elders followed his example, my resin prison dissolved.

"W - what?" was all I managed to stutter, still shaking on my feet from my sudden release after a full night of imprisonment.

The Cardinal looked up at me with eyes filled with existential fear. "We've been heretics, it seems," he said. "Please, pardon our ignorance. We should have listened."

"What should we do? What is our purpose?" A chorus of cries echoed behind him, and all eyes were on me – as if I would have any answers.

"D-don't do this to me!" I said, my voice trembling. I walked over to the Cardinal and tried to drag him to his feet but the ancient Spark wouldn't budge and kept deflecting my grip, deadset on groveling before me. "How should I know of any purpose?" I screamed at him and the rest of the cowering elders. "I've never believed in *any* predestination! And what in the Allspark's name is a Catalyst? Stop acting as if I'm some cursed chosen one! You had me confined, for crying out loud. It's just me, *Harold!* The outcast asshole, the thorn in your side, remember? The one you had to knock cold for ruining a poor human's life?" At that, the Cardinal found a fresh source of untapped tears somewhere deep in his heaving, frail body.

It took over two hours before all emotions, including mine, had settled enough for the Council and me to actually speak on the previous day's unparalleled events and their meaning. It required me to get a crash course in Spark mythology and history – something I'd avoided like the plague until that day.

You see, we Sparks do not have many things in common with mortals, be it humans or any other species. We have elders, but not parents – only Sparks who arrived before we did. We come into existence, but as far as we know, not through procreation or duplication. The birth of a Spark - or its casting, as we like to call it - is a blink, and we are here. At least a few of us arrive in every season – I was cast in Winter's heart. As far we know, none of us has yet departed. What shapes us then, you ask? That has ever been our mystery to solve but, as it turns out, there were clues. Nine, to be exact.

"What you are about to hear has never been shared outside the Council of Nine," the Cardinal said as he thoughtfully studied the countless twinkling lights of they who part the darkness: the Gods above. "We, whom you call the Council, were the first, back when humanity was still in its infancy. In fact, I believe I might have known the very first human, although her species still differed significantly from the wonderful bipeds we know and serve today."

"Back in humanity's Spring, Eve was a unique primate," he continued, "and the first of the lot bestowed with the first sparks of creativity and true practical and emotional intelligence. This was long before the birth of all the wonders that make humanity such a unique species like speech, art, and technology. But there *was* one: fire. Eve had knowledge of fire."

"The world is such a big place. How can you be sure that you were first?" I asked the Cardinal. "I can't imagine you scoured the Earth for that knowledge."

"There was no need," he said in a solemn tone. "For with my blink into existence – a Winter casting, like yours – came a message of sorts. A lesson to carry, to teach my future kind. There were no words per se, but it was a message of emotion; not a dictated meaning, but an implied purpose nonetheless. It named me. Not that I understood that at the time. It was not until eons later that I learned the meaning of my name – First." He frowned and offered me a sad smile. "It seems our greatest turning points all take place in Winter."

The Cardinal explained how many years after his casting, during a cold season when Eve's tribe had grown with several generations and were about to discover the wheel, the second elder joined him in existence, and Sparkdom was born. Each following Winter, another joined their number, but things changed after the birth of Ix, the Ninth spark.

"'I am the last,' were Ix's first words," the Cardinall recalled, and Ix, seated on the other side of the circle, nodded in confirmation. "'We are all here,' he said, and all nine of us knew it to be true. At that moment in time, Eve was no more, but her tribe thrived in industry, creativity, and invention. She had passed on her intelligence and her drive to excel onto her offspring, who in turn passed it on to theirs. With the coming of Ix we elders knew that, between us, we possessed full knowledge of our purpose and that we were meant to keep that purpose alive."

He rubbed his eyes and sighed. "Arrogant, blind fools as we've ever been, we must still have gotten some of it right, for it turned out we guessed correctly. After us many others followed, scattered across all seasons. Still, no other Sparks, even Wintercasts like us, seemed imbued with our sense of purpose upon their creation and thus all others started to look to us for guidance. Hence the Council of Nine was created."

"But there never were actual words of guidance, only

these...feelings, and instincts?" I asked him, trying to make eye contact, but the Cardinal kept his gaze on the ground. I found all this new knowledge confusing, contradictory, and hard to process. "Where then did you learn this title 'Catalyst' you give me? You say that your sense of purpose has always been merely emotional and instinctual - where then did your reading of our intended destiny as shepherds of human inspiration originate? Did you make all of that up?"

Dark looks passed between the nine elders. For a long time they remained silent. "After a long study of humanity, and the conditions in which new Sparks blinked into being, we realized that it was moments of unique creativity - specifically the birth of original ideas that had not been witnessed before - that sparked the creation of our kind. The moment we realized this correlation we knew it to hold our purpose. Then, as years progressed and human communication evolved into language, certain words and terms humanity used stood out to us. The moment they did, we knew them to hold meaning for our purpose. Inspiration. Catalyst. Weave. Pattern. Destiny. We know so many parts of the great puzzle, but as I now fear, we might have been wrong about its intended image."

"You've always told us that we are the source of human creativity, but now you tell me that it's the other way around - that their inventiveness is what created us? Why would you spread such a lie, Cardinal?" I looked at him and the others with disdain. "You arrogant zealots ruined my existence for so long; you banished me! And for what? Just because I felt something off in your tellings of our 'glorious purpose'?"

"What would you have had us tell you instead, Harold? That we knew we had a purpose but hadn't the

340

faintest what it entailed? What would that have done to your spirits? As you must have learned by now, a Spark without purpose is miserable..."

"I just know what living a lie did to my spirit... and how exile only worsened it. What happened yesterday... my outburst...the darkness I let slip into the world, you awakened that in me – I was not born with it. If indeed I am this Catalyst, as you name it, then it was you nine who turned my purpose into a dark one."

"Don't you dare put that blame on us, Harold!" the Cardinal spat at me, startling me with an unexpected out-of-character burst of anger. "You were always the bitter one, the skeptical one – the one who went against the grain, just to spite us."

"It is true. I've always gone against the current, but never to spite you, Cardinal. I saw the river and knew it to flow in an unintended direction."

The Cardinal paled, started trembling, and fell silent. When he found his voice again it was but a whisper. "Then it seems we were not far off when naming you at your casting all those Winter moons ago, Harold, but two letters. You are our Herald."

Weaver

I've known so many names in my short and mostly miserable existence. Harold was my first. Over the years I have learned that my name means 'strong.' It means 'a fighter.' These meanings always fill me with a deep sense of melancholy. For I have fought, and I've always felt that need to be strong, hold on to my convictions, and carry on. Might the elders have seen that stubbornness in me from the very start, that cold Winter morning of my casting? They may well have.

For the longest time, those convictions are what gave me my second name: Outcast. Being different, my alternate worldview, my disconnected sense of our reality and purpose set me apart from the rest of my kind, and they resented me for it. It's been an essential part of my journey, for only on the outside can you see the whole, as lonely and bitter as it left me. Destiny is a cruel master.

My third name, Catalyst, my prophesized title, foretold my awakening. Not my blink into existence, no. My awakening required observation through my years of misery, without which I could not have changed the course of my species' evolution, and through it, that of humanity. It made me the Herald of what was to come, our true purpose.

Only if one sees the pattern can one recognize the odd strings that stick out - the strands that are not in their proper place and distort the whole fabric. Only once one acknowledges the dissonance can one work towards harmony.

We Sparks, born from human ingenuity and creativity, we fruits of your creation, are the bookmarks of your greatest moments - like the Gods above we are the light at year's end, the flickers of hope that light the path ahead. We are not here to inspire but merely to help those who got misplaced in the fabric of creation - the tortured, the tired, the uninspired - and guide them to their intended place in the great weave.

That fateful Winter night on the night of my awakening, Tobias was my first correction. What I did to that young man felt too harsh, too evil, too dark. But you know what? I saved him from a tortured existence and ended his Winter. He never became an artist, a creator, but that was never his intended destiny. In the wake of my correction, Tobias found his Spring. He became a music teacher – a role he was born to fulfill. Like us Sparks, he had followed his passions onto a misinterpreted path. All he needed was a little nudge to find his happiness.

After Tobias, there were so many others. Once I understood my gift, the signs for my intended destiny were everywhere. You see, I *know* your inner doubts. I hear them gnaw at you as you struggle through life. I *see* you, and I know that you do not *belong*.

And even though you cannot see *me*, I know you can hear me just fine – it's my gift, my curse, my purpose. I've told you my story, I mean you well. Do not despair, and do not fear me or what's to come. I am here to enlighten you and guide you to your proper place. After all, eventually, even the darkest Winter turns to Spring.

My name is Harold, but they've come to call me the Weaver.

As a rock journalist for Metal On Loud Magazine, Randy watches the world in search of both rhythms and answers. As an author, host of the Twitter poetry prompt tag #vsspoem, and a lyricist for four different bands, poetry is part of his every day – it even found its way into his novels.

His first self-publication: a collection of micro poetry forged into a single, two act epic poem called The Rhythm of Life, is now available on Amazon.

Randy's first published short stories Rain Must Fall and Days Gone By are now available in the anthologies Of Silver Bells and Chilling Tales and Of Mistletoe And Snow by Jazz House Publications.

YOU CAN'T SEE ME

Kate Longstone

Ellie stopped as she reached the crest of the hill and let the cord fall from her gloved hands. It curled as it fell, landing partially on the bright red plastic sledge resting beside her. Not far from where she stood was the beginning of a well-marked groove in the snow which showed the many trips down the hill she had made in the last hour. Nearby was a similar, but less well defined, path, broken frequently by the boot prints left as she dragged the sledge back up the slope.

She took a moment to breathe out gently and watched her breath dissipate in the cold morning air. Her gaze was drawn down the hillside, following the single line of footprints back to the gap in the hedge at the end of her garden. This was the first time in her life that she had seen the house and surrounding countryside completely covered in a blanket of pure white snow. Not for the first time that morning, she paused to take in the beauty of the scene laid out before her, grateful her school had been closed for the day.

Feeling more confident in her ability to control and guide the sledge, Ellie decided to try a different, more difficult, way down. Picking up the cord she began crunching through the unbroken snow, pulling the sledge towards the highest point of the hill. As she reached it she scanned the slope to look for any obvious obstructions on the steeper gradient she had chosen. There was a small group of trees at the foot of the hill, but they were several feet away from where she planned to come to a halt, so she disregarded them.

Placing the sledge in front of her, Ellie lowered herself onto the raised seat at the back and braced her feet against the front. After pushing herself away with her hands she clutched the cord securely in her fists as she began to descend. The cold breeze rushing past her face made her eyes water, and she laughed in excitement as she picked up speed.

Thirty feet from the base of the hill, there was a sudden thump and scraping noise as the sledge caught on something concealed beneath the snow. Fighting hard to stay on the sledge, Ellie found herself hurtling towards the copse of trees. Letting go of the cord, she instinctively raised her arms to protect her face, closed her eyes and shrieked as she careened into the bushes.

Ellie heard a soft thud and lurched forwards as the sledge came to a stop. She sat back heavily, and waited for a few moments before opening her eyes to see where she'd ended up. The sledge had come to rest against the trunk of a mature oak tree, and her arms were tangled amongst its low hanging branches. Feeling dampness on her face, she retrieved a tissue from her coat pocket and dabbed it against her cheek, coming away with a small amount of blood. Carefully, Ellie freed her arms and stretched out her legs, checking for any indications of injury. Satisfied that she seemed to have escaped without much damage she looked around for the best way to leave the thicket.

Heading towards a gap between two shrubs, Ellie stopped when she heard the faint snapping of a twig from her left. Catching a glimpse of movement just a few inches above the ground, she lowered her gaze, and was astonished to see a pair of tiny blue eyes looking directly at her through a gap in the leaves. Unsure what was looking at her from behind the branches, she kept as still as possible. However, the creature continued staring at her and – as it was showing no signs of moving away – Ellie edged closer for a better look.

Stopping an arm's length away, Ellie could hear a soft voice repeating over and over, "You can't see me, you can't see me, you can't see me."

Her curiosity roused, Ellie stretched to move the leaves and branches aside with her hand, revealing a small bearded figure sitting in the snow. They were wearing an off-white fur cloak, with a matching hat covering most of their head, leaving a hint of blue-black hair visible around its edges.

"I *can* see you," Ellie said, "and I can hear you too."

"Oh dear," said the figure. "You're not supposed to be able to hear or see me when I say that."

"If you didn't want me to find you why didn't you just hide or run away?" Ellie asked, slightly perplexed.

"I couldn't." The stranger sighed, standing up to

brush away the snow which had been covering his waist and legs. "I've been caught in a trap."

The figure was slim and about twelve inches tall; Ellie could now see tiny dark red stains around his waist, from which a thin wire fastened him securely to a sturdy branch.

"Oh, I didn't see that before. Are you badly hurt?" asked Ellie.

"It only hurts and bleeds when I move," he replied, "and I've not had the strength to free myself."

Ellie thought she recognised what had captured the stranger, and believing she knew how to release him, she said, "I might be able to get you free, if you're willing to let me try."

"I would be most grateful," said the stranger, clasping their hands together. "I've been stuck here since the moon set, and I'm getting rather hungry."

"I'm going to go back to the house now and get some things," she said. "You stay right there, I'll be back soon."

He gave a small laugh. "Well, I'm hardly going anywhere am I?"

* * *

Ellie returned to the copse of trees about twenty minutes later. She had gathered all the things that might be useful in freeing the stranger and placed them into her school rucksack, which she now removed and placed on the ground beside her. It had taken her slightly longer than she had anticipated; her mother was working from home due to the snow, and Ellie hadn't wanted to explain what she was doing.

Opening her bag, she was about to retrieve the tools she had taken from her father's toolbox when it occurred to her that she didn't know anything about the little man who was trapped – not even his name. Keen to remedy this, she introduced herself, "Sorry, I forgot to say before," she said, smiling, "I'm Ellie."

"Hello, Ellie," he replied, "my full name is rather difficult to pronounce, but you can call me Eduric, as that is close to how it sounds in your language."

"I'm pleased to meet you, Eduric," said Ellie, and continued, "I don't want to appear rude, but you seem too small for a person. Are you a fairy, or something else like that?"

"No, I'm a Snow Pixie," Eduric replied, his chest swelling slightly as he spoke, "and I don't think you're rude at all. We don't normally come into contact with people, so I wouldn't expect you to have heard of us before. We rarely travel around, and only when the snow is thick on the ground; the rest of the time we spend hidden away in our homes in the highlands and mountains."

Pleased with the trust Eduric had shown by sharing so much information, Ellie moved towards him, asking, "Is it alright if I have a closer look at your waist? I want to see how close the wire is to the skin."

"Of course," he replied. "It hasn't cut into the skin that badly though; my fur coat protected me well. I did struggle against the wire a lot at first, which probably made it worse than it might otherwise have been."

"How did you get caught?" she asked, examining the

wire closely. "You don't seem the type to not check where they're going."

"It's a bit silly," Eduric said, looking slightly embarrassed, "I got startled by a fox and was running into the trees to hide when I blundered straight into it. I was too busy looking behind me and didn't see the wire at all."

"I don't see any signs of a fox," Ellie said. "So I assume it didn't catch you?"

"No, they didn't," he answered. "Luckily the 'you can't see me' trick worked that time."

"I wonder why it didn't work on me, then."

"It doesn't always work," Eduric admitted. "There are a few special people who seem immune to it."

Having finished her examination of the snare wire, Ellie decided that trying to unwind the end of the loop was better than attempting to cut the wire, which was still digging into Eduric's waist in a couple of places. Retrieving her father's pliers from the rucksack, she explained her decision to Eduric. "This is a rabbit snare. I'm going to try and unwind the wire holding the loop in place. It might hurt a bit, but please try to keep as still as possible."

"You seem to know a fair bit about snares," Eduric remarked.

"My father showed me how to make them," she explained. "We have quite a problem with rabbits around here. I think this might be one of his snares."

"They're nasty things," Eduric muttered.

"What, rabbits?"

"No, the snares," Eduric said, sighing. "They cause a

lot of pain and suffering. I wish people wouldn't use them."

Working slowly and methodically, Ellie was able to remove the wire from around Eduric's waist. "There, that's got that off," she said, feeling quite pleased at how smoothly it had gone. "Now can you lift your coat and shirt up, so I can tend to the wounds?" Using a wet tissue she gently cleaned the areas where the wire had cut into his skin, before applying a small amount of antiseptic cream to the affected areas, prompting a small cry from Eduric.

"Sorry," said Ellie. "I should have mentioned that it might sting when I put the cream on." She finished by taking a small roll of bandage that was little bigger than her thumb and wrapped it around his waist, fixing it in place with a piece of tape.

Leaving Eduric to adjust his clothes, Ellie returned to her rucksack, retrieving a small piece of bread and a bottle of honey. "I don't know if you can eat this," she said, "but I thought you might like some bread and honey."

"I like bread," Eduric answered. "But I've never tried honey before. What does it taste like?"

"It's sweet and very tasty. My mother gives it to me when I haven't been well. She says it's good for you."

"In that case, I would like to try it, please," he said, taking the bread from Ellie after she had squeezed some honey on it.

"Oh my! That's really nice," he exclaimed. "May I have some more?"

"Of course you can," said Ellie, and handed him a second helping.

After Eduric had finished eating, Ellie asked him if there was anything else she could do, as she needed to be home soon. Eduric thanked her again for her help, but advised that although he would need to rest for a few days before moving on, he should be fine. Although he did say he would like it if she could come back tomorrow – with more honey, of course.

* * *

Eduric recovered in the copse for a few more days. Each morning, Ellie would bring him more bread and honey, and they would spend the time talking, sharing stories about their lives. It turned out that Eduric was a lot older than she had first assumed, and he was able to tell her about the changes in the weather he had noticed over the years. That was why this year was the first in nearly a decade that he had been able to travel this far South, as the warmer winters and lack of snow had prevented it before now. He also explained the subtle differences in the seasons he had observed, and the effect this was having on wildlife across the country.

Ellie was enjoying the time she spent with Eduric – it had given her someone to talk to on the days her school had been closed. Her family had only recently moved to the country, and their house was fairly isolated, so there were no other children living nearby for her to play with. Ellie thought she had probably learnt more from Eduric than she would have from her teachers, anyway.

On her visit to the hill that morning Eduric announced that he would be leaving later that day: the cold spell was coming to an end, and the snow would soon begin to melt. Ellie quickly rushed back to the house to collect a tiny pot of honey, which presented to Eduric to take on his journey. Thanking

Ellie again for her help, he handed her a small parcel in return, saying, "Please, take these, they will bring you luck."

As he was making his final preparations to leave, Ellie asked him, "Will I see you again?"

"I hope so," Eduric replied, "I have really enjoyed your company, and I won't forget the debt I owe you for the help you gave me. I don't know what would have happened if you hadn't freed me from the snare, but I will try to return the favour one day."

Pausing to look up at the sky before continuing, he said, "It will depend on the weather though, as I can only get here when there's been heavy snow."

"I shall hope it snows every winter from now on, then," said Ellie. "When it does, I'll come and look for you here."

"And I'll be waiting," Eduric confirmed, as he turned to leave.

Ellie watched Eduric depart from the copse of trees with tears rolling gently down her cheeks, giving him one last wave as he disappeared from view. "I'm going to miss you, Eduric," she whispered, remaining alone on the hillside for a moment longer before returning to the warmth of her home, clutching the small pair of fur gloves that Eduric had given her as a parting gift.

* * *

Each winter, whenever there had been the slightest fall of snow, Ellie returned to the copse of trees at the base of the hill to look for Eduric as she had promised. But, as he foretold, the heavy snowfall they had experienced that year did not reoccur.

Although she didn't see him again, the meeting with

Eduric changed Ellie's life. Their conversations led to her taking an active interest in environmental issues throughout her remaining academic years, during which she regularly participated in demonstrations and marches, much to her parents' surprise. She became a keen supporter of animal rights, too, taking part in many animal welfare campaigns and events. She even persuaded her father to stop using snares to trap the rabbits, which she was sure would have pleased Eduric.

Ellie went on to study climate change at university, and after graduating with honours, she was keen to find employment in a related field. She was naturally excited, then, when what appeared to be her dream job – studying the effects of climate change on wildlife in the Scottish Highlands – was advertised not long after she graduated. She eagerly applied, but sadly didn't make the shortlist.

She had thought it unusual when the job was advertised again a few weeks later, but she still reapplied. Yet there was more disappointment waiting for her; although Ellie made it through to the interview stage, she was again unsuccessful. It therefore came as a pleasant surprise when the head of the interview panel called her two months later asking her to come back for another interview.

Ellie thought the second interview was strange – to say the least – as she was the only person they were talking to at the time. In fact, the interview had practically started with them offering her the job. It was when Ellie had questioned the reasons why the role had become vacant, for the *third* time in just a few months, that things really began to get odd.

Reluctantly at first, the recruiting manager, with a significant level of embarrassment, explained that the previous post holders had been too scared to continue staying in the house which was provided with the role. Ellie still accepted the offer of the job despite the accounts she heard of cupboards opening and closing themselves at night, along with contents moving around of their own accord, and small objects disappearing then reappearing again several days later. This was, after all, the opportunity she had always hoped for, and she was determined to take it.

* * *

When she arrived in the Highlands on a cold but sunny afternoon , Ellie fell in love with the house straight away. Built of grey stone, it was set against the lower reaches of the mountains, and covered with early winter snow. It was absolutely beautiful, and brought to mind her childhood home during the winter she had met Eduric. Inside the rooms were in good repair, even though they were decorated in a rather old-fashioned style. There was an open wood fire in the main living room, and Ellie spent a cosy evening in her new house before retiring to bed, where she quickly drifted off to sleep after a tiring day.

She spent the following days getting settled into her new home. There had been no strange noises or any weird things happening, and Ellie began to think that her predecessors must have been imagining them. She went to bed as usual, thinking how well things had turned out...until she was suddenly woken just after midnight.

Now, during what should have been one of the happiest moments of her life, Ellie was lying wide awake in bed in the early hours of the morning, her bed clothes pulled tightly around her, listening to the strange noises coming from the kitchen of her new home.

After reflecting on past events and the recent decisions that had led her here, Ellie gradually found the courage to face the situation. This was her dream job; she was not going to cower in her bed, and she would not be frightened away like the others had been. Determined, Ellie got out of bed and pulled on her dressing gown. Retrieving the small pair of fur gloves she kept under her pillow for luck, she placed them in a pocket and went downstairs to investigate.

Moving as quietly as she could, Ellie opened the door to the kitchen. There in the shadows she could see what looked like a small person standing on the work surface, reaching up to one of the cupboards, which they opened and shut quickly creating a loud thud. Turning the lights on, Ellie recognised the bearded figure immediately – especially when he began to repeat, "You can't see me, you can't see me, you can't see me."

"Eduric!" she shouted, "What are you doing here?"

"How do you know my name?" he asked. "And why can you see me? I don't understand."

"It's me...Ellie," she explained. "Don't you remember? I freed you from the rabbit snare many years ago."

"I remember being freed from a trap," Eduric said, tilting his head slightly to peer at Ellie more closely, "but you don't look like her. She was much smaller than you, for a start."

Recalling the gloves in her pocket, Ellie showed them to him, "It *is* me, Eduric. Look, you gave me your gloves for luck, remember? It was such a long time ago though, and I've changed a lot since then."

"Ellie! Is it really you?" he said, his eyes widening.

"What are you doing here?"

"This is my new home," she answered. "I moved in a few days ago. But what are you doing in my house?"

"My home is nearby," Eduric said, smiling, "but in a way, *you* are the reason I'm here."

"Me?" Ellie replied. "How did you even know I would be living here now?"

"Oh, I didn't know that," Eduric admitted. "I grew rather fond of honey though, after you gave it to me back then, and I've been coming here now and again hoping to find some more."

"So it was you who scared off the other people who were living here!" said Ellie, laughing. "Well, thanks to you I've been able to get my dream job."

"I'm glad I could finally repay my debt after all this time," said Eduric, bowing extravagantly. Still smiling at her, he asked, "Now for a far more important question... do you have any honey?"

"No," said Ellie. "But I can get some tomorrow, if you'd like to come back then."

"I'd be delighted to," said Eduric. "Perhaps I could visit regularly, now we're neighbours – I have to stay near the mountains most of the year now because of the warmer weather."

"That would be lovely," said Ellie, returning his smile. "I think this job is going to work out just fine."

Kate Longstone is a writer of fantasy and other fiction.

She has a passion for telling the stories of strong female protagonists overcoming adversity, drawing inspiration from her interests in myth, folklore, history and nature.

Kate lives in Essex in the United Kingdom with two adorable cats, and when not writing can be found enjoying the local countryside, or exploring fantasy realms in books and games.

ACKNOWLEDGEMENTS

H. L. Macfarlane, editor

Well, I made it.

In June this year I decided to organise an anthology of fairy tales. I love them, after all, and I'd like to think I'm rather well-versed in them. So it should have been easy, right?

Oh, I was a sweet summer child if ever there was one.

Regardless of the difficulties that come from organising a group of seventeen authors across multiple time zones, the benefits far outweighed any problems caused. I have since found a group of remarkable, talented, funny and, above all, lovely people who I consider my friends. Therefore, I'd like to thank each and every one of them for making this anthology possible. I can't wait to work with them again.

I hope you enjoyed this anthology. Here's to the next one!